Ravens and Roses
Part Three of the Spirit Sword Series

By Jonathan W. Thurston

A THURSTON HOWL PUBLICATIONS BOOK

ISBN 978-1-945247-29-3

RAVENS AND ROSES

Copyright © 2018 by Jonathan W. Thurston

First Edition, 2018. All rights reserved.

A Thurston Howl Publications Book
Published by Thurston Howl Publications
Lansing, Michigan

jonathan.thurstonhowlpub@gmail.com

Cover design by Scott Lewis Ford

Printed in the United States of America

Table of Contents

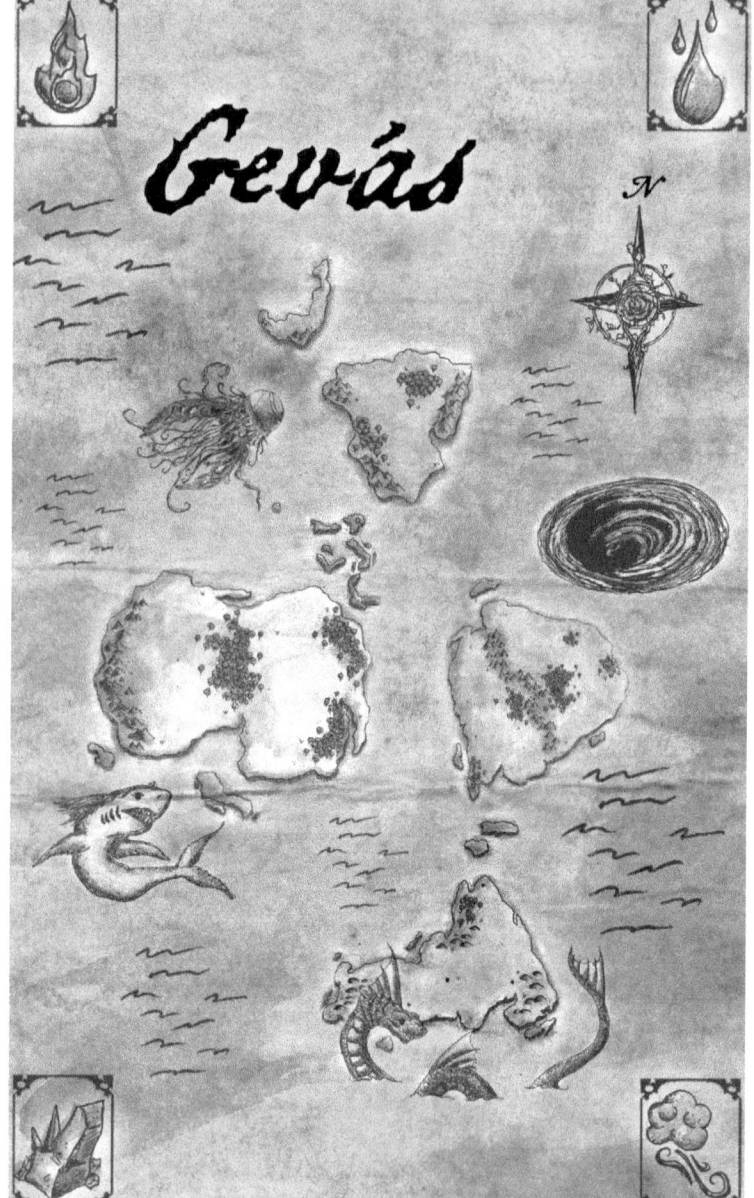

Northern Continent

Golden Plains

Astra

Libris

Ruvion

Aurale

Western Continent

Pureau

Rulia

Saldir

Temple
of the
Spirits

Arvon

The
Pyramid

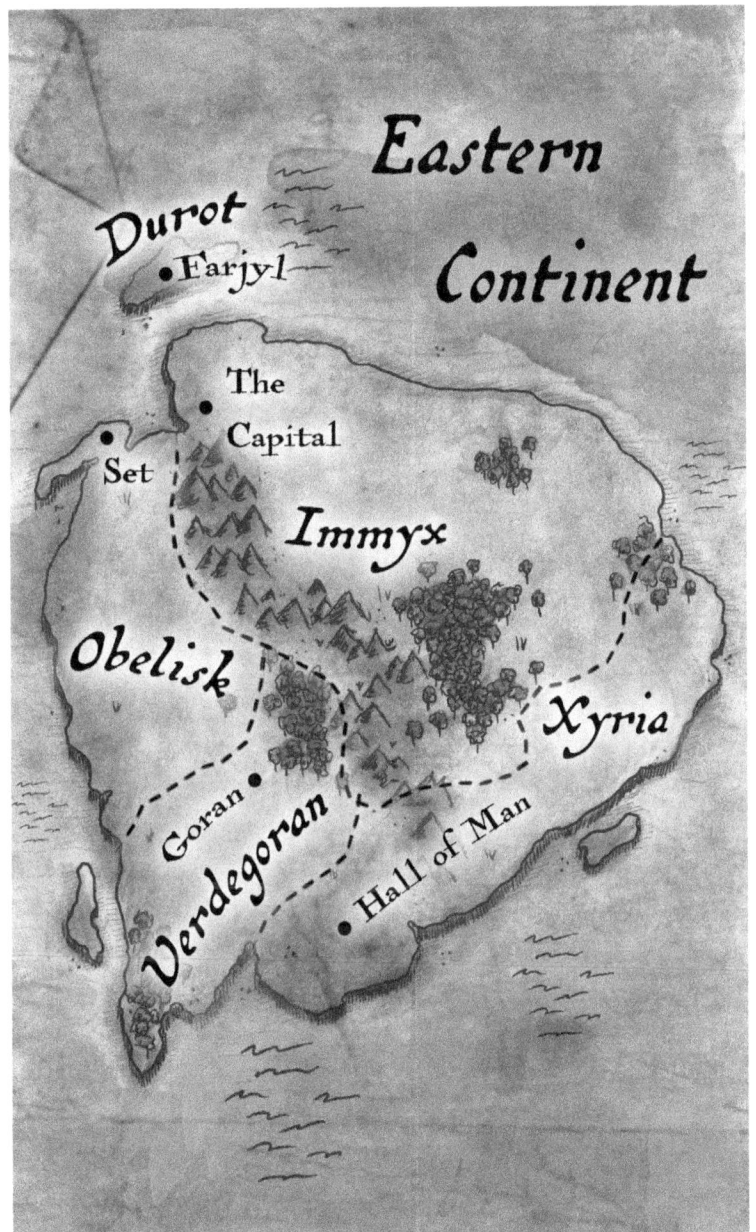

Southern Continent

Macela

Heaven's Isle

• Dream City

Mashan Telis

Helio

Varyx

Alerris

Terin •

Leik •

• Apolis

Gryphos •

Norlante

Prologue –
Without Words

H IS FALCON-LIKE EYES darted across the scene, searching for anything salvageable in the wreckage. However, every piece of equipment appeared to be destroyed. The charred remains of the once-spectacular machine filled the room with a thick cloud of pollution, though his employer had said that a spell had destroyed the machine days ago.

To clear the haze, he thrust his wings forcefully to create a powerful current in the water. The mechanical remnants shifted slightly before him, and he could only grimace. This task would be far from easy. Stepping forward, his talons clicked on the metallic floor, and his hopes gradually diminished.

Shouldn't he have hired a mage to do this? he thought to himself. Working with digital codes and assembling wires were his specialties, but performing miracles was a job for those who could wield the legendary force of *mysteria*. He shook his head doubtfully. The griffin bent over the pieces of metal and assessed the damage.

The computer had definitely exploded, though he was not sure why. Every piece should have been working properly according to his employer, so such a malfunction did not seem plausible. This destruction had to have been caused by some external force, possibly someone else. He did not have the ability to sense *mysteria,* so that was out of the question, but he could still identify any physical evidence of who had done this.

His talons traced over a part of what had once been a large screen. As he carefully reassembled the broken glass, he could make out a small, circular hole from where the glass spider-webbed into several shards.

Hmm . . . This appears to be the work of a scepter or rod . . . The hole is too perfectly circular for it to have been anything besides a weapon. It had to have been a scepter or a rod. Will the Emperor believe that logic, though?

It had been the Emperor of Light himself who had employed Feranx's services, and the griffin was more than happy to help as well. Nonhumans had only recently been claiming jobs in the south end of the world, and, having a knack for technology, Feranx had been attempting to find a job with many of the technological corporations of the Eastern Continent. However, the Emperor Regin had denied him because of his species. Going to the Southern Continent where the Emperor of Light held reign was the only logical option remaining.

Lord Helius had found Feranx via a man with long, red hair and a golden robe. The robe had borne on its front the emblem of a crimson phoenix, and the man would not say anything about himself—only his purpose of seeking out Feranx.

Of course, the conversation had been rather one-sided due to Feranx's lifelong muteness.

He pressed a button on his electronic belt to activate his own personal computer, and one claw waved in the water in front of him to create a green digital keyboard and screen. Both were as thin as a sheet of metallic paper and were the highest forms of technology in Gevás. His talons darted rapidly across the green keyboard as he constructed a message to the Emperor of Light regarding his findings:

"Your Majesty,
I truly do not think that any of these parts are salvageable. The damage was too strong, and there is simply no way to recover the data. However, I was able to find out that this destruction was caused by someone with either a scepter or a rod. I am going to stay here and investigate a little further. My devices have indicated more machinery further underground.
Your servant, Feranx."

One claw moved in front of the screen, and the screen divided into six panels that swam through the water to surround him in a ring that followed his every movement, each panel always staying at least three feet from his body.

He returned to the staircase. Several yards above him was a field that only recently began to recover from a fierce attack it had suffered years ago. Grass had started to grow there again, and there were a few roses as well. This island was known as Heaven's Isle, and according to the legends he had heard, the place had been well-known for causing shipwrecks and disappearances, but the Prince of Light, Dragenopn Helius, had supposedly purified the unholy ground. Lord Helius certainly possessed the power, too. Feranx had never had the experience of witnessing the Emperor of Light in battle, but there were many stories of the Emperor that stayed constant, regardless of the continent on which he was standing. Along with that, the Emperor of Light was the reason he was able to walk freely on this island. The young lord had removed the exile that had plagued the nonhumans for years.

So, why does someone so great need someone like me to survey some technological remains?

Stepping through the open door, he found himself at the

staircase once more. The stairs continued further down than this room, and his computer was definitely sensing some concentrated signals from that area. His green screens illuminated the area as he descended, and the light shimmered eerily on the metal walls. The talons on his feet clicked with each step. Then, one of the panels reported the increasing strength of the signal: he was getting closer.

What could be down here? he wondered. The signal was obviously a powerful one, but his technology could not identify the type of machine. *What long-forgotten device had been concealed under Heaven's Isle?*

Suddenly, the stairs stopped. They did not run into a wall or even a door. There was only a shadowed pit below him. The spiraling staircase had merely ended into nothingness. The screens suggested that the source was farther down still, however.

He moved to the edge of the stairs and jumped. He plummeted into the water, the green panels still surrounding him, and then his wings unfolded and propelled the water downward, halting his fall. He had reached the floor. The floor was a silver disc that bore several strange markings on its surface, and they did not seem the slightest bit familiar to him.

One claw waved in front of a green panel, and the screen spread itself out to form a long, glowing rod. The rod hovered above the ground and proceeded to scan the whole ground, attempting to recognize and analyze the inscriptions. After a few seconds, the bar returned to him and reverted to its panel form. Lines of text appeared on the screen. Feranx was stunned to discover that the characters were that of an ancient code used in the time of the Obsidian Wars by Dagan and the Y'mordi. He growled at the thought of this place being a base for those filthy murderers.

He had heard rumors of the Y'mordi returning to Gevás. Tales of their chaos had trickled into the Northern Continent slowly, but they were there.

Examining the rest of the data, Feranx was finally able to understand the inscription.

Cronus 624? What is that supposed to be?

Then, his panels began displaying the red alert: there was another person in the chamber, above him, on the staircase.

A voice called down to him, "Who's there?"

However, he could not answer.

His panels instantly revealed that the person was no longer there, as if he had spontaneously vanished. His beak curled into a snarl. The person had used a Gate. The person was a *mysteria*-wielder.

The Gate appeared in front of him, and he was terrified to behold a black-robed figure step out of it to face him. "I said, 'Who is down here?'"

Feranx was immediately suspicious. He flipped one of his panels with a turn of the claw and began typing his name onto the screen so the stranger could see it.

"Feranx, huh? Can't talk?"

Though he could not speak, his talons spoke as fast as the stranger's voice could. *"No, but I think that this will suffice. Now, who are you?"*

"Heh," said the stranger. The voice was clearly that of a male, though Feranx still did not know who he was. "My name is Mali. I am one of the seven Lords of the Shadows." The man pulled back his hood to reveal a young man with blonde hair and golden eyes. He was smiling almost wickedly. "It is a pleasure to meet you, Feranx. May I ask what you are doing here? I had not expected for the Emperor to find this place so easily."

"I am here merely to investigate. How would you know of my employment with the Emperor, and why are you here, Y'mordi?"

Mali smiled again and walked to the center of the room. "I came here to activate the Cronus program, actually. It seems that the time to set our plan in motion has come. Six years is simply too long."

Instantly, Feranx waved his claw in the water, and his panels turned into discs that flew threateningly toward Mali. However, the panels dissipated inches from the Y'mordi's face. The man was protecting himself with an invisible barrier. The screens reappeared around Feranx, and he prepared to fight. He doubted that he had the ability to defeat one as powerful as an Y'mordi, but it was worth a try.

"You are a fool, griffin, for thinking that you could raise a weapon against me."

Feranx retorted, *"Is it foolish to fight for what one believes in?"*

Mali's smile faded at the words on the screen. "Perhaps not foolish but dangerous, nonetheless. I will give you the chance to live if you withdraw from your stance of battle and leave. As it were, I have no reason to harm you. Regardless of what you do, Cronus shall be activated. May the Darkness take over this world." He held out a gloved hand with his palm facing the engraved ground.

"The time has come, Cronus 624." Suddenly, the inscriptions began to light up with a white glow. "Earth is in dire need of your assistance, and the unclean humans have stained its surface. Eradicate them, Cronus 624."

A digital voice resounded through the chamber. "Cronus 624 activated. Initiating Gate sequence . . ."

Above them, the water shimmered, and the ground began vibrating.

"What's going on?" asked Feranx, his eyes wide and his neck craning to get a scope of what was happening to the chamber.

"Heh, the ground you stand on is not the ground of the chamber but the head of the master computer Cronus 624. It is only the main console, and its remaining 623 components are already scattered throughout Earth. The thing that makes this computer unique is its ability to utilize *mysteria*."

Feranx took a step backward. *"How is that possible? It doesn't have a heart!"*

Mali lowered his arm and walked toward Feranx. "No, but the other Lords of the Shadows and I have been able to create a spell inside it that allows it to feed off others' emotions and *mysteria*. Even now, it is using both of our hearts to create a Gate that will take it to Earth. It is a rather clever machine, actually," he explained.

Feranx looked upward and watched the water above him ripple more and more. It was about to be split into a massive Gate. He needed to get out of there fast. Still, he could not help but wonder if there was a way he could at least hinder Cronus 624's entry to Earth or perhaps maim the Y'mordi.

A rapid movement of his claw flipped the screen to face him, and he typed a single command. It was by no means a permanent thing and would not harm the data in any way. This command was merely his greatest defense. After allowing the computer to execute the command, he made one more motion to send the panels to rotate around Mali, and Feranx flew upward to escape the chamber.

Three ... two ... one ...

As soon as the countdown ended in his mind, the explosion happened below him. He smiled to himself, knowing that, perhaps with both himself and the Y'mordi away from the computer now, Cronus 624 could not summon enough energy to construct the Gate.

Suddenly, light from behind him lit up the stairs above him as he soared. He became aware of the Y'mordi that was rapidly catching up to him. Shock overcame him as he realized that the explosion had hardly affected the robed figure. All he saw was the flash of the Y'mordi's deadly katana.

Only Mali was surprised when the blade was deflected by a green panel. Feranx aimed a disc-shaped panel at Mali, but the Y'mordi blocked it with his own weapon. Before he had time to block the second panel, it collided with his arm, cutting deep and spilling blood into the water. Feranx smiled and continued his barrage, some panels blocking while others darted at Mali.

When Mali vanished into a Gate, Feranx pressed himself to the wall and forced his panels into one massive screen just in time to block Mali's next attack as the Y'mordi reappeared through a new Gate. Feranx's claw moved forward, his screen knocking Mali backward.

"Gate complete. Transportation initiated . . ." roared the voice of Cronus 624. Below the two fighters, the Gate had been finished, and the floor began moving upward to enter the Gate.

Realizing that it was too late, Feranx shot upward, beating his wings as fast as he could to escape the underground base. He directed the screen to stay directly below him to shield him from any attacks that the Y'mordi might aim at him. As he neared the top, he forced the screen to shift so that it was above him, suspecting that the Y'mordi would use a Gate to move to the door that led back outside and attack him there. Another motion from his claw signaled a piece of the screen to split into a sharp bar that fit comfortably into his claw as a makeshift sword.

He grasped the railing of the stairs at the top and slammed his screen through the door forcefully. He heard a cry of pain instantly, bringing a proud smile to his face. Not wasting a moment, he bolted through the doorway and flew into the watery sky of Gevás. He needed to give this information to the Emperor of Light. As he flew, he turned his head over his shoulder to see if the Y'mordi was following him, but no one seemed to be on the island at the moment. Feranx hoped desperately that Mali would not use a Gate to sneak attack him. The screen split into panels that circled him as a cautious barrier.

However, each passing second only brought silence. At first, that silence gnawed painfully at his mind. His eyes darted to each side, expecting the Y'mordi to appear at any moment. After a few minutes, he realized that he was not being followed. He breathed out a sigh of relief and allowed his wings to beat at a more relaxed pace.

He shivered beneath his fur and feathers. It was the coldest season of the year in Gevás, and the Southern Continent was particularly freezing at this time. Still, the ice of the south was always so beautiful to him. It was surprising to him that a place could look this amazing even with its presence in the middle of a war.

Feranx could remember the terror of the Third Obsidian War so many years ago. All the nonhumans had had their loyalties tested entirely. Many of the griffins—including Feranx's own family—had fought against the Emperor of Light and his Council. Nevertheless, Feranx had stayed out of the conflict altogether. He had realized the stupidity of the war and had avoided its destruction.

However, the peace that followed the war had hardly been a long one. Many of the Eastern leaders had banded under the leadership of the Emperor Regin to contest the Emperor of Light's removal of the exile. It was a dangerous thing for a nonhuman to touch the waters of the Eastern Continent now. However, nonhumans had been given the chance to fight in the terra and navy of Helio. One respite was simply the fact that the Emperor Regin and the Emperor of Light were careful strategists: full battles were rare and only really happened two or three times a year. The Emperor of Light had countered each attack by the East with a large enough force to incapacitate it. The Emperor Regin had done the same. Neither side had truly gained anything through the war as of yet.

Just as he had earlier, Feranx had chosen to stay out of this war as well. Working for the Emperor of Light had been the best job he had ever had, and it was not one he would give up so that he could fight in a futile and foolish war. The

Emperor of Light had summoned him five years ago with the request of helping him construct a master computer program similar to the ones at Heaven's Isle and the Academy of Gryphos. However, the mysterious thing about the project was that the Emperor of Light had mentioned a component of the computer that would be added last, after the construction was completed. For years, Feranx and the Emperor had been working on the computer and had been siphoning data from Master Marqest's COM into the Emperor's computer. That sharing of data had lasted until COM had been recently destroyed. Now, it seemed that the Y'mordi were involved.

Before he could think any more about it, Port City appeared beneath him. It would probably be a better idea to stop there and find a mage who could bring him straight to Apolis with a Gate. He could not understand how these humans could walk around with such thin and loose clothing or, in many cases, hardly any at all. The men of the town were mostly wearing only some jeans, while the women were wearing skirts and bikini tops. He was shivering even with all of his feathers and fur.

Landing in the city, he approached the first person he saw and typed, *"Excuse me, but do you know of a mage who could summon a Gate for me, mam?"*

The woman seemed to be rather surprised at the sight of the griffin, but she replied anyway, "Yeah, if you go that way, you'll find the hut of the Khaosdog."

He felt a shiver shake his wings before responding, *"The Khaosdog?"*

She nodded. "Yes, she is a rather . . . eccentric artist who actually moved here a few years ago from Earth. However, she has a knack for creating Gates and loves all nonhumans. She can help you."

Feranx grinned at the woman's helpfulness before offering her a metallic sheet of paper. *"May the Light protect you,"* he said, as she accepted the Imperial favor in awe.

"Thank you, Master Griffin," she muttered.

The idea of Imperial favors had been a new one to Feranx when he had come to Apolis, but they had certainly come in handy. They were ways of payment to those who aided a Loyal Servant, Council member, or member of the Imperial family. It was much more valuable than salt because it could be valued for a service or higher-valued salt.

He turned to walk in the direction to which the woman had pointed. It did not take him long to find the hut with several paintings outside it and the name *Khaosdog's Wonder Works* scribbled on a sign. The griffin smiled as he approached the building.

His rapid knocking resulted in a call from inside the hut, "Please, come in!"

He opened the door and entered the small house. The place was filled with several paintings and small jars with colored paints trickling down their sides. Then, he saw a thin-framed girl with thick glasses hovering over a canvas.

"A griffin?" she said with apparent excitement, pushing her glasses up her nose. "What can I do for you today, sir?"

Moving one of the panels in front of him to face her, he typed, *"I need a Gate to Apolis. Would you be able to help me?"*

"Eh? What's the matter? Can you not talk?"

Feranx smiled. He had been asked that question so many times. Why was it that he had never gotten used to it? *"No, I've been mute for as long as I can remember. Now, please, can you help me get to the Palace of Light?"*

"The Palace of Light?" exclaimed the girl as she rose, almost knocking over one of her pots. "What business would you have there?"

The griffin was beginning to become impatient. *"I am one of his Majesty's Loyal Servants, and I need you to make a Gate. Now,"* he demanded.

The Khaosdog folded her arms over her chest and remarked, "Oh, and what will be your payment, griffin?"

"Whatever you want! Just make me the Gate already!"

She smiled at him. "Fine, the price shall be . . ." Suddenly, her eyes lit up, and Feranx knew that he was about to find himself in a heap of trouble. She reached into her pocket and pulled out a metallic flyer. "Give this to his Majesty. Perhaps one day, I could move to Apolis. With the Emperor of Light's blessing, I could have a pretty fair start at it. That's my price."

The griffin frowned, but he was not going to go back on his word now. He used a sharp claw to snatch the sheet from the girl's hand and moved it into a pouch on his belt.

"Thank you, Master Griffin," the girl said happily. With a wave of her hand, a hole appeared in the water of the room, and, to Feranx's amazement, the room became colder. He shivered as he approached the Gate.

"I can't take you to the Palace, but this is right outside its walls. The Emperor has had barriers placed so that only people inside the walls can use Gates to move around the city."

Feranx offered her a grateful nod as he entered the city of Apolis, Helio's grand capital.

1

The Third Great Servant

MALI COUGHED uncontrollably for several minutes as he breathed in the stench of the Dark Realm. The black haze of the air was thick around the Palace of Shadows, and it had caught him off guard. The concentration of the darkness there was perplexing to him: it had never been this strong, not since the Dark Lord, Dagan, had ruled.

His eyes scanned over the immense castle. Recently, he had been asking himself if becoming human would be a decent possibility for himself. After all, his best friend Victor Ferro was attempting that nearly impossible feat.

When he had served under the Lord of Light, Lux, he had been a dedicated servant. Yet, he had not been fairly rewarded for his efforts. In his mind, Lord Lux had not led as good-willed a life as most people had thought for centuries. Then, he had decided to switch to the service of the Dark Lord, Dagan, who promised long life and power to those who served him well.

Mali stepped forward and the gate to the Palace dissolved around him. Only Servants of the Darkness could enter this place. To others, the gate would be solid iron, enchanted with spells of almost perfect invincibility.

A Gate appeared beside him, and a black-robed figure stepped out of it. "Mali, is Cronus 624 deployed yet?"

He nodded softly in response. Mali did not have a prejudice against the Adviser, Xarden. He had always been utterly surprised by Xarden's phenomenal abilities in both fighting and *mysteria*. The other Y'mordi was rather old, and his past had always been a mystery to Mali. However, he was not one to question those who were his elders. "Yes, I sent him out a little earlier. As your sources had predicted, the griffin indeed showed up to witness its launch into Earth, and I gave him the information. Has Lord Y'tal found the third Great Servant of the Darkness yet?"

Xarden smirked. "Patience is a good quality to possess, Mali. As a matter of fact, he *has* found the next Great Servant. However, all shall be revealed in the meeting."

With that being said, the two walked toward the entrance to the Palace. Mali sensed only the thinnest stream of *mysteria* move from Xarden to open the massive doors. The older Y'mordi had always tried so hard to hide his heart from those around him, but whenever Mali caught a glimpse of Xarden's heart, he saw that it was broken. Division was an ancient spell that had always been rather mythical, but the state of Xarden's heart had proved otherwise to Mali.

As they ascended the stairs to the open doorway, they sensed another figure entering the courtyard, and they turned to face the newcomer.

Xarden smiled as he said, "Randir, I had been wondering if you were going to come. I suppose you're eager to find out this information so you can go haywire again?"

Without any hesitation, Randir summoned his lengthy hammer into one hand and muttered, "If you wanted a fight, you should have said so to start."

Just as rapidly, Xarden drew his own scepter. Being beside the elder Y'mordi, Mali could feel the air freeze around him, though it was clear that Randir was generating his own heat.

Mali called out to his best friend, "You are a fool, Randir. Step down. You couldn't beat Xarden if you tried." Ever since Mali had sided with Randir rather than Pullatus, the need to lie about his intentions had become apparent. If the third Great Servant was to be revealed, then Mali and Randir needed to kill that individual before the other Y'mordi wasted too much time trying to manipulate that Servant. However, they had to kill the Servant in a way that would not point to either Randir or Mali.

Xarden smiled before turning and entering the Palace of Shadows, leaving Mali and Randir behind.

"He could beat me, huh?" joked Randir knowingly.

Mali stepped back down the stairs and approached his friend. "You know I was kidding. Don't play dumb." In a soft voice, he added, "Did you find anything?"

Randir shook his head in disappointment. "I'm afraid not. The Emperor Regin is still planning his next attack from what I have heard, and the Emperor of Light is preparing his own counterattack. This is the slowest war I've ever seen."

"What about away from the Eastern Continent? Have there been any unusual events around the rest of the world?" Mali was eager to have some information. For the past six years, the two had been searching for signs of the next Great Servant's existence, but they could not interpret the Voice of the Darkness as Y'tal could. However, Mali doubted that it mattered now, since Pullatus had already found the individual.

"I have heard only rumors from the East. However, one such rumor mentioned a Southern kingdom switching its loyalties . . ."

Mali raised an eyebrow at the thought. "A Southern kingdom? I have not heard this, but I am sure it would be kept a well-hidden secret from the Emperor of Light."

"So, you've been keeping your eye on the kid?" asked Randir, changing the subject.

"Yes, the Emperor of Light is nothing like his father was. Dragenopn Helius does not rely on others to make decisions for him, and the Council is hardly an advising unit any longer. Aria has been handling affairs of the capital while taking care of her kids, as well."

Randir was almost shocked by the words. Because the couple were in their late twenties, both Dragenopn and Aria still seemed so young. Randir could remember fighting Mali off to help the three kids escape that small island years ago when they had first arrived in Gevás.

"Hm, then, I suppose that Y'tal's plan will work better than what we had originally thought," murmured Randir faintly.

Mali gestured to the door before saying, "We should get inside before we are late."

His high voice filled the room, "The third Great Servant of the Darkness has been revealed to me . . ." The other six Y'mordi were silent in anticipation. A gentle breeze filled the large ballroom, and Mali could sense the restless *mysteria* of Sarn creating that wind.

"It is the Emperor Regin."

The twins instantly began chatting amongst themselves, while Ixion paled at the thought. Xarden put a hand to his chin in deep puzzlement. Mali and Randir glanced at each other in astonishment. Neither of them had thought about investigating the Emperor Regin himself.

Pullatus ventured further, "For years, the Emperor Regin has been suffering a Heartbind curse. I have yet to identify the mage who cursed him, but regardless, he has been under the control of someone else."

Naturally, Randir was the one to interrupt, "Y'tal, are we going to interfere with it if we truly cannot identify the person who is possessing him?"

Xarden commented, "Who said we had to reveal that we know he is possessed?"

All eyes went to Xarden, and Pullatus inquired, "What do you mean, Xarden?"

"It's simple, isn't it?" When it became obvious to him that no one else knew what he was talking about, he continued, "At the moment, he is one of the world's most influential political leaders, and he likely already has several guards and servants. It should only take one of us to aid him. That one of us should not reveal our knowledge of his possession. The possessor will be rather shocked and will realize who he is working with. From there, he could do one out of three things: he could either exit his predicament, try to take advantage of us, or be cautious and not try anything funny."

Randir countered, "What if he tries to take advantage of us?"

"I wasn't done, hothead," retorted Xarden. "Meanwhile, another one or two of us will be looking for the possessor. Regardless of what happens, we will have the possessor and the Emperor Regin in our grasp."

Before anyone could truly think about what Xarden had just said, Y'tal responded, "It is settled, then. Mali, get to the Emperor Regin's side and protect him from getting killed. Randir and Ixion, I need the two of you to track down the possessor. Xarden, I need you to see what you can find about the Captain of the Enigma Brigade. I need to know more about Maksimilian, as it so happens."

Randir's head rapidly faced Pullatus in a frightened bewilderment. "What did you just say?"

"Oh, yes, I suppose that you had not been there when that had happened. Maksimilian seems to have survived the past few centuries. He is certainly not an Ancient, but he has survived nonetheless. He is the Captain of the Enigma Brigade, it seems," was Pullatus's simple response.

Randir felt a sinking feeling in his stomach as a memory came to the surface of his mind. Years ago, he had felt a powerful connection to a captain of one of the Emperor Regin's armies named Stehl. She had been disguised as a man to legally fight for the Emperor Regin. He had needed her help to defeat Maris at one point, but he had grown rather close to her. However, when saving her from a band of assassins, he had needed to fight their leader, a red-haired male with rapid reflexes and a deadly sword. It dawned on him, then, that the leader of those assassins had been Maksimilian. "He never aged at all, did he?" asked Randir vaguely.

Pullatus's silence was answer enough.

Maksimilian had been Ophelia's lover before Randir. Ophelia had been a few years younger than Randir and a few years older than Maksimilian. On many occasions, the two of them had fought. What was Maksimilian doing here now? Randir had been confident that Maksimilian had died all those years ago. Pullatus had said that he had been hiding as the Captain of the Enigma Brigade. Still, the means of Maksimilian's survival over the years were puzzling to Randir.

Y'tal continued, "Sarn, go to the Academy and see what you can find out about the Demons. The library here tells us everything about the Demons except for their present locations, so perhaps you can aid us by searching at the Academy's library. Arnim, I need you to go to Earth and ensure that Cronus 624 will complete its mission."

"What exactly is happening on Earth?" asked Arnim with slight curiosity.

"Now that that fool, Regin, has been revealed as the next Great Servant of the Darkness, we shall use him to win this war the way we desire. Apolis has become more heavily guarded, and Regin will do everything possible to crush the Southern Continent. However, everything is moving too slowly. We must alter this war. The first thing to do is to get the Emperor of Light out of the way. He is still young, and confidence will be his downfall this time. With his own plans of counterattack already in motion, he will see no problem with going to investigate a light disturbance on Earth that his new computer will reveal to him. Cronus 624 will activate its barrier to prevent the Emperor from moving back to Gevás. Then, it shall activate the other 623 components to take over Earth. This time, the Guardians will fall. You are all dismissed."

"He doesn't seriously expect me to find some possessor for him, does he?" roared Randir. His steaming anger was all too apparent to Mali, and Mali could not figure out what the problem was.

"What is wrong with it, Victor?" asked Mali finally, using Randir's birth name.

Randir's red hair seemed as if it was on fire, and his chambers burst with an uncanny heat. "Maks is back, Hector. He never died."

Mali shook his head doubtfully, "Victor, you heard Y'tal's orders. You are to find the possessor. Xarden is going to seek out Maksimilian." He, too, was well aware of Maksimilian's connection to Randir. The two had often been in petty quarrels around Ophelia back then. However, Mali had stayed out of those conflicts. According to Randir, in the Final Battle, the last thing that Randir had done was fight Maksimilian. In the middle of that fight was when the light had flashed through the field and ended the Wars.

"You know . . . I bet it is the effect of one of the Spirit Swords . . ." explained Randir.

"What?"

Randir walked to one of the windows and glanced out at the barren plains of the Dark Realm. "Before the Final Battle, Maksimilian had been seeking the five Spirit Swords. Perhaps he found the Steel of Life."

"Did you see it in the Final Battle?"

"No . . ." he responded, shaking his head in puzzlement.

Mali joined Randir beside the window and muttered curiously, "Why do you care so much? What happened between the two of you ended in the Battle. You cannot still bear a grudge against him after just finding out that he lives still. He has not sought you out. What do you intend to do?"

The room heated eerily, and Mali could sense the stress that Randir was feeling. "Hector . . . I have no intention of following Y'tal's orders. This possessor of the Emperor Regin shall be revealed in time. I have no interest in learning of it."

"You will follow Maksimilian?"

Randir shook his head, and the heat subsided. "No . . . A long time ago, I met this woman. She was beautiful, strong, clever, and she fought for what she believed in."

"Like Ophelia?"

A smile crept across Randir's face at the name. "In many ways, yes . . . I want to be with Ophelia again. I want that more than anything."

Mali placed a hand on Randir's shoulder, and the darkness of the Dark Realm seemed to brighten around them. "Victor, you cannot be with her yet. We are still tied to the Darkness. Do you want this girl you have met to replace Ophelia in your heart?"

"Of course not!" Randir snarled in response. "But . . . in this era, I need some healing. I have been without love for too long. When I was with this woman, she made me feel young again, full of life. Even after these years, I miss that again. I wish I had her beside me . . . Stehl."

Mali was always amazed by Randir's ability with women. "Perhaps you should try to find her then. At least you could act like you are looking for this possessor. Y'tal would not know the difference if you were looking everywhere for this person. Do you have any idea where she could be?"

"Apolis."

"Apolis! How do you expect to get in there exactly? The

Emperor of Light has erected a barrier around the city that prevents using Gates to enter. Certainly, the guards will not let you in the front door, either. If you roast them, the Emperor of Light will only suspect that something is amiss. You need to think this through a little better, I believe."

Silence held. Then, Randir ventured, "Hector, what were you before the colonization of Gevás?"

Mali was immediately stunned by the unexpected question. He shuffled his feet, and the light dimmed in the room. "I was just a boy when the world split, Victor. When it split, Gevás chose me."

"Are you sure that you didn't choose it?"

Mali's head turned quickly toward Randir, causing his hood to fall and his blonde, spiked hair to blaze with a golden light. "Of course not!" Realizing how loud his voice had been, he lowered his gaze. "I mean . . . my family was made up of a bunch of farmers. My life was really nothing special . . . but when I came here, I had the chance to make something of myself, and I started working in Helio. It didn't take long for me to get into the Emperor of Light's favor."

"Do you regret what you've done? What you've become?" Randir's question was just as much to himself as it was to Mali, but he awaited Mali's own response.

"I . . . I do. I wish I could sever the ties to the Darkness just as much as you do, but I don't see a way around it. Unlike you, Victor, I cannot just go and alleviate my pain with some woman I barely know." Wishing he could take back his words, he quickly added, "We're stuck like this; Servants of the Darkness. I see no way out of it."

Randir turned his red gaze back to the ashen plains outside the Palace of the Shadows. "Hector . . . I think that I have indeed found a way to sever the bonds, but it shall not be easy."

"What? Why did you not say something sooner?"

A grin spread across Randir's scarred face. "I wanted to

hear you say that you regretted the past first." He turned his back to the window and leaned against it. "Like the old spells, there is an artifact that has remained since the time of the First Obsidian War. The artifact is known as the Dusk Lyre. It is a relic that existed in Lux's treasury."

"How could a lyre help us exactly?"

A bright red flame appeared in Randir's outstretched hand. "This Lyre has the power to sever Dark connections." The flame flattened and spread across his fingers.

"And why is it that you have just now discovered this instrument?"

Randir closed his fist, and tongues of the fire licked at the edges of his hand. "Simple. I didn't think there would be a way to learn the Song."

"The Song?"

Randir nodded with a slight amount of impatience. "Yes, the catch is that a very specific song has to be played in order for the instrument to work its spell. There is a riddle that describes the Song. 'If you want to keep the Shadows long at bay, listen to me and repeat what I say: three strums, three knocks, no fear, no locks.'"

"A true puzzle indeed . . . Do you have any idea where this Lyre could be hidden?"

Mali received a heated glare from Randir and sighed with disappointment. Randir added, "We have roamed this world for around a thousand years, and we have never learned of such a thing. The books here in the Palace tell us almost nothing about the Lyre. If only . . ."

"What?"

Suddenly, Randir smiled again. "Hector, you are to protect the Emperor Regin, correct?"

"Yes. Those were Y'tal's orders. So?"

"So, you could check my old library then. Clearly, you will not have to be watching the Emperor every second, and you will have unlimited access to that library. Perhaps there is something there that might mention the Dusk Lyre."

Their senses tingled as they felt a Gate swirl into existence in the middle of the room. Out of it, green leaves fell to the ground. As the Gate grew, a man in a black robe stepped from it. The man pulled back his hood to reveal a green-eyed face with brown hair. "What are the two of you doing hunkered out in the dark?"

A ball of Fire immediately exploded into Randir's hand as he roared, "What are you doing here, rat?"

"I heard some whispering and thought I should check it out. Is that alright with you, hothead?"

Mali smirked at their bickering. Randir and Ixion had hated each other ever since they met. He supposed it was understandable: Randir was ranked second in the Y'mordi, while Ixion held the lowest position as the Spy for the Y'mordi.

"No, it is not alright with me! Now, get out of here before I decide to make barbecue out of you."

Rather than scampering away as Mali had predicted Ixion would do, the Y'mordi summoned two of his dangerously long knives. "Come at me, dragonbreath."

Without hesitation, Randir swung his arm, throwing the fireball at Ixion, and Ixion cut through the heat with his knives and then leaped forward to slash at Randir. Dodging Ixion's crazed flurry, Randir summoned his lengthy hammer and used it to block many of Ixion's attacks.

Mali stood back and merely watched the struggle. If he aided Randir, there was no telling what the red-haired Y'mordi would do: having been a General and a King, Randir knew much of honor and pride in battle. Mali could not help him here.

Randir was utterly stunned by Ixion's sudden speed. Though every attack was certainly stoppable, it was nearly impossible to get in a strike of his own. He could not even find the time to blast some Fire in Ixion's direction. Then,

Randir realized that Ixion had indeed been training over the past decade. The last time that Randir had fought Ixion, he had used a Heartlock on Ixion and killed him. Struck by the memory, Randir prepared to perform the same maneuver. Waiting for a single moment, he found his opportunity.

In a single dash, he reached his hand out to Ixion's heart and turned the hand as if he were twisting a doorknob. His body went straight through Ixion's as a ghost would, and Randir then stood back to back with Ixion. The Heartlock was a means of sealing a person's heart in the physical realm while keeping it connected to the caster of the spell. With that power, the caster could manipulate a person's heart in his or her own hand. In the Second Obsidian War, the Y'mordi had all bore witness to Y'tal as he had angrily killed a soldier who had tried to remove Y'tal's black hood. The leader of the Y'mordi had performed the Heartlock and then allowed thin snakes of Darkness to move out from the person's insides. The man had been screaming for mercy as those dark columns had shot out of his eyes, ears, nose, and mouth. Y'tal had brutally murdered that person, and ever since that day, not one of the Y'mordi dared even consider touching Y'tal's hood.

Randir raised his hand in order to roast Ixion from the inside, but as he did so, Ixion whirled around, plunging his knife through Randir's wrist. The hand landed against a wall, and a yell of pain escaped Randir's lips. Ixion slashed again, hoping to kill Randir this time, but Randir transformed into a tremendous, long Red Dragon. Twisting around the room to dodge the blade, he shot through the chamber windows, shattering them in his escape of the Palace.

The room was silent.

Mali did not know if he should try to fight Ixion or if he should do nothing and leave. Thinking quickly, he summoned his katanas, and Ixion whirled toward him with knives flashing.

❀ ❀ ❀

Ixion breathed in the frigid water of the Southern Continent. He did not truly mind being there all that much, though it was hardly his choice. Y'tal had told him to search there first for the possessor of the Emperor Regin. He had no intention of doing such a thing, though. He was tired of following everyone's orders and constantly being punished. He was on his own now. Ignoring Y'tal's orders for the past six years had led Ixion to gain enough strength and skill to defeat Randir and even kill Mali. That was only a taste of his new power, though. He had grandiose plans, and showing Randir that he was not to be messed with was only the beginning. His rank would hopefully change by the time the Emperor Regin's blood was taken.

He walked through Terin proudly. Ten years ago, he had been here to take three of the Guardians of Light. Unfortunately, the Golden Dragon had incinerated him before he could kill them. As much as he had contemplated revenge over the years, the Golden Dragon had not returned from Sharl Drake. The Light had indeed spread across the Southern Continent, and Terin had been influenced by this time of Light. Travelers came through a lot more frequently. Many had come just to speak to Varyx's new king, Lomeo.

King Lomeo had used his skill in *mysteria* to create a forest around Terin. Never before had Varyx held true flora. Ixion grinned wickedly. Indeed, King Lomeo had created something spectacular, a treasure that Ixion probably knew more about than Lomeo's own people.

Pulling the hood over his face, he entered one of the inns and asked for a room.

"Sorry, we're full."

When Ixion pulled the hood up a little, the innkeep saw the glint in his eyes and stammered, "Oh, I'm sorry, I didn't recognize you, sir. Right this way."

As Ixion followed, he realized that his redemption was

well on its way. Soon, the other Y'mordi would be bowing to
him. He was the one making the rules of the game now, and
no one could possibly beat him. The stairs creaked noisily as
he stepped across them and wondered with what poison he
was going to kill the innkeeper.

Sarn paced in the library of the Academy. She hated this
whole scenario. She had to do this mission without the help
of her twin sister Arnim, and she had to do it in disguise.
Before Arnim had departed for Earth, she had transformed
Sarn into an image of her younger self and then changed her
hair color from blonde to black. It would be an easily hidden
spell in the Academy since many teenage girls used similar
spells to hide pimples or freckles. Still, in order to remain in-
cognito, she would have to follow the rules of the Academy.

Despite her obvious impatience though, she did enjoy
being back there again. Before Arnim and she had become
Y'mordi, they had been studying here at the very same Academy. It was Sarn who had become bored with the place and
mastered most of the Academy's secrets first. When she had
learned the Dark Lord was seeking soldiers, she enlisted immediately and trained ceaselessly for it. Not wanting to leave
her sister to such a dangerous task, Arnim had joined her.
The one thing they had not expected was the mission to destroy the Academy at Gryphos.

The memory of the burning school brought tears to
Sarn's eyes. Remembering the task at hand, she wiped her
tears away with one hand while summoning her wand with
the other. She sent a blast of Air through the water in the
hopes that it could trace the metallic sheets of the books in
the library and find anything about the Demons. She sat
down at one of the computers and made a basic search for
the beings.

"'Demons . . . These monsters were servants of Dagan
during the Second Obsidian War and destroyed thousands

of soldiers. Dagan imbued five animals with his dark powers, and they grew to monstrous proportions, capable of casting spells and fighting with Dagan's own terrible ferocity . . . Tell me something I don't know," sighed Sarn. "This is going to take forever."

"And why are you so interested in Dagan's Demons, young one?"

Sarn whirled around to behold the Prophet of Nature, Mistress Leona. "Oh, Mistress Leona!" Having hardly ever played the good person, Sarn was at a loss for words. "What brings you here?"

Mistress Leona raised an eyebrow in puzzlement and replied, "I teach a few classes here every once in a while. Now, answer the question. What has called your attention to the Demons of legend?"

"It's just . . . I heard that one of them had been found and killed on the Northern Continent by that anima. I just wanted to know a little more about them."

"One was killed in the Northern Continent? Where did you hear this?"

Sarn realized then that she had given Mistress Leona some new information. Her mind scrambled for the best action. If she revealed herself now, it would be impossible to even begin her mission. "I . . . I overheard one of the Lords of the Shadows say it, Mistress Leona. They were . . . at the top of the Academy, where the input module is."

"How do you know where the input module is?"

Sarn rubbed the back of her head. She really did know too much information to give a good lie. "Mistress Leona, they said it was a spider that the horse anima killed—the Guardian of Light."

The Prophet's face paled at the knowledge. "If you are even partially accurate, the Demons did not vanish as much as we had hoped then. I must alert the Emperor of Light." Immediately, she summoned a Gate. Before she entered it, she turned back to Sarn and said, "What is your name, girl?"

"Um . . . my name is Iona . . . Iona Cabot."

"Well, Miss Cabot, you had better head to bed soon. You know the rules."

Sarn stuck out her tongue at the spot where Mistress Leona had stood seconds before. "Now I have to find the Demons before the Guardians do. Great . . ." Her spell of Air returned to her, but no interesting information about the Demons existed in the books of the library. Perhaps she should spend some time at the input module.

She left the library and strode to where the elevator was. As she walked, her high heels clicked against the hard floor. Then, she became aware of someone else's footsteps trying to match hers: She was being followed.

Sarn whirled around, releasing a blast of Force at the same time. The teenage boy did not know what hit him. She watched as he soared into one of the walls and his head slammed against it, his blood spattering the floor where he landed. He was fine, although his head would certainly be hurting in the morning. Again, she sighed. More than anything, she needed to be more careful. If Arnim were with her, she would not have gotten into as much trouble as she already had.

The elevator hummed to life and rose steadily to the peak of the Academy. Sarn's heartbeat slowed to a more even pace, and her nerves finally settled. She stepped across to the balcony railing and looked out at the Southern Continent that surrounded the castle. The world seemed so vast from up there, and it looked beautiful. She could remember all the times she had come up when she had been a student. From this place, the world did not look as if it had changed at all. However, she knew the truth. The world had certainly changed. The Academy had been her home, and when she had been forced to destroy it, she had been devastated. Then, after a few years, the Academy had been rebuilt, and she had

had nothing to do with it. She was an outcast, whether it was by choice, or force, or even fate.

"Tatsu and Kohana . . ."

The input module shimmered into visibility, and its mechanical voice responded, "Password confirmed."

"What can you tell me about the Demons?"

Screens appeared around the circular room, each one depicting one of the monsters of legend. The only one of the Y'mordi who had been able to control the Demons had been Y'tal. He had been able to ride the Demons into battle and command them to do his bidding as the Dark Lord had been able to do. Y'tal was such a puzzle, even to Sarn. His voice was high, and he was so short. He had to have been younger than her when he had taken the Trials. The surprise was not that he was good enough to be an Y'mordi, but that he was good enough to be the leader of the Y'mordi.

"The Demons were Dagan's dark pets, which he used to decimate whole forces on the field of battle. The five of them were unbeatable, and it is said that they could not even think for themselves. Dagan had supposedly had all of them under a strange form of possession."

Sarn muttered to herself, "Possession is becoming such a nuisance. The Demons, the Emperor Regin—and we are even trying to possess him ourselves. I would hate to ever have that happen to me." Then, she addressed the input module. "Do you know anything of their supposed whereabouts?"

"The Demons were destroyed in the Final Battle of the Second Obsidian War."

Sarn roared, "No, they weren't! They are still here, under your nose, and they have been here for centuries! How can you be so blind and stupid?" Her wand waved, and a spear of pure force launched itself at the input module, but the spell went straight through the machine. "Oops . . . Forgot about that . . ." she murmured. The input module was well-enchanted to protect itself from being touched. "Clearly, Pullatus thinks that the information is here somewhere. It might just take me a while to find it. I can do this." She closed her eyes and imagined Arnim standing beside her, giving her more confidence. "I can do this."

Xarden could remember the first day of his life. Before that, there had not been darkness, or light, or even nothingness. He had not even existed. The day he came into being, he stood there in a black robe and took in his first breath. He discovered that he could sense things around him, people, fish, and other hearts. He made those people explode with his power, and he saw no wrong in his actions. When he compared himself to the others around him, he saw himself as incomplete. After all, he only had half a heart.

Xarden had asked Y'tal a dozen times what had happened to him, what his life had been like, and what he had been before his heart had been sliced in half, but Y'tal offered only silence. He had learned the ways of this world quickly and had apparently returned to what others called his former level of skill, but he still felt distant. He wanted to know who the other half of him was and why the person had split himself. Clearly, the person had been able to separate himself from the darkness by concentrating it in one part of the heart. That concentration and Division had created Xarden. So, who was he before the Division?

"Pullatus, what are you going to do while everyone is out following your orders? Are you going to stay holed up in here as usual?" He knew he was pushing the limit, but he also knew he was acting as Pullatus's Adviser. "When are you going to take part in the fight?"

Y'tal's response was calm. "If we fail with Regin, then I shall lead the next fight. If world conquest is impossible with the Great Servants of the Darkness, then we shall use them solely to fight and kill the Guardians of Light. We shall let the Darkness itself worry about taking over the world. For now, I shall watch the world from afar. This is your test."

"Our test? Have we not been tested enough?"

"Hardly." The bluntness of the answer caught Xarden considerably off guard. "You all still have a long way to go, and our true conquest is yet to come. If we were to try it now, we would all fail miserably. We are not ready yet. All of you need to return to your former glory—even you, Xarden." Now, Xarden could hear the sneer in Y'tal's voice. "You have fallen as well. You would do well to train as you seek Maksimilian."

"Yes, Lord Y'tal." Xarden knew when to be a follower rather than a challenger. Instantly, he summoned a Gate that led to the Water Realm of Gevás where most of the other Y'mordi were. There in the Water Realm, the world was real. Fish swam, and Apolis existed in all its golden light. The question was of how to enter Apolis. The place was well barricaded thanks to the Emperor of Light's spells and well-trained guard. Even the walls were enchanted there. Still, Apolis would be the first place to check on the whereabouts of the Captain of the Enigma Brigade, Maksimilian.

He manipulated the light around him and became invisible. His eyes went to the shimmering sky in search of a vehicle preparing to enter Apolis. Once one finally came, he flew up toward it. His gloved hands grasped the bottom of the vehicle, and he allowed himself to be carried toward the city. Once they came closer to the gates, he transformed himself into pure water and shifted through the gears of the vehicle so as to be completely hidden inside the machine.

"Identification, please?"

The driver of the vehicle offered a badge of sorts, and the vehicle was allowed into the city. As soon as they were in, another couple of guards came up to the car to search it. The security of Apolis certainly had increased. The Emperor of Light was more paranoid than his father was. Xarden smirked from inside the vehicle. Emperor Helius was much smarter than his predecessor. Perhaps this one could last longer than the previous one. At the very least, Dragenopn Helius had proved himself in battle far better than John Helius had. Perhaps Dragenopn's being a Guardian of Light had something to do with that superlative strength.

The vehicle moved forward again, and this time, there were no more security stops. As soon as they turned onto a minor street, Xarden seeped out of the vehicle and allowed himself to splatter through the water of the city, sinking toward the houses. He landed between two buildings, and the water formed his natural outline. Darkness filled that figure, and he breathed. He was himself again.

"Now, where are you, Maksimilian?"

He turned right to see the enormous Palace of Light towering above him. Maybe the answer was in there somewhere. With caution at the forefront of his mind, he stepped forward, eyes darting back and forth among the buildings. This mission needed to stay as covert as possible. Then, he whispered through *mysteria*, "Valdridge, come to me. I need your aid in entering the Palace. Come to me, Servant of the Darkness. I need your aid."

As soon as he had spoken, he saw a dark figure approaching him from the direction of the graveyard.

2

Ace Helius

MATTHEW HELIUS STOOD outside his house and approached a bench made of pure silver. As he sat, a sigh of contention left his lips. The cold current of Apolis swept around him, and he reveled in that soothing wave. His black shirt rippled around his body, and he ran one hand through his dark hair. Though the world was hardly at peace now, he had found his own form of serenity there in Apolis. After living in the Western Continent with his father for years, he had never thought that he would love the city so much—but here he was with his own house and a family.

He heard William cry inside the house and got up to see what was wrong. As soon as he did, he sensed his wife Lilian move to take care of their son. Lilian was a being known as an anima, half-horse and half-human. Though Lilian had been worried that her being half-horse would make Matthew think she was less beautiful, he had loved her regardless of which form she took. William was their fully-human son who had Matthew's hair and face and Lilian's silver eyes.

A squirrel anima from Lilian's hometown, Senagul had become Matthew and Lilian's adopted son. When his real parents had died two years ago, Matthew and Lilian had taken him in and raised him alongside William. However, Senagul was practically a teenager now and a little more than rebellious.

At the sound of William's crying, Senagul came outside and sat beside Matthew. Much to Matthew's own surprise, he had never truly become accustomed to seeing Senagul's human form. The boy had preferred his squirrel form while in the Northern Continent, but there in Apolis, Senagul was usually guised as a human.

"Hey, Matthew, how's it going?"

Matthew smiled and responded, "I am doing well. What's wrong with your brother?"

Senagul rolled his brown eyes. "He ran into the door."

The bluntness of the remark made Matthew laugh. Maybe William was not the brightest kid for his age, but he certainly had a hard head, a desirable quality there in Gevás. Then, he heard Lilian speak into his mind, "Matt, William's fine. He just hit his head on the door. I am going to finish getting him ready, and then we can go, alright?"

"Sounds good to me." Anima had the ability to open mental communication with anyone around them. Though Matthew could respond effectively enough, he could not start such a conversation. "I'll make sure that Sena is ready."

Sena was Senagul's preferred name, and he was always frustrated when people did not call him that. Matthew turned to his adopted son and gave him a fond look.

Matthew himself had been called adopted for half his life. His mother Elizabeth had lied to him, his brother, Drage, and his sister, Helen about Matthew's origins because her husband, the deceased Emperor of Light John Helius, did not like Matthew at all. In reality, though, Matthew's mother was indeed Elizabeth, but his father had been the Prophet of Wind Derek Janus. Senagul truly was adopted, though. He never seemed to mind it.

"Hey Sena, is all your stuff packed?"

"Yeah, what little I'm bringing."

"Oh?"

The boy put his arms across the back of the bench and leaned back against it. "I am just bringing my gadg and a few books."

The gadg was an interesting piece of technology that was unique to Gevás: No other world had a device such as that one. In some ways, it served as a personal computer, but it was different in the device's ability to read its user's heart. By doing so, it could scan the world news for matters of personal interest. Along with that, the gadg noticed when its user was sad and provided articles or music to cheer up its user.

"It's almost time for the disq tournament, and I have to keep my eye on Jiron Mackey."

Unlike the Earthan sports with which Matthew was most familiar, disq was a game of individuals. One person would represent an entire city in this sport, and through years of competition, every kingdom would have one athlete representative to compete in the tournament that took place once every four years.

"When's the tournament start again?" Matthew asked jokingly, though he knew the answer already.

"It's in a week! It's gonna be the biggest, the grandest, the most spectacular event of my life!"

In that moment, Matthew saw a much younger Senagul.

Matthew laughed and ruffled the kid's hair. "Alright, well, make sure you are ready to go through the Gate."

Matthew left his son there and entered the house. The hallway held the same silver luster as the bench, and white lights illuminated the place. At the end of the hall, he turned to enter his and Lilian's bedroom. In the corner, his wooden staff stood against the wall. It was long and thick with an orb inside its head and ravens etched across its body. It was one of the greatest gifts his father had given him. The ravens were symbols of an ancient and mysterious group known as the Keepers.

His fingers traced the strong wood and felt every depression that the ravens' outlines made.

"I wish you were here, Dad. I really do."

His fingers closed around the staff and lifted it from the ground. He walked briskly out of the house, and a white light shot from his staff, creating a hole in the water in their front yard. The hole swirled the water around it to create what looked like a glowing whirlpool that was only a foot thick but six or seven feet tall.

"Are we ready?" said Lilian's voice in his mind.

"Yup, we're ready."

Lilian came out of the house with little William, and Senagul joined them from the bench. Matthew hoped that they were doing the right thing for their kids. After all, they all had been living happily in their cozy house in the city. Senagul would still be able to go to his school, but William had never really seen that much outside his own home.

Senagul was first to enter the Gate with his tote bag across his shoulder and gadg in his hands. William and Lilian followed. Finally, Matthew entered the Gate, and a world of light accompanied them. Golden walls surrounded them, with electric torches illuminating the hall. They were in the Palace of Light. The Gate closed behind them.

William gaped at how humongous the entrance hall of the Palace was and promptly ran in circles, while Senagul stepped forward and headed toward the guest bedroom he wanted.

Lilian stopped William and whispered in his ear, "Hey, you might want to beat Senagul there, or he'll get the best room."

As she had predicted, the little ball of fire went running straight past Senagul and down another hallway.

"You think that will tire little Will out?" Matthew asked

his wife.

"I do not think that at all, and you should know that."
She offered him a beautiful smile, and he gave one back to
her. They stepped together toward the Throne Room. To
Matthew, the place looked the same as it had ten years ago
when he had first come here. The only difference was that
there were two thrones now: Matthew's half-brother sat on
one, and one of his best friends sat on the other.

Drage rose and exclaimed as he approached Matthew,
"Hey, Matt, how is life, my friend?" Drage's brown hair
had gotten a bit longer, and most of the spikes of that hair
drooped over his eyes now, no longer able to carry their own
weight. Drage's eyes were back to their regular brown color,
though they had undergone a few changes several years ago.
He was dressed in a golden robe, similar to the one his father
had worn almost a decade ago.

Matthew hugged his half-brother. "All is well, Drage.
Any news on Regin?" Though Matthew was now a member
of the Emperor's Council, he had went on a temporary leave
for the past month to spend more time with Lilian and the
kids. Now was the time to delve into the most important
stages of the war, and Matthew had decided to move the family into the Palace for a while. He needed to stay here at the
Palace to take care of things, but he did not need to neglect
his family, either.

"Nothing too spectacular. At the request of many nations, I have been in contact with the Emperor Regin about a
period of truce on the day of the disq tournament. It is a big
deal here as you probably remember—don't understand why
though. Soccer is so much cooler, and it doesn't get as big a
crowd as this."

Though Matthew had never been that much into sports,
Drage had certainly been on most of the sports teams that his
high school and elementary school had had.

"Everyone is getting excited about the disq tournament."

Matthew had not watched a disq tournament yet, though he had been there long enough in Gevás to see two of them.

"Aren't you going to say hi to me?"

Matthew looked over Drage's shoulder to see Aria in her own golden robes. Her brown hair stretched across her back, and her blue eyes were as dazzling as ever. "Of course!" He went over to Aria and hugged her as well. "How has everything been?"

"Unruly, with the kids running around. Apollo turned four the other day, so she has been bragging to everyone about how old she is now."

Lilian nodded in understanding. "William has been a handful as well, though he is only three at the moment. How are the other two doing?"

Drage laughed at the question. "Well, Ace has been staying in trouble still. He seems to believe that the Palace servants are Shadows and feels the need to tackle every one of them he encounters. Alison is surprisingly still for a two-year-old." Drage rubbed the back of his head in embarrassment. "This parenting thing is harder than I thought, y'know?"

Matthew patted his shoulder and laughed with him. "Yeah, I know it, but it's a job that's not so easy to quit. Besides, I'm sure they'll be the best kids around when they're older."

"I don't know . . ." Drage said with his eyes squinted in skepticism. "That Ace might be a bit of trouble then, too."

As if he had heard his name, the little boy with black hair and white clothes came running into the throne room. "Hey Dad, I think I found one of the Y'mordi! It's that guy who keeps burning my fish at supper!"

While Aria, Matthew, and Lilian smiled in amusement, Drage rolled his eyes and picked up his son. "I'll be back in a minute," he muttered.

Drage, Matthew, and Aria had all heard of the name 'Ace' before this boy had been born. Years ago, a strange man had saved their lives and guided them on numerous occasions, and his name had been Ace. When Aria had done research on him, she discovered that there was a young man six hundred years ago who had been looking for a place called Paradise. In an image she had discovered at the Academy, the man had been surrounded by five marked circles, and a beautiful world thrived behind him. At the time of her son's birth, she had no intention of naming him after that man. Actually, Mistress Leona had suggested it at the time, believing the birthmark on the side of his knee to be in the shape of a spade from a card.

When Drage left the room, Aria asked Lilian, "So, how is Senagul doing? It's been a while since I've seen him."

Lilian gave a warm smile and replied, "He is doing well. He is heavily anticipating the disq tournament more than anything. His neglect for his studies is becoming a problem. However, on the whole, he is doing well. His grades are still considerably above average, and his manners remain flawless. I worry that he is lonely, though. Since his parents died, he has not been the same, cheerful squirrel that he once was. I am not sure if that is what is affecting him or just the coming of age."

Matthew wrapped an arm around her shoulder, and she grasped his hand tightly.

Aria smiled with a secret pleasure. When they had been just children, she had wondered when Matthew would ever get a girlfriend, and now, he was married with two kids of his own. In her mind, the two of them made a cute couple, though she thought it was a little weird that he would have fallen for a horse of all things. "I'm sure that he'll be better soon. Perhaps being here at the Palace will do him some good."

"Well," started Matthew, hoping to cheer up his wife. "There is no doubt that this place will do William some good. It's big enough to sate his adventurous curiosity, eh?"

Lilian looked him in the eye and glared. "I wonder from where he got that particular quality."

Matthew brushed a hand through his hair and grinned.

Aria stepped forward and said, "Oh, Matt, Drage wanted to show you something. Since he's busy, I can show you. It's that project of his he was wanting to keep a surprise. Well, he's finally ready to show it off."

"Really? It has taken him years to make it, whatever it is."

It had been shortly after Drage and Aria's marriage that Drage had told Matthew about a special project that would "revolutionize the goings-on of the Palace." Drage had refused to give any more information under the claim that it was not ready for showing off yet.

"Should we wait until Drage gets back? Surely, he wants to be the one to show me."

"Neh, he'll catch up. Come on." Aria gestured for the two of them to follow her, and they acquiesced in silence.

Despite himself, Matthew marveled at the architecture of the Palace. After Drage's father had been killed, this place had fallen into ruin, and the Emperor's Council had not helped matters. Under Drage's leadership though, the place had been restored. Every wall was back to its shimmering brilliance, and beautifully designed electric lights decorated every hallway. Servants ran the maintenance of the Palace, and Drage had taken every measure to get the best servants in the Southern Continent.

"Hey Aria, what happened in the last Council meeting?"

She put a hand to her chin in concentration. "Well, we discussed the temporary truce for the disq tournament. We fortified some of our defenses. Master Marqest is insisting that we forego honor and send an assassin to take care of the Emperor Regin. Master Valdridge is still claiming that we should forget the barriers around the city and focus more on making the first move."

"And Mistress Leona?"

"Well, she has recently brought us some disturbing news: the Demons of legend still dwell here in Gevás. They were never properly destroyed. It seems, Lilian, that you killed one in the North. Is this correct?"

Lilian's blank expression did not change, though her tone gave away her confusion. "You mean the Spider? I suppose so . . . What are the Demons exactly?"

They turned a corner, and another long, golden hallway extended before them. "The Demons were tremendous monsters that Dagan himself created. He used them as powerful weapons during the Obsidian Wars, and they were almost unstoppable. The books say that when Dagan and Lux fell, the Demons vanished as well. However, Mistress Leona has gathered information from a student at the Academy who overheard the Y'mordi speaking: they are seeking the remaining Demons. Supposedly, the Demons were once under Dagan's control, but with him gone, I guess that the Demons are a lot weaker now. So, the Y'mordi would be looking for them in order to gain control of them once more."

Matthew nodded in understanding. "So, we have to find these Demons before they do. How many people do we have on the search now?"

Aria shook her head. "No one. The Council is wanting to focus on the war now, and Drage doesn't even want to change that focus for the Demons. Once the Emperor Regin is dealt with, he will want to worry about the Demons immediately. He called it 'second priority stuff.'"

As they turned a final corner, Aria said, "Here it is." The three of them were now standing in front of a massive mirror in one of the hallways.

"He's been working on a mirror?" Matthew inquired in disbelief.

"No . . ." muttered Lilian. He felt her heart glow with the power of *mysteria,* and then, the mirror shimmered. "It's a Light spell." She dissolved the spell gradually, and a chamber appeared before them.

"He's getting better with *mysteria,* Aria. Have you been teaching him?"

"Nope. He just trains a lot. I don't see how he does it with no formal training. I keep telling him he should employ the aid of one of the Prophets. He has three on his Council, for pity's sake. He could be as strong as any one of them if he just gave up the tough-guy façade. Now that he's Emperor, he thinks he can't afford to show any weakness."

The three of them stepped forward into the dark chamber. Aria waved a wand, and a ball of Light appeared in front of them to light the way.

Matthew stated simply, "He can't, though."

Aria gave him a sharp look.

"It's understandable that he doesn't want to show any weakness, even to his own Council."

"How?"

"He's probably the youngest Emperor of Light this world has seen. If it had been up to the Council, they would have taken the throne themselves. He gained his position through confidence and a refusal to relent. If he weakens that for even one second, the Council will step all over him. Half of the time, you and I are the only ones who agree with what Drage says—and even we sometimes disagree with him."

Aria's diamond eyes softened as she looked at Matthew. "I'm just worried about him. He is so stressed all the time, and it always seems as if he takes it out on Ace."

They entered the end of the chamber where a massive machine occupied the space from ceiling to floor. Metallic parts shimmered in the light of Aria's spell, and wires lay exposed all around them.

"What is it?" Matthew said in utter awe.

A voice behind them ordered, "DATA, awaken."

The machine hummed to life, and lights flicked on all through the mechanical parts. In the middle of the titanic device, a box of light appeared and grew to create a cube of six identical screens. "Hello, your Majesty. How are you doing today?"

Drage stepped into the group. "I am doing well, DATA. How are you feeling? Are all of your systems doing okay?"

"Yes, they are. Who are your guests?"

Two green eyes appeared on the front screen and looked straight at Aria, Lilian, and Matthew.

Drage nudged Matthew forcefully and muttered, "Introduce yourself."

"Um . . . My name is Matthew. I'm Drage's—"

"Half-brother," replied DATA. "Yes, the Emperor has told me. I just hadn't seen your face in order to associate the two. So, that means you must be Lilian, correct? And you, Aria?"

"Yes," was Lilian's cold reply. Aria nodded.

"It is a pleasure to meet all of you," responded the machine.

Matthew was still in shock by the intelligence and personality of the device. "Drage, what is this thing? It's almost as smart as Marqest's COM back at Heaven's Isle."

"No, Matt . . ." Drage walked up to the screen and smiled. "DATA is a computer, like COM. She is packed with information and can research stuff all around the world. She has a few advantages over COM, though. For one, I have installed subunits for her module all across the world, giving her nearly unlimited sight across Gevás. She is the Digital and Arboreal Total Archive."

"Arboreal?" asked Matthew. "What does it have to do with trees?"

"Trees?"

Aria said, still staring up at the machine. "Yes, trees. Arboreal means having to do with trees."

Drage's eyes widened. "Really? I just thought it sounded cool, and I couldn't come with a better word to fill in that 'A.'

Oh well. I'm keeping it." He cleared his throat before continuing. "Anyways, the most defining feature of DATA is that she has a heart."

Now, even Aria was gaping. "What?!" she exclaimed.

At the moment, Drage was beaming with pride. "Over the past several years, I have been working on a computer that could not only think but could also feel; an ultimate machine that can cast spells as well as fight. However, DATA is not a weapon, but an asset to the Palace of Light itself. When I am finished with the programming, she will have full control over the barrier around Apolis, and I will have a lot more mages at my disposal."

DATA interrupted, "Yes, but unfortunately, you still have quite a bit of programming left to do, your Majesty. I see several glitches in the programming that I can point out for you but cannot fix myself. Also, in case you have forgotten, I am still missing a part."

Drage winced at the computer's words. "I'm sorry. I'm still working on that."

"What?" Matthew asked, his curiosity piqued.

"Matt . . . there was another reason for me asking you to spend more time here in the Palace. Something has come up, and Earth might be in danger. It seems that the Y'mordi are focusing on that world for the moment, and if Earth falls, then the Y'mordi will have far too much power. For us, the Y'mordi are a greater enemy than Regin could ever be. One of my servants discovered that the Y'mordi destroyed COM and set up a computer of their own by using Marqest's programming. However, they are planning on using their computer as a weapon against the people of Earth. To make matters worse, they took a part of the heart component I was using for DATA. I have no idea how they got in here to steal it, but they did. Now, DATA is incomplete, and Earth is in real danger."

Matthew crossed his arms, a little upset. "So, you expect

me to go to Earth and take care of this problem? I came here
so that I could spend a little more time with my family while
working, Drage."

"No, no, no, no. Matt, I want you to stay here and take
over for me while I go and fix the problem on Earth. Technically, you have full rights to it. Even if my father didn't say
anything about it, you are a Helius, and you can lead this
place as well as I can, if not better. It should just be for a few
days. Of course, Aria and the rest of the Council will be able
to help you. I really need a break from politics. I need to see
what's happening on Earth."

In all honesty, Matthew was perfectly okay with doing
this favor, as long as Drage was only gone for a few days.
However, he turned to his wife and asked her silently, "Is that
alright with you?"

"Yes, that shall be fine. The kids will still get to spend
plenty of time with you, and so shall I. Plus, there should not
be a battle for a while now."

Indeed, the war had been progressing at a snail's pace.
Neither the Emperor Regin nor Drage had made many major attacks, and each side had been well-defended such that
neither side was truly *winning* yet. If a battle was on the rise,
the Council would know about it several weeks in advance.

"Alright, Drage, just make it quick then."

Instantly, the golden robes vanished from Drage's body,
and in their place, a leather jacket and t-shirt covered his tor-
so while a simple pair of jeans stretched tight over his legs.
"Thanks a bunch, Matt! I was getting tired of being Emperor,
y'know."

"Yeah, I know. When are you leaving?"

Aria gave her husband a glare. "He will be leaving in a
few days. You can't just decide to leave all of a sudden. So, you
were just planning on leaving the kids with me?"

Drage's face gained a reddish hue, and his form shrunk in
embarrassment. "Um . . . No, I was planning on leaving them

with Matt and Lilian, too . . ."

"Matthew, Lilian, you two might want to get out of here."

Matthew smiled at Aria's words and gave Drage a farewell salute. "See you later!"

The two exited the secret chamber, and the mirror illusion reset itself behind them. "Hey, Lil, do you want to go check on the kids?"

"Yes, that would be fine." She held his arm to her side, then he leaned over and kissed the top of her head. "What if William starts learning to act like one of their kids?"

"I don't think we have to worry about that. If anything, he will learn to quit running into walls. Maybe Ace or one of the others can teach him something more productive to channel all that energy into. They're a bit older than him."

After a few minutes, they found the Throne Room again and saw Marqest standing there with his foot tapping the tile floor.

"Master Marqest, what are you doing here?" Matthew asked.

"I am here to speak with his Majesty about someone who wants to see him. It is hardly any of your concern."

Matthew ignored the remark. "What is this I hear about you advocating a stronger attack and less strategy? You are the Emperor's greatest advisor, so why do you not tell him to look before he leaps?"

"Because there is a time to wait and a time to fight. Now is the latter, as it happens. Regin and his Majesty are at a standstill, and the only thing that will happen from it is the division of Helio, chaos from its people, and possibly their deaths. His Majesty needs to do something that Regin will not expect. *There* is wisdom for you. Now, leave." Marqest's graying hair waved in the warm current of the Palace, but his stern face remained as cold as the weather outside.

Again, Matthew decided to leave it be and walked away from the Prophet of Water. Lilian stayed where she was, though. "Marqest, how can you be so mean? The two of you used to be friends. What has caused this sudden loathing? Are you troubled by your lack of closeness with his Majesty and therefore take out your rage on his half-brother? Explain to me who you are to be able to tell guests of his Majesty to leave at *your* convenience. His Majesty invited us to stay, so wish us a good day rather than being so cold." She walked away with Matthew.

When they had almost reached the door, Marqest called to them, "Wait." Lilian kept going, but Matthew stayed put.

Lilian turned to Matthew and muttered, "I'll be with the kids," and then she left.

Marqest approached Matthew with his arms open wide as if to embrace him. His eyes were soft as he started, "I am sorry, Matthew. Perhaps she is right. I have been rather frustrated with his Majesty, and I am taking it out on you. You have done nothing wrong to me, and you are ever patient." The older man grasped Matthew's shoulders and grinned proudly. "I remember when I first met you. You were just a bit shorter and looked a lot more confused. You've grown quite a lot. You truly have. I just hate that your half-brother has not done as much growing."

Matthew grinned as well, more than willing to drop the dispute. "Marqest, I do not think that he does wrong in his choices. In his mind, his actions are in the best interests of his people, not of his own pride and not of his own position. He would love not to be Emperor, I am sure, but he knows it is his responsibility. Our job as members of the Council, is to tell him what we think is best for the people, to give him ideas he does not think of, show him new flaws or advantages, and then *accept* his choice. We can't do any more than that."

"Marqest, what are you doing here?"

The two of them turned to see that Drage and Aria had returned. Marqest stepped away from Matthew but gave him a nod and a smile that communicated clearly, "Thank you." Matthew gave Drage and Aria his own glance of acknowledgment, then turned toward the door and headed back to Lilian and the kids.

In one room, Senagul was fascinated by his gadg, probably keeping track of the disq stats at the moment. Down the hall, Matthew heard the fervent yelling of several young children. He entered the large room to see William and Ace playing tag, while the two girls, Apollo and Alison, were trying to read a couple of picture books. At least Apollo was trying to teach her younger sister how to read.

Apollo had Drage's brown hair and Aria's light blue eyes. She seemed a bit tall for her age, but her most stunning characteristic was how calm she was. Alison was an exact replica of Drage in female form. Her short brown hair went barely over her muddy brown eyes, and a single freckle dotted the center of her nose. She was two years younger than her brother and sister, but she seemed just as captivated by the children's story about the Dragon and the fish as much as Apollo was.

Matthew's eyes went back to William. The boy was certainly enjoying the company, and hopefully the exercise would tire him out more. On the other hand, Matthew decided that as long as William was not running into doors, he would be fine.

"What are you thinking about?" Lilian whispered from behind him.

He jumped. "Don't do that!"

She wrapped her arms around his waist and kissed the center of his back. "What are you thinking about? You look pensive."

He sighed and relaxed under Lilian's touch. "I am just thinking about the future. These kids are growing up in a world plagued by monsters. On Earth, we didn't have to worry about the Y'mordi, or Regin, or people like that."

"Sure you did. From what you have told me, the crime is much higher on Earth, and wars are far more destructive with those powerful bombs about which you have previously told me."

Matthew raised his eyebrows and nodded in agreement. "That is true, I suppose. So, why does it seem as if we will be sending our children into the middle of something that we started? It doesn't seem right."

"The Eastern Continent shall be defeated before William has to start school. Do not worry about that. Have a little faith, alright?"

Matthew smiled as she stood on tiptoe and kissed his neck. As she turned around to leave, she glowed with a white light and transformed into a beautiful white mare. Matthew always thought she was just as pretty a horse as she was a human. Her hair was immaculate, and her tail and mane appeared as if they had been brushed a thousand times a day. She turned her head back to him, and those silver eyes stared deep into him.

He mouthed the words, "I love you."

Her eyes brightened, and in his head, he heard her respond, "I love you as well, Matthew." Then, she left the room.

He glanced back at his son and smiled. Perhaps there was some hope for him in the future. Every time Matthew had thought about his son and the future, he wondered if his son would be as adept at Time spells as Matthew was. William could have the blood of the Keepers in him as well, and one day, Matthew might make a staff of ravens for his son as well. William turned from his game to face his father, and he exclaimed, "Daddy!"

Ace sped past the three-year-old and tapped his shoulder. "Tag, you're it!"

At this point, William's face wrinkled as if it were about to cry. "That's not fair!" Without another moment of hesitation, he chased the older boy around the room.

Matthew squinted his eyes, watching Drage's son. Ever since he had learned of the son's name, he had been trying to see if it was indeed the same Ace who had saved his, Drage's, and Aria's lives back on Earth. His memory of that Ace was rather weak, but the voice had been permanently branded into his mind. Still, Drage's Ace had a long way to go before his voice changed. Time knew all answers, but Matthew was not yet ready to traverse the stream of time to find those answers.

He turned away from the room and searched for Lilian. By opening his heart a little, he could sense the memory of Time: he could sense the most recent events in the area, allowing him to see where Lilian had gone. When he found her, he realized the significance of the upstairs room. It was the room he had used in the Palace his first time here. "How did you know this was the one?"

She smiled at him. "I made a good guess," she communicated mentally.

"You never guess though, Lil."

"You are correct. You have shown me before, but you must not remember it."

Matthew smiled at her and hugged her long neck, rubbing his fingers through her white mane.

3

Digital Heart

YOUR MAJESTY, IS something wrong with DATA? She is not functioning the same way." These words appeared on the green screen in front of the griffin. "What happened?"

Drage put his hands on the keyboard of the massive computer and leaned against it. "Feranx, the Y'mordi have taken a piece of my secret component. DATA cannot function the same way without it. It seems they are using that piece in Cronus 624, that machine you encountered on Heaven's Isle."

Feranx's claws clicked against his own luminescent keyboard. "But your Majesty, why would they need that piece? What is so special about this component I don't know about?"

With a sigh of surrender, Drage explained. "Feranx, the component I was installing into DATA was a heart." Feranx's eyes widened, but, before the griffin could start typing, Drage held up one hand. "When a person is born, that body develops a heart. However, hearts are not just inherited. There is a connection between the physical realm and the realm of hearts. Birth is one such tie. Death severs that tie, which is why resurrection was supposedly a type of Darkness. Those spells would summon heartless bodies, monsters. After studying the heart, I found a way to actually create one with one slight flaw: the heart needed a physical vessel along with stronger connections to the physical world. Inside DATA, I have planted thousands of memories of my own and others. In actuality, she has the ability to scan a person's heart if the person is willing and inherit all of those memories."

Finally, Feranx had to interrupt. "Pardon me, your Majesty, but how did you actually create a heart?"

At this question, Drage smiled. "Simple. It's one of the most basic things you learn about hearts. Every heart is comprised of every basic Element in every form. Every person is born equal on the level of hearts, but the person's environment, experiences, and family all affect the heart over time, shifting the balance to one or two Elements. I had to combine the exact amount of each Element in the midst of a vessel in which memories were waiting to be grabbed. DATA was that vessel."

"So, whatever the Y'mordi took from DATA has a great potential to be dangerous, right?"

"Right. They took a piece of the memory drive. If they put that into Cronus 624, it will probably think that one of them is me and will do whatever it takes to defend and serve that Y'mordi, even destroy a world. However, based on the scan I ran, they only copied some of the programming code for DATA. Most of the defense and offense capabilities were scanned, and it should be able to use *mysteria* as well. The machine won't be as knowledgeable as this one, but it could pack a little more punch."

"What are you going to do, your Majesty?" Feranx's wings twitched nervously. He could predict what the Emperor of Light was going to say, but he was not excited to hear it.

Drage gestured for Feranx to follow him back to the

Throne Room. "You and I are going to go to Earth and stop the Cronus program. Recent information has shown that the Y'mordi are seeking monsters that have remained hidden since the first two Obsidian Wars. Perhaps they shall use Cronus to find one on Earth. Regardless of how they intend to use Cronus, we need to shut that program down and get the piece of the memory component back."

As they walked, Feranx's head ruff flattened against his skull. The griffin had never been much into politics or war, and he did not like the idea of going to Earth on some impossible mission that would mean confronting a military machine. He was a mechanic and a programmer, not a soldier. Grudgingly, he typed, "Yes, your Majesty. When do we leave?"

They arrived in the Throne Room. "In three days. Be ready to leave by that time." Out of the corner of his eye, Drage could see Marqest standing impatiently at the main entrance to the Throne Room, waiting to invite Drage's next visitor. Drage hoped that the old Prophet had not heard too much of what he had been telling Feranx. He had not revealed to the Council yet that he would be leaving for Earth in a few days. "You are dismissed, Feranx."

"Yes, your Majesty," typed the griffin with a bow. The screen and keyboard faded into nothingness as the device at his waist went into sleep mode. The griffin made another bow to Marqest as Feranx passed him.

"Come in, Master Marqest. Show our guest in."

Marqest stepped forward, and a teenage girl followed him into the room. "Your Majesty, I present to you . . . the Khaosdog." He sneered as he said the name that he considered too odd for a young lady.

"Thank you, Master Marqest. You are dismissed." The Prophet bowed and left the two alone. "What can I do for you, Miss Khaosdog? I recall receiving a flyer from Feranx that portrayed some of your works not too long ago.

'Khaosdog's Wonder Works,' if I remember correctly?"

The girl bowed to him and replied as she rose, "Yes, your Majesty, that is correct."

In her eyes, the Emperor glowed with a golden brilliance. His aureate robes extended from the throne itself and seemed to meld with the floor, sparkling just as much as the well-polished walls, floor, and ceiling. "Well, child, what can I do for you today?"

"Your Majesty, I would like to show you some of my works. I would greatly appreciate the opportunity to work for his Majesty. As an Earthan artist, I would think that you would have an interest in my style of art and would employ my services."

Drage's eyes widened in surprise. "You are from Earth?"

"Yes, your Majesty. I come from the United States there. You are from there as well, your Majesty?"

"Yes. I am from Massachusetts, actually. Tell me: What purpose do you think you will serve by being an artist here at the Palace? How will your work benefit me?"

She stammered in return, "Your Majesty . . . I can . . . make paintings of your choice to place across your elegant Palace of Light."

"I have plenty of paintings, though. Throughout every hall, there are paintings of past Emperors of Light. Why should I throw away that history? I mean you no disrespect, Miss Khaosdog, but I see no need for your employment."

"Pardon me, your Majesty," she pleaded, "but from what I have heard about you, you are revolutionary. You are different from every Emperor ever to rule Helio, and praise of your name whispers across the sea. Even with a bloodline of treachery and civil unrest, you have led your people out of the darkness. I would not mean to throw away or discredit the past or even to make a shrine for you. I only wish to make the art in this place more representative of your Majesty's brilliant work and ideas. When has there ever been a painting of a nonhuman in these golden walls? When has there been an image of the gorgeous landmarks of this city in this Palace? When—?"

"Alright, alright!" He laughed loudly. "I get the picture, no pun intended."

The Khaosdog exhaled heavily. "Sorry, I am a bit nervous." Then, what he said dawned on her. "You mean you'll hire me, your Majesty?"

A nod was enough answer for her, and she leaped in excitement with an ecstatic cry of joy. "Miss Khaosdog, I will arrange for your things to be moved to one of the bedrooms here. I trust you are staying at a hotel around here?"

"Yes, your Majesty."

"Very good." Drage cast a simple Light spell to signal one of his servants, and the man entered the Throne Room seconds later.

"Did you call, your Majesty?"

"Yes, follow this young lady to her hotel and help move her stuff here into one of the guest bedrooms."

The servant bowed and escorted the Khaosdog out of the room. Drage was glad for the quiet at last. First, Matthew and his family had come, then Marqest, Feranx, and the Khaosdog had followed. It had certainly been a busy day. He could not wait to go back to Earth. Of course, it was mostly a business trip, but hopefully he would get to see his sister and mother while he was there. He had not seen them since his wedding five years ago. The illusion of his gold robes faded, and his regular Earthan clothes became visible again.

His heart scanned the area to make sure that no one was coming this way before summoning his Sword. Both the hilt and blade were bright silver, showing his reflection as clearly as any mirror. The Sword of Destiny was a Spirit Sword capable of slashing through almost anything with the utmost ease. Over the years, Drage had learned that holding the blade facilitated his powers of *mysteria*. The fragment of the Great

Spirit that dwelled in the Sword had a strong attachment to his heart. At all times, the Sword fed itself on a portion of Drage's heart, though *mysteria* did not have a limit even in one person's heart. *Mysteria* did not have to follow the laws of physics and science that governed the physical realm.

He waved the blade experimentally, and it swished in the water, flowing gracefully as it cut the water. The blade lowered to make a diagonal line in front of his lower legs. This form was the starting stance that his old mentor Draconis had taught him. It had been called the way of the Dragon, and it had served Drage well on numerous occasions. With fluid motions, he slashed the water around him, staying on his toes and ready to change directions instantly. He maneuvered the blade around him effortlessly, forming a deadly dance of sorts.

Then, he heard a whooshing sound, and a Gate opened in the middle of the Throne Room. Drage ceased his practice and turned to face the newcomer. "Captain Bryco, I was not expecting you today. What is amiss?"

The man in the golden robe rose from his bow, and Drage beheld the crimson phoenix that adorned the chest of the robe. "Forgive me for interrupting, your Majesty."

Drage put his fists to his hips and took on a lecturing tone. "What have I told you about calling me that? We work closely enough together to where we can speak to each other on a more familiar basis. You're the Captain of the Enigma Brigade, and I am the Emperor of Light. I feel we can dispense with the formalities."

"Of course, Lord Helius." Drage grinned at the other title. It was much better than "your Majesty," and it was sufficient, he decided. "We managed to reach some negotiations with a couple of the Eastern kings, and it seems that they are willing to come to this truce."

"And Regin?"

"He still will not even see us, Lord Helius. He refuses to

allow us entry into his castle."

Drage sighed as he crossed over to the throne. "Very well. I will probably have to send a Council member for that particular task. I suppose the Brigade is ready for the next task, Captain?"

"Yes, sir." Bryco's dark hair reminded Drage of his own son's black hair. He was not sure where Ace had gotten that hair, As both Drage's and Aria's parents had had brown hair. "What would you have us do?"

After Drage had announced to the world the existence of the Enigma Brigade, its Captain at the time, Maksimilian, had left without a word. Bryco had been next in line to be the Brigade's leader. The Brigade was presently made up of five members: Bryco, Sume, Gaspard, Thera, and Nilram. Of course, Drage had not revealed the identities of the Brigade's members to the public, but he felt it was important that his people at least knew of their existence, though Maksimilian had clearly felt otherwise. His disappearance was hardly a nuisance to Drage though: the two of them had had considerable tension between them, and they had hated each other.

However, Drage had liked Bryco almost instantly. Bryco knew his place and never turned down a mission. "I have not done a good enough job with the new king in Varyx, Lomeo. I think I would like for you all to go over there and settle some negotiations with him. I want reassurance that he will be willing to aid me in this time of war. I have heard that he is quite the leader, and his people love him all over his kingdom. Do you think you all could handle him?"

Bryco replied immediately, "Yes, Lord Helius. It shall be done."

Drage nodded in confirmation. "Good. This is a little more of a low pressure mission, so there is no real rush. Maybe you can relax around Terin yourself, Bryco."

The slightly older man replied with a smile, "Perhaps I shall, my Lord."

"Good. You are dismissed, Bryco." The Brigadier prepared a Gate, but, before he stepped through it, Drage called, "Actually, Bryco—could you summon the rest of the Brigade quickly? I would like to have a word with all of you. It has been a while since I have addressed the group, would you not agree?"

Bryco nodded. "Of course." At his heart's command, the other four Brigadiers appeared.

All four knelt before the Emperor of Light. Sume was bowing the deepest. Drage noted that Sume was getting older each time he saw the man. Drage could see a few gray hairs on that wrinkling head. All the same, Sume had been in the Brigade longer than any of the others. Drage's own father had recruited Sume. Even if he was old, Sume was a fighter, in both the literal and the figurative sense. "Sume, you may rise."

Drage shifted his focus to the next member. Gaspard had the same short blonde hair now that he had had six years ago when Drage had fought him in the Temple of the Spirits. The one thing that was noticeably different was the standard military sword at his waist. For a couple of years, Gaspard had wielded the Spirit Sword known as the Behemoth, but, one night, it had been stolen. His skill in swordplay had fallen considerably ever since. "Gaspard, rise. How has your training been progressing?"

"All has been well, your Majesty." Drage grimaced at the name, but he allowed Gaspard to continue. "I am steadily returning to my former skill, sir."

"Good, I am glad to hear it." He turned to the next member. Thera was the first female ever to be in the Enigma Brigade, and Drage himself had recruited her. He had seen her fight in one of the battles against Regin, and her skills with *mysteria* were simply amazing. When testing her, he had discovered that she had a certain knack for manipulation and negotiation, qualities he looked for constantly in the Enigma

Brigade. "Thera, you may rise." When she stood, he marveled at her soft blonde hair and deep green eyes and shook his head immediately afterward. He knew better.

The final member was a tall, red-haired man named Nilram. He was a lion anima and the first nonhuman ever to join the Brigade. Even in his recruiting, Drage had been keeping an eye open for anyone who was skilled enough to be in the Brigade, regardless of species or gender. Nilram had moved to Apolis after Drage had removed the exile, and the anima was a true master at fighting without weapons. A martial arts expert, Nilram had been able to win one of the local fighting tournaments that allowed the usage of a sword. Drage had watched Nilram with keen interest and had hired the lion anima on the spot. "Nilram, you may rise as well."

"Yes, your Majesty."

Drage stepped back and addressed the whole group. "You all did well on that mission, and I am pleased with all of you. I trust that Captain Bryco is keeping all of you in shape. Your next mission should be a much easier task, but that does not promote laziness or lack of vigilance. I have sent your Captain the next mission over at HQ. I expect this one to be handled with finesse, understood?"

"Yes, your Majesty!" all five of them called in unison.

The Emperor of Light shivered in disgust at the title. "Very well. You are all dismissed."

As soon as the words were spoken, they each summoned a Gate and exited the Throne Room.

He considered summoning his Sword again for practice, but thought better of it, guessing that someone would need him again shortly. With a defeated sigh, he walked toward the playroom for the children. Perhaps Matthew was still there.

As he walked, he regarded the paintings he passed. This hall had the most recent rulers. He passed Lord Seth Mentiris, the Emperor who had outcast Marqest and exiled all nonhumans; Lord Bral Helius, the man who had hired Draconis as his protector; and Drage's own father, Lord John Helius. Several painters had come to him previously and had offered to make a portrait of Drage himself for the halls, but Drage had declined, not thinking himself worthy of such an honor yet. He felt as if most of what he was doing was cleaning up after the other Emperors' messes, especially those of Mentiris.

Finally, he reached the playroom. Ace and William were both passed out on the floor, while Apollo and Alison were still reading. However, Matthew and Lilian were nowhere to be found. He walked over to the nearby guest bedrooms and knocked on a few doors until Matthew opened one finally.

"Drage?"

"Oh, there you are. May I speak with you?"

"Of course." Matthew stepped into the hall and closed the door behind him. "Did you finally take care of all your visitors?"

Drage shrugged. "Hopefully. I guess we will have to wait and see, though, huh?"

The two walked down the hallway for a while in silence, then. Finally, Drage summoned a Gate that glimmered with golden light. Matthew followed him into the portal, and they both stood on top of the Palace of Light itself.

Matthew was enthralled by the sight before them. The city of Apolis glowed beneath, but the world beyond was cold and dark, the shadowed depths of an underwater world.

The two breathed in the still night. "Matthew, this is where I go when I'm tired of being Emperor." They were standing on a flat part of the roof of the Palace, a form of battlement that had never been finished during John's rule. "It's so quiet here."

Together, they stared out at the world.

"It is also where I train, Matt."

Immediately, Drage summoned and swung his Sword,

while Matthew sidestepped away from the blade and summoned his own staff. Every slash Drage made was blocked by Matthew's rapid whirling of the wooden, raven-engraved staff. Though they were fighting each other as fiercely as they would have fought any other enemy, they were smiling. They had not dueled in several years. Neither of them cast any spells, though both could not help but grasp the tantalizing power and sense each incoming attack. That ability had become second nature to them. Occasionally, one of them would be forced to the edge of the circular arena and would stumble, but a *mysteria*-induced leap sent them over their opponent's head and to the opposite side of the area.

"Matt, how'd you get so fast, huh?"

Matthew laughed after blocking another attack. "I'm tempted to say the same to you, but quite frankly, you are just too slow." He stabbed his staff at Drage, but Drage dodged it with ease and launched a counterattack. Neither weapon touched the flesh of its target, but both wielders grew tired.

After half an hour of the struggling, they both lay down with exhaustion overcoming their bodies. "Matt, how many years has it been since we've done that?"

Matthew started to count his fingers before realizing that he did not have enough fingers. "I think it's been ten, Drage. It was back when we were on the beach, the afternoon before Ace showed up."

Drage rested his head on his arms as he looked up into the blue. "Yeah . . . Ace . . ."

"He is the Wolf, the Shadow, the Remnant, and the Seeker of Paradise."

"And he could be my son." Drage's voice was deep and grim, full of fear and foreboding.

Matthew turned to face his half-brother. "What would be so bad if he was? The guy saved our lives and helped us out often enough. Sure, he was more than a little enigmatic, but he wasn't a bad person."

"I don't want my son to be nothing more than an illusion."

Matthew could sense the amount of thought Drage had put into this idea. "Drage . . . An illusion is what you are called when you travel the streams of time. It is not that the person isn't real. It's that the person *shouldn't* be real . . . at least, not in that time period."

Drage did not respond. He pondered what Matthew had said and wondered if that definition was any better than what he had been thinking. Finally, he said, "Do you think he ever made it back to his normal time?"

"I think there is more than a good chance of it. My father told me that anyone who learns to travel through time has to learn the rules first. The Keepers acted as a police of it, even through time, probably even as far forward as Ace, if your son is indeed the same Ace. So, that means that Ace would know the importance of staying alive and not causing too much trouble as he traveled time. However, one thing struck me as odd about Ace and his time travel . . ."

Drage turned toward Matthew. "What?"

Matthew sighed in his own thoughts. "Well, when one travels through time, you are not supposed to mess with things that did not travel through time as well. It's against the rules. You can go through time and stay hidden, disguised, and learn things you didn't know. That's fine, but you can't change things. Ace has done just that. He stopped us from being killed on Earth, and he helped us a few times around Gevás our first year here. So, how did he get away with that?"

"Maybe he didn't . . ."

To that statement, Matthew did not have a response. He did not think that the Keepers stopped Ace, because the things Ace did were too far apart in time. On the other hand, though, Ace could have transported himself a few days forward after helping them on Earth. Too many unanswered questions revolved around the mystery of Ace, and Aria's information had not helped matters. She had mentioned a

Seeker of Paradise that had existed six hundred years ago. Was that the Ace they had met, or was Drage's son the Ace that had helped them? Even more puzzling, were all three Ace's the same person? "Maybe . . . no, never mind."

"What is it, Matt?"

"Well, perhaps it's time I tried traveling the streams of time myself. Maybe I could try going back to when Ace was here and talk to him. Perhaps he won't be so elusive this time, and we could actually solve this mystery for good." Still, Matthew was hesitant. He had not truly learned all the rules of Time yet, and it was truly complex. He worried about what might happen to him.

Drage noticed Matthew's hesitation and ventured, "Well, is there any way you could find out more about that traveling? I mean, is there anyone who can teach you?"

Matthew shook his head. His father had been the last of the Keepers. His fingers naturally went to caress the ravens on his staff as he thought back to his father's words of advice on traveling through time. "But I have to learn it at some point, I suppose. Maybe, I will try it."

"Do you think I should go with you?" Drage asked curiously. He genuinely was captivated by the idea of traveling through time itself, though it was also a bizarre and almost frightening prospect. "I could, if you needed me to."

"No. I think that if I do it, I might take Lilian with me, though. She has a better grasp on *mysteria* than I ever could. Plus, I am sure that Aria could watch William and Senagul anyways, right?"

"For sure. She wouldn't mind. You would have to act like I didn't say that, though. She hates when you assume she'll do something for you."

Matthew laughed. "I'm sure she does. Well, are you ready to go back down?"

"Not yet . . ." Drage lifted a hand, and a shower of fireworks lit up in the dark water above them, providing a brilliant display for the people of Apolis. Drage's eyes closed, and his hands moved with the fireworks. One firework turned into a lion that danced all the way down the Palace, while a Dragon roared above them and spewed dazzling fireworks across the city. Matthew was entranced by the display. Even after all that Drage had been through, he had not forgotten the beauty that light could make, and that would be something that Drage's own people would never forget.

"So, you have no idea where Maksimilian is?" It was the sixth time that Xarden had asked Valdridge, but the answer had never changed.

"No, Y'mordi. I know nothing about the Enigma Brigade, apparently less than you did. I have heard about him only from some stupid soldier a few years ago. He was apparently the one who killed several of Regin's guards and servants while the exile still existed."

Xarden tapped his scepter impatiently. He needed at least some lead in order to find the Captain of the Enigma Brigade. "Well, then, make it your top priority. Bring it up at the next Council meeting. I need to know where to start looking as soon as possible."

"I'll do it when I can, Xarden. I make no promises."

Instantly, Xarden raised his scepter, and a wave of Force grabbed Valdridge's throat, strangling him. "You have yet to learn your place, Servant. I could snap you in half right now."

Valdridge scrambled for breath but could not take in a single gasp. "I . . ."

"—am becoming a nuisance. Even Pullatus tires of your antics. Our next puppet has been found, and you are here playing leader of the Emperor's Council? You are a disgusting waste of flesh." In anger, Xarden threw the man against the wall and tightened his hold on Valdridge's neck. "Why should we even bother keeping you alive?"

Valdridge managed between gasps, "I can still . . . provide

info! The Council . . . knows about the Demons, Xarden. Someone apparently overheard one of you at the Academy."

Xarden growled at the news. "Sarn . . ."

"What are you going to do about that? The Emperor is planning on holding off on the Demons for the moment, but he will have his eyes and ears alert to any strange happenings. Does that interfere with the plan at all?"

The Y'mordi considered it for a moment. "No, I do not think that this news changes anything. The Emperor will still go to Earth. In the meantime, you would be doing well to keep Matthew in the Palace at all times." Using a more serious tone, he added, "And in the next meeting, find out about Maksimilian. This is it, Valdridge. I have Pullatus's permission to kill you if you disappoint me."

"What?" said a now flustered Prophet of Light.

Xarden smirked. "Yes, it seems that you truly are not as valuable as you once thought. Even Pullatus is fine with disposing of you if you continue to provide trouble for me. So, that means you had better do a better job of following orders. You think because you are an elder, you deserve more respect, but I am centuries older than you are, Valdridge. Do not forget that." He summoned an icy Gate in the nearby water and finished, "I shall be back in two days. You had better have the information I need, Valdridge. Your life depends on it."

Valdridge glared at the closing portal and snarled viciously. "The Rebirth is on its rise. Soon, the Division shall be undone, and this world shall fall into its deepest darkness. Then, even the Y'mordi will bow before me."

Lilian finished tucking William into bed before checking on Senagul. The teenage squirrel anima was still checking his gadg for the latest disq stats, but she figured that he could stay up a while longer. He would probably fall asleep keeping up with the incoming schedule for the tournament.

She walked past his room and reverted to her horse form.

It felt so much more natural to her. Appearing human took some level of conscious control, and when she retired for the night, a horse is what she became naturally. She had never heard of an anima being able to sleep in its human form. It was just too unnatural. Matthew was just taking off his shirt as she walked into the bedroom.

"Did William get to bed alright?" he asked her with concern.

"Yes, he is fast asleep." She glanced at his strong, muscular chest while he was not looking, and her eyes went to the blankets, moving them with the slightest trace of *mysteria*. With that, she was able to lift the covers and get into bed without trouble. Then, the blankets landed comfortably on her back.

When Matthew had finished undressing, he joined her in the bed. "Tomorrow, it might be a good idea to take Senagul and William out to check out the Imperial Gardens. I'm sure they would like that."

"You are probably correct. They have never been." She turned her white snout to him and kissed his face with her large lips.

"Hey, that tickles!"

She smiled noticeably, and she placed her hooves softly across his body, feeling his muscles relax as her feet massaged his back. "We have a rather big day tomorrow then, if we intend on showing them bits of the city."

"Yes, we should probably get some sleep." Matthew yawned deeply as he wrapped his own arms around his beautiful wife. Usually, they started falling asleep in each other's arms, but as soon as they both fell asleep, Matthew frequently rolled about too much for them to wake up in the same position.

"Yes, we probably should." With a quick spell, she turned off the light in the room and rested her head softly against her husband's thick, dark hair. She had never thought that she would fall in love with a human, and now she was married to one with an anima child and a human one as well. She was so glad to have met someone as wonderful as Matthew. He was patient, charming, thoughtful, and, most of all, an animal lover. She smiled again as she rubbed her snout appreciatively against his face and closed her silver eyes, welcoming the dreams that would soon follow.

4

King Lomeo

"So, what are our orders, Captain?"

Bryco scanned the room to make sure the barriers were all erected around the room. Silence was always key in their meetings, and caution was one of his strengths. Once he was satisfied with Thera's spells, he began, "We are to negotiate with King Lomeo in Varyx. His Majesty, the Emperor of Light, wishes to reaffirm their close ties in these times of war." These were the types of missions that Bryco had always thought they should do.

When Maksimilian had been Captain, Bryco had always questioned a lot of Maksimilian's violent and heartless methods. The Enigma Brigade had been assassins for the Emperor of Light and had been that way ever since Lord Mentiris. Maksimilian, that red-haired tyrant, had left the Brigade as soon as Lord Helius had informed the public of the Brigade's existence. Bryco knew that Maksimilian had been the one who had stolen Gaspard's Sword, the Behemoth. Maksimilian's hunger for the power of the five Spirit Swords had led to his corruption. Six years ago, the Captain had ordered Bryco to kill his second-in-command, Tilgé, though Bryco had helped Tilgé fake his own death instead.

Thera replied, "That does not seem so bad. It's still a Southern kingdom, so the King should be pretty compliant. I guess that's why his Majesty, the Emperor of Light, told us that it would be an easier mission."

Gaspard nodded. "Yes, but we have to stay determined and treat this like it is any other mission. No mess-ups." Gaspard now held the third rank in the Brigade, and he was a proud holder of that position.

Their headquarters were an abandoned Gatemaster's house. Gatemasters were people whose sole profession was summoning Gates to transport other people around the world. Of course, longer distance trips meant higher cost, and in general, Gatemasters were rather costly. They were for high class people who could not wield a sufficient amount of *mysteria* to create a Gate themselves.

Supposedly, the Gatemaster who had owned this building had passed away a few years ago, but in the war, there was simply not a strong enough reason to demolish the building. So, the Emperor of Light had allowed the Enigma Brigade to set up headquarters there.

"When do we leave for it?" Nilram asked with his deep voice.

"At dawn. However, we are going to try our long approach."

Thera groaned in disappointment. "But those missions take forever. I can't stand doing everything the long approach."

The lion anima beside her laughed and replied, "That's why it is called the long approach. Besides, it usually gives us time to relax. But, as his Majesty said, we need to stay focused even while we relax."

Sume added, "We need to play this one by the rules. Step one: we settle into the city. Step two: we announce ourselves and our intent while waiting for the King to respond to us.

Step three: we take every step to gain the favor of the towns-people and learning of the area's customs. Step four: we ar-range a meeting with the King."

Bryco smiled at Sume's well-versed knowledge. He had always been able to quote from the manual that Bryco and Lord Helius had written a few years ago. For the first time in centuries, the Engima Brigade had standard procedure. The change of pace was a great improvement for Bryco and Sume, who had been with the Brigade for a very long time. With the Emperor of Light finally having a direct involve-ment with the Brigade's methods, Bryco felt that the Brigade now better represented the Light and its true purpose. Still, not knowing where Maksimilian was worried him. Assum-ing that Maksimilian had two of the Spirit Swords now, he would still be seeking the other three. Bryco realized that the Emperor of Light had one of these Swords, but clearly Maksimilian had no interest in that particular weapon.

"Very good, Sume," Bryco stated simply. "For now, you are all dismissed. We shall reconvene here at dawn to settle into Terin."

The Brigadiers all made a bow to their Captain, and three of them disappeared. Only Bryco and Nilram remained. "Can I help you, Nilram?"

Again, Nilram bowed before stating, "I'm sorry, Cap-tain, but I was wondering something if you would be so kind as to satisfy my curiosity."

"Go on," Bryco said warily to the dark-skinned anima.

"I was wondering if you would mind if I reverted to my lion form more often." Bryco raised an eyebrow in surprise and some confusion. Nilram hastily added, "Well . . . it's just . . . When I first joined the Brigade, I stayed in human form as much as possible to be polite, to show that I could function as well as everyone else even if I was an anima. There is still some prejudice in the world, and I didn't want anyone thinking lowly of me."

"So you are wanting to know if I would be okay with you switching to your animal form more often?"

"Yes, sir."

Bryco smiled warmly at the other Brigadier. "Of course you can. Lord Helius has lifted the exile, and I shall not have any prejudices here in the Enigma Brigade. We represent the Light at its brightest, and we shall not think less of you if you show us your true form. That is the way of the Light, Nilram."

"Yes, thank you, Captain." Immediately, he glowed with a red light, and he fell onto all fours. Light brown fur sprouted all over his body as he grew, and a full mane sprang forth around his head. For the first time, Captain Bryco was seeing Nilram as the lion he had always been. Those deep, dark eyes stared at Bryco expectantly, awaiting a response.

Bryco laughed in his own shock. "You look great, Nilram. You really do. As strange as it sounds, you look more like you than you do in your human form."

Nilram's light chuckle was full roar in this state, and he communicated mentally to his Captain. "Thank you, sir. I am glad that my true form does not lessen your opinion of me. It seems that his Majesty truly has done a good job of eliminating the biases that once plagued Gevás."

Though he had never told Bryco or Lord Helius, Nilram had fought alongside Maris and Gaspard in the Third Obsidian War. He had always been against the exile and had been grateful to Lord Helius when he had assumed the Throne and removed those laws. The world was in a state of change, and that change was certainly for the better.

"It seems so," Bryco agreed. "Can you still fight well in that form?"

Nilram placed a humongous paw forward and leaned down, taking an aggressive stance. "Shall we spar for a bit, Captain?"

Bryco drew his own sword with a confident smile. He

charged at the lion, and, to his surprise, the lion dodged the attack at lightning speed and swiped a paw at Bryco's back. He barely ducked low enough to dodge it. When he tried to stand again, Nilram stood on his hind legs and roared as he pounced upon Bryco, pinning him to the wall. Bryco's sword clattered onto the floor.

"Well, it seems you certainly are just as good a fighter. That shall come in handy in the future. You have quite the element of surprise."

Nilram released his hold on Bryco and fell down onto his paws again. "Thank you, Captain. I find that I am a much better fighter in this form. It flows more naturally to me."

Bryco sheathed his sword, still in shock from the rapidity of the battle. "Yes, well, you should probably go back home for the night and prepare for the morning. As I said, this shall not be a short mission."

"Yes, Captain. I shall be ready at dawn. Thank you again, sir." Then, Nilram disappeared into a Gate of his own, leaving Bryco in the orange light.

In all his years of serving in the Enigma Brigade, he had never thought that he would one day be its Captain. He had always been a higher member, but never even second-in-command, not until Tilgé left. The Brigade had changed, and Bryco was glad to be heading that change.

Bryco walked over to a chair, sat down, and leaned his head back. He closed his eyes and watched the orange light filter through his eyelids.

"That was some display, Bryco."

His eyes snapped open and leaning over him was a man with long, red hair with green eyes. "Maks!" Bryco practically fell out of his chair as he scrambled to stand up. "What— what are you doing here?"

The taller man smiled his wicked grin. "I found out that Tilgé was still alive, Bryco. You lied to me. You lied, Bryco."

Immediately, Bryco reached for his sword and unsheathed

it in one fluid motion. Maksimilian already had his Steel of Life out and pointed it at Bryco. The katana stabbed toward Bryco, but a sidestep caused the blade to hit the wall. Bryco counterattacked, but Maksimilian merely jumped onto the table and slashed at Bryco's head.

Bryco whirled his sword to block the attack, and, as he prepared his next attack, Maksimilian struck his sword with a powerful blast of Light, causing Bryco's sword to once more fall to the ground. Bryco looked up in time to see the Steel coming toward his face.

His eyes snapped open, and he fell out of the chair. His heart was pounding heavily, and his breaths were rapid. He looked around, but he was entirely alone. A sigh of relief left his lips, and he rose steadily, using the table for support. He did not know how many times he had had a similar nightmare. He just kept hoping that they stayed nightmares and never became real.

With a shaking hand, he summoned a Gate and entered his home near the Palace of Light. It was a well-furnished apartment with some of the higher-class portraits and lightings throughout the place. Being a member of the Enigma Brigade certainly had its benefits, even if it was one of the most dangerous jobs there were.

Gaspard woke the next morning and kneeled in front of the small altar he had placed in his hut. He had finally come to terms with the fact that the Great Spirit was no more. It was now divided into five pieces across the world, and one of them had lived in his Sword, the Behemoth.

"Oh spirits, please hear my call. I apologize for my past mistakes. I have wronged so many through my actions, yet I beg forgiveness. As his Majesty, the Emperor of Light, has done, I ask you to see past my mistakes and believe me when I say that I shall do better in the future, as I strive to do every day of my existence. Please bless me with the luck that the

Great Spirit once blessed me with by offering me one of its Swords. Thank you, oh spirits." He left the candles burning around the altar. He believed that such fires enticed the spirits. They were used to a realm of shadows, and sometimes, all they wanted was a light.

Years ago, he had almost changed the tides of war by accidentally working for one of the Lords of the Shadows. When he had realized his grave error, he had submitted himself to the Emperor of Light, but instead of being executed, Lord Helius had given him a position in the Enigma Brigade, a group of his finest soldiers. However, Gaspard had never been able to forgive himself.

Steadily, he rose and made a final bow to the shrine before returning to his room. The water was much warmer here in the Western Continent. He had made himself a home in the forests of Rulia, and it was certainly comfy enough. The house was filled with a large number of books, some suits of light armor, and an empty scabbard that had once held his fearsome Sword. He had kept the scabbard with the promise to himself that he would one day regain that weapon and wield it with as much power as he had once possessed.

He felt the call in his heart. With a couple of basic spells, he adorned the golden robes of the Enigma Brigade and summoned a Gate to his Captain. In training, all Brigadiers had to learn to come immediately when called no matter what. Gaspard had needed quite a bit of *mysteria* training when he had entered the Brigade, and even now, he could only muster the most basic of spells.

Bryco began sternly, "Alright, now we march to Terin."

Once Bryco summoned the Gate, the Brigadiers marched into it one by one, until they were all standing in the middle of the already-bustling city of Terin.

Gaspard had never seen a city so lively at this time of day. The sun had just barely risen over the horizon, and all the stores in Varyx's capital seemed open and packed. On edge, he put a hand to the hilt of his sword under his robe. He felt a hand on his shoulder and turned his head to see Bryco standing there.

"You would do well to not even think of touching that sword, Gaspard. There are some here who would recognize that gesture."

Once Bryco released his grip, Gaspard lowered his hand from the sword. Bryco was probably right. This place was just a major city, much like Apolis, and there was no reason to be suspicious. Doing that would only cause more trouble than good.

"Captain, are we paying with Imperial favors or salt here?" asked Gaspard.

Bryco nodded in acknowledgment. "Favors. It will look better for us. Remember, everyone, play all the cards right while we are here. We want the citizens here to not feel threatened in any way."

Gaspard knew that the Brigade rarely got into skirmishes, but they had to stay in shape in case they ever did run into any trouble. Lord Helius had wanted them to be more than just negotiators: the Enigma Brigade was a team of the Emperor's most powerful soldiers. He wanted them to be able to fight if it came down to that.

The five Brigadiers divided, and Gaspard started heading in one direction, seeking a nice-looking hotel among the tall buildings. Occasionally, a passerby would ram into his shoulder, causing him to snarl with discontent, but he did nothing more than that. Finally, he saw a likely building and approached it. He pushed back the metal door and entered the well-polished halls. A young maid approached him and said, "Please follow me, sir. The innkeeper is this way." Indeed, this place appeared to be a nice hotel.

He followed her into the main lobby, where a man behind a desk greeted him. "Ah, welcome to Twenty and Silas Inn! I'm Barrius, the manager. How can I help you today?"

The man seemed polite, but Gaspard could tell how fake the man's smile was. "Oh, I'm just looking for a room for a week or so."

"Alright," started Barrius as he took out a keyboard. A computer screen appeared above the keyboard as he typed into some program. "What is your name?"

"Gaspard."

"What is your address?"

"Um . . . I don't think I will be needing one, sir. I am here on business for his Majesty, the Emperor of Light, Lord Helius." At these words, the man's smile faded.

"I see . . ." said the now gruff voice. "Well, I hate to have made your travels for nothing, but we don't have a room of your caliber here, *sir.*" The innkeeper practically spat the last word at Gaspard, and even the maid had a disgusted look on her face.

Gaspard was in utter awe and confusion at the sudden hostility of the innkeeper. Nevertheless, he remembered Bryco's words and did not press the matter. "Well, thank you very much," he said as he left the hotel.

He had not met such dislike for the Emperor of Light since the Third Obsidian War. He ignored it for the moment and pushed onward, looking for the next place to try. As he stepped out onto the busy path, cars whizzed above him. The traffic up there looked unbearable from where he was standing. While he gaped, someone shoved him out of the way and yelled, "Hey, get out of the way!" The temptation to draw his sword was stronger than it had been all day, but he did nothing.

Then, he saw a parting in the crowd ahead. The split grew, and he watched their faces turn to slight fear or shock, not fear of him but fear of something below them. Finally, enough people divided for him to see a lion in their midst. The lion approached him, and he realized it had to be Nilram. "Nil, what are you doing here?" Gaspard had honestly never seen Nilram in his animal form, but the chances of another lion being there in Terin in the same area were slim to none.

"Same as you: looking for a place to stay. I tried one place, but they kicked me out when I told them I serve the Emperor of Light." Nilram's words came to Gaspard through his mind, a form of communication with which he was fully familiar, having grown up in the Western Continent.

"They did the same to you?"

Nilram accomplished what a lion's version of raising an eyebrow was and said, "So, it wasn't just because I was an anima, then. Apparently, there is something going on here then we hadn't anticipated."

Gaspard looked around him with disbelief. "The people here don't like the Emperor of Light . . . Why is that, I wonder? The Emperor has only offered his full help to King Lomeo as he took the throne, so why the cold shoulder?"

The lion glanced in both directions, seeking some clue that was probably not there. "I don't know, but I really don't like it."

Suddenly, they heard screaming. The two ran toward the source, and at a path intersection, a group of watchmen had beaten and then bound a girl. As they started to put her into their vehicle, Nilram and Gaspard both realized that it was Thera the watchmen had arrested.

Gaspard unsheathed his sword, saying, "Now might be a good time to use this."

At the sight of the blade, many people ran away screaming. Nilram stretched out a paw and leaned down in his own aggressive stance. The two of them charged at the vehicle, and the two watchmen lifted their own guns. Before Gaspard could reach either of them, Nilram had leaped the distance and swiped both guns out of their hands with one paw. He let his momentum carry him into spin, allowing him to generate a powerful punch that knocked one of the watchmen unconscious. Gaspard knocked out the other one with the flat of his blade.

As they started to get Thera out of the vehicle, her eyes widened, and she screamed, "Hey, behind you!"

An electric jolt from one gun took Nilram out, and Gaspard dodged another shot. Using his sword and his Light-imbued reflexes, he deflected many of the attacks.

"Gaspard, duck!"

He did as he was told, and Captain Bryco shot a bolt of Light right over his head through one of the watchmen. Out of the corner of his eye, Gaspard saw Sume coming as well. Now that three of them were at fighting capacity, they would be unstoppable, Gaspard thought. Still, the challenge was that they needed to avoid as much carnage as possible: This area was still in the middle of a large city.

Gaspard called to Bryco, "Hey, what do we do, Captain?"

"Sume, grab Thera! Gaspard, get the lion out of here! I'll hold these guys off!" Bryco leaped into the middle of the battle and attacked at the speed of Light, disarming the watchmen and knocking them back. Gaspard saw Sume run toward the vehicle and start untying Thera.

Gaspard summoned a Gate that would take him to the fringes of the city and pushed Nilram through it. He entered the portal and closed it behind him immediately.

He heaved with exhaustion as he slumped against the wall of the back alley. A little light came in from the main street, but otherwise, the area was dark. Nilram was still unconscious, and Gaspard was not doing much better. His eyes kept looking at the main street, watching for anyone heading their way. He could not even feel Captain Bryco calling them.

"Nil... what's happened?"

At the sound of his name, the large lion stirred. "Uhnnn... Gaspard...?" His eyes opened fully, and he tried to stand on his wobbling legs. "What happened? Where's

Thera?"

"The Captain came, and so did Sume. The Captain told me to grab you and told Sume to grab Thera. Then, I brought you here, and it's been several minutes since."

Nilram growled fiercely, so much that it startled even Gaspard. "We need to find them. We need to find them now." He took a step forward, but then stumbled.

"Nil, you are not fit to fight now, and, besides, we need to wait for the Captain."

"What if something happened to him?" Nilram's growl was sharp and almost threatening.

Gaspard was taken aback by the immediate reply. "What if something happens to us, and he has to come and save us later?" To this question, Nilram was not so snappy with his reply. "We need to wait and see if he calls us. If he hasn't by nightfall, we will investigate a little further. Deal?"

The lion nodded in reluctant compliance. "Deal."

The two stayed there in an awkward silence for several minutes. Finally, Nilram ventured, "So, Gaspard, what were you before a Brigadier?"

Gaspard laughed heartily at the question. "I was a General in the Third Obsidian War, actually."

"A General!"

"Yes, I was a General. Is that so hard to believe?"

Nilram replied bluntly. "It is, a bit. I say that just because of your fighting skills."

Gaspard's smile vanished. "Oh . . ."

The lion growled in pleasure. "It is a surprise, yes, Gaspard, but do not take it so personally. I have heard that you used to be a great fighter, and I am sure that you shall return to your former glory. You just need more confidence, you know. If you believed in yourself a little more, perhaps your skills would be better honed."

Gaspard sighed in defeat. "Perhaps you are right, Nil. I just . . . I was once blessed with the powers of a mighty Sword.

Then, it was stolen from me. That Sword allowed me to be a great swordsman."

"Were you a swordsman before that?"

Gaspard's eyes lowered. "Yes, I was . . . but these past few years, I've gotten worse than I've ever been."

"Then, perhaps that Sword did you more bad than it did good."

"What?"

Nilram grunted. "Figure it out."

Suddenly, they both felt it: a pull on their hearts so strong that it made them think of nothing else but answering the call. Immediately, they both summoned a Gate and stepped through it. Captain Bryco stood before them.

"Captain!" Nilram and Gaspard said in unison.

The three of them were on top of a building in the middle of a city. Cars drove over their heads, and bright lights from the city illuminated the sky. "It seems that King Lomeo is no friend of the Emperor of Light. He has taken Thera and Sume into custody, and from what I have gathered, an execution is soon to follow."

Nilram took his offensive stance and roared mightily.

"Relax, we are going to try to rescue them tonight. I found out where the prison is. It's going to be dangerous, though."

Gaspard replied, "We are ready for it, Captain."

"Glad to hear it," Bryco said. "Follow me."

After moving through a Gate, the three of them were standing right outside a massive fortress. Gaspard asked, "So, what's the plan?"

"Circle the perimeter. Find any weak spots in the fortress and rendezvous here."

The two other Brigadiers nodded in confirmation. They all split up, seeking an unguarded door or a window, even. Gaspard ran quickly but quietly. Guards seemed to be everywhere, and it took all his concentration to make as little noise as possible.

"Their guard is too heavily fortified. There's no way to get in there without using a Gate."

Gaspard was well aware of the dangers of summoning a Gate in the middle of the prison, though. If that were to happen, someone innocent could be killed, or something worse could happen. Making Gates was a tricky business. One could not just make a Gate and hope that it took its user to an open area. There were risks involved, especially when making them in buildings.

Finally, he rounded the final corner where Bryco was already waiting. Nilram leaped down to them from a ledge.

Bryco started, "Anything?"

The Brigadiers only shook their heads in denial.

Bryco stomped his foot silently. "Damn . . ." He thought about a plan of action, but this place was just too heavily guarded. "If only there was a way to get one exit open . . . Oh, wait, if we made a distraction, that could work." Bryco's eyes scanned the area for something that could make a sufficient distraction.

A roar filled the water. Bryco and Gaspard turned to see Nilram running into the distance, roaring as loudly as he could. Two guards left their post, and Bryco and Gaspard ran to that door, entering the prison. Once the door was closed behind them, Bryco looked through a crack in the door to see if Nilram was alright.

"Did he get caught?" Gaspard asked.

"No . . ." Bryco replied with uncertainty. "I think he made it."

Together, they turned to face the dismal fortress. Cells lined one side of the hallway, and they could hear one man singing terribly off-key in the distance. "Alright, let's split up. We are going to need to do this as quickly as possible."

"Right," agreed Gaspard.

The place was filthy and dark. He looked into each cell,

hoping to find either Sume or Thera, but he only found ragged, dirty old men. "Where are you guys?" he asked softly. He pushed forward a little faster, but the whole prison was like a labyrinth to him. "I hope the Captain is having better luck than I am."

A man screamed behind him, and Gaspard turned, his heart pounding in shock, but it was only one of the prisoners. This place was putting him on the edge.

"And what do you think you're doing?"

It was one of the guards. He had been seen. Drawing his sword, he charged at the men so as not to raise an alarm. As soon as he did so, he sensed another watchman appear behind him. Now, he was trapped, and he realized he was not strong enough to face these opponents alone. However, Bryco was nowhere to be found.

One of the guards called to him, "You are under arrest. Lower your weapon!"

That was when he saw Bryco being led into the hall in handcuffs. "Captain . . ." Gaspard muttered. The guards ran at him, and it took little effort for them to disarm him. He was simply no match for their numbers now. He struggled violently, punching in a crazed rage, and he certainly felt his fists hitting flesh.

Finally, he felt the handcuffs click around his wrists. When he tried to kick at the guards, one of them tripped him, and his face slammed into the cold stone floor. Blackness came.

5

Stehl and Mirah

STEHL LOOKED OUT THE window, deep in thought. The water looked the same everywhere she went. Half the time, she was not sure what she was even searching for anymore. The surroundings seemed to blur together as much as the past did. She could remember being a highly respected captain for the Emperor Regin. She could remember walking into his fortress and watching the Enigma Brigade kill off her friends and what little family she had ever really had. She could remember meeting the Lord of the Shadows with the handsome face and the red hair. She could remember lying there beside him under the stars. She had saved his life once in the first battle of the Third Obsidian War, but she had not seen him since then. In all honesty, she hated that man for making her have any feelings for him. Then, she had encountered her newest companion.

"Are ya alright, Stehl?"

She turned to face Mirah Silverpike and smiled at him. "Yeah, I'm fine. Just thinking."

Mirah turned the car a little to the right and said, "Well, what's on yer min'?"

There was too much on her mind, though. Her eyes scanned over her lover, and she admired his hair-covered face, his tattooed chest, and his muscled arms. "I'm just thinking about how handsome you are today."

Mirah chuckled deeply. "I'm sure dat's zactly what y'were t'inkin' about. Ser'ously, what's wrong?"

Her smile faded. "I just don't know what I'm doing anymore. We've been looking for the Enigma Brigade for years, and the Emperor of Light finally announced their existence, but if anything, they've become more elusive. We can't find them anywhere."

He reached over and patted her lap softly. "Ah, don' y'worry about a t'ing, Miss Stehl. We'll find 'em fer sure."

"I hope you're right, my love. I really do." Then, she returned to staring into the abyss of the sea.

Mirah could tell that something was still bothering Stehl, but he knew better than to push the matter any further. Ever since he had met Stehl, he had been entranced by her beauty, her fiery personality, and her mystical Sword, Kohana's Fang. That Sword supposedly made its user older but acted as a shield against all *mysteria*. Mirah had never been one to like sorcerers himself. He found *mysteria* to be a dishonorable way to fight. However, Stehl was, in his mind, the epitome of an honorable soldier. She had fought as a man to serve her country, and when she had seen a terrible act committed, she had fought against it.

Mirah had always been one for cars and ships, though. Driving vessels had been his life for years, though he had spent some time as a regular soldier and a merchant. His life was centered around honor, but once he met Stehl, he found a reason to quit the soldier's life and aid her in her quest to destroy the Enigma Brigade. Plus, that Sword of hers caught his eye just as much as she did.

"How much longer till we reach the Capital?" It had been quite a while since she had been back home, but she had not missed the place truly. She had no friends there, and her family was all gone as well.

"Jus' 'alf an hour left. Then, we'll be at yer old home."

"I don't know if I'm willing to call it home anymore. I suppose it used to be, but now . . . I'm just not so sure . . ."

Mirah sighed. These past few days, Stehl had been in a particularly foul mood. It was not uncommon for her to stare off into the deep as she presently was, and Mirah had started to give up on consoling her. At first, his jokes had put a bright smile on her face, but over the years, she had stopped laughing. If only they could find one Brigadier, she would probably be alright again. "Y'know, Miss Stehl, in a few days, dat disq tournament is supposed ta be happenin'. Maybe we should check it out too, eh?"

Stehl squinted her eyes in confusion. "Why would we do that?"

"Well, it would be a great way ter relax, an' maybe da Brigade'll be dere too."

She imagined all the disq players running and swimming, fighting over the all-elusive Crystal Trident. In her lifetime, she had never been to a tournament, but she had seen a few matches in the Capital. Usually, the athlete from there won the highest place in the Eastern Continent, though some years had certainly brought exceptions. "That actually sounds like a good idea. Do you think the tickets would be expensive?"

Mirah laughed deeply. "Mos' certainly." They laughed together in their ship in the sea.

Outside, they could see land far below them and far out into the distance, but they were so high that most of their vision was occupied by the blue sea. Above them, they could see one of the rare atmosdomes of the world. Though Mirah had never been inside an atmosdome, Stehl had had the privilege of entering one of those pockets of air that existed in Gevás. Every decade or so, a new atmosdome would appear, and the area would be more or less off limits and marked as a dangerous area. It was actually a very frustrating idea to her: humans like her struggled in air and they sometimes made it a game, trying to reach the end of the atmosdome before running out of water. However, the anima, those half-human monsters, could survive easily in the waterless place. As if there was not enough reason for her to hate anima, she held that jealousy as well.

After they stopped laughing, Mirah asked, "Alright, Miss Stehl, tell me dis: what do ya love da mos' about me?"

Stehl put a hand to her chin in mock consideration. "Hm . . . your way with words?"

"Hey, play nice!" he said.

"Alright . . . hm . . . I guess I love how much you respect me. Where I came from, men were disgusting pigs. They talked about all their intimate relationships with their friends as if it was some contest. 'Oh, I got five different girls in one week,' or, 'You should have seen what we did,' or . . ."

"I get it, I get it!" Mirah exclaimed, still smiling. "Dat's pretty rough, though, isn't it? It couldn't 'ave been easy living wit' a bunch of moronic guys like dat."

"No . . . it wasn't . . ." Breathing out a sigh, she looked forward and watched as a school of silver fish swam over them. "You know what, my love?"

"What?"

She grasped his hand and held it tightly. "After the tournament, maybe we should quit looking for them. I've taken care of a lot of the people who were in the Brigade, and I've done my part. Maybe it's not my responsibility any longer. Who knows? Maybe the spirits are telling me to just quit now."

"Could be . . . but what'll ya do after?"

"Maybe we could just settle down, just you and I." Yet, somehow, Stehl knew that could not work. She loved Mirah, and she felt safe with him. However, settling down did not seem right. She still felt incomplete. For some reason unknown to her, she still felt a burning hatred and equally burning passion for the Lord of the Shadows, Randir. Why was it so hard to love Mirah when she so greatly hated Randir? "Maybe we could get a house in Port City. You always talk about how nice it was there."

"Ya, Port City was a real nice place, I 'member. Not too chilly, and da business worked out swell. You'd like it, I'm sure." Mirah wondered if he could just settle down that easily as well. He and Stehl had certainly become close, and he did love her. He loved everything about her. Sure, he was not the most romantic guy, but he knew how to respect her. He knew how to be honest with her, and he never faked anything when he was around her. He found that life was too short to try being somebody you are not: it was far more important to perfect who you already were.

Sighing, Mirah looked at the meters on the screen above the steering wheel and lowered the vehicle toward the ground.

Stehl said, "Pit stop?"

Mirah nodded. "Yup, just real quick. We nee' more fooel anyway."

Stehl smiled at his long pronunciation of the word "fuel." There were some words that she just loved to hear him try to say. She never made fun of him for his strange accent, but she did smile occasionally at the odd word.

"Alright, but hurry up." She kissed his lips, feeling the whiskers of his moustache scrape roughly against the cheeks of her face. "Hey, that tickles." He rubbed his face against hers, and she pushed him back into his chair playfully. "Oh, go get the fuel, silly."

He smiled as he exited the vehicle. Seaweed covered the ground outside, and no hills were in sight. Just by rolling down her window, Stehl could tell that this place was the Eastern Continent. It was one of the warmest areas in Gevás, though Immyx was by no means the prettiest place. The kingdom was one vast plain that extended as far as the eye could see in any direction. Somewhere among this expanse, she had spent a night with a Lord of the Shadows.

For once, she succumbed to the memory. She could picture Randir's strong, angled face with his long scar and his few burn marks. To her, they were not marks of pain, but marks of beauty. She imagined how his muscular chest bulged from his robe, and how deep and entrancing his red eyes were—how much they pulled her into his very core.

Furious with herself, she shook her head. "I have got to quit thinking about him. He's gonna drive me as crazy as the Enigma Brigade have!"

She returned her thoughts to her lover, Mirah Silverpike. The man was sweet, sweeter than most guys she had ever known, and he had been able to make her laugh more often than not. There was some spark in him, somewhere, and that spark was what made her truly love him. When he laughed, she could tell it was genuine. When he complimented her on her looks or her thoughtfulness, she knew that he meant it. Mirah was the real deal, the kind of guy she had always hoped to be with one day. The times she dreamed about him, she imagined them rolling in a field of flowers, laughing the whole way. She did not see him as a great warrior she should respect, and she did not see him as some lifelong friend. He was Mirah, and no one could be like him.

Finally, Mirah returned from putting fuel in the vehicle and urinating into a bush of seaweed. "Y'ready ter go?"

"Yeah, do you know how much farther the Capital is? We should probably grab a bite soon. I'm starting to get hungry."

"Jus' a bit longer, Miss Stehl. We should be at da Capital real soon. Then, you can have as much lamazza as ya want." Lamazza was Mirah's own personal favorite fish. In Gevás, fish was the only meat that could be used for food, but spices were what made cooking extravagant. "I wonder if we really could just settle down?"

Stehl was silent, though. A bright smile still lit up her face, but her own mind wondered the same thing. Her heart was divided in three ways: her love for Mirah, her hatred for Randir, and her desire for something else—something that could bring her back to her old life. Everything was so much simpler then.

The vehicle rose high into the sea again, and they sped off into the blue. They had been traveling in this ship for years, and it had never served them poorly. It was endurable: probably not the fastest or prettiest of ships, but it worked. Had Mirah and Stehl not deserted the Emperor's army, they would have had a decent enough income, but now that they were on their own, salt was scarce. Even if they had jobs, salaries had been cut to finance the war. The two Emperors were doing everything to tear each other apart, and the lower and middle classes were suffering for it.

She was tired of it. She had fought for the Emperor Regin and Emperor Helius. In her mind, war was just a fact of life. It never ended in good for anyone. Now, she was stuck in the middle of nowhere with nowhere to really go, while those anima ran free and were as happy as could be. This new order did not make sense to her, and she was genuinely glad that the Emperor Regin was striving to fix the problem. The last time she had been at the Capital, something had been gravely wrong with the Emperor Regin.

By the sounds of this war, he was no longer in such a strange mood.

"Mirah, watch out!"

He swerved to avoid the incoming vehicle, and bubbles swirled around them fiercely. Stehl saw flashes of light, and within seconds, they crashed into the ground below them. A sharp pain filled her head as smoke filled the vehicle. "Mirah . . ." she moaned. "Are you alright?"

However, Mirah only groaned. He was badly hurt. She

could see the blood seep out of a wound in his side into the water around them, staining it. A shaking hand slid over to the door, and she opened the vehicle. Stumbling out onto the seaweed-covered plain, she staggered to her feet. Her vision blurred everything around her, making the ground become entirely green with seaweed.

A roar came to her ears, and she thought she was imagining the wreck that had just happened. However, the incoming lights made her think otherwise. A second vehicle landed beside her, and a man stepped out of it. "Hey, are you guys alright? I didn't mean to be driving like that."

Stehl put a hand to her waist, where a gun was concealed by a flap of cloth, but she fell forward accidentally into the man's arms. She looked up to see his face, and she saw his dark hair sway in the current.

Stehl woke up before Mirah did. The three of them were riding in a Helian transport, a vessel much faster than their own had been. Though she still felt weak, she tried to appear alert.

"Hey, where are you taking us?" she asked the driver. She realized that she was in the front passenger seat, while Mirah was laid out in the back.

The man turned toward her. "To the Capital. Isn't that where you were headed?" The voice was sharp. "I figured the least I could do would be to get the two of you to a Healer. I don't touch that *mysteria* stuff."

Gradually, her vision came back to her, and she could make out more of his features. His black hair swept slightly down the back of his neck and covered his ears. From the angle at which she was sitting, she could see his hair almost cover one of his eyes, but not the other. A few pale scars lined his face, but these were quite faint. As she glanced down his body, she realized that her rescuer was rather scrawny, a man of sticks, and she found it amazing that such a person could have lifted Mirah and her into his transport.

She decided not to attack him after all. Her eyes looked around, trying to gather her bearings, but only sea surrounded them. For all she knew, they could be heading in the opposite direction from the Capital. "Hey, who are you exactly?"

The man sighed before starting. "I'm nobody. Really, I am."

She knew that feeling. At one point in her life, she had been a well-known captain for the Emperor Regin, and at another, she had been a great general. Now, she was nobody. "Well, do you have a name at least?"

"Yeah, but it's not even worth sharing. I'll get you guys to a Healer, and then I'll leave you guys alone. Deal?"

"No," Stehl replied bluntly. The man did not twitch in the slightest at her response, which came as a surprise to Stehl herself. "How do I know you aren't taking us somewhere else?"

The man laughed. His voice was neither too high nor too deep, though it was certainly higher than lower. "I guess you don't. Ever looked up the word 'trust?'"

She folded her arms against her chest and turned away from him. Being insulted by strangers was not among her favorite things, and she awaited an apology. However, she only kept waiting. The man refused to offer any regret. The silence became awkward. She was expecting him to start some conversation, regardless of the topic, but he did not oblige her. His eyes stayed focused on the sea in front of him, and, worst of all to Stehl, he seemed to have no interest in talking with her whatsoever.

"What is wrong with you?" she asked.

"Excuse me?"

"You almost kill us, and then you save us. Now, you won't even say a word to me and expect us to trust you."

He smirked. "No, I don't. I expect *you* to trust me. I couldn't care less if the one unconscious person trusts me or not."

She felt like punching him in the face, even if he was driving. Yet, she knew that technically he could have easily left them to die. They owed him, so she did not press the matter. Regardless, she did not like him at all. "Well . . . Where are you from?"

"I was born in the Western Continent, but I have lived most of my life in Apolis."

"Apolis?" Stehl raised an eyebrow, interested. "What have you been doing there? I was there for a few years, but I never saw someone like you."

Again, the man smirked. "That's good. I would have been worried if you had." He laughed to himself for a moment before adding, "I moved around a lot actually."

"So, what's your name?"

Suddenly, he snapped at her, "I told you it's not important!"

Stehl sensed a strange hostility in his voice, but she watched him calm himself down immediately afterward. He was certainly an interesting character.

She turned around in her seat to check on Mirah again. His breathing seemed to be fine, but he was still bleeding in numerous places. This mysterious driver was right: Mirah needed a Healer. Neither she nor Mirah had ever cared too much for the cheating powers of *mysteria,* but in the past, Stehl had needed it to take on the guise of a male soldier in order to serve in the army.

The driver was wearing tight silver clothes that revealed how skinny he was. He drove the vehicle with one hand, though his other hand was buried deep in one of his pants pockets. It was driving her crazy, not knowing anything about this guy. Still, it felt awkward to keep pushing him for more information. "Alright, next question. Where do you work now?"

"Unemployed." The answer was short, blunt, and, for Stehl, not enough.

"Do you have family?"

"Nope."

"How did you get this transport?"

"Hmm . . ." he acted as if he was considering how he should answer, and Stehl eyed him curiously. Suddenly, he roared, "None of your business!"

She turned her head so that she could not see his frustrating existence and acted as if she was observing the fish they passed occasionally. Now, she had nothing left to say to him, but she knew better than to just tell him to let them out. That would be quite a walk if she had to drag Mirah with her.

Another vehicle passed them, and minutes later, another one did as well. Stehl realized that they must be getting closer to the Capital now.

"I was a soldier for Helio most of my life," he finally offered. Her head whipped around to face him. "I lived near the Palace of Light, actually. I got paid quite a bit because I was high-ranking, second-in-command in my regiment. I left, though, and I've really . . . I want a new life—one without killing or wars." The look in his eyes was sincere enough, but deep within those coals, Stehl could have sworn that she saw something much deeper, as if she were only seeing a single layer of this enigmatic driver. "So, what's your story, lady?"

"My name is Stehl." She had never felt so introverted that she could not tell her basic story, though she was amazed that this guy was even slightly interested. "At the start of the Third Obsidian War, I switched from the army in the Capital to the army in Apolis and became a general. Six years ago, I deserted them. I had seen enough of fighting, just as you had."

"And how did you get with bubble-belly here?"

She glared at the man and considered defending Mirah, but she felt that it was too much of an obvious truth to try arguing. "I met him when I left the army. He was in the navy at the time. We just sort of stuck together, I guess."

"So, are you two . . . ?"

Despite herself, she blushed at the implied question. "None of your business . . ."

He laughed at the remark and then reverted to his previous focus. "Good, I quite frankly am tired of hearing it." The urge to hit him was only growing in Stehl's heart, and it took all her energy to refrain from doing so.

"Good, I was tired of talking to you."

"Good."

Neither looked at the other, and a fuming tension burned between them for the rest of the ride. The transport approached the massive walls to the Capital, where lines of guards protected the entrance. It seemed that even the Eastern Continent was fortifying their defenses in fear of impending attacks from the enemy nations.

"Identification, sir," commanded one of the guards with a monotone voice that revealed how many times a day he had to request such identification.

The driver turned to Stehl, "You have I.D., right?"

Her eyes widened in surprise. She had been expecting him to have I.D. Nevertheless, she pulled a card from her pocket. It served as proof that she was born in the Capital and therefore had rights to enter it.

A couple of the guards looked into the transport and saw Mirah in the back. "What's wrong with him?"

Stehl passed the driver her card to give to the guards.

The driver said, "Here is the I.D. He had just a few too many sizzlers at home and managed to get himself all bloodied up. We were going to be heading this way anyways, so we thought he should see a Healer. Wouldn't you?"

"Well, I don't know, sir . . ."

The driver yelled, "Oh, just hurry up and open the damned gate!" His voice was sharp with a tone of command. It made Stehl wonder what kind of military authority he had held in the army.

The guards obeyed and promptly opened the gate for

them. When the driver handed her the card back, she whispered, "You're pretty good at this lying thing . . ."

"You have no idea," was his strange reply.

She was constantly taken aback by his mannerisms, but she did not argue. "Just make sure you know that you're lying to the right people," she said with a slightly warning tone. She had always had a respect for good liars, as long as they did not lie to her. That was, of course, something upon which she heavily frowned. "Let's just find a stupid Healer."

"So, what are you guys doing in the Capital anyways?"

She did not speak at first, not out of anger, but in thought. "Well . . . We are looking for a group of people, some murderers."

The driver looked straight at her this time. "Murderers? I could help with that. I am good at finding people like that."

Stehl laughed. "No, I don't think you're this good. These people supposedly didn't exist, and they are trained to hide."

His eager look faded. "What?"

Her gaze became hard and deep. "I hunt the Enigma Brigade." His eyes widened. "Ten years ago, they killed the one person I cared about, along with most of the Emperor Regin's staff, and I watched them die. I tried to fight their leader, but he was too much for me. I hunt them for revenge."

The man countered, "Bah, you won't be able to get them. You really are wasting your time."

"What? You don't believe in the Enigma Brigade? Even the Emperor of Light himself has announced their existence."

The man nodded solemnly, "Yes, I had heard as much. This new Emperor is different from the others. He's revolutionary. Custom means little to him, and change means everything. I am not quite sure if that is a good thing or a bad thing, though."

"What are you talking about?" Stehl asked, perplexed.

He shook his head. "Nothing, just thinking aloud. Now, where is the nearest parking space?"

Finally, he spotted one in the distance, and he landed on its surface smoothly. He opened his door and paid the fee at the exit of the spot. Then, he turned back and saw Stehl get out of the vehicle. Seeing her in full made him freeze where he was.

"What?" she asked.

His mouth lowered slightly, and he muttered simply, "Nothing . . ." Then, he went past Stehl and opened Mirah's door.

"What did you do with our vehicle, exactly? Just leave it there?" she asked him accusingly.

"Would you rather me have left you there?"

She did not have a witty answer.

"Help me grab him. He's not exactly light, your lover-boy."

This time, she did punch him in the arm. As she started to grab Mirah, she noticed that the driver was not removing that one hand from his pocket. "Aren't you going to use two hands, genius?"

He smirked. "I can't use two hands if I don't have two."

Stunned, she asked, "What?"

Reluctantly, he lifted the arm that was in his pocket, and the arm ended in a stub. He was missing that hand altogether.

She had never felt so stupid. "Oh . . . I'm sorry . . . I didn't mean to—"

The man shook his head. "Now, don't start feeling sorry for me or anything. There's a reason I keep it hidden, and it's not because it's just ugly, which it really is." They both laughed at it, though Stehl found herself laughing a bit more awkwardly than he was.

"So, what caused the stump?" she asked as they managed to lift Mirah with three hands.

"I was tired of being right-handed, so I cut it off." He smiled sarcastically at her as they started to move Mirah to the elevator.

"Haha, what happened?"

"Oh, it wasn't anything spectacular, just another casualty of war."

In his eyes, she could see some grim acceptance, so she did not press the matter. The elevator reached the ground level, and they exited it, still carrying Mirah with their off-balance support.

Stehl called to the first person she saw, "Hey, do you know where the nearest Healer is?"

When the person saw Mirah's blood, the woman paled. "Yes, you're going to have to go down that road and take the slight right, and then the full right."

The man and Stehl shifted their positions in order to carry Mirah a little better and immediately sped off in the direction the woman had been pointing.

"So, why exactly are you helping us, stranger?" Stehl asked her one-handed companion.

"I caused this. It was the least I could do." His voice did not reveal an inner kindness, just a feeling of debt.

"Well, you're almost done with us, and then you can go back to your regular life."

The man nodded strangely. Stehl could have sworn that she saw some reluctance in his face, but she did not know what to think of it.

Finally, they found the full right and turned on it. "Stehl, would you mind if I stayed with the two of you for a while?"

Her head turned to him sharply.

"I mean, I don't really have anything better to do."

She snapped at him, "Well, that is certainly not a reason for me to let you start following me around! I'm sure you can find *something* better to do."

He cringed visibly. "Sorry, I guess I chose the wrong words there. I guess I just find you interesting. I guess I would like to help you find this Enigma Brigade."

"I thought you didn't believe in them."

The man laughed. "Oh, I believe in them, alright. They're

the ones who made me lose my hand. Or, at least, it's the fault of their Captain. He wanted me dead."

Stehl was now fully stunned. "Why did he want to kill you?"

"Because . . ." He gritted his teeth as he muttered the words, "I apparently am not as good a soldier as I thought. Now, let's drop it."

It was clearly a sensitive subject. Stehl was finding this man to be more and more unpredictable. She was not quite sure that she could afford to have someone like that with her all the time. "I don't know . . . We just met, and I don't even know that Mirah would like you."

"Do you like me?"

She stopped walking. "You're just full of surprises, aren't you?"

"Here's a deal then. If you like me, I can stay. If you can't stand my guts, I shall leave once we got the big guy here into the Healer's. Deal?"

"Deal."

Finally, they saw the sign for the Healer's office. They made the final trek to the door, and the man knocked against it heavily. A man answered the door, and, upon seeing Mirah, he invited the three of them inside.

As the Healer worked, Stehl looked to the man with one hand and said, "Alright, here's a counter-deal for you. If you tell me your name, your *real* name, then you can stay with us. Otherwise, you're on your own. Deal?"

He laughed at the suggestion. "Deal."

The two watched as the Healer prepared a few poultices on his table. Stehl asked expectantly, "Well?"

The man sighed before finally saying, "My name is Tilgé."

6
Being Emperor

"H EY, SWEETIE, IT'S TIME to get up."
Drage opened his eyes gradually and was amazed at the beauty of his wife's face above him. He reached one hand up and stroked Aria's light hair softly. "Good morning, my love." He brought her face closer to his, and he kissed her carefully. She closed her eyes and kissed him back. "What time is it?" he asked, wondering how late he had stayed in bed this time.

"It's nine, but this is going to be my last day with you, so I wanted to spend more time *awake* with you. Is that alright, or would you rather go back to sleep?"

Her blue eyes were dazzling this morning. With the sunlight glimmering through the window onto them, he felt as if he were looking at diamonds—genuine, beautiful diamonds. He stroked her hair again and whispered into her ear, "I love you."

Half the time, he could not believe that he was married to such a wonderful woman, and he truly did feel blessed for it. He had known Aria ever since they were kids, and they had dated for quite a while as well. Still, he had never imagined that he would be where he was now.

He was the Emperor of Light, had a Palace, was married to the most beautiful woman in the world, and had three kids. If only he were not in the middle of a war, life would have been just shy of perfect. However, a war turned daily affairs rather sour for an Emperor.

"I love you, too." She kissed his nose delicately before resting her head against the side of his neck. It was then that Drage realized that she was laying on top of him. He wrapped an arm around her back and started rubbing the tight muscles of her back. Her breathing deepened as he relaxed each muscle one by one.

"You're more stressed than usual . . ." he commented.

"I'm just worried about what's going to happen tomorrow . . ."

He smiled and kissed her neck warmly. "Don't worry. I'll be back in just a few days. Those Y'mordi scum are up to something, and I need to put an end to it. You wouldn't want anything to happen to my family, would you?"

"Of course not," she muttered softly as Drage pushed his fingers into another tight muscle.

Drage sighed as he thought about how busy the day was going to be. "Well, today, I am going to have to confront the Council about the issue. We have a big meeting, and I truly am not looking forward to it."

"They are not going to be fond of the idea of Matthew taking over, especially because he is a member of the Council."

"Well, I am not going to leave them a choice."

From the first day he had become Emperor, Drage had been aggressive in his command of his kingdom, and he had made short work of his own Council, who had worked under the assumption that the new Emperor of Light would be easy to overcome and manipulate. Drage had been suspecting some sabotage in the Council, and he was anxious to know who it was.

The Council was made of eight members: Valdridge, Leona, Marqest, Matthew, Aria, Jallun, Ocrum, and Quella. Though Master Valdridge was clearly the most annoying of the Council, he was still the Prophet of Light, and Drage never fully despised the elderly man. Because Aria trusted her, Drage had no real problem with Mistress Leona, and of course, he trusted Matthew, Aria, and Master Marqest fully, since they were already Guardians of Light. Master Jallun had been in the Council since Drage's father had been Emperor, yet Drage was not yet sure if the silent man was trustworthy. Master Ocrum, a man who had entered the Council four years ago, had been Drage's greatest advisor in terms of military advice. Having been a well-established captain in the Third Obsidian War, Master Ocrum had been a great asset the past few years. Mistress Quella was the new Prophet of Earth who had ascended to the title after Mistress Daghda's death at the hands of an Y'mordi ten years ago. The woman was certainly hard-faced enough to be the Prophet of Earth, yet Drage had no real problems with her.

For years, Drage had pushed and prodded at the members of his Council, seeking the person who was leading his nation into ruin behind his back, but he had not discovered the traitor.

"Aria, just make sure that the Council does not try anything funny while I am gone. I trust Matthew fully, but I am not sure that he can be aggressive enough to deal with them if they become unruly. Though they will complain about my leaving, they will likely abuse that once I am actually gone, y'know?"

She nodded solemnly. She, too, had suspected something fishy happening in the Emperor's Council, and she was focusing on enough mysteries at the moment. Her thoughts had constantly returned to the elusive Ace who had saved Drage, Matthew, and herself years ago. She wondered about her ex-master, Mistress Daghda, and the secrets she had carried to her grave. Someone also had given her all their powers in *mysteria* at her birth in a process known as Gifting, and she was desperate to find out who that person was.

Another mystery to her was the secret of one of the Y'mordi, Y'dax, who was missing a large part of his heart somehow. Master Marqest had once told her about an ancient spell known as Division that could allow a person to split his or her heart into pieces. According to him, his own brother Bastion had attempted the same process a millennium ago. To make matters worse, she was a mother of three, wife to the Emperor of Light, and a trainee to become the Prophet of Fire, a title that had not been gained in centuries.

"I will try, Drage, but just please hurry back."

He raised his head up to her face and kissed her lips warmly. "I will be back in no time, I promise. These few days will pass in the blink of an eye, and there is a good chance that the Council won't be able to do anything major while I am gone. It's not like they could have planned anything: they don't know what I am about to do."

"Alright . . ." Aria's turned lips revealed her skepticism, but Drage knew that if he had not convinced her by now, there was no use in even trying further. "Get dressed while I go make breakfast, alright?"

"Isn't that what we have professional cooks for?" he joked with a bright smile.

She smiled as she rose. "You know, Drage, you are a real handful."

When she left the room, he sat up and stretched in the sunlight that was still brightly shining into the whole room, lighting up every corner of the massive chamber. He pulled back the covers and placed his feet on the lukewarm floor. He managed to find a pair of pants that did not look too regal, a shirt, and a light jacket in case he went outside today. Opening his heart a little more as he gradually awoke to full awareness, he sensed Aria summon a great amount of

Light, and he knew it was her beacon to him that breakfast was ready.

He walked outside the room and summoned a simple Gate to move down to the dining room. The massive table held two plates, each carrying some pancakes, skander eggs, and rapjalia, one of the more expensive breakfast fishes in the Southern Continent. "Wow, breakfast looks great. What are the kids going to have? They are usually awake by now."

"Actually, Lilian and Matthew woke up before we did. They took all the kids out for breakfast this morning. It's been a while since ours ate out, anyways. Lilian had asked about it last night."

"Wow, you always do amaze me, Aria." He sat down beside his wife and proceeded to eat his home-cooked breakfast. Most mornings, he had to help Aria take care of the kids, so it was certainly nice to just spend a morning alone with her. After swallowing a mouthful of eggs, he said, "After breakfast, do you want to walk through the Gardens? It's been a few months since we have had the chance to do that."

"Sure, I would love that." Ever since she had come to the Palace of Light, she had been fascinated by the Imperial Gardens. The Gardens were a labyrinth of beautiful trees, flowers, and hedges that contested every garden she had ever seen or imagined during her time on Earth, and she was glad to live right beside such a gorgeous place, even if she frequently did not have the actual time to go there. "But after that, I think we will need to get ready for the meeting. You know how Master Valdridge gets when you are late." She decided not to bring up how often it was that Drage *was* late to a meeting. She usually lectured Drage on his tardiness as much as Valdridge himself did.

"Fair enough," Drage responded, fully indulging in his food.

Already half-finished with her own plate, Aria said, "Hey Drage, when you get back, do you think we could go to that disq tournament? It seems that it is only in a few days, and you said you should be back by then. Besides, the head of the tournament has actually invited you to preside over the initiating ceremony. It would be a great honor . . ."

Drage chewed in meditation. "Hm . . . Well, I suppose that if I get back and the kingdom isn't in a state of ruin, that would not be a bad idea. This is still all assuming that Regin decides to allow the temporary truce in order for the disq tournament to work."

However, Drage's words were assurance enough for Aria, and she smiled despite herself. She had not seen a disq tournament yet, and she had really wanted to see it this year. It happened too rarely for her to miss it every time. Plus, she was married to the Emperor of Light. That meant that she should know enough about their world's customs enough to have actually seen a disq tournament.

After a while, the two of them finished eating, and servants came to collect their dishes. As they headed out of the Palace, Drage asked, "So, how is the Regiment doing? It's been a while since *I* have heard any news from them."

The Phoenix Regiment was Aria's personal military force, the fourth division of the Emperor's military, though he had no control over it whatsoever. She had originally commanded it solely as a regular section of the terra, but now it was a special force, designed to be a fighting unit stronger than the Enigma Brigade and made up of only females. However, with the slowness of the war, Aria had put the Regiment into strict training, waiting for the right chance to strike. Frequently, she had tried to convince Drage to change the mascot of the Enigma Brigade because it was the same animal symbol as her own, but Drage had not relented because of the timelessness of the symbol for the Brigade. Another reason for this stubbornness was his high approval of the new Captain wearing such a symbol. The phoenix looked much better on Bryco than it ever had on Maksimilian, that treacherous snake. However, Drage knew that Maksimilian had given him one piece of useful training: he had trained Drage to get used to people wanting to use him and had accidentally taught Drage how to deal with such people.

"They are doing well. My second, Urin, has been training them still, and they have gone on basic reconnaissance missions—nothing too special. They are becoming anxious. They want to see some real fighting." She smiled at Drage. Though she represented the Regiment in most matters, she knew that Drage was doing the right thing by taking this war slowly. With his pace, he was able to counter moves effectively, plan ahead, and hurt the least amount of people through careful strategy. Even if it was a long and drawn-out war, it was one that would protect his people, and she did not want to bring out her Regiment until they were sorely needed. After all, they were her greatest weapon. When they came into battle, she wanted it to be a complete and catastrophic surprise for the enemy. What Aria did not know was that Drage was planning on doing much the same with his Enigma Brigade. He had kept them well-trained in combat, too, and he was quite confident that his Brigade could defeat the Phoenix Regiment with little to no effort. "More than that, they are wanting some change of pace."

"Why don't you throw them a surprise visit? Maybe a test?" Drage offered.

Aria found the idea to be a sound one, but she did not like Drage even giving such simple suggestions about the control of her Regiment. She thought about lecturing him about it. However, she replied, "Perhaps I shall."

A servant entered the room in a white robe. "Your Majesty, the Council is here for the meeting."

Drage gave the man a dismissive nod, and the servant left. "It seems that the Council is here considerably early. I wonder what warrants this particular bit of nonsense." He sighed loudly and lowered his eyes in thought.

Aria bit her lower lip. Usually, when Drage had that pensive look on his face, he was easy to anger, and Aria could not help but feel sorry for him. He had such a tremendous weight on his shoulders, a weight that she could not truly fathom, even if she was his wife. She stepped toward him and grabbed his hand. His skin was still soft, and he still retained that warmth that she loved about him. His fingers tightened around her hand affectionately, but his eyes remained pointed into the distance.

"Let's go," was all he said.

Together, they walked toward the meeting room, a circular area with a long, rectangular table that started at the door and extended to the opposite side of the room. The whole Council was already seated, including a bewildered Matthew.

"What is the meaning of having this meeting so early?" Drage demanded.

Master Valdridge responded, "Your Majesty, I heard a recent complaint of which you would most likely wish to hear. I felt that the matter would occupy enough time to have the meeting a little earlier."

"You are half an hour early, and if this *matter* of yours is not worth it, then you and I shall have some rather grave words." Drage and Aria took their own seats at the table as Valdridge began with a slight tremor to his voice.

"Your Majesty, I recently spoke to a general in your terra. She admitted to me that the only reason she had joined your forces was to track down a murderer. She said that the murderer lived here in Apolis and was of the upper class. The murderer had killed most of her family and friends in her hometown solely as a display of his power."

Drage felt his face reddening in anger and shock. "Why have you brought this matter to the Council, Valdridge? That is a matter left to detectives and crime enforcement. That is not our purpose, no matter how vile the murderer is."

"Your Majesty," Valdridge interrupted, "the murderer's

name was Maksimilian. He is the Captain of your Majesty's Enigma Brigade, according to this general. Is that correct?"

Now, all eyes went to Drage. However, Drage himself was looking down at the table. Had his father truly allowed a criminal to lead the Enigma Brigade? "No, Valdridge, that is not correct." A number of things about this whole discussion reeked to Drage of treachery and lies, and he did not know why. Maksimilian had always been a problem, but he doubted that the ex-captain could have committed such a wrong. "Maksimilian was an unregistered soldier that I once knew, but he deserted the terra several years ago. He helped me on numerous occasions, and for that, I do not condemn him. As I previously said, why did you not call a detective?"

Valdridge's eyes widened. "You mean . . . Maksimilian was not part of the Enigma Brigade?"

"Yes, that is what I mean, Valdridge. What is your point, and what made you think that he was part of it? Back then, people did not even know that the Brigade existed fully, so why would a general of mine feel such doubt in me or my father? Who was this general anyway? When did you speak to her? Where is she?"

The Prophet of Light's head lowered in shame and embarrassment. "Forgive me, your Majesty . . ."

"Leave."

Again, all eyes returned to Drage as Valdridge muttered, "What?"

Drage's eyes were cold and hard as they glared at Valdridge. "I have no inclination to forgive you, Valdridge, so you do not have the right to be at this meeting. I shall speak with you later."

Suddenly, Valdridge's expression turned to flustered anger. "I am the head of this Council, your Majesty!"

Drage countered immediately, "And you shall not be if you choose to argue with me. Leave." He had chosen to lie to the Prophet of Light for numerous reasons. For one, he had noticed that Valdridge himself had been lying. There was an entire façade around Valdridge's demeanor today, and Drage was not going to fall prey to it. Maksimilian was no longer in his jurisdiction, anyway. That red-haired man had indeed deserted him, but desertion was a much better fate than what would have awaited him had he stayed in the Enigma Brigade. Now, Drage suspected Valdridge of some betrayal. What had created such a sudden interest in Maksimilian? Drage watched Valdridge storm out of the room in an embarrassed hurry. Valdridge clearly did not know his place, and that rebelliousness would lead to Valdridge's demise if he continued with such antics.

As the door slammed shut behind the Prophet, Drage asked, "Now, I call this meeting officially to order. Master Marqest, do you have any news for me?"

The old Prophet of Water responded calmly, "Yes, your Majesty. It appears that we have heard a response from the Emperor Regin. He has accepted your peace treaty for the day of the disq tournament."

Drage sighed. "That is good news. Our kingdom needs a day of resting after fighting for so long." He addressed the rest of the Council. "Is there any other top-priority news?" When he noted that the room was silent, he continued, "I have some news for you all to hear. I will be away from Gevás for a few days."

He noticed Marqest raise an eyebrow, but no one said anything. They knew that Drage was not finished yet and eagerly awaited his explanation.

"I have received knowledge that the Y'mordi have sent a massive weapon to Earth. There is a very real chance that they are trying to distract me from going there by manipulating me to look for the Demons. Because of that, I really need to go there and investigate this machine of theirs. In my stead, Master Helius shall be acting as Emperor."

Marqest opened his mouth as if to protest, but no

argument escaped his lips.

"It shall only be temporary, but I trust his judgment to be equivalent to mine, and you shall treat it as such."

Master Ocrum responded, "Your Majesty, what if Regin makes an attack during your absence?"

"Master Helius has had as much training in the military as I have, and besides, I have no doubt that he will always be open to your excellent military advice. You have served me well, and I do not doubt you. Do not question me." Though Drage had said this comment in response to Master Ocrum, he directed it more toward everyone.

"Your Majesty," Mistress Leona began. "Might I suggest you make use of the Enigma Brigade to take care of the affair on Earth?"

Drage shook his head at the thoughtful suggestion. "Actually, I have my own reasons for wanting to go to Earth. As many of you know, I know it better than any person in this world does." He addressed the whole Council then. "However, as I said, I shall be back in only a few days. So, do not worry too much, alright? It shall not be all that bad."

Marqest stroked his white beard as he muttered in a flat voice, "Your plan actually seems relatively sound. My only concern is for the possibility that the Y'mordi *mean* for you to go to Earth. How sure are you that this is not a trap of some kind?"

In all honesty, Drage had not considered this idea, but he did not see any option that could lead away from going to Earth. "I am not as sure as I would like to be, Master Marqest. What would you recommend?" His voice was not harsh or even accusatory. He generally trusted Marqest's advice and held it to be valid, so long as it did not clearly contrast Drage's own plans.

Marqest crossed his arms before replying, "Is it a reasonable assumption that you shall be well defended during your time on Earth?"

"Yes, I shall enlist the help of the Ring of Elders, along with my chief mechanic, in order to disarm the weapon."

"Very well . . . your Majesty."

Drage smiled.

Walking through the Palace that night, Drage pondered his dilemma. Finding the Y'mordi's weapon on Earth would not be an easily accomplished feat, and disarming it would be even more difficult. Feranx would probably be a considerable help in the destruction of the machine, but if they got into trouble with the Y'mordi, it would be hard to protect Feranx. They definitely needed the help of the Ring of Elders. Drage had found out five years ago that his mother was the head of the Ring of Elders, the council on Earth in charge of *mysteria* regulation. He had seen both his mother and his sister at his wedding, then. Thinking about how beautiful his wife had been that day, the day of his proposal and their wedding, brought the slightest tears to his eyes.

After making two turns down a hallway, he found himself face-to-face with his half-brother. "Matthew, what are you doing here? I thought you would be going to dinner with the others?"

Matthew brushed a hand through his hair. "Neh, Aria gave me that look that said that, for some reason, you were not coming to dinner, so I took note of her hint and decided to follow you. Is that alright?"

Drage laughed. "I suppose." The two walked side-by-side through the long halls. "Matt, something stinks about this whole thing. If Marqest is right, then the Y'mordi could become a real nuisance."

"Haven't they always been?" Matthew joked.

"Very true . . ." They turned another hallway, and Matthew knew he had been this way before, but could not remember where it led. "But if things get too bad, do not hesitate to reach me on Earth."

Matthew put a hand on Drage's shoulder as they walked. "I think I can do that." As they turned another corner, Matthew realized that they were headed toward Drage's computer, DATA. "The Y'mordi are still acting in the background. The forces of the Darkness remain too well-hidden. Whatever their plan is, it is not going to be good."

"I agree. Unfortunately, none of us have much of a choice. I'm sure we can handle it, though. I mean, we've fought Maris, the Y'mordi, sea serpents, and even Dragons. Whatever the Y'mordi have to throw at us, we can beat them."

Matthew remained slightly skeptical though. "Yes, but do not forget what Draconis told us last time we were at his castle."

"Hm?"

"The Y'mordi are planning more than what we thought. They manipulated that Black Dragon Cairon just like they did Maris. Then, they killed him and dragged him into the Darkness. There is more at work than we previously thought, Drage."

"True, but usually they had the Behemoth on their side."

Matthew shook his head. "But you don't know that they don't have it now. The Sword disappeared, didn't it? How do you know that the Y'mordi weren't the ones to take it? They took some of your computer parts, so they could very well have been the ones to take the Behemoth from Gaspard."

Drage considered Matthew's words. However, the possibility did not give him any form of hope. The Y'mordi were definitely up to something. What could he do about it that was different from what he was already doing, though?

"Hey Matt, if something does happen to me, take Aria to see the disq tournament this weekend. She really wants to see it this year, and as Emperor of Light, I should be more involved in the affairs of this world, including the recreational aspects."

Suddenly, Matthew stopped walking. "Drage, if there's

one thing you've taught me, it's not to give up. You will make it back, so don't even worry about that. You are leaving for just a few days, so don't lose confidence now."

Drage smiled. "I guess you're right. It's just . . . been a while since I've been back to Earth. I guess I really worry since it was our home for so long. Even if it is a trap, I can't let them mess with that world. Mom told me that the Y'mordi came there a few years ago, so maybe they have been planning this for quite a while."

Finally, they were at the room that held DATA. Drage dispelled the mirror illusion, and they entered the dark chamber. "DATA, are you asleep?"

Blue lights lit up the room. "I was, but it is fine. What can I do for you?"

"DATA, I know you're missing some parts, but I need your advice."

"Certainly."

Drage took a step closer to the blue screens. "You remember me telling you that the Y'mordi were active on Earth at one point?"

"Yes."

"Well, with the knowledge that they are there again, I wonder if this move is some grandiose plan of theirs. Is it that or a trap for me? What do I do?"

Matthew kept his eyes on Drage. In front of this machine, Drage could be open. Out in the world, he had to hide everything. He knew that Drage had lied about Maksimilian, but regardless of the necessity, politics had caused Drage to keep his feelings to himself. A moment's weakness would make the Council overpower him. He could not imagine being in such a terrible position, yet he was taking over for Drage starting tomorrow morning.

"Well," the computer responded, "my readings indicate that Earth is not in any overly powerful danger now. A trap is still possible, and the machine is still probably there.

However, with the calm state it is in now, I would recommend working with the Ring of Elders as quickly as possible to locate Cronus 624. Difficulty is not the issue as much as speed itself is. If a trap is to be set, I do not see it set yet, or else the readings would be much worse. Speed is of the essence."

Drage nodded in understanding. "Thank you, DATA." He sighed heavily before adding, "Well, I suppose that now is the time." He turned back toward the entrance and raised a hand. With concentration, the water split to allow a beaming light to enter the chamber. The light became a glowing vertical whirlpool: a Gate.

"I thought you were leaving in the morning," Matthew said in surprise.

"Goodbyes are always hard," Drage muttered with his eyes directed at the ground.

"Aria won't be happy."

Drage did not change his vacant stare. "I know. But sometimes, I would rather her be mad than sad, y'know?"

Matthew was so confused. With his wife, things were much simpler. Sure, they had their arguments every once in a while, but there was never a time when he had to choose between making her sad or mad. Still, he supposed he could not judge Drage based on a relationship that was entirely different from his relationship with Lilian. "What about that mechanic?"

"He is already waiting for me. We set up a rendezvous point earlier."

Matthew raised an eyebrow. "You had this all pretty well planned out, didn't you?"

Drage turned and smiled at Matthew. "A bit. When you say goodbye, it implies at least some permanence. When you leave without saying it, the other person expects you to come back so that that person can yell at you for a while."

"In other words, Aria, right?"

"You got it." Drage turned back to the Gate and stepped

forward. "I'll see you soon, alright?"

Matthew gave a confirming nod and replied, "Definitely. Don't take too long."

Then, he stepped through the Gate and felt air for the first time in years.

7
End of the World

"Y OUR GRACE, THE ENIGMA Brigade has been successfully imprisoned." The servant bowed deeply before his
king.

"Good. Now, tell our commander to ready the troops for
battle. We strike the Emperor of Light in a few days. With
the Brigade out of the way, the Emperor will not have any
secret weapons at the ready."

"Yes, sir." The servant left the king in his round throne
room.

Lomeo, King of Varyx, rose from his great chair and
walked down a few steps. He had used a platform for his
throne due to his short stature. As he stepped across the
white stone floor, the potted flower he passed grew a few
more inches, straightening immediately. He looked out the
window at the kingdom that was now his. He had never
imagined that he would own an entire kingdom. Life had
never been so gracious to him.

A malicious smile spread across his face. It was not as
though he had genuinely earned the position. The last king
was weak, and it had taken Lomeo little effort to manipulate

the man into doing his bidding. Before too long, Lomeo had become the well-renowned advisor to the king, and when the king finally did die, Lomeo had simply taken the throne, much to everyone's approval. What the people did not know was that Lomeo had killed the king in his sleep. What they did not know was that their new king was not a normal human.

With the Enigma Brigade now in his well-secured prison, defeating the Emperor of Light would be one step easier. Of course, Lomeo had planned it from the start, but the hardest part had been hiding his intentions from the general public. By manipulating the media and even gossip, he had brought suspicion and hatred of the Emperor to the people of Varyx. He had committed all of these acts without proclaiming his hatred for the Emperor directly. The good news was that He-lio would not see an attack from Varyx coming. It would be a complete shock to them, and the element of surprise would be the deciding factor for this battle. However, there was a good chance that it would be the last battle. He had let the Emperor of Light and the Emperor Regin play their long games, but now, Lomeo was going to give the final aid to the Emperor Regin—assistance that would turn the tides of war in favour of Emperor Regin once and for all.

"Darkness . . . come to me." At his words, three Shadows appeared. Though Randir and Pullatus had much greater control over the creatures than he ever could, simple control was within his grasp. "Go to the Palace of Light and test the defense fortification there. I want a full report." As quickly as they had come, they vanished.

His comrades had always treated him like dirt, and now, that was all going to change. It would be because of him that the war changed. Regardless of what Pullatus's orders were, he had a responsibility here, and what he did would make a much greater difference than anything Pullatus had planned. For the first time in almost a thousand years, Ixion was on top of things, and this time, he would not fall—not to Randir, not to Pullatus, and certainly not to the world.

Arnim stood in front of the monstrous computer and found herself shivering despite herself. The air was so cold there. The main component of the console rose up twenty to thirty feet above her, a terrible colossus that would bring about the destruction of this world.

"I never thought that Earth would end by a technological apocalypse." She had always imagined Y'tal destroying the world himself through some dark *mysteria,* but instead, he had chosen to bring about its end by stealing the Emperor of Light's technology. A ring of smaller mechanical towers surrounded the main component.

For the first time since she had been there, a period of a few days, Cronus 624 awoke, and red screens surrounded each of the towers. "Y'mir, is that you?" the computer asked.

It had been a while since she had heard herself called that name. "Yes, Cronus 624. I am glad to see you have awoken at last. So, that means that the Emperor of Light has arrived."

A digital face appeared on the red screens, and its eyes glared at her. "The Emperor of Light? Who is he?"

"The Emperor of Light is your sworn enemy, Cronus. He has committed numerous great wrongs against your makers, and we would like for you to destroy him and this pathetic world, while you are at it."

The eyes looked skyward as his deep voice droned, "Say the words that shall allow me to initiate this program, Y'mir."

Arnim smiled beneath her black hood. "Cronus 624, activate program Ragnarok."

As soon as the last syllable left her lips, the ground shook. Each of the outer towers glowed deep red and shot hundreds of balls of green light into the distance. "Ragnarok initiation: 2% complete."

"What's going on?"

Cronus 624 spoke even though it was clear he had the program initiation moving at full speed. "I am starting by creating an anti-*mysteria* barrier across all of Earth except for my own vicinity, so I can defend myself if needed. Then, I am going to awaken the other 623 models and begin world destruction. Each computer will tap into any technological components this world has to offer to aid in the coming of Ragnarok."

Arnim's eyes widened. Y'tal was right. This machine would bring about this world's destruction. With such a magnitude of power, nothing could stop it. Because of the disabling of *mysteria*, not even the Emperor of Light would be able to stop this apocalypse. Gates would be impossible. The Emperor would not be able to even track the location of Cronus 624. The Y'mordi had indeed created the perfect weapon. If it succeeded here, Y'tal would likely use it to conquer Gevás as well. The remaining Great Servants of the Darkness would fall under such power.

"Ragnarok initiation: 14% complete."

As long as she stood inside Cronus 624's ring of towers, she could sense the world around her becoming dead of *mysteria,* but any person outside of those towers would lose even their sensing capabilities. Such an emotional silence as that seemed terrifying to her, but at the moment, she just smiled. She was safe as long as she stayed here with Cronus 624. Her orders had included staying with the computer to ensure the Emperor of Light's death. Of course, Cronus 624 could sense when the Emperor of Light was dead. The computer had such tracking abilities detailed in its programming.

"Ragnarok initiation: 19% complete."

"Cronus, what will happen to this place when everyone is dead?" It was merely a curious musing, but she figured that Cronus 624 would know the answer to that question better than Y'tal or Xarden would.

"Then, I will kill the heart of this world. If there are still hearts thriving on the ever-flowing stream of *mysteria,* then my task is not complete. Would you not agree?"

Such a mindset could not have been accidental. They wanted to destroy Earth, not just take it over. Since when had that ambition changed? Nevertheless, she knew better than to question her leaders. "Yes, that is correct, Cronus 624. Continue with the initiation process."

"Thank you, Y'mir. Ragnarok initiation: 28% complete."

Arnim looked around at the icy landscape that constituted her first view of Earth. Was the whole world ice like this area? She could not fathom a world being so cold all over. It seemed torturous, but she knew at the same time that judging a world was a hard concept. There were whole societies on this world, and they would find Gevás equally strange and complex.

Sitting there, waiting for Cronus 624 to complete its initiation was not a problem for her. She prided herself in her patience, but she wondered what her sister Sarn was doing now. Y'tal had sent her to do research on the Demons at the Academy at Gryphos. Usually, Sarn was impatient and did not think before she made a decision, and that hastiness was what got Sarn into so much trouble. The two had always been a pair.

"Ragnarok initiation: 36% complete."

She could remember life before becoming Y'mordi. The two of them had been dropped off at the Academy when they were only infants. Neither of them could remember their parents, and the instructors at the Academy became their parental figures. They had both loved studying there, learning the enchanting ways of *mysteria,* history, science, and even alchemy. It had been Sarn who had become bored with their life after their twenty-first birthday. Seeking a real change and the promise of power, they had taken on the Trials set forth by the Dark Lord, Dagan. The Trial of Will had been easy for Sarn, though she had considerable trouble with the Trial of Body. Arnim, on the other hand, had suffered at the Trial of Heart but did really well during the Trial of Body.

"Ragnarok initiation: 46% complete."

After being inducted into the Dark Lord's greatest soldiers, the Y'mordi, the two of them enjoyed having the black robes, the notoriety, and even their newly found dark powers. However, after a few years of service, the Dark Lord, Dagan, had given them a mission to destroy the Academy, the place of their fondest memories and friends. At the thought of this mission, even Sarn had hesitated and had had to think.

In the end, they had realized that they did not have a choice and destroyed their home. The whole building had gone up in flames, and screams had filled the night water. That night had been forever branded into Arnim's mind, and she was pretty sure that it was in Sarn's mind as well. Ever since then, the two of them had always been together on almost every mission, and, despite their differences, they were twin sisters and comforted each other when necessary. Being an Y'mordi was not an easy task.

Arnim leaned her head up to face the clear blue sky above her. The Emperor of Light was somewhere on this icy world, and she needed to find him and aid Cronus 624 in killing him. How could she do that if there was an anti-*mysteria* barrier all around Earth?

"Ragnarok initiation: 61% complete."

"Hey, Cronus," she started. When his red eyes focused on her, she continued. "Is there a way you could exempt me from the anti-*mysteria* barrier? I would like to aid you in killing the Emperor of Light. You would not have to change the programming for the other Cronus computers. I could deal with them easily enough, but I cannot even help you if I cannot use *mysteria*."

Suddenly, a beam of red light shot from one of the towers at her. The red glow enveloped her, and she could feel her own *mysteria* swell inside her. "What just happened?"

"I enhanced your *mysteria* such that, in this field, your power is doubled, but outside of the field, you will have your normal abilities. I have done as you requested."

She smiled up at him, though she knew how clearly not human he was. "Thank you, Cronus."

"Ragnarok initiation: 69% complete."

"What do you mean by 'not a member of the Enigma Brigade?'" Xarden roared at Valdridge.

The man in the white robe crossed his arms just as angrily. "It seems that the Emperor of Light suspected me. However, despite that obvious lie, I think that he told the truth. Maksimilian is not here in Apolis or probably even in Helio at all."

Xarden growled, "How can that be? Where am I supposed to look now then?"

Valdridge smiled at the Y'mordi's frustration. "I do not know why you are so upset. I did exactly as you asked."

"Yes, but at what risk? Now, the Emperor of Light is suspecting you of treason or something. This could not have gone any worse, really."

Valdridge's face became stern, then. "Y'dax, why have the Y'mordi not come out of hiding yet?"

Xarden calmed as well. "Valdridge, the world has not become terrified enough yet. It is not a world that dwells in the past, and therefore, we are merely nightmares for children. Every parent warns their kids not to hurt others for fear of Y'tal the Dark consuming their souls. As long as we remain hidden, we can manipulate the world with utter ease. Look at us. I can talk with the head of the Emperor's Council without the Emperor suspecting that you are a Servant of the Darkness."

"And what if the Emperor decides to reveal you?"

Xarden laughed. "If that happens, we shall throw secrecy to the wind and loose our wrath upon this world freely."

"And what of the Great Servants of the Darkness? Have

you found the next one yet?"

Gradually, Xarden was becoming frustrated with how much Valdridge knew. Y'tal had given the man too much information, and in all honesty, Xarden wanted to kill him. He could not understand why Y'tal had trusted Valdridge so much. "As a matter of fact, yes. However, he is being possessed. We are trying to simultaneously manipulate him and his possessor, though I am not aware of what progress has been made. I am focusing on Maksimilian, actually."

Valdridge smirked. "I do not know why you are so interested in that man."

"Because I have been ordered to be interested in him. But I suppose you would not understand the meaning of loyalty, would you?"

Finally, Valdridge's patience broke, and he drew his wand, casting a blast of Light at the same time. Xarden blocked the attack immediately and prepared an Ice spell. However, he sensed Valdridge creating a rather powerful spell and focused on creating a shield of Ice instead. He felt for the proper emotions, a simple task, but the feeling of *mysteria* was not there. He floundered for the depths of his heart, but he felt a cold resistance. "You . . ."

Valdridge smiled. "Yes, I have learned the ancient spell of cutting one off from *mysteria*. It is not that hard of a spell, now is it, Y'dax?" When he saw Xarden's teeth clench, he added, "I am more powerful than you could realize, Y'dax. Perhaps you would believe me if I told you a little secret about me."

Xarden's eyes widened. "What are you talking about?"

"I am an Ancient, Y'dax. Older than the First Obsidian War—old enough to know the other two parts of your heart, Y'dax."

"Ragnarok initiation: 75% complete."

⊛   ⊛   ⊛

The Emperor Regin was no longer his usual vibrant self. Whoever was possessing him hardly spent any time with the old man, unless he was in a meeting of some sort. Mali felt so bored being with him. Only when the possessor was spending genuine time with his puppet was the Emperor Regin even slightly conversational.

The large hall of the Emperor was bare of any decoration and had poor light. Mali hated the darkness that filled the room. It made him think of the small torture chamber in which Randir had been imprisoned a decade ago. He returned his golden eyes to the book he was reading, a history book about the Second Obsidian War that had been hidden in the Emperor Regin's personal library. The Emperor had certainly not minded as he was for the most part brain-dead, and Mali saw no better use of his time. He was seeking information on the legendary Dusk Lyre, the mythical instrument that Randir claimed would free them from their Y'mordi bonds.

Then, he heard the Emperor Regin mutter something.

"What was that, your Majesty?"

"I said, 'What are you reading?'"

Mali sighed. "Just an old book. It's been a while since I have heard the story of the Second Obsidian War told this way."

"Heh, most of those books are nothing special. The past can be told a hundred different ways, and each way reveals something new about the cultures that existed, but analysis of it all doesn't change the past."

"Very true, your Majesty."

"What's happened to me . . ."

Mali looked at the old man in his pitiful throne, and he realized that the possessor's hold had temporarily weakened. He was seeing the Emperor Regin fully now. "Your Majesty . . . you have been under someone's possession recently. Do you know who it is?"

The old man shook his head sadly. "I do not. I remember that man with the red hair sent by the Emperor of Light killing everyone in my court, and then I remember that filthy horse anima's destruction at Apolis. What happened after that?"

Mali's eyes widened. The Emperor Regin had been under possession for around a decade. Who was this powerful possessor? "Your Majesty, a lot has happened since then. That was almost ten years ago."

"Ten years!"

"Yes, your Majesty."

Then, the Emperor Regin's head lowered as he went into a deep slumber. Mali wondered what was wrong with the fallen king. He had to have been in an already weak state of mind for someone to control him this thoroughly. It was almost unbelievable. Usually, people who were possessed were capable of putting up at least some fight, but the Emperor Regin seemed to have lost all will to live. No mage was so powerful that he or she could put an end to the will of the possessed.

"Servant," commanded the Emperor, now fully under the possession, "the time to destroy the Southern Continent is upon us. However, I fear that my own strength has dwindled. How can I possibly lead the East to victory if I cannot stand at its head?" The man rose and faced Mali. "You came to me as a Lord of the Shadows, and yet, you did not seek to kill me. Now, you are my servant. Tell me your darkest secrets. Tell me how I can obtain the powers of the Darkness that you have."

Mali had been instructed to awaken the Emperor's dark abilities only in dire circumstances, but somehow, the Emperor Regin was expecting such powers now. Without having much of a choice, Mali lifted a hand to the Emperor Regin, and a white glow surrounded Mali's body. A blast of Darkness shot from his heart, through his arm, and out his hand.

The sphere of pure dark energy forced its way through the Emperor Regin's chest, and the old man fell onto his back, the spell working through him.

"My Lord Regin?" Mali asked curiously.

Darkness filled the room as the Emperor Regin's heart surged with the dark energy that had lain dormant in Regin's veins since the day he was born. Mali had never experienced a Great Servant of the Darkness with such raw power. Maris, the horse anima, had been relatively weak, and, from what he had heard, Cairon, the Black Dragon, had been slightly stronger. The man in front of Mali was the strongest user of the Darkness he had seen since the first two Obsidian Wars, excluding Y'tal.

Through the darkness, Mali could see the Emperor Regin standing on his feet again, glancing at his hands and relishing his newfound power. When he opened his mouth to speak, Mali sensed something else different about the Great Servant: He could feel the heart of the possessor deep within the Emperor Regin's heart.

"Mali, we attack the Southern Continent on the day of the disq tournament." The Emperor Regin's voice was doubled. Though the deep voice of the Emperor was loudest, a younger voice spoke beneath Regin's own words.

"But your Majesty, what about the truce you made with the Emperor of Light?"

A spell of Darkness wrapped around Mali, constricting his movements and suspending him in the water. He groaned in pain.

"It is long past time for this child Emperor to fall. Ever since he came to this world, chaos has reigned. His Enigma Brigade killed my family, and he freed the anima from the exile that his family had supported for decades. He is a traitor to his kingdom, his people, his family, and his allies. For his crimes, I shall sever his head from his neck."

Mali looked up at the empowered Emperor Regin.

Though Mali did serve the Darkness, he did not think that the Emperor Regin was just in his breaking of the truce. The lack of honor in such a move was appalling to him. "You would kill without any honor like that? As if no one would notice the lack of any pride you have?"

The Darkness constricted Mali's body tighter, and he groaned more loudly. "Servant . . ." the Emperor Regin began, "I need a sword. If I am to kill Dragenopn Helius, I shall need a blade far superior to any one sword I have here."

"What—what are you talking about?"

"I once held one of the five legendary Spirit Swords in this castle, but it was stolen from beneath my nose. Now, somewhere out there, some filthy thief has my Kohana's Fang."

"Kohana's Fang?" Mali muttered. "That was the blade that Tatsu used during the Obsidian Wars. That blade was hidden here for centuries?"

"Yes, the King Ferro hid it here after the Final Battle. Now, tell me: where are the others? Surely, someone as ancient as yourself would know the location of at least one more." The Emperor Regin stepped closer to Mali. "I cannot defeat Emperor Helius without one of the Spirit Swords. After all, he has the Sword of Destiny."

"I—I don't know. I know that the Emperor of Light has the Sword of Destiny. I know that one of his soldiers named Gaspard has the Behemoth."

The Emperor Regin growled. "Where is this Gaspard person? The Behemoth was the strongest of all the Swords. Where is it?"

Mali yelled as the dark constrictions solidified further and pierced through his skin.

"Ragnarok initiation: 83% complete."

"Lord Y'tal, it would seem that Maksimilian has fled the

confines of the Engima Brigade. He left years ago and has evaded all detection ever since then. I forced Valdridge to speak with the Emperor of Light, and that only yielded the Emperor of Light's slightest suspicion of Valdridge and the information that Maksimilian did leave years ago."

Pullatus considered the kneeling Y'mordi before him. "Well done, Y'dax. That would mean that Maksimilian has feared our coming after him. He is wise, and he regrets revealing his presence to us entirely. It is possible that he hopes to avoid us another several centuries."

"Surely, we are not going to allow that, my Lord?"

"No, we are not." Pullatus rose and walked past Xarden. "I have obtained information myself from another of our Servants. It would seem that Maksimilian left Helio with two Spirit Swords, the Steel of Life and the Behemoth. The Steel explains his survival over the years, but I believe that he only recently stole the Behemoth from Gaspard. This fact would mean that Maksimilian is weak now. He is more than well-aware of the wildness of the Spirit Swords. He shall be spending quite a bit of time trying to train the Behemoth to his will."

Xarden remembered a legend about the Spirit Swords. "'Every Spirit Sword has an ideal master, a person with whom it can truly be at ease and mold itself to its master's desires.' However, every master has to go through a long training session with the Sword first. Does Maksimilian honestly believe that he is one of the destined masters of a Spirit Sword?"

Pullatus was silent, and that was answer enough for Xarden.

"Well, would you like for me to chase after him? I suppose that it is possible that we could find him. After all, if he is in the middle of training, now would be his weakest time, as you said."

"Yes . . . Search for him. He will not have left many signs for you to follow, but if he is in training, there will be a time when he needs to test the Sword at its maximum. Seek the world for signs of high energy. One cannot train with a Spirit Sword and not use a lot of energy. *Mysteria* will be overflowing wherever he is."

"Yes, Lord Y'tal." Xarden summoned an icy Gate and left the Palace of Shadows.

In the silence of the throne room, Y'tal shook his head. "They are all growing soft. They have forgotten my power and therefore are lazy. The twins and Mali remain loyal, but the rest are turning to treachery. I can feel this much. If Regin fails, then I shall have to rise when the next Great Servant appears."

"Ragnarok initiation: 89% complete."

Arnim stood on top of a warm mountain now. Trees covered the rocky sides all around her, but she could feel the hard earth calling to her. Her heart reached out, tracing over every mineral, every gem, and every glistening stone of the summit. Mountains like these were nonexistent on Gevás. She had never imagined a place so full of earth and rock. She had heard that every mountain could fall, given the right pressures, but somehow, being on this mountain gave her such a sense of security, as if this terrestrial monument would last a lifetime.

Perhaps Earth had more going for it than she had originally thought.

She opened her mouth, and for the first time in years, let her voice fill the world around her. The first note held, and then the next three came rapidly in succession. Her mother's lullaby filled Earth's air and resounded through the trees below her. She neither knew nor cared if anyone could hear her. She had never felt as at peace as she did now on this mountain.

As the last notes faded away, she smiled, an expression

she rarely showed. This world was beautiful to her. Absolutely beautiful.

When Arnim opened her heart, she could sense the presence of the Emperor of Light west, across the vast seas of this world. The end of this world was coming, and the Emperor of Light must be destroyed. Raising a hand, she summoned a Gate that would bring her closer to the Emperor of Light and felt a slight regret for leaving such a gorgeous mountain.

"Wait!"

She stopped but did not turn around. Rather, she rapidly cast *mysteria* behind her to wrap around the heart of the speaker, trying to identify the person. The person was not a mage and seemed relatively normal. "Who are you?" she asked stiffly.

"I'm Aksel. Sorry, but I couldn't help but overhear . . . You have an amazing singing voice."

Arnim turned around to face the man. He was slightly taller than her and was carrying tons of strange equipment. "What are you carrying?" she asked.

"Hiking and climbing equipment. What does it look like?"

She noted that there was not sarcasm in his voice, only confusion. "What gives you the right to stab your tools into the sacred earth here? Do you think to master the beast of the earth?"

"No," he replied instantly. "The earth is definitely sacred. I come here to respect its beauty. It is beautiful, isn't it?"

Arnim cast aside her hostility and turned back toward the Gate that Aksel had for some reason just not registered. "You would do well to stay up here. The end of this world is coming, and if you value your life, you will not return home. Technology is no longer safe." She stepped through the portal, allowing it to close behind her and leaving a dumbfounded hiker staring at an empty space where a beautiful woman had stood seconds prior.

◦   ◦   ◦

"Ragnarok initiation: 95% complete."

Xarden cursed himself for his failure. Pullatus was clearly not pleased with him, and now he knew that Valdridge knew more about Xarden than Xarden himself knew. He had bullied the Prophet ceaselessly, but the old man had not budged. It was so puzzling though: Xarden heavily doubted that Valdridge could be an Ancient, because Xarden had seen Valdridge being considerably younger thirty years earlier. Yet, the Prophet of Light knew quite a bit about the past and Xarden's own past. What was going on?

"Valdridge . . . who are you?" Xarden asked the cool waters of the Southern Continent. His heart released tendrils of energy, sensing the area for miles around and hoping to find the elusive Maksimilian.

He knew now that his heart had been divided centuries ago into three pieces. Somehow, the body had been copied, but altered as well. Xarden himself knew very little about Division, though he was a product of it. Valdridge had explained to him that when a heart was Divided, the body replicated itself with modifications based on the piece of the heart it inherited. Though the spirit was not bound by the body, the heart was heavily connected to the body. No heart could exist without a vessel in which it could travel.

Somewhere out there, the other two pieces of his heart existed. He could not help but wonder if they were as bound to the Darkness as he was. Perhaps they were equally as immortal, if they had survived. Xarden had wondered if by some stroke of unfortunate luck Valdridge was one of the missing pieces, but upon examination, Valdridge had his own full heart. Still, something was definitely out of place about that Servant of the Darkness.

Xarden had always been fascinated by the differences between the Servants and the Great Servants. Some people served the Darkness through choice and offered their souls to the Shadows, ones such as Valdridge and the Y'mordi. However, seven people had been predetermined to serve the Darkness by the Hand of Darkness itself. The latter were the Great Servants of the Darkness. When the Darkness that marked their genes was awakened, they became fearsome indeed. Xarden had initially questioned the choices of the Hand of Darkness, but after a while, he realized the logic behind its choices. Only Maris had the will to lead nations into war, using the powers of the Darkness. Cairon was already at the top, but needed the Darkness to finalize his rule. The Emperor Regin could use the Darkness to destroy the Southern Continent if he knew how to use it properly. Ideally, Mali would help him with that if the Emperor Regin was to be awakened. They still needed to find the possessor of the Emperor.

For now, Xarden needed to figure out how to deal with Valdridge. He was too vital to kill now, especially if he spoke truth about knowing the identity of Xarden's other two thirds. How could he deal with Valdridge if he was so busy searching for Maksimilian, though?

He growled in frustration before summoning a Gate. The quicker he dealt with one problem, the sooner he could deal with the next.

"Ragnarok initiation: 97% complete."

Randir finally stood and beheld the ring of smoking bodies that surrounded him. He had thought that he had been exercising considerable caution, but apparently, some of Apolis's guards had tracked his occasional disturbances. He sighed. He had not wanted to kill people tonight.

"It seems that she is not here after all."

The ceiling caved in behind him as he left the still-flaming hotel. That was the third fire he had caused in the past twenty-four hours. His skills in stealth were fading, it seemed. His head turned northward. "She left the terra, then. By the sound of it, she left some time ago . . . to the East. There, stealth will be even more crucial, though. I do not want to get caught by the Emperor Regin." He summoned a blazing Gate and stepped into the Eastern Continent, several miles north of his present location.

"Ragnarok initiation complete."

8

Strange Company

S TEHL!"
   She snapped awake and looked at Mirah. "Hey, what
is it?"

He looked around wild-eyed. By the look of the pale
walls, he realized he was at a place of Healing. "Stehl, what
'appened? All I remember was da otha' transport comin' toward us."

"Yes, we had a wreck, Mirah. You're fine now. We just
had to take you to a Healer. We are back in the Capital."

He smiled and grasped Stehl's soft hand, his large palms
engulfing her smaller hands. "Wait . . . we?" That was when
he saw the other man in the room. "Hey, who are you?"

The other man was silent. Mirah observed the man's dark
hair cover one eye. Scars traced the man's pale skin.

Stehl explained, "Mirah, this is Tilgé. He saved us from
the wreck." She felt no need to mention that he was also the
one to cause the wreck in the first place.

Mirah rose with a groan—much to Stehl's worry—and
held out his hand to the scrawny man. "Pleased ter meet ya.
Mirah's da name. Spelled em-eye-ar-ei-eich, but said like

mee-rah. T'ank ya very much for da help. Was Miss Stehl hurt bad at all?"

Tilgé offered a slight smile as he shook Mirah's massive hand. "No, she was fine. She just had a few cuts and bruises. Nothing the Healer couldn't handle." He could not help but smile at Mirah's accent.

Mirah smiled back at him gratefully and offered, "Is dere somethin' ya would like in return, Mister Tilgé?"

Tilgé was utterly stunned by the request. Stehl definitely traveled with strange company. He had imagined that Mirah would be as rough and tough as Stehl herself was, but he seemed to be the complete opposite. How were they so close? "Well, Stehl is allowing me to travel with you as reward for saving your life."

Stehl turned to look sharply at him. That was not what she had said at all, but she did not comment on it. She merely waited for Mirah's reaction.

He did not turn his head to face Stehl but smiled even more broadly instead. "If it's fine by Miss Stehl, it's fine by Mirah."

Tilgé was utterly stunned. Mirah and Stehl were a couple, and Mirah was fine with allowing him to come with them? Furthermore, he did not sense Mirah's words to be a trap of some kind. "If you're sure . . ."

Though Stehl blushed at the words, Mirah laughed heartily. "Mister Tilgé, it's not a prob when yer wit' us. I t'ink we'll be here a while, do'. Are we not, Miss Stehl?" Mirah figured that at least having someone else with them would get Stehl out of the rut she was in. It could be good for her, especially if it was her idea to begin with.

Stehl brightened. It seemed that bringing Tilgé along would work out rather well. She had been worried that Mirah would oppose the idea. However, she realized that Mirah had never told her "no" unless it was to protect her. "Right. We need to check things out and see if we can find any of the members of the Enigma Brigade." She added as an after-thought, "And, don't get caught by any of the guards around here. The Emperor Regin's soldiers are certainly overwhelming the place. He knows how to make a solid defense."

Tilgé crossed his arms but did not change his blank expression. "So, are we all splitting up to find this mysterious Brigade? Is that your great plan? It's no wonder you haven't found any of them yet."

"Oh? And what is that supposed to mean? Do you have a better idea?" Stehl snapped.

After snorting, Tilgé responded in amusement, "Of course, I do. I'm not so silly as to go looking for something so aimlessly." He leaned back against the wall of the room and smiled.

At that moment, the Healer entered the room and scolded the group. "Miss Stehl, I told you to inform me as soon as Master Mirah awoke. Master Mirah, how are you feeling?"

"Good enough ter walk, I suppose. T'ank ya so much for the Healin', do' I am usually not one fer *mysteria.*"

At the mention of the word, Stehl put a hand to the hilt of her Spirit Sword, and Mirah noticed the movement. Though she had hardly used the weapon since she had obtained it, she knew well the powers against *mysteria* it possessed and felt the need to remind herself it was there, a practice in reflex she hoped to perfect in case they ever did find other members of the Enigma Brigade. However, Mirah was not the only one who noticed. Tilgé also caught the subtle movement. He had not really had the chance to observe her weapon yet, but once he saw how quickly she was to hold its hilt, he wondered about her own prowess with the blade. Was she as skilled in combat as she was in sheer physical attractiveness?

The Healer nodded. "You are most welcome. When you are ready, you can check out at the front desk. The receptionist can work out the billing. Have a good day, the three of you."

◉   ◉   ◉

"So, what is your grand plan for finding the Enigma Brigade?"

"Well, for starters, assuming the Enigma Brigade is actually here, you would need to know that they would probably not be looking for you. Rather, they would be doing their own missions."

"So? How does that help?"

Tilgé snorted. "In other words, you need to limit your search to areas the Enigma Brigade themselves would actually visit. Checking every alley in the hopes of a random encounter would be an act of pure futility."

Mirah interrupted, "Where do ya t'ink dey would go?"

"I have no idea, but you can't honestly think that wandering around aimlessly will all of a sudden bring one of the Enigma Brigade into your arms. That's crazy!"

Stehl crossed her arms in silent anger. She knew that Tilgé had a point, but more than anything, she did not want to admit it. Honestly, she had been doing it this way for years: constantly seeking the Brigadiers just by covering every inch of the cities they searched with an open ear to any phenomenal news or exciting events that might point to the elusive Brigade. After all, she had first found them by witnessing them massacre a group of people in the Emperor Regin's castle.

Finally, she sighed and said simply, "Alright, Tilgé. Would splitting up really be a bad idea? It would still save time if we split up to find the major areas. I suppose if the Brigade were to appear in this city, they would go to either the training facilities or a lord's house. A few years ago, there were some Brigadiers in the castle, so I suppose they could very well be there again. It would explain a lot . . ."

Tilge raised an eyebrow, confused by the reasoning for her distant look. Still, he merely cleared his throat. "Sure, we can split up. You and Mirah can go and look through the training facilities. I will tackle the castle." He thought Stehl needed to be alone with her lover, since he had only just awoken from his injured and unconscious state.

However, Mirah shook his head. "No, Mister Tilgé. You can go with Stehl. I need some time alone anyway. We can meet back at dat one bar, alright, Miss Stehl?"

Stehl was as perplexed by Mirah's offer as Tilgé was. He was genuinely trying to show Stehl that he meant to give her space. She almost felt guilty. Perhaps she had not been paying as much attention to Mirah as she should have the past few days. It was only that her life seemed to be a chaotic mess. However, with her promise to soon quit hunting the Brigade, it could be possible to let all of that stress fade away. Hopefully, she could find it in herself to settle down after it was all over. "Alright, Mirah. We will meet you there."

The large man smiled contentedly and turned to head toward the castle, assuming that Tilgé and Stehl would search the training facilities that were scattered throughout the Capital. It had been quite a while since they had traveled this way, but Stehl was confident that she knew where she was going. Tilgé tagged along at a comfortable distance, a good three or four yards from Stehl. For now, he wanted to observe her, not be beside her. There was something about Mirah's attitude and Stehl's own personality that warned him to be cautious.

Stehl noticed. "What is wrong with you? People are going to think we look suspicious . . ."

Tilge snorted his disagreement. "No, people would think it was suspicious if you were to travel with that fat guy at your side."

This time, Stehl snorted. "Mirah is not fat. He's just . . . larger than the average guy."

"Hey, you don't have to justify it to me. I'm just a companion for the moment." Though he said that, he did not really know what he meant by that. He hoped Stehl did not read too much into it, wanting to tease himself more than her.

"Whatever," she replied. "Anyway, we need to start scout-
ing all of these training facilities. It is certainly not going to
be easy." Changing the subject, she added, "So, what made
you the expert Enigma Brigade hunter?"

Tilgé shuffled his feet. Stehl noticed the gesture and
wondered what secret he was hiding. "Well, I have had some
experience in undercover work. I know how to think like my
enemy and try to put myself into their shoes." He sighed, disappointed with his own lie. He knew that that would not
satisfy her, so he came up with a better one. "Actually, for a
while, the Enigma Brigade has been after me. They are more
than a little responsible for what happened to my hand, or
the present lack thereof." He watched as Stehl's eyes widened
in quiet horror. "They have been trying to kill me, so I have
had to learn how to avoid them, know when they could be
where I am, and even think just like them. You are right. The
Brigade is a group of monsters, though I would not say that
they are all that way, I guess . . ."

"Huh? What's that supposed to mean?"

"Well . . . the Captain of the Brigade—the one with the
long—red hair, tried to have me killed, but another member
of the Brigade, a man named Bryco, warned me of it ahead
of time and helped me escape the Captain. He told me that
the Captain demanded my head as proof of my death. I cut
off my own hand so that Bryco could tell his Captain that he
had killed me with a blast, that only my hand had survived
the attack. I am sure that Maksimilian could tell that it was
indeed my hand and not some fake. Still . . . I fear that he
could be following me now. I think that he might know that
I am still alive . . ."

Stehl did not say a word. Rather, as they walked, she
merely thought about what Tilgé said. He was not just a random wanderer, or at least not the kind of wanderer she had
originally thought him to be. He was a survivor of the terrible
Enigma Brigade, and he was also proof that the Brigade was

split. There were those that followed the demonic Captain of the Enigma Brigade, and there were those that followed what the Emperor of Light truly preached. So, perhaps they were not all as evil as she had originally thought.

That notion made her a little sad, actually. With Tilgé's information, that meant that there was a good chance that some of the men she had killed had actually been entirely just, not evil at all. Still, all of the Brigade had been present and had served their Captain when they had massacred those people in the Capital's castle. Regardless of what good each member individually had, they had sacrificed it to be a part of the Enigma Brigade. She simply could not see them as good, or at least, not as good as the people of Helio saw them. To her, they were a band of murderers, and this knowledge incited her anger once again, as it had almost a decade ago. What was she to do? Could she really keep hunting them down until either she died or she killed them all? Or should she try to settle down with Mirah?

As her eyes looked deep into Tilgé's own, she wondered what would happen to him. If the Captain of the Enigma Brigade was genuinely looking for him, could she afford to stay in one place with him? It would make it extremely dangerous for him. Suddenly, she realized what she had in her grasp. It was a blessing that she had Tilgé with her: he could be bait for the Captain of the Enigma Brigade. "Well, Tilgé, if he wants you dead, perhaps we should advertise your presence a little better."

"What?"

"I told you: I want that Captain dead. I have been looking for him for years. Don't you see?" She was smiling now. "You are the answer to all my prayers. Having you will lead me to the Captain of the Enigma Brigade, and this time, I will kill him. He will not be the victor of this fight, and I won't have the foolish aid of some stupid Lord of the Shadows to stop me from trying to kill him." She said this last part more to herself than to Tilgé.

Tilgé felt his temperature climb. What mess had he gotten himself into? He thought Stehl was stunning: she was smart, clever, brave, strong, but apparently foolish as well, and that was not the most ideal combination. He did not need for her to summon Maksimilian. If Maks knew that he was alive, then Bryco could die just as easily as Tilgé himself would, and Bryco had done everything in his power to keep Tilgé alive. It would be poor repayment if Tilgé allowed for Bryco to be killed because of him. He simply could not allow that to happen. "Stehl, look. You can't just use me as bait. Listen: if he truly does know I am alive, then the person who saved me is in danger, too. I can't allow him to get killed, not because of me. Don't you know of honor? You are a military woman yourself, are you not?"

At this call to duty, Stehl's heart steeled. "Yes, I do know of honor." She tried to calm the voice in her mind that compelled her to use Tilgé to her advantage anyway. Above her hatred for the Enigma Brigade, she had a duty in this world. She knew to serve the Light as much as she could. If she were to cause such a dishonor to Tilgé and his rescuer, then she could not honestly call herself much better of a person than any of the Enigma Brigadiers themselves, for they killed without honor, and she would be sending that rescuer to his death without honor.

She pitied Tilgé in that moment, for he was in a rough situation. He, too, wanted the Enigma Brigade dead, but he did not seem wise or brave enough to be able to overcome them. Perhaps with his missing hand, his strength had subsided altogether. She found herself wondering if he could indeed fight with just one hand. Did he honestly think that they were never going to find the Brigade? Was he using Stehl as a means of avoiding the Brigade entirely? This masking of purpose was frustrating and perplexing to her. She wished he would be more direct. In anger, she retaliated, "What are you doing here? Is it to avoid the Brigade?"

Tilgé exploded in anger then. "I am staying with you, and I am not out to betray you! I have done nothing wrong, and I just like your company. Is that so wrong?" Blushing, he realized what he had said. Nevertheless, he did not turn his head. Though embarrassed, he was not ashamed of his words. He knew his place: he had not meant to come into this companionship and throw that balance into chaos. He merely wanted to be a companion to the two of them, not a pack-mule, just a friend. It had been a long time since he had had any true friends.

Stehl kept walking and did not look directly at him. She had not been yelled at for a while. When she had worked for the Emperor Regin in his terra, yelling was common for officers, but as a General in the terra of Emperor Helius, she was treated very much like a female, even though her own nature had not been altered in the slightest. Though Tilgé's yelling had clearly been in frustration, it reminded her of her time back in the Emperor Regin's terra, where she had truly felt at home. Though Mirah certainly took care of her, he was not the masculine type she was used to, the kind of person she had always imagined herself with. Tilgé seemed to fit the standard she had once held. He did not have that twinkle in his eyes that Randir had, and he did not have that gentle care that Mirah had shown her. Still, he had a rough edge that made him seem strong, powerful, and strangely attractive.

"No, it isn't wrong, I guess. I get lost when I think about the past and what's happened to me." When she felt Tilgé's eyes looking at her in confusion, she added, "It's not like my life was perfect before the Enigma Brigade came along or anything. I just never really questioned anything. I was fine with life being simple, working in the terra, and I thought that that was all I would ever really need. Then, when I witnessed them murdering the people at the castle, I found something to fight for for the first time. I ran into that Lord of the Shadows, and he only thrust my thoughts into greater chaos." She rolled her eyes at the memory of Randir. "Maybe finding and killing the Brigade is supposed to help me find something out about myself. I don't really know. I just know that I have to do it. I'm sure that sounds really stupid, though . . ."

Tilgé stepped beside her and brushed his hand against her cheek. "Not at all." He himself had had a similar feeling after his time in the Enigma Brigade. He had always followed Maksimilian blindly, thinking that he would always have a place there. Since he had left it, life had lost its original safety and comfort. Yet, he knew that he needed to find his true calling. Perhaps that was why he wanted to stay with Stehl and Mirah. He lowered his hand.

They continued on in silence, regarding all of the training facilities in curiosity. Tilgé's eyes went in every direction, hoping that if by some chance, they did come across the Enigma Brigade, he would see them before they saw him. It had been several years since he had been in the Capital. He remembered when he met the Emperor of Light here. The former Prince was such a strange character, young, but mature. He barreled through battles and even Maksimilian's strict façade. Honestly, Maksimilian had probably tried to manipulate the Prince, but that had proved to be a harder task than Maksimilian had hoped. Tilgé could not fathom how anyone could stand up to Maksimilian the way Dragenopn Helius had. Tilgé himself was certainly terrified of doing anything like that, especially now that he would be killed on sight if Maksimilian ever found him.

A door opened to one of the training facilities, and a soldier stepped out of it with a heavy rifle in his hands. "Clear the streets!" he roared.

Other doors opened at the same time, and soldiers filed out of the buildings in a rush. "What's going on?" Stehl asked the soldier. "I demand to know what's going on."

The man smirked. "Ma'am, just step back. Don't worry your pretty self with the matters of war."

"Excuse me?" Stehl asked in the utmost anger.

"You heard me, lady. Move it."

She was upon him in an instant. Her Sword flashed once, and his rifle went flying into the water. Before he could react, she pointed the tip of the Sword at his throat. "If you know what is good for you, you will show a little more respect to a former captain of the Emperor Regin's terra."

The now flustered soldier countered, "You? A captain? Are you crazy?"

"Surely, you remember Captain Terrell?"

The young soldier was not the only one to gape. Tilgé was in equal awe. Ever since the day that Maksimilian had encountered the Lord of the Shadows and the Emperor Regin, the Enigma Brigade had been hunting down that Lord of the Shadows and Captain Terrell. Tilgé could remember that day well. They had killed innocents in the Emperor Regin's fortress, and Tilgé himself had killed a large number of those people. Though he had hardly thought about the incident all that much, the memory came to him vividly. If she was indeed Captain Terrell, then perhaps she might have a chance at beating Maksimilian after all.

The soldier muttered, "Captain Terrell was a traitor. He abandoned his station at a time of war."

Stehl growled, "No, I went to the army at Apolis to hunt down the very people who murdered his Majesty's court."

"There were . . . there were whispers that he had a Lord of the Shadows for an accomplice."

"Never!" Stehl snarled, now pushing the tip of her Sword against the man's neck. "I would have killed the assassin, had that Lord of the Shadows not stopped me!"

From what Tilgé could remember, though, she had almost been killed. The Lord of the Shadows that had appeared had saved her from total annihilation. "Stehl, I need to speak with you."

Stehl turned in surprise. "What?"

"Now," he repeated, turning into an alley. He realized that the street had become quite a scene, with other soldiers lined up in formation, but all eyes were drawn to Stehl and the soldier she was threatening. As soon as Stehl realized the same thing, she lowered her weapon and ran after Tilgé.

"What is it? I was kind of in the middle of something, in case you didn't notice!"

"Did you mention something about a Lord of the Shadows?"

She rolled her eyes again. "What is it with everyone talking about it? So, he came to me looking for the Guardians of Light, and I told him I would help him if he paid good money. I planned on killing him afterward, but he saved me from the Enigma Brigade at the fortress. We had one night under the stars, and that was it!"

"Stehl . . . I think that you can beat Maksimilian." Her anger subsided slightly. "I don't think you can do it alone, though. You will need my help and probably Mirah's as well. But you definitely can't do it alone."

"Oh? And what makes you say that?"

Tilgé lowered his eyes in aversion. Now was definitely not the time for a confession on his part. If he were to tell her the truth, then she would leave him there, and he would be no better off than where he was. He needed to keep the lie going a little longer. "It's just . . . that sword you have. You look like you definitely know how to handle it, especially if you were really Captain Terrell. I heard a lot of good things about that particular soldier." While it was definitely true that Tilgé had heard many things about Captain Terrell, few of them had indeed been good. Most of them were Captain Maksimilian's rantings about the filthy soldier.

Stehl's features softened. Her eyes lowered and lost that angry glare. Her jaw unclenched, and her fists opened. "I don't see how you could have heard anything good about me. By the looks of things, all that ever spread about me was bad. I am a traitor to these people, and I fraternized with the Darkness."

Her words only made Tilgé feel guiltier though. While Stehl had talked with a Lord of the Shadows and was associated with evil, Tilgé had killed almost a hundred innocent people and was associated with the Light. He shivered despite himself, and he wondered where Maksimilian was right now. That long red hair had haunted Tilgé's nightmares ever since he had cut off his own hand. "You are not evil, though . . ."

Her eyes sparkled with a look of pity. "Tilgé, why did the Captain of the Enigma Brigade want you killed so badly? What did you do that upset him so badly?"

"I don't really know. I was loyal to the Light. I followed every order I was ever given, and I never stepped outside my bounds. I guess that that is what years of loyal servitude gets you: a bad name and a death order. Hopefully, Maksimilian still thinks I am dead."

"Maksimilian? Is that the Captain's name?"

Tilgé cringed. He needed to keep his mouth shut about information on the Enigma Brigade or else she would want nothing to do with him. He had trouble distinguishing between what most people knew and what he knew. "Yes, I believe so. That was the name that Bryco gave me, anyway."

Not wanting to push the matter further and seeing how uncomfortable it made Tilgé, Stehl changed the subject. "Well, I hope you are right about me and my Sword. This is not an ordinary blade." She unsheathed it to show off its intricate design. "It is known as Kohana's Fang, a legendary Spirit Sword from the time of the Obsidian Wars. It has the ability to ward off *mysteria*. I think it will help me defeat Maksimilian. I found it six years ago when I first met Mirah, and we were hunting down the Enigma Brigade here in the Capital. It seems as if I am constantly returning here. This is the only place I have ever actually encountered the Enigma Brigade. Perhaps this is where we should all settle down."

"Settle down?"

"Yes—I have been playing the role of adjudicator for too long. I promised Mirah that, after searching here, we will go to the disq tournament and then perhaps find a place to settle down. I told him that after this city, I would quit hunting the Brigade. I just can't see myself wasting both of our lives looking for some people that seem to have vanished from the world completely. Once the Emperor of Light announced that they were not a myth, all traces of them vanished. I don't know that I can do this all my life. But . . . I also don't know what else I can do. I mean, fighting is all that I have ever known."

"I know that feeling well enough." Stehl looked up at Tilgé in shock. "I was raised fighting, and I have been a part of all the wars and have killed more than my fair share. Looking back on it, though, I am tired of the all the fighting. I would take back all those people I have killed if I could. I really would. I just wish it were that easy." Tilgé was just now realizing the full damage he had caused during his time with the Enigma Brigade. Realizing that Stehl had been the one to stand against Maksimilian put his life in a new perspective. She had thrown away everything to pursue a cause that was truly serving the Light. Such an act was admirable to him, and he envied her. He had never committed such a selfless act. Serving Maksimilian, he had always thought that what he did was in the best interests of the Light, but he was realizing more and more that Maksimilian's actions were helpful to the Darkness.

"Hey, let's go back to Mirah and see if he's found anything. On the way back, we can find out what those soldiers were doing." She put a hand to her Sword and smiled when she noticed Tilgé's eyes follow her hand.

❊   ❊   ❊

Tilgé exited the inn with his cloak wrapped tightly around him. Though the Capital was quite warm in the day, it became a little chilly at night. He was not used to the night world of the city. Most of his life seemed to be covered by a thick shadow, dark as the night sky itself. He shook his head. He could not get any sleep in there. Though it would be easy to blame Mirah's excessive snoring, he just had too much on his mind.

As he rounded a corner, he saw a figure stand in the pool of pearly light that emanated from one of the building signs. The figure wore a white robe, but Tilgé did not turn his head to face the stranger. Attracting attention was not what he meant to do on this night. He passed the stranger with no problems and proceeded into one of the side streets. The street was thinner there, and the lights were dimmer. Yet, the quiet and dark relaxed his nerves.

"I thought you would never come out of there."

Tilgé did not have to turn around to recognize that voice. His hair stood straight up, and a chilling tremor rolled down his spine. "Captain . . . I didn't think you knew I was still alive."

Tilgé heard Maksimilian step closer to him. "I knew once Bryco gave me that hand that you were still alive. Unfortunately, I had other matters to attend to. Guess what, though? I have pushed aside all those problems just to find you. You lucky dog."

A sword moved from its sheath, and Tilgé drew his own sword with his only hand, turning to block an attack, but Maksimilian had only drawn his blade. "Get out of here! I never did anything wrong to you! I did everything you ever asked me to, and this is how you repay me? By killing me?"

"Oh, Tilgé. You always were loyal, but you thought too independently as well. You were becoming a tiring nuisance, and I couldn't keep hearing that yapping. It was time to get you out of the picture, as it were." When Maksimilian rushed, his white hood fell back, and his red hair sprawled behind him.

Tilgé struggled to block the rapid flurry of attacks. His sword was much smaller than Maksimilian's own massive katana, but now was not the time to complain about sword sizes. Without the use of his other hand, he could not press his own attacks against Maksimilian, and he already felt his strength ebbing. Each deflecting maneuver sent powerful jolts of force up Tilgé's arm. Soon, that sword would come flying out of Tilgé's hand, and the fight would be over. "What you're doing isn't for the Light, Maksimilian. You're serving the Darkness even now!"

Maksimilian leaped backward, lowering his blade. "Why, Tilgé, you're not getting soft for that girl, are you? What's her name again? Stehl? Or, was that Captain Terrell?" The man smiled devilishly, and Tilgé gaped.

Raising an aggressive stance, Tilgé charged at Maksimilian, who pointed his sword at Tilgé and charged as well. Metal met metal, and the ringing tone rippled through the water of the Capital.

The sword fell beside Tilgé's feet, and his chest heaved sharply. His enemy's sword tip was aimed at his throat, and his eyes looked deeply into Maksimilian's own green ones.

"Hmph, what a pity you have to die, Tilgé. I suppose I shall have more enjoyment killing Captain Terrell and that fat ogre she's been traipsing around with." His muscles tensed to push the sword straight through Tilgé's neck.

"Don't hurt her!"

Stehl sat up and turned to look at Tilgé. After making the yell, he rolled over, but he stayed asleep. Mirah did not seem to have budged: he appeared content with his obnoxious snoring beside her.

She wondered if Tilgé had been married before all of this drama had happened to them. He had certainly never mentioned anything of the sort, but he still seemed as if there was something he was intent on hiding.

Yawning, she wrapped her arms around Mirah and snuggled up to him, falling back asleep.

9
Of Ravens

V ALDRIDGE ROARED above the other voices with a powerful authority. "Master Matthew, if the Emperor Regin is genuinely offering a truce for the day of the tournament, we should strike him then and end this war once and for all. Can't you see the wonderful opportunity we have?"

To Valdridge's words, Ocrum added, "If there could be a time to end the war, this *would* be it, Master Matthew."

However, Marqest would have none of it. "Master Matthew is not the Emperor of Light, and he knows not to force such an act of rudeness and injustice."

Matthew sighed heavily. Now, he was understanding what Drage had to go through on a daily basis. Fighting the Emperor's Council in a debate was harder than any fight with the sword or staff. He would rather be fighting Maris again than go through this torture. "Mistress Quella, what do you think of the matter?"

"I think that Master Marqest is right. We cannot make such a bold action when the Emperor of Light is away. He would have your skin, Master Valdridge, if he knew that you were trying to start a battle."

Mistress Leona glared at the elder man as well. "Yes, you are not usually so forward. I question your motives almost as much as his Majesty did the other day."

Valdridge was flustered and did not press his argument.

"Don't you all see?" Aria started. "The Emperor Regin, against his better judgment, is trusting us not to attack and have a day of peace amongst our people—a day without war, fighting, and bloodshed. And you, Master Valdridge, seek not only to continue the violence, but also to do so without any national pride or honor? As the *Prophet* of Light, I would think that you would know well the voice of the Light and preach only its soundest advice." She emphasized the word "Prophet" with a bit of jealousy. For years, she had been training in the arts of Fire in order to further her abilities in *mysteria,* striving to become the next Prophet of Fire.

Marqest snapped, "Aria!" The glare he gave her was enough to tell her that she knew better than to disrespect a Prophet, no matter how right she knew she was and how wrong she thought Valdridge was. "Master Ocrum, you were taught well in the military the meanings of discipline, honor, and chivalry. Do those codes not apply to this particular suggestion?"

Ocrum closed his eyes in thought and snorted. "Yes, I suppose they do. If we attack on the day of the tournament, it would be a terrible act. I am in agreement with you, Master Marqest. It is only that I do not think that Master Valdridge's claims are necessarily foolish. He wants what is best for the people of Apolis, even if it is not the most morally right thing to do."

Matthew was truly tired of hearing this debate. Lilian was sitting at his side, but was only taking in all the information. She had not said a word the entire time, though she did grab his hand when he was at his most nervous. Going through a meeting such as this one every week was unfathomable to Matthew. How did Drage do it?

Seeking to distract himself from his thoughts, he looked forward to the end of the meeting when he would try going into the past to find the mysterious Ace. He had never tried moving through time, but surely it could not be that hard. After all, he had had a great teacher: his own father. He was the last known descendant of the legendary Keepers, and he intended to use his abilities to their fullest. Lilian was, of course, going with him, and after talking to Aria about it, she wanted to accompany him as well. Aria's scholarly attitude and her own stubborn persistence would not allow anything to the contrary to occur.

The kids were enjoying their time with the artist, the Khaosdog, at the moment, and Matthew wished he were playing with them rather than sitting in this terribly boring and frustrating meeting.

Then, he noticed the raven at the window. Its black wings flapped against its back once, and its head tilted, as if it were regarding the people in the room with a hint of curiosity. Matthew cocked his head in puzzlement, mimicking the bird. He squeezed Lilian's hand, and her head looked to the window as well.

"It is not one of my kind. That bird is just an animal," her thoughts spoke into his mind.

In all his time in Gevás, he had never seen a raven. Plenty of birds thrived in the Eastern, Northern, and even Western Continents, but hardly any flew above the South. What was this one doing here?

It pecked the glass once and then flew off into the sea. The black shape became a dot in the distance over time.

Matthew realized that Marqest was staring at him in wonder.

"I think that Master Helius needs a brief respite from this session, fellows." However, none of the Council members regarded Matthew and merely stood, groaning. Matthew smiled at the Prophet of Water and left the chamber.

As he took Lilian out into the hall, he said, "What was with that bird? It was like it was just watching us."

"I do not know," she replied in honesty. "As I said, it is not an anima like I, and it was not capable of communication. I do not think it was any more than just a regular animal."

"Still, I've never seen a raven here before." He looked back into the room at the window, but the raven had not returned.

Lilian stroked his back. "Perhaps you did not get enough sleep last night. Tonight, you should retire early."

"Maybe you're right." He smiled at his wife and kissed her forehead. "I cannot wait to try this time-traveling thing out after the meeting. I'm sure Aria is excited as well. We have been wanting to know the truth about this Ace character for ten years now. Aria has done her best to research him, but little seems to be known about him, although he has carried quite a few names."

"Yes, and the greatest concern is of the connection that Ace has with Aria's son, Ace."

Matthew looked in the direction where the children were probably playing. "Yes." He felt an urge to go through the winding hallways to see if his children were doing alright, but Lilian's hand closed around his.

"We should probably go back to the meeting room. They are more than likely waiting on us to finish it."

He nodded and followed her inside.

"Now, Master Matthew," began Ocrum, "I just received news that there has been a stirring near the Capital. It seems that they are planning an attack soon, and from what my intelligence informs me, the attack will be made here against Apolis." Matthew's eyes widened. The Emperor Regin had never been so sudden with his attacks, and he was choosing now of all times to launch an attack against Helio? There could not have been worse timing.

"Master Ocrum, are you certain?" Mistress Leona asked.

Matthew looked around, and everyone was as surprised as he was.

The military advisor nodded.

"How soon?" Aria asked.

"My report says that it is planned to happen on the day of the disq tournament."

Matthew clenched his fist. "That can't be right. He is not so foolish that he would throw away honor for this war. Neither side is losing enough people for him to resort to that. He just signed a truce, and now he is going against that?"

Valdridge sniffed. "It would seem so, Master Matthew, and if we do not reassemble all our troops, then we shall lose this war. I demand that you listen to reason!"

Despite the seriousness of the situation, Matthew could not grasp a clear action. Then, he saw the raven at the window again. It tapped its obsidian beak against the glass and flapped its wings as if it was trying to get Matthew's attention. The thought finally came to him: he *had* seen ravens in Gevás before, on his staff. They were the symbols of the legendary Keepers of Time. Slowly, Matthew raised his staff, and the raven dipped its beak as if in acknowledgement. The carved outlines of the black bird on his staff glowed with a white light, and several members of the Council stood from their seats as they felt Matthew's *mysteria* surge through his body. What was happening?

Lilian grasped his hand as if she knew something he did not, and Aria put a hand on his shoulder as if she too was somehow aware of what was going on. The white light filled the room, and, when it finally dissolved, the three of them were the only ones in the room. All of the Council's metallic sheets and staffs were gone. It was as if a meeting had never occurred.

"What—just happened?" Matthew muttered.

Aria turned her head to him. "You didn't do that?"

"No, I didn't! I mean—I felt my own *mysteria,* but I was

hardly controlling it. I think . . . I think it might have been the staff itself or maybe the raven."

"Raven?"

Lilian looked Matthew in the eyes. "I did not sense anything. I did not even sense that the raven was there again. This raven is curious. I wonder if it serves a mage. If it channeled your *mysteria,* I would think that it has to be controlled by a mage."

Aria looked around. "Well, what exactly did it do? I honestly thought that you were going back in time in the middle of the meeting. That's why I grabbed you."

Lilian nodded, showing that her thoughts had been the same.

Matthew went to the window of the room, where he had seen the raven stand only moments before. "Well, I wonder if we did move back in time. If so, how far back did we travel? I felt the spell, so I suppose I might be able to repeat it when we need to return to our time."

Aria followed Matthew and peered into the outside world. "Look, Apolis has shrunk so much. Even the wall is lower." The city outside was indeed different. Most of the buildings they all knew were either gone or had become smaller.

"That," began a voice from behind them, "is because you have moved 500 years into the past."

The three of them turned to face several robed men. Their silver robes bore hoods that hid each person's face and stretched down to the floor beneath their bare feet. The one in front continued, "We, Matthew, are the Keepers of Time." Then, Matthew noticed the raven that was perched on the man's shoulder.

He grasped his staff tightly. "What—what's going on here? What do you want with me?"

"Matthew, we have predicted our doom. There will be a day when the Keepers nearly fade from existence, and our ways could be lost to time. You, in 500 years, will be the last remnant of the Keepers unless you do something about it."

"What can I do? To my knowledge, I am the only one who can use the powers of Time. How can the Keepers continue if there is no one left to learn? Not even regular Wind mages can utilize those abilities."

"Matthew," continued the leader of the Keepers, "if you will learn what we have to teach you, then you could be the greatest wielder of Time in your era. However, your son can learn to be even greater if you train him."

Lilian said, "William? He is to become a Keeper?"

"We have not seen all of what would happen in your time, but I can tell you this: what the Guardians have done up to your time is only a beginning. The children of the Guardians are the ones who shall come to fight the greatest Darkness."

Matthew, Lilian, and Aria each felt their faces turn pale. What they had done was only a beginning? Would their children have to face monsters stronger than Maris? Gaspard? The Spider? Of course, they had all planned on training their children in the ways of *mysteria* and basic fighting, but they had never thought that the Darkness would be stronger in the coming years—not to such dangerous levels, at least. Being all Guardians of Light, they figured that they had seen the worst of the Darkness already. Would the Y'mordi be the cause of such chaos, or some other unearthly evil? Matthew shook his head. Thoughts like these are what made Time wielders crazy. Knowing the future was dangerous.

"What do I need to learn from you?"

The raven made a rattling noise deep within its throat, and the man said, "You need to learn the rules of traversing the stream of Time. You need to learn how to predict the near future naturally, and you need to be as a raven, in battle and in life. When you have mastered all three of these things, you shall be free to return to your own time."

Of course, Matthew and the others knew there was no

real pressure in staying here until Matthew learned what he needed to know: when they returned, they could go back to the moment when they left, not losing any time at all.

"Alright, that sounds fair to me," Matthew replied, "but I would like to see your faces rather than have our whole time here shrouded in mystery."

"Oh, on the contrary, we want you to be left as much in the dark about us as possible. Assuming you do train William, after him, the Keepers may be no more, and we are content with that. In the era that exists afterward, there shall not be a need for the Keepers. Our primary goal is not to wield Time, but to regulate its use throughout all of Time, and we have learned to sense potential rifts in the timeline of the universe. We have looked forward to each of these and corrected them."

Aria raised an eyebrow in confusion. "Corrected them? How?"

The Keeper addressed Matthew, "Do you know the answer?"

Matthew hesitantly answered, "Well—time is very much like a stream that is moving over new territory. It is constantly expanding, but with enough training, you can see the path it will take, all the way out to the sea. However, when you do that, I guess you could see places in its path where it would stop working altogether."

"Yes," continued the leader. "Such places are called rifts, or at least potential rifts—places or times when wielders of Time could use Time improperly and cause the very flow of Time to shatter around them if they allowed it. The Keepers try to find the person responsible for the rift and educate them and warn them. As we do so, we see the stream of Time shift just slightly enough to avoid the rift."

"But if you could predict the rift, then shouldn't it actually happen? Or does the stream split?" Aria said.

The Keeper laughed. "You are quick, my lady. No, the

stream does not split at all, but you have to understand the weight of such a rift. We cannot see the rift itself. However, the stream of Time itself can sense its coming, and we, the Keepers, can feel Time's stress, its worry, and its pain. We can pinpoint the source for the potential for chaos and stop it."

"So, you could not move to the rift through time?"

"Any person who tried would be destroyed instantly. That is the power of Oblivion, the ancient Element."

"Oblivion?" Aria asked.

The leader of the Keepers cleared his throat. "Though I am sure you have many more questions to ask me, I cannot answer all of them. While you all have all the time you need, we have other matters to which we must attend, and our laws forbid us from telling you everything of this time. Some remnants of the past should remain remnants and possibly fade into ashes. For now, Matthew, you are to be properly trained."

"I am ready," was Matthew's immediate answer. He had relaxed his grip on his staff, but he still held Lilian's hand softly.

Now alone with the Keepers of Time, he prepared for his first lesson, how to move through Time itself.

"Now, the first thing you must understand is that Time is vast and ever-flowing. When you maneuver through its current, you are not just manipulating a few of its drops as is necessary for many of the tricks you have probably learned. You have to put yourself at the mercy of Time itself. At that point, you do not display aggression or dominance, but lowliness and submission. When you can float in the stream of Time, then you are moving correctly."

Matthew tried to understand what was metaphor and what was literal, but he struggled to understand the meaning of the words even without such distinction. "Can you explain it another way?" He was far from frustrated, and he simply wanted to approach it another way.

"When you cast a simple Time spell, you seize its great power. However, when you travel through Time, you cannot even attempt to assume such authority. Usually, when using *mysteria,* you allow your mind to flow in the river of your emotions, where *mysteria* lies. Take that a step further. Allow your emotions to ride the stream of Time itself. You can sense it out there."

"How will I know what to do once I am in the stream?" Matthew asked, wanting to know each step before he attempted anything.

The head of the Keepers stepped up to him. They were in one of the massive training rooms of the Palace of Light, and it was easily one of the coldest rooms of the castle. They were in no danger of running into any of the other inhabitants of the Palace because the Keepers had frozen time once Matthew, Lilian, and Aria had entered this era. "When you are in the stream of Time, you will feel the weight of a trillion eras pressing against you, each imploring you to enter its foreign realm. However, the temptation is easy to resist. To find an era you wish to enter, just feel for it with your heart, and the break in the stream shall appear."

"You make it sound easy," Matthew commented.

"Perhaps," began the Keeper with a tone that revealed he was smiling beneath his hood, "it is because I have done it so many times. Nevertheless, if you wish to equal or surpass my power, then you must learn to yield to the stream of Time."

When the Keeper did not say anything else for a while, Matthew stammered, "You want me to try it now?"

The Keeper's silence was answer enough.

"Alright, I'm ready. You'll be able to find me if I land somewhere where I am not supposed to?"

"Of course. Begin," commanded the voice.

Matthew clenched his jaw. The Keeper did not expect that Matthew would learn the ability quickly. He was expecting Matthew to fail, but Matthew had no intention of failing. He closed his eyes and focused on that energy that rested within his heart. At first, he reached out to grab as much of that calming power that he could possibly grasp. Then, he tried yielding his heart to that same power, giving in to it without losing sight of it. Gradually, he felt a blue light fill his heart. He could not see it, but he felt it. The light was most certainly blue.

At first, he thought he was simply imagining the light, but the more he focused on it, the more it seemed to grow. He relinquished his grip on the stream, and it flooded through him, a blue storm that swept through his very being. He could not see anything—at least, not in the conventional sense of seeing. Rather, he felt the colors and images around him. He was drowning in a sea of blue water, yet bright lights shimmered through the ocean all around him. When his heart scanned across such a light, he felt the pains, the pleasures, and the millions of hearts that dominated each era.

Then, the era he had hoped to see appeared before him. Though he knew almost nothing about it, he knew that it was the time in which the Seeker of Paradise would live. He almost reached for it, but he stopped himself. He needed to wait for Lilian and Aria before he went there.

Concentrating, he looked for the era he had just left.

"Matthew, the stream of Time is beautiful. It is eternal and infinitesimal. It is not a physical stream, but a stream of the heart, and that is what makes it so great. However, that is also what makes it terrible." Matthew could hear the voice in his head. These had been his father's words to him years ago. "No one knows what happens to your body when you travel through time, but it can be affected if you stay there too long. Respect the stream's beauty, but do not dwell in it. Do not give in to it so much that you lose yourself as well."

In response, Matthew's heart stopped searching for where the Keepers were and admired what was around him.

The way the lights of different eras reflected off his heart and illuminated the water, causing it to sparkle beautifully. He felt as if he were looking at the whole universe, a million worlds spread before him, each waiting to be explored. The whole scene was so relaxing, and Matthew could see how it would be easy to lose himself in this comforting atmosphere.

However, taking heed of his father's warning, he prepared to return to Aria, Lilian, and the Keepers. The light of that era came easily enough, and he embraced its warmth.

He was standing exactly where he had been standing when he left.

"You did it." The Keeper was clearly surprised at Matthew's accomplishment. "How was it?"

Matthew smiled. "It was amazing. It was so beautiful, yet I could see the danger in it as well. I can see why we do not try to foster that ability in every mage. It could be easy to abuse, and it could be even easier to lose yourself in it."

"Yes, the current is strong, but if you keep your wits about you, you can ride its flow without a problem. Now, do it again. I want you to go to five days after today."

"Hey Matthew. How is the training going?" Aria asked as he came back to the meeting room for a break.

"Incredibly tiring. You have no idea . . . What have you been doing here?" He saw the several metallic sheets she had spread out across the long table.

"I am merely writing out all that I know about Valdridge. I am trying to piece together what is going on. When we had that break, Mistress Leona pulled me aside and warned me about Valdridge. She said that he has been more than not acting his normal self. She said that he reeks of some strange spell—foreign to her, anyways."

"What? Do you think he is being controlled?"

Lilian asked, "If he is being controlled, would that not mean that the plans that the Emperor's Council makes are in extreme danger of falling into another's hands?"

"Yes," Aria agreed, "but not necessarily into enemy hands. If Valdridge is indeed possessed, we need to find out who is controlling him and why. Though Valdridge does seem to be in the wrong more often than not, he is not evil. We need to discover the intent of whoever has control over him."

"That will be easier said than done," Matthew commented. "How long do you think it has been going on for?"

"Well . . ." began Aria in thought. "For the most part, he's always acted strangely, but when he called Drage out on the Enigma Brigade the other day, that was the worst he has ever been."

"Well, then, all we can do is wait until Lord Helius returns, correct?" Lilian asked.

Aria shook her head. "No, if we can find proof that Valdridge is not really himself, then the Council as a whole can vote him off, and that would settle that. While Drage can appoint and remove members of the Council, the Council itself also has a right to appoint or remove members."

Matthew inquired immediately. "How many members have to agree in order for Valdridge to be removed?"

"It always takes at least three-fourths of a vote for it to pass. Since we have eight members, it would take six to agree."

"So, Valdridge would get his vote too," Lilian stated simply.

Matthew started counting all the members off. "Well, we should definitely have at least four: Aria, Marqest, Leona, and me. Valdridge will clearly stand up for himself, but what do you think about the other three?"

Aria put a hand to her chin. "Well, Jallun is pretty quiet. I would think that he will stick with whatever the majority is, but I don't feel confident enough to count him. Ocrum is on the fence. He will think for himself, though. That is for sure. Mistress Quella . . . I don't even have a guess for her."

Matthew added, "So, all we can do is explain the situation

and hope for the best. All we need is for two of those three to vote our side."

Lilian countered, "But Valdridge also only needs two of those people to vote on his side. We are at equal ground now."

One of the Keepers appeared at the door to summon Matthew. Aria looked to Matthew and said, "Lilian and I will try to come up with something while you are training. Good luck!"

Before leaving, Matthew smiled at his wife, and she stepped forward, kissing his lips before returning to help Aria. Matthew turned and followed the Keeper to the training room.

"Your next lesson will be to feel Time as naturally as you feel the water flowing across your skin. In order to be a Keeper, you need to be able to sense attacks before they are made, predict chaos itself, and sense when someone is reaching for the powers of Time." While the Keeper summoned his own *mysteria,* Matthew waited for the Keeper to explain. He did not interrupt the lesson and did not question what he was being told. "As you try to control *mysteria,* you feel its enticing pull. That pull allows you to sense all that is going on around you. If you grasp Fire, you can see the world in its thermal levels, seeing heat, in essence. If you grasp Light, you can see through the most blinding of lights and notice things that would have otherwise been invisible. And if you grasp Time, you can see actions before they happen. However, your foresight must be harnessed well. If you expand your power too far, you will see an outcome. If you look for the outcome of an action and try to prevent it, you are finding yourself in a paradox, and paradoxes can be disastrous. Predict what an enemy is about to do, and fight accordingly."

"How does one harness such an amount of *mysteria* without actually manipulating it? You mentioned that one could have such awareness at all times, but that seems like it requires quite the amount of concentration."

The Keeper folded his arms across his chest. "It takes a little getting used to, but then it is easy. It is similar to breathing or blinking—things you do all the time that require little to no thought. You only need a small amount of *mysteria*. It is as simple as holding on to that power. You do not even have to let it fill you."

Matthew experimentally reached for *mysteria* and touched the stream of Time, allowing it to trickle into his heart, not filling him but still flowing into him. "I feel it, but how will I know if someone is about to attack me?"

Immediately, the Keeper summoned a staff and swung it one fluid motion. The Time energy swelled inside Matthew's heart sharply, and in his heart's eye, he could see the attack coming before it even began. Rather than dodge as reflex demanded him to do, he had plenty of time to draw his own staff and raise it to block the incoming attack.

He felt another attack coming from behind him, and he whirled his staff instantly, blocking an attack from another one of the Keepers. "Whoa," he said, appalled at the ability. "Why didn't Dad ever show me this? It could have helped me so often."

"He didn't show you many things, Matthew. You needed to master the basics before you tackled such spells as these. You needed true discipline and practice and even your own trials."

Matthew was having a hard time understanding what this Keeper was saying. "Wait—is my Dad here? Did he travel to this time? With the ability to travel time, could I find him?"

The Keeper nodded. "You know the rules of traveling through time, so, as long as you follow them, there is no reason you could not see your father again. However, there is no need to travel. He is here in this Palace. He is one of the Keepers working with me."

"Where is he?" Matthew asked. His voice was calm, yet his heart beat heavily against his chest.

The Keeper sighed before calling, "Derek, it is time."

The door to the training room opened, and Matthew did not even notice the leader leave the room. All he saw was his father standing in the doorway. "Dad . . ." He ran to his father, throwing all calmness away and becoming a child again. He wrapped his arms around his father's body, taking in his warmth and the smell of tea that still lingered on his robes. "I've missed you."

Derek smiled lightly. "Matt, I don't know my future, so do not tell me anything past what I already know. I come from the era in which I was training you in the ways of Time. Your brother Drage returned to Earth, and you stayed with me. Do you remember this era?"

Matthew returned the smile, "Of course, I do. How could I forget?"

"How old are you now? You've grown up so quickly." His eyes sparkled with the light of a mild joke, and Matthew could not help but laugh.

"I'm twenty-seven now, Dad."

"It has been a while then . . ." Then, Matthew caught something in his father's eye, a slight distress.

"What is it?"

"It's just—I don't know where to begin. Um . . . did I ever get to tell you the real reason why Liz told you that you were adopted?"

Matthew's heart sunk then. All thoughts ceased in his head, and his smile shrunk. "What do you mean? I thought it was just because the Emperor didn't like me."

Derek grimaced. "Well . . . it is very true that John did not like you, but there is a big reason for that. I passed something on to you—something that Helen did not inherit. Some call it a gift, and others call it a curse, I suppose. Its abilities made Lord Helius and even your mother think of you as a demon child. You see, she didn't know I had the ability. She found out when you accidentally exhibited this ability one day.

That was when she left me to go to Apolis."

A lump built in Matthew's throat, and his mouth was starting to dry. "What is it I have that makes me so demonic?"

"No, no!" Derek rushed. "You are not a demon for it at all. It can be a gift, too. In a few years, it will definitely be a gift. I am sure of it."

"What is it?"

Derek stood back and held Matthew by the shoulders. "You are not a pure human. Your mother was certainly human, but I am an anima. You are part-anima, yourself." Matthew could not believe what he was hearing. "Of course, you are mostly human, but you do have some anima in you— enough to make you change while you were a little toddler and make your mother take you and Helen away, calling me a monster."

"I don't understand. How could I go through my whole life without knowing that I had some anima in me?"

"Because your mother did everything she could to hide that part of you. She tried to shelter your mind. Changing involves embracing your true nature, and she tried to make you feel as if you were not wanted—at least, not as much as Dragenopn or Helen."

"But—how can someone be part anima and part human?"

Derek smiled. "Yes, it is quite the interesting hybrid. Walk with me." Matthew followed his father out of the training room and up the stairs. "It seems as if you can still call yourself human. An anima is an animal with the ability to become human. If a human can turn into an animal, that being is still a human. Your animal form is just a small part of you, Matt."

"What is my animal form?"

Derek gave his son a wink. "What would you think it is? It's the same as mine, son."

They continued to climb the stairs, higher into the

Palace. "I'm a raven, then? Are all the Keepers ravens?"

"Yes, they all are. It is a secret organization of raven anima who have mastered traveling through the stream of Time. The raven is associated not only with the Element of Wind, but also the form Time. Though there are some humans that can manipulate the flows of Time, they cannot handle it as well as we raven anima can."

"And Mom hated me . . . because of that?"

Derek swallowed. "She didn't hate you, Matt. She cared about you deeply. She really did, and I have no doubt of that. She thought I had defiled you, that I had caused you a great harm. She tried to raise you as if you were a full human, and for the most part, she succeeded. I think she knew that that would change once you came here, though. Coming to Gevás meant facing the past she tried to keep from you. That's why she never came back for you. She could have so easily summoned a Gate to see you, but she knew I was taking care of you, and I'm sure that Dragenopn conveyed as much. She and Lord Helius just grew up in cultures where that was seen as a terrible thing. Your mother did care about you. She just thought that being part anima was unnatural. It's not exactly accepted for an anima to have such relations with a human, you know."

Matthew smiled. "That is something I definitely know, and I have faced my fair amount of judgment for it."

"What? People already could tell that you had anima in you?"

Matthew shook his head, still grinning. "Don't tell me this back in your time, but do you remember that girl I was with, the one with the beautiful white hair?"

"Yes, of course. I could tell that you two were close. So, what?"

"She's my wife now, and she's a horse anima."

Derek burst out laughing. "I'm sure your mother was glad to hear about that."

"She came to the wedding and told me she was proud of me and all. I could tell she was a little put-off though. I didn't know she had such a resentment toward anima. I guess that since I am part anima, it's not that strange though, right?"

Derek put an arm around Matthew's shoulder. "No, it's still pretty strange. You are so much more human than you are anima. You've probably only changed to an animal once in your whole life—not that the number of times you change is the defining factor here." Then, Derek opened a door, and they were standing on one of the balconies of the Palace. "Still, she is definitely beautiful. I guess you also got your good tastes from me as well."

Matthew wished he could take his dad with him, back to his time, but he knew that he could not. He would be breaking so many laws of Time, yet he wanted to stay here forever with his dad. The current was still around them, and the world was just as still. The city was definitely smaller in this era, yet it still had its brilliant luster. "I saw the stream of Time. You were right, Dad. It was so beautiful. I felt as if I could stay there, and all my problems would just melt away."

"Yet, you came back," Derek commented.

"Yes, I had to. I felt that more than anything. Floating in that stream was like no feeling I had ever felt before, not one, but I knew that there were people needing me in my own time."

"You would do anything to help your friends, even if it meant throwing away Paradise?"

Matthew turned to stare at his father. The older man was gazing out at the city, deep in thought. "What do you know of Paradise, Dad?"

Derek sighed heavily. "It is a legend, nothing more than a fool's dream. I have met him. I have met the man who calls himself the Seeker of Paradise. We, the Keepers, spoke to him once. He had never been trained in the laws of Time, yet he felt the need to travel the stream as if he were one of us. He is strong—stronger than all of us put together, yet he is not stupid. He has not broken any of the laws, though he was never taught them. He worries us."

"What did he do 600 years ago to put him in the books?"

"That is something you shall have to find out on your own. Now, son, before I must return to my time, won't you fly with me?"

Matthew nodded with a reluctant tear in his eye. "Of course." Without being told how to do it, he reached inside himself, allowing *mysteria* to light up his heart, and he embraced his being. He pictured the raven and sought its form in his heart. As if his desire alone had summoned it, the raven overcame his being, and he no longer stood on the roof. Rather, he flew side-by-side with his father, each wing-beat a natural action that pushed him farther into the sea.

"Matthew, where have you been? We were looking all over for you!" Aria demanded.

Matthew smiled in response. "Are you guys ready to find Ace? I think I can take us there now."

10
Level 1

DRAGE COULD NOT believe what had happened to his
little community. Although Paradise Shores had once
been a peaceful little suburb, it was now ashen ruins. The
devastation was far from old. He and Feranx had entered
Earth a few miles south of the area. Wrecked cars dotted the
way to Paradise Shores, but Drage still did not expect the destruction that had awaited them here. What had caused such
chaos?

He thought about using *mysteria* to repair the neighbor-
hood, but he decided that such an action could only cause
more harm than good: the area would be considered haunted, at best, if it were mysteriously destroyed and just as mysteriously rebuilt. Then again, the cause of destruction might
only be a mystery to him. "Any ideas, Feranx?"

The griffin sent a screen to float in front of Drage, flashing the words, *"I'm not noticing anything particularly useful. I
mean, it genuinely appears as if it was just a regular fire."*

Drage replied in frustration, "What about this seems
regular to you?"

"I mean just in terms of the fire. The source of the fire just came from these primitive electric outlets."

Drage examined an area of a destroyed house where an outlet was likely to be. Just as Feranx had said, the blackest spots in the rubble indicated the outlets were indeed the most likely causes of the fire. Still, how could everyone's houses have spontaneously combusted at the same time? Something about this whole disaster seemed more planned than Feranx was thinking. "I don't sense anything odd about." In truth, he had not sensed anything since coming here. The world was so quiet here. Of course, he loved breathing in the salty air again, but the dead quiet made the place of his dreams seem a nightmare. "A lot of people have died, but I don't see Mom anywhere. She must have escaped it, whatever it was."

Feranx typed, *"Why don't you create a* mysteria *signal? If she is a particularly good mage, she should be able to detect it."*

"That's right. She is the head of the Ring of Elders, after all." He raised his hand, preparing to cast a spell of Light, but when he grasped the power, he discovered something. A resistance pressed against his heart, cutting his heart off from the world around him. He could feel the energy inside him, but he could not release it. "What—what's going on?"

"What is it, your Majesty?"

"I can't use *mysteria*. There's some kind of barrier here. I can't even cast the simplest of spells. I wondered why I couldn't sense anything."

The griffin shook his head. "But that's impossible. You used *mysteria* to get us here. How could it not get us out?"

Drage found his breathing had increased. He had no idea what was going on, but it was definitely reeking of a trap. Somehow, the Y'mordi had known he would come and set a trap so he could not return to Gevás. Matthew was the one in real danger. "We have got to find my mother and fast. What can you do with all your gadgety stuff, Feranx?"

"My gadgety stuff, huh?" Feranx typed these words with a smirk on his beak. *"Well, I can try hacking into any computers*

this world has and take over any surveillance system there is. What can you tell me?"

"Well, the world has a humongous network system called the Internet. It's sort of like the overall features of one of our master computers, without personality or its own real intelligence. Still, most people here have access to it. Oh, and you might be able to tap into the satellites around Earth as well."

A few more green screens appeared in front of Feranx, and in seconds he had access to the Internet. He frowned in confusion. He did not know quite what to expect, yet he knew that something was definitely off about what he was seeing. *"Lord Helius, I believe this Internet is frazzled. There is this strange code blocking off access to even the most basic functions."* Drage walked over to Feranx, considering the screens. Feranx was right. Somehow, the Internet had been disrupted, entirely locked.

"Well, it seems the Y'mordi came up with a really clever trick this time. No *mysteria* and no Internet. I guess we should just start walking toward the city."

"Wait, Lord Helius," Feranx frantically typed. *"I cannot access the Internet per se, but I can certainly analyze the code that is locking the network."*

"Huh?" Drage looked closely at what Feranx was doing, but could not understand it.

Feranx waved a claw in front of the screens, and each panel revealed a flashing mixture of white symbols. *"These are of the same language that marked Cronus 624. The Y'mordi are indeed behind this barrier."*

"Can you translate it?"

Feranx smirked again. *"Of course, I can, your—Lord Helius."* Though he knew he had almost called Drage "your Majesty," he only smiled. *"By the way, does your Sword at least work here? If the Y'mordi found a way to knock that out of commission as well, we could be in serious danger."*

"Right," agreed Drage, unsheathing the Sword of Destiny.

He was glad he had brought the sheathed weapon this time rather than merely relying on summoning it, as he usually did. "Besides, you can't fight, can you, Feranx?"

This time, Feranx snorted. *"Of course I can fight! I would be lying if I said I could handle a sword as well as you or some of the terra can, but I would not be too terribly easy to kill. I may be mute, Lord Helius, but I can still fight."* He typed a few more keys rapidly, still decoding the flashing white text. As the translation appeared on another screen, Feranx typed a summary onto the screen closest to Drage. *"It would appear that Cronus 624 is behind the barrier. It has instilled a firm root of control into the technology of this world, hacking into every computer this world has."*

Drage clenched his jaw. "Why would it do something like that?"

Feranx rubbed the bottom of his beak thoughtfully, *"I wonder . . . Could it have caused the computers in these homes to short-circuit? That would explain the seemingly controlled fires, I suppose."*

"Do you mean—do you mean that fires like this one are occurring all over the world? Has this world been totally destroyed?"

Feranx examined the code more closely. *"It is not likely, though I do think that that is the program's ultimate goal. It is a program called Ragnarok that was executed only minutes ago. It is striving to hack into every computer in the world to destroy this world. There are 623 other modules in this world, each one expanding the program's reach."*

"So, we have to find the main module and shut it down, right? How could we track down such a machine out of 624 of them?"

"Well . . ." Feranx lowered his beak in thought. *"Well, all we really need to do is find one. If we can disable one module, I can analyze some of the programming and really crack through this code, opening up the Internet and locating the*

main module."

Drage nodded. "Okay, to the city, it is, then. Hopefully, we can find some survivors and find out where the nearest module is."

Feranx waved a claw in front of the screens, and they all dissipated. Hesitantly, he followed Drage out of the wreckage of Paradise Shores. Feranx was not impressed by what he had seen of Earth so far, yet he did like breathing in the air. It was far thinner than the water in Gevás, and this thinness prevented him from being able to swim upward, but he could still fly by using his wings. The wind felt relaxing here.

"I lived here for so many years, Feranx. I loved it here: the breeze, the sea, the clouds, and the sun. I called this place home all the way through college."

Feranx typed, *"What made it not your home anymore?"*

Drage rubbed the back of his neck. "Destiny, duty, I don't know . . . I had suffered quite a lot back in Gevás, and I didn't feel I was ready to be ruler of it all. But, eventually, I realized that no one else was going to set things right. If I didn't like the way Gevás was functioning, then I was the only one who could change it. I had to change my definition of home. Here, I have some relatives, a few friends, and the wind at my back. On Gevás, I have my real family, my true friends, and a kingdom to rule. It's certainly harder, but it is where my heart belongs now."

"No regrets?"

"Regrets?" Drage repeated as they walked down the black asphalt. "No, I don't think I have any regrets. I mean, my life has been far from perfect, but I don't think I would have done anything differently. My mistakes are part of what made me what I am now." Drage felt as if he should have regrets of some kind, but he was for the most part content with his life. "What about you, Feranx?"

Grudgingly, Feranx acquiesced, typing away rapidly. *"Well, I came from the North. My family all fought in the Third*

Obsidian War, but I stayed out of it. I was always a techie griffin, and I was glad to have the opportunity to work after the Exile was lifted." He noticed Drage's eyes gleam. "*What is that look for?*"

"I hate that Emperor Mentiris ever passed that exile. I hate even more that the following Emperors of Light kept that law going, my father included. How could they allow such wrongs to go uncorrected, even if it did mean starting a war with the Eastern Continent?"

Feranx countered without conviction, "*Well, if you lose the war, would you have committed an act of justice or a wrong?*"

Drage opened his mouth to call the question absurd, but after thinking about it, he realized there was some truth in Feranx's words. "We will win this war. I refuse to allow the nonhumans to go back into exile. The Light shall prevail."

Feranx continued, "*I remember hearing of a Black Hope, a horse anima who would free us from our imprisonment. Then, that hope faded when you killed him, and, in his place, people looked to the Golden Dragon who protected you and your family, Rexam Draconis. Yet, it was you who saved us. My family was so confused. Most nonhumans had gained the idea that in order to be free, we would have to fight your system, your government. We never expected that a human would lift the exile. We saw it as immovable from your end.*" As they walked, Drage and Feranx stared ahead at the skyscrapers of Boston that were finally coming into view. "*Once that exile disappeared, so many were confused and did not know what to do. Some joined the fight against the Emperor Regin, of course, but others stayed where they were, holding on to their old hatred and thinking your actions to be a trap. My family, of course, enlisted in the war. I sought merely to go after my own skills and interests, and I ended up being hired by the Emperor of Light himself.*"

Drage sneered, more at himself than Feranx, "And do you feel that you are doing a greater service to your race than your siblings are?"

Feranx side-glanced at the Emperor of Light. *"I did not know pride before I came into your service. Now, I would definitely put myself in a higher level of duty than my brothers. Still, I do not think of them less for it. I am using my strengths to my maximum, as they are theirs. I do not brag of my intellectual superiority. We each have our own duties to fulfill."*

"True," Drage agreed.

Their eyes widened as a wave of sound washed over them. A skyscraper exploded in the distance. Drage gaped at the sight of the burning spire ahead. "Even Boston is falling apart." Drage clenched his fists. "This really could be the end of this world if we don't do something about it." He turned to Feranx. "Do you think you could fly while holding me?"

Feranx smiled at the idea. *"Well, sort of."* He waved a claw, and a screen appeared, laying itself flat against the road and expanding slightly. *"Hop on,"* Feranx implored with another screen. Drage stood on the screen, surprised it was so solid. As Feranx flew toward the city, the green screen flew beside him, Drage crouched on its thin surface. Drage nervously held the edge of the screen, not wanting to fall.

"I didn't know your screens were so versatile."

"They are how I fight as well," Feranx replied.

Drage could not help but laugh at the thought. "I think that that is one of those things that I will have to see to believe. I am sure you will get your chance, especially if the Y'mordi are to be found here . . . I wonder if the Y'mordi are as limited to *mysteria* as I am. How extensive is this *mysteria* barrier that Cronus 624 created?"

Feranx shook his head. *"I could not tell you. I can only analyze what I see hindering access to the Internet. I do not even know where to begin on examining the link between the program and mysteria. It would seem that that is more of your department than mine, Lord Helius."*

Drage snapped back, "Alright, for at least the duration of this little excursion, call me Drage. On this mission, we are not Emperor and servant. We are partners, alright? Here, you are my equal, unless you want me to refer to you as Master Mechanic Feranx every two seconds. Deal?" Drage extended a hand for Feranx to shake.

The griffin considered the gesture hesitantly. Then, he flew closer to Drage, smiled, and reached his claw out to shake Drage's hand. With his free claw, he typed, *"It's a deal, Drage."*

Boston was indeed in ruins for the most part. All the computers had gone haywire, but there were survivors here. Drage and Feranx spent several hours sifting through the survivors to see if there was any word on Drage's mother or any of the other Elders, but no signs revealed themselves to Drage and Feranx. Everyone seemed entirely disoriented as to what was happening to the world, their lives, and their own sanity.

Drage sighed in frustration, "Feranx, I really don't think the Elders are here. They must be looking for the main module themselves if they have half as much information as we do. Do you think there is any chance of a module being near here?"

"I would think the chances would be pretty high, actually. Especially in big cities like this one, there would have to be a central module to extend the program just the right way."

"A central module? So, we just gotta find that central location... How would we know what the general area of such a module looks like?"

Feranx rubbed his beak in thought. *"Well, I would think that it would be the area that is least damaged right now. So, perhaps we should look for the one area in Boston that has not been ruined by machinery."*

Drage looked around and finally saw a skyscraper that was for the most part intact. It was near the center of the city. "A central location and not too damaged? Could that building over there be it, Feranx?" He pointed to the building, and

Feranx nodded.

"It is definitely worth a shot . . . Drage." The griffin summoned a screen on which Drage could stand, and the two flew off to the upper floors of the building, the least damaged part. As soon as they approached it, a beam of electricity shot out at them from a window. It narrowly missed the flying pair, and they crashed through one of the windows, falling onto hard stone floor.

Drage stood and unsheathed the Sword of Destiny. "Feranx, get behind me!" He raised his Sword in time to block another searing blast. The module was a huge machine that stretched from floor to ceiling and filled half of the area. Several desks had toppled over, and papers were strewn all across the floor. The module had several guns pointed at Drage and Feranx, and they knew those guns to be the source of the lightning. Still, without being able to use *mysteria,* Drage could not predict attacks as easily.

Calming his mind, he relaxed his grip and lowered it to his legs, summoning the Way of the Dragon that Draconis had taught him years ago. He blocked several more blasts that came from the module, each defensive maneuver a quick and graceful blur that Feranx barely caught up with himself.

Feranx typed, "I can't get through to the machine. We need to find a way to shut it down."

"Can't I just destroy it?" Drage asked in frustration. "How can I do anything else with just a Sword? I can't even use *mysteria,* remember?"

"Well, can you at least cover me for a bit?" Though that was already what Drage was more or less doing, Feranx wanted assurance that he could do his work without being zapped. Feranx saw Drage's nod and summoned five green screens. They each shot off in different directions, wrapping around the module and accessing its programming. It took only seconds for the module to figure out what was going on, but, by that time, Feranx already had most of the information

transferred to his belt computer. The module zapped the screens around it by erecting an electric barrier, but it was too late. Feranx summoned another screen and accessed the programming codes. By making a few adjustments on his screen, he knew how to disable the machine. Throwing one more screen toward the module, it made the desired edit directly, and the module went on standby before it could blast the screen.

Drage exclaimed, "How did you do that? I didn't think you could do all that much with those screen things. What was it you did exactly?"

Feranx smiled, glad he had impressed the Emperor of Light with his skills. *"I sent the first screens over to examine the coding of the machine. Then, from here, I made the suggested edits to the coding to put the module on standby. It would normally not be an edit of code, but it can be done that way. Then, I sent the screens a final time to execute my commands. Pretty simple."* Though he called it simple, he knew it was far from easy.

Drage was in awe of Feranx's abilities. He had not realized Feranx's green screens could be so versatile. "Well, can you use any of its codes to find out anything? Maybe get into the Internet?"

"It's certainly worth a try," Feranx typed. *"Just give me a few minutes to analyze the data. Sure, it's easy, but it is still time-consuming."*

"Alright, fair enough." Drage walked over to one of the broken windows and examined the remains of Boston. Decrepit buildings towered across the massive city, and cars were turned over on every street. Fires lit up the once-dark alleyways, and the survivors of the massacre were either cowered in corners or trying to help those who were injured. Drage shook his head. How in the world was the Ring of Elders going to fix this problem? They had been known to work on people's memories of incidents such as these, but this particular catastrophe surely had affected too many people to be in the Ring's capabilities any longer. What could they possibly do? He shook his head again. He was thinking too far ahead. He needed to worry about disarming Cronus 624 before he thought about repairing all the damage the computer had done. Wishing he could do something for the people of Boston, he reached out for *mysteria,* but again found it impossible to exert such energy into the world. "Any luck, Feranx?"

A screen came to Drage with the words, *"Not yet. Almost."*

Drage sighed. He held his Sword up to the sky, wondering if it was as limited as he was. Channeling his power through the Sword, a beam of Light shot into the clouds and caused a rainbow to form across the city. "Oh, wow. It seems that the Sword can slice through even Cronus's barrier. Still, I can only cast limited spells through the Sword. I certainly can't fix a whole city with it. I am not even strong enough in those Elements. It's hard to cast even this much energy outward."

Another screen came. *"You are going to have to leave some of these matters for the Ring of Elders. Even if a part of you still considers this place home, this world is not your responsibility. Weeding out the evil that the Y'mordi placed here will be doing more than enough. You cannot do it all, Drage, even if you are the Emperor of Light. You have your own duties on Gevás, a war to attend to."*

"Yeah, I know, Feranx. I just don't want to leave this world in such shambles. I mean, I grew up here."

"It is done, Drage."

Drage turned around and approached Feranx with his multitude of green screens. "What have you found?"

"It seems I have access to the router map for the whole Cronus network. I can locate every one of the Cronus modules. The problem is that it does not give the model numbers. It only gives a power rank. There are four modules at the top rank. We can

actually go and find those with this information, but it could still take days, even with me flying us there. Is there not an alternate method of travel on this world?"

Drage shook his head, "Not one that would be that much quicker than your flying . . . *Mysteria* is the quickest way, but we can't summon Gates. How are we going to do it in time?"

Feranx looked over the data again. *"Well, you know, a lot of this data was programming from DATA, your computer. We might be able to make it summon a Gate for us."*

"Can you really do that?"

"I can certainly try." Feranx put his green screens to work, examining and putting in the occasional command. Only a few seconds later, a Gate appeared in the middle of the room. *"Yes, it worked!"* his words flashed across a screen, blinking with his excitement.

Drage smiled, "Nice work, Feranx. Now, where does this thing lead?"

"Straight to the first Rank 1 module."

"Alright, let's do it then. What rank was the module we just went up against?"

Feranx's grave answer was immediate. *"11."*

Drage and Feranx entered the Gate and found themselves falling into the sea. They splashed through the cold surface, and the water enveloped them. Rushing upward for air, they saw the massive module piercing the ocean's surface in front of them. It was a mechanical behemoth that towered over the nearby lighthouse and had one tremendous red eye in its center. Gradually, the eye shifted downward to focus on them.

Drage pointed his Sword upward at the module and sent of beam of Light at it, but the whole module disappeared. In a roaring boom, it reappeared behind them.

"Feranx, did you see that? The whole thing just moved! How did it do that?" When he turned to Feranx, the griffin was gone, though. "Feranx?"

A flash of green above revealed his companion's location. Feranx was already flying above him and held a bar of green light in each hand. He sent one green screen down to lift Drage, and the Emperor rose up to Feranx's level. "So, you really do have a weapon after all."

"It's not as powerful as a sword, but it definitely does the trick. I am interested to see how it will fare against this clunky monster, though."

Then, a voice called out. "Drage, hold on!"

Drage whipped his head around to see the whole Ring of Elders coming toward them, riding on metallic scepters, as if they were the witches on broomsticks of folklore and legend. "How did you guys find me?" he called.

Elizabeth called back as they came closer. "We felt someone use a Gate nearby."

"You guys can still use your *mysteria?*"

"Sort of. We will explain later. For now, let's take this thing out. Full circle, Elders!"

The Elders scattered, creating a large circle around the module. Its red eye shot beams of fire in every direction it could, but each of the Elders was well protected by an invisible barrier. Elizabeth called out, "Now!"

What seemed to be a million bolts of Lightning came flying out of the scepters and wrapped around the module, frying it in its place. At first, it seemed to resist the spells, but then, it exploded, sending shrapnel in all directions. Smoke and fire combined in a monstrous cloud. Drage and Feranx found themselves already protected by the Elder's spells: the heat dissipated around them, and the smoke and metal avoided their bodies altogether.

"Wow!" Drage said. "Kick-ass, mother."

Elizabeth smiled at her son. "It's been a few years. I told you to come and visit me."

"He was probably too busy with Aria." Despite the sarcasm in that voice, Drage was glad to see his sister on her own scepter. "How's it going, bro?"

"I'm doing well, Helen. So, how are you guys still using *mysteria*? All I can manage is what my Sword can." Elizabeth explained. "Whatever is the mastermind of these computers has created a barrier between our hearts and the physical world. However, there is a slight loophole. We can channel our energy through other objects to exert our spells. So, wands, scepters, and even your Sword work fine as means of using *mysteria*. However, Gates remain pretty hard to create. We have had to utilize two or three scepters at once in order to create a decent one. It seems that this world could fall apart for good. We need every bit of strength we can get. What brings the Emperor of Light to the world of Earth anyways?" Though she was very much Drage's mother, she knew how to act the head of the Ring of Elders as well. "And with a griffin, no less?"

Feranx and Drage approached the head of the Ring, and Drage explained, "We found out that the Y'mordi were sending an intelligent computer called Cronus 624 to Earth, and we came to disable the machine. Feranx here is my tech genius, and he is an expert with handling such programming."

Then, Cameron spoke up, appearing from behind Elizabeth. "But, do we not need to destroy this computer, not alter its programming?"

Feranx typed, *"Destroying Cronus 624 would be much harder than disabling it. Plus, the Y'mordi stole some parts from his Majesty, and we indeed plan on taking them back intact."*

Elizabeth took note of the griffin's inability to speak verbally and said, "Drage, you seem to know quite a bit more about this whole ordeal than we do. I suggest we work together to defeat this computer."

"Sounds like a plan. Basically, this is the strategy: There are three more really powerful modules on Earth, one of them being the main module Cronus 624. So, all we have to do is shut down that main module, and that will shut off the whole Ragnarok sequence."

"You make it sound easy," Helen smirked. "Where are we going to find these modules?" She lost her sarcastic tone. "Do you have an idea?"

Drage smiled. He could tell that Helen had grown up, but sarcasm had been their only connection. It was only natural for that to be her reaction toward him now as well. "Well, Feranx here can hack into this module and use its power to take us to the closest module."

"How can the module link to a Gate?" one of the Elders asked curiously.

Feranx answered, *"Because his Majesty has found a way to give a computer a heart. Part of that technology has been installed in this computer."*

The whole Ring was dumbfounded. Elizabeth was the one to break the silence. "You managed to give a computer a heart, Drage?"

"It is almost finished, I suppose. It just needs a few last minute corrections, and that should be it. When it is done, it will be able to cast spells, have its own personality, give advice, and defend my city."

A few Elders whispered to themselves. Elizabeth called them out on it, "What is that chatter? Speak up."

One of the whispering Elders responded, "How do we know we can trust him, Elizabeth? He is responsible for this monster, and this world could end because of him. Now, he wants to disable the machine? So that he can unleash it later on another world?"

Elizabeth said, "You certainly speak words of wisdom. After all, we have been handling the situation well, have we not?" This remark was full of sarcasm, and she noticed the Elder flinch. "He knows more about the computer than any one of us does, and if you want to see this world return to its original state, you will not frown at his offering us aid."

Drage looked fondly at his mother, then. She was certainly getting older, but she still had that sharp edge that warned others to back off. From what he had heard, she had rebuilt her home after one of the Y'mordi had wrecked it six years ago and had trained both Cameron and Helen there. Also, he had heard that Helen and Cameron had begun dating last year as well. "Mom, do you think we could rest somewhere before we go off to the next module? Feranx and I are pretty tired. We've been working all day fighting computers and all."

Elizabeth laughed, and the tension of the situation diffused. "Sure, the beach is not too far. Can Feranx keep that screen going a while?"

Drage looked to his mechanic, and the griffin rolled his eyes with a smile. Drage laughed. "I will take that as a yes. We are set to go."

Drage awoke and sat up in the cold, hard bed. It had been a while since he had slept in a hotel. He had become so accustomed to sleeping in a luxurious Palace. He rubbed the stiff muscles in the back, trying to alleviate some of the pain, but it was to no avail. On the other side of the room, Feranx slept peacefully. The griffin had never slept in such a nice bed in all his life.

As Drage's eyes made their way across the room, they stopped on the alarm clock. It was already noon, and he felt the urge to jump out of bed immediately. He had not meant to sleep so long. Why had the alarm not gone off? An even better question was of why his mother had not come to get him. He stood and put on his clothes. Clearly, his mother had washed them while he had been sleeping, and he smiled gratefully. Though he considered waking Feranx, he thought better of it since the griffin looked so content in his dreams.

He walked outside the hotel to find himself looking out at the sea. Only his mother was standing there. "Hey, Mom, what's going on? Where are the Elders, and why didn't you wake me?"

"Oh, Drage, I thought you needed some more rest. I scanned your body for injuries with *mysteria,* and you seemed pretty exhausted."

Drage shook his head. "I have suffered much worse. We don't really have time to waste. We have to stop the Ragnarok program from destroying this world. What do you plan to do once we get the program taken care of? It won't undo all of this chaos."

Elizabeth looked back out at the sea. "No, it won't. It will take us so many months to rebuild this world, and it will take even longer to erase all memory of it ever happening."

Then, Drage had an idea. "Actually, Matthew might be able to help us."

"Matthew?" Elizabeth repeated.

"Yes, his powers in Time are above par. He just might be able to reverse the state of this world if it doesn't disobey some rules of Time or something. It is certainly worth a try, and it is definitely something we can hope for."

Elizabeth smiled. "Most teenagers had to worry about girls, school, and getting a car, yet you had to rule a nation. How did my Drage grow up so fast? I remember when the three of you used to play around at the beach back home. You have all grown so much."

Thinking about home made him think about Aria. He really hoped he could make it back home before the disq tournament. It was not looking good overall. He had to disable Cronus 624 no matter what. "I grew up because I had to, Mom, and I don't regret that. I have an amazing wife, three beautiful kids, and a great home."

"Well, son, you had better go and wake your friend if you are ready to tackle this next module."

"Right," Drage agreed as he turned to go back into the hotel.

11

Execution

CAPTAIN BRYCO AWOKE to Gaspard looking out the window of their cell miserably. Luckily, they had managed to get inside the same cell, but that hardly did any good if neither of them had the strength to break through the solid iron bars. Somehow, King Lomeo knew how to enchant the cells so that they could not escape via *mysteria,* either. They needed to get a message to the Emperor of Light regarding King Lomeo's evil treachery. Locking away the Enigma Brigade was nothing short of blasphemous, and he would pay for it. His thoughts shifted to the figure in front of him. In the sunlight, Gaspard looked so dismal, one knee up and the other leg flat across the ground. His hands had been manacled to the wall, though Bryco's had not been chained at all after having been released from his handcuffs.

"Hey—Gaspard, how are you holding up?"

However, Gaspard did not answer. His eyes just stayed fixed on the window as if some angel hovered outside their cell, but Gaspard was not sure if the angel was a beacon of hope or a harbinger of death.

"Gaspard, answer me." Bryco's voice was soft now, not its

usual sharp, commanding tone.

Finally, Gaspard's eyes lowered. He still did not answer.

Bryco sighed in frustration and submission. "I don't know what we are going to do, Gaspard. We have to get out of this place. I don't know what Lomeo is planning, but it can't be good."

"Can you sense Nilram anywhere?"

Bryco lowered his own eyes this time. "No, I cannot. That means he is not here in this infernal prison, but that also means he could be dead. The best case scenario is that he returned to his Majesty, and they will send a full military force soon." However, both of them knew that such an event was unlikely to happen now if it had not happened already. The chances of Nilram being dead were much greater at this point.

"And what of the others?"

"Sume and Thera are fine. They are on a lower level than us."

Gaspard hung his head. "Well, what do you think is going to happen to us now? What can we do? Is King Lomeo just going to let us rot here?"

Bryco considered Gaspard's words deeply. "I suppose it is definitely possible." He sighed before approaching Gaspard. "Let's see if we can get rid of these manacles." Bryco had no real experience with lockpicking, but he figured it would at least be worth a try. It definitely could not hurt, and it might be a way to pass the time. Breaking through the chains seemed an easier task than getting through the gate to their cell, never mind escaping the whole prison unscathed. "I wish the bond of the Enigma Brigade was stronger. If it were, I would be able to sense if Nilram was elsewhere in Gevás, but his Majesty thought it would be a waste of *mysteria* since we should always be together."

Gaspard smirked. "Well, now would be a great time to have such a skill."

Bryco responded roughly as he handled the manacles, "Do not speak ill of his Majesty's decisions. I am merely commenting that it might be advisable in the future, and I shall pitch the idea to him when we get out of here."

"If we get out of here," replied Gaspard smugly.

"Look, we will get out of here soon. Usually, the Emperor expects communication within 24 hours, and he has not received that yet. He should know that something is wrong, and when he does, he will definitely investigate. It should not take too much time to realize that King Lomeo is against him."

"Yes, I suppose that that is true," Gaspard agreed. "I just wish I had my Sword. These gates would be nothing with that Sword, and we wouldn't have even been caught in the first place."

Bryco shook his head. "Enough with that Sword business. You have to let it go, Gaspard. You have been obsessing over it ever since you lost it. The weapon does not make a warrior. You act as if the Sword did all the work in all of your battles, and you know that that is far from true."

"Forgive me, but you don't know what it was like, Captain. That Sword gave me unbelievable power. I was even able to stand against his Majesty with that Sword. I was so strong, then."

Bryco's voice rose. "Gaspard, Maksimilian stole that Sword from you years ago, and you will never see it again for as long as you live." He regretted his words as soon as he said them.

"What?" Gaspard's jaw hung, and his eyes had widened. "Why would Maksimilian take it? I didn't think him to be a thief."

Bryco kept working on the chains, though his eyes could not look into Gaspard's at the moment. "Well, Maksimilian is actually a lot older than he looks. He's sort of an Ancient. That sword he had was no ordinary sword. It was the Steel of Life, a Spirit Sword that enabled to him to live as long as he wielded it. However, he has been spending several years searching for the other four Spirit Swords. I guess that, when he left the Brigade, he did not plan on leaving without your Sword."

Gaspard's teeth clenched then, and his fists tightened. "Maksimilian . . . I'm going to kill him when I get my hands on him!"

Bryco shook his head. "No, with two Spirit Swords in his possession, he would be nearly invincible now. No one has ever beaten him at hand-to-hand combat, and I have only seen him outwitted once."

"Which was?"

Then, Bryco smiled. "That was when I did it to him. There was a Brigadier named Tilgé right before you joined. He was Maksimilian's second and more than a little rough around the edges. He was short-tempered and enjoyed killing, but he always did what he was told." Bryco gave up on the chains for a few seconds. "One day, Maksimilian ordered me to kill him. He wanted Tilgé's head presented to him as proof of the death. However, when I came to Tilgé, I realized that I really could not kill him. I told him to flee as far away as he could, but we both realized that Maksimilian would need some form of proof. Before I could protest, Tilgé cut off his own hand and gave that to me to show."

"And Maksimilian believed that you killed him?"

Bryco nodded. "Yes, he had no reason to think otherwise. I was almost as obedient as Tilgé and less wily. Maksimilian probably still believes that Tilgé is long dead."

"Have you heard from Tilgé since?"

Bryco lowered his eyes again. "No, I have not. I guess he would not have to go into strict hiding, but he would still have to lay low."

"But Maksimilian is no longer the captain. You are."

"Sure, but Tilgé does not know that. The Emperor of

Light never released *that* information. As far as Tilgé knows, Maksimilian is still the captain and has eyes everywhere."

Gaspard shook his head. "Was Maksimilian really all that bad? I mean, I never noticed him doing anything crazy, much less ordering anyone to kill someone else."

"That's because of the new Emperor. His Majesty changed the purpose of the Enigma Brigade. We were once a group of the Emperor's greatest assassins. With the new Emperor though, we became ambassadors and scouts. We became more than just weapons."

"Maksimilian did not want that?"

Bryco examined the chains more, searching for some flaw in them, but nothing stood out. "Maksimilian said that everything he did was in the name of the Light, but he killed without mercy and without necessity. His interpretation of the Light was more than just considerably flawed."

A third voice interrupted. "Oh, come now, Bryco. You do not think that I am *that* terrible, do you?"

Though Gaspard was able to shift his head to the direction of the voice, Bryco was paralyzed in fear. their hearts froze in their chests, and their eyes widened, disbelieving the terror their ears perceived.

The voice continued, "What? No words of greeting for your former captain, Captain Bryco?"

"Why—why are you here, Maks?" Bryco stammered. Finally, he turned to face the black robed, crimson-haired man. He was standing outside the cell, and his face was well-hidden in the shadows. Despite that darkness, his hair seemed to burn and ignite the water around them, with a heat that rose, yet sent shivers down their spines.

"Of course, I came to help out the Enigma Brigade, and now I find out that Tilgé is still alive. I was wise to leave the Brigade after its grave fall. I had more important matters to deal with." His voice was low, yet sharp, like the hiss of a snake winding its way through a dark cavern.

Bryco growled, "You came to help us? Not likely, Maks."

The former captain flashed a Sword, and the bars of the cell fell apart. "You are free, Captain Bryco."

Once the bars were destroyed, Bryco was able to use *mysteria* again, and he freed Gaspard from his chains with a quick Wind spell. Before even thinking of exiting the cell, he faced Maksimilian. "Why are you helping us? What is it in it for you?"

Maksimilian crossed his arms. "Why, I want Lomeo to fall. I have been in this city for a few months now, seeking the Swords, and I discovered the truth behind the evil king: he is one of the seven Y'mordi in disguise. That explains his skill in deceit and lies."

At the mention of the Spirit Swords, Gaspard protested, "I want my Sword back Maksimilian, and you are not going to get away with it this time."

Immediately, Maksimilian drew the Behemoth and pointed its deadly tip at Gaspard's neck. "If you want it, then summon it. The Sword has a spirit of its own and will come to the wielder it chooses. So, call it, Gaspard. If it chooses you over me, you can keep it."

Gaspard closed his eyes and felt in his heart for the will of the Great Spirit, imploring it to give him the Sword. However, his prayers were met with silence. "It . . . it won't come."

Maksimilian whirled around and headed toward the hallway of the prison. Bryco and Gaspard stood behind. "Gaspard . . ." Bryco began, unsure of what to say. "Don't trust him. Something about this is far from right. If he tries anything funny, do not hesitate to kill him." The Emperor of Light had taught them that killing without necessity was an abomination, but certain crimes had to be punished by death. Maksimilian had already committed many of those crimes. If Maksimilian gave either of them any reason to further doubt his intentions, they would be justified in getting rid of him.

Gaspard nodded. He meant to have his Sword back. Bryco created two swords of pure light and threw one to Gaspard.

They followed Maksimilian into the hall, and the black-robed man said, "Where are the others? Are they trapped here as well?" The hall had a low ceiling, and the place was for the most part dark. However, the light of their swords kept the stone area visible.

Bryco looked to Gaspard. "Thera and Sume are in here somewhere, and I know they are on the lower floors. I can tell more when we are closer."

"Well, then, we go this way," Maksimilian said, opening an iron door to a stairwell. "Follow me."

"Why do I not like the sound of that?" Bryco muttered to himself.

The two Brigadiers followed Maksimilian into the dark, winding stairwell, and each footstep was fast and loud, echoing through the dark. When they arrived at the next door, Maksimilian looked to Bryco to see if the other Brigadiers were on this floor. At Bryco's denial, they continued down another flight of stairs, and this time, it was the correct floor. As soon as Maksimilian swung the door open, guards attacked. Bryco and Gaspard were quick to respond, waving their swords immediately, but Maksimilian pushed them out of the way and swung the mighty Behemoth once. A wave of purple light shot from the Sword and split each of the guards in two before them. Though Bryco grimaced, Gaspard was in awe at Maksimilian's wielding of the blade.

"Maksimilian, how did you get the Behemoth to do that?" Gaspard asked.

The red-haired man sighed. "It took a long time, but it finally submitted to me. Training a Sword is not an easy thing, and it has not yet chosen me to be its true master. But, perhaps it shall just take a little more time."

However, Gaspard had no intention of letting

Maksimilian wield the Behemoth any longer. He had craved the power of that Sword for years. "I just don't know why the Sword would choose him over me," he muttered inaudibly.

Bryco ran over to a far cell and called, "Thera! Sume! Are you two alright?" The two were sitting in the back of their cell with their hands wrapped around their knees.

"Captain, is that you?" Thera asked, overjoyed.

Summoning *mysteria,* Bryco blasted the cell door into dust with a Light spell. "Yes, now, let's get out of here." The three ran back to the stairs, and Thera and Sume stopped when they saw Maksimilian.

"Surprised to see me?" Maksimilian grinned.

Sume growled, "What is he doing here, Captain?"

"Sadly, he is the one behind our rescue." Bryco was still unsure of his full intentions.

"I serve the Light, as I always have. I left the Brigade because I realized I could better serve the Light outside of the Brigade's constricting barriers. I have made a much more significant difference of late, but when I discovered that the Emperor of Light's Enigma Brigade had been imprisoned, I knew that you all had been treated unfairly, so of course, I came to free you." Still, the fiendish grin that lit up his face set all of Bryco's nerves at edge.

"Maks, if you dare cross me, I shall have you beheaded. Do you understand me? No matter what you believe, I now outrank you, and you shall do nothing to disrespect me or the Brigade. Is that understood?"

The Brigade watched as Maksimilian's smile faded, and his jaw clenched. "It is understood, Captain Bryco."

"Good. Now, we all need to return to the Palace and warn his Majesty." Bryco summoned a Gate by the stairs.

Gaspard commented, "What about Nilram, Captain? Are we sure he's not in Terin somewhere?"

"Nilram?" Maksimilian repeated. "Is he the lion anima?"

"Yes," Bryco confirmed. "Have you seen him?"

"Well, I believe he is to be hung this afternoon. Lomeo— or Ixion, if you know that name—wanted to show the people of Varyx how anima should be treated."

"What? We cannot let that happen. Maks! where are they holding him?"

"He should be in the town square. They are making a mockery of him presently, I believe. Ixion is certainly making a mess of things."

"And you didn't think to stop him? And you go around preaching that you serve the Light!" The Brigade had never seen Bryco so angry. His face was turning red at this point. "I cannot believe how damned heartless you are, Maksimilian!" As soon as his voice had risen loud enough, he felt in his heart the guards that were moving down to his level. He muttered, "They know we've escaped . . ." He turned to the rest of the Brigade and commanded, "Everyone, get to the city!" He changed the destination of the Gate, and Thera and Sume ran through it. "Gaspard, go!"

However, Gaspard was frozen in his position. "Bryco . . ." he whispered. "We are not letting him go with us, are we? After what he did to Tilgé and what he has done to you? Since when are we on his side?"

Bryco yelled, "Gaspard, go!"

Gaspard threw his sword at the staircase, creating a blinding explosion of Light, and then he grabbed the hilt of the Sword at Maksimilian's side. Pulling with all his weight, he grabbed Bryco so they fell into the Gate behind them. As soon as their feet were clear, Gaspard closed the Gate.

They panted in the middle of the street. Bryco asked, "What just happened?"

Gaspard stood and admired the lengthy katana that was now in his hands. "Well, I had meant to grab the Behemoth, but I guess this shall just have to suffice. The Steel of Life, you said?"

Bryco's eyes widened. "You stole—stole Maksimilian's

Spirit Sword?"

With a laugh, Gaspard replied, "I believe so. I guess that that is what you call payback, though. If he thought he could just come up and steal my Sword, he was sadly mistaken."

"Don't you see? He will spend every waking moment trying to find and kill you now! You are as stupid as he is!" Realizing he did not even know where they were, Bryco looked around and found that he was yelling in a side street. Several people were staring at them, and Bryco ran to the nearest alley, gesturing for the rest of the Brigade to follow. "Now, how are we going to get to Nilram? If we run into Maksimilian, we will—we will . . . I do not know. I suppose we will just have to stand up to him. I mean, what you did can hardly be called theft since he stole from you in the first place and refused to return it, and we certainly cannot just let him butcher you, either. So, we shall stand against him if need demands it."

Though he did not show it outwardly, Gaspard smiled on the inside. Bryco really was a much better captain than Maksimilian could ever have hoped to be.

Sume added, "Yes, I would like to put a sword in that man myself. If it weren't for his Majesty, Lord Helius, we would still be living in Maksimilian's terrible grip."

Thinking about the Spirit Swords, Gaspard hazarded a question for Bryco. "Hey Captain, will Maksimilian go after the Emperor of Light to take the Sword of Destiny at some point? I mean, if he is genuinely seeking the power of all the Spirit Swords, will he not have to come back for the Sword of Destiny at some point?"

"I suppose he will at some point, but I think that, because the Emperor of Light will always be easy to find for someone like him, he is not worrying about getting that Sword yet. He's going for the harder Swords first. That is probably why he did not take the Behemoth sooner. He knew you would be in the Enigma Brigade as long as he kept you in it."

Thera commented, "I think he was terrible, this

Maksimilian guy. I didn't really know him—at least, not like everyone else here did—but from everything I have heard, he was terrible. It's a pity he's not easier to kill."

"Brigade, attention!" Bryco roared. Immediately, the three Brigadiers straightened their positions, eyes forward, chest out, feet together, and arms at their sides. "Have you all lost sense of your purpose? We are the Enigma Brigade, his Majesty's greatest military force, and we shall damned well act it. Thera, tell me: is the rogue Maksimilian a designated factor of our mission?"

"No, sir!"

"Sume, what is our top priority as the Enigma Brigade?"

"Serve the world in the Light's best interests, not the Emperor's, the Captain's, or my own."

"Continue, Sume. What do I always say?"

"No matter what, we stay together."

Bryco nodded fiercely. "That is right. And, that means we shall certainly not leave Nilram here on his own to die. However, we also have a mission to worry about. Gaspard!"

"Yes, sir!"

"I want you to return to the Palace of Light and inform his Majesty of the goings-on here. Stay with him in case he needs to assign you to another task."

Gaspard stammered, "But—Captain, you need me to help you—"

Bryco raised a hand, and Gaspard became silent. "Do not disobey me, Gaspard. Besides, it will save us a great deal of trouble if we run into Maksimilian and you are not here. If you are not here, we cannot very well give him the Spirit Sword, can we? Get out of here, now."

Managing a respectful salute, Gaspard summoned a Gate back to Apolis and disappeared.

Bryco sighed. "And then there were three. Alright, move out. We need to get into Lomeo's castle and save Nilram."

"Look, there he is, Captain!" Sume whispered.

The three of them had managed to reach an upper-level window that looks into the throne room. With a sack tied around his head, Nilram was secured in a corner of the throne room with two guards in front of him. King Lomeo was nowhere to be seen, but the castle was crawling with soldiers.

Thera offered, "Well, I do not see how we are going to take care of the guards without killing them, Captain. Those guys do not look as if they would fall for a distraction, and their armor is too heavy for it to be easy to knock them out."

"Well," Bryco said with a sigh. "You are the only sorcerer out of the three of us. Is there not anything you can do to take care of them?"

"I suppose I could mess with the gravity a little bit. But, it will cause chaos if I do that. Are we looking for an entirely covert operation or a get-the-job-done mission?"

Bryco looked inside the throne room closely. There were considerably good chances that they could get in there, grab Nilram, and escape if Thera went berserk with her spells. "Alright, do it." Sume shattered the window with a Light spell, and the three jumped into the throne room, Thera's Water spell cushioning their fall. As soon as the windows had shattered, the soldiers charged toward them. While Thera dealt with the guards, Bryco and Sume unleashed several Light blasts, knocking the soldiers back toward the front door of the room, and occasionally, they would create shields of Light to block incoming arrows or spells.

Thera created a Gravity spell that made the guards "land" on the walls and not be able to move from that spot. Then, using the same type of spell, she pulled Nilram toward them. A new presence entered the room, and she felt the Darkness in her heart. As she turned to face the enemy, a blast of Darkness hit her in the face, knocking her into the wall. More blasts of Darkness flew from the man's wand, knocking Bryco to the wall as well.

Sume acted quickly and ran to Thera and Nilram, creating a Gate in the process. Even as blasts of Darkness flew toward him, he escaped the throne room with Thera and Nilram in his arms.

Bryco stood, brandishing his sword against a roomful of guards and soldiers. Lomeo stepped forward in his black robes. "Well, Captain, it would seem that you shall have to take the anima's place for today's execution. I can't just have my people disappointed because a prisoner got away." Lomeo smiled as he stepped closer to Bryco.

12

A Collar Around His Neck

XARDEN ENTERED THE courtyard of the Palace of
Shadows and breathed in deeply. For the lungs of an
Y'mordi, the Darkness-laced air was divine. He was about
ready to give up on finding Maksimilian. Valdridge was of a
much greater interest to him. Nevertheless, he had felt Y'tal
call him, and so he had answered the call. However, as soon
as he had come, Y'tal had asked him to wait out in the courtyard. It was not that he minded being bossed around. Rather,
he felt proud of himself for being so loyal.

More than anything, though, he wanted to know what
knowledge Valdridge had kept hidden. Somewhere out
there, the other two thirds of his heart lived out their lives.
They would have to be Ancients. They could be anyone, and
there was a relatively high chance that he had encountered
one of those pieces of his heart in his life. The fact that the
frustrating Prophet of Light knew the truth was the worst
part about it, though. Xarden was certain that Valdridge was
not an Ancient, yet he had professed to be around since the
first Obsidian Wars. "Valdridge, what is your secret?" Xarden
asked the air around him.

"Every man is entitled to his secrets, Y'dax."

Xarden had not sensed Y'tal's arrival, yet he did not turn to face his master. "This is true, Lord Y'tal, but does not the entitlement change when one is an inherent part of another's secrets?" He turned to face the shorter Y'mordi. "My Lord, Valdridge knows who the other two pieces of my heart are, yet he will not tell me their identities. I do not know what to do about him. He professes to have survived the centuries, but he is not an Ancient. I have noticed him age."

"Y'dax, why do you worry about such things? Whoever has the core piece of that heart has made it clear that he is not interested in uniting all three parts. You would be wise not to dwell on such matters, Y'dax."

"Yes, my Lord," Xarden acquiesced. "What news do you have?"

"I have much, actually. Come. Let us walk through the courtyards around the castle." Xarden followed the head of the Y'mordi silently but expectantly. "First, it seems that many are not following their orders. Randir is seeking a woman, while you have been obsessing over your past. Ixion has also failed to follow his mission, though I am not exactly disappointed in him this time."

"No?"

"No, I am not," Y'tal confirmed. "As it would seem, King Lomeo is Ixion."

"What?" Xarden stopped walking for a moment, dumbfounded. His eyebrows were raised, and his jaw hung.

Y'tal grinned under his long hood. "For the past several years, Ixion has been worming his way into the advisory of the former king of Varyx. Ixion killed the king and took the crown for himself. He is planning on leading Varyx into a side attack on Helio soon. I have gathered information that he is planning on executing a member of the Enigma Brigade as a display of his new power."

Xarden continued following Y'tal. "That *is* news. I did

not think that Ixion had it in him to do something like that."

"Neither did I, but I am glad. He is returning to the level of power he possessed during the Obsidian Wars. Also, Y'dax, I summoned you here for a rather private matter."

"Yes, my Lord?"

"This secret is never to leave your lips, not even in my presence, unless I specifically choose to discuss it with you again. Is this understood?"

"Yes, my Lord."

"The Dark Lord, Dagan, lied to all of the Y'mordi, except myself. One of you is a false Y'mordi, although still blessed with his powers. However, the bond to the Darkness is slightly different, altered."

"So . . . there are only six of us?"

Y'tal shook his hooded head. "No, Y'dax. There are still seven. You have just not met the seventh yet. The Dark Lord, Dagan, meant for her to stay hidden until the right time had come."

Xarden was beginning to understand. "And that right time is near?"

"Yes. The Darkness rising in them has an eagerness to decimate the forces of the Light. Their time is coming quickly."

"Do you know who the fake Y'mordi is, Lord Y'tal?" Xarden asked, begging for an answer.

"I do know, Xarden, but I shall not tell you the answer today."

Disappointed, Xarden changed the subject. "Do you still intend on stepping into the fray yourself if this Great Servant fails?"

Y'tal's silence was confirmation enough for Xarden. Thinking of Y'tal fighting again was a nervous thought. In the past, Y'tal had been quite a ruthless fighter, incapable of showing mercy and never fond of a quick death. He had tortured so many prisoners during the Obsidian Wars. Xarden had never seen Y'tal use a weapon, but he had no doubt that he was proficient with almost every weapon imaginable.

Xarden remembered when Y'tal had faced his own Trials before they all became Y'mordi. During the Trial of Body, all the competitors had to face three battles. In the first battle, the opponents were an army of Shadows, some with swords and some with bows and arrows. Y'tal had stood there, completely calm, and Xarden could remember watching him and not sensing even the slightest amount of *mysteria* being used. Of course, the Dark Lord, Dagan, had forbidden for any defensive or offensive spells to be used, though sensing was allowed.

The army of Shadows had charged, and a flurry of arrows preceded them. Y'tal leaped high above all the arrows, allowing them to stab the ground, and then he fell into the midst of the Shadow army. As swords lunged at him from every angle, he dodged each attack without even the slightest effort, and the Shadows found themselves accidentally killing each other. Y'tal had grabbed two fallen swords and spun around, cleaving every Shadow that came near him. Once he had some genuine space, he threw the blades in two different directions with considerable force, destroying tens of Shadows at once.

From a higher level, Xarden and the others had watched the display in amazement. Y'tal certainly took his time with the battle, but he did it so effortlessly and wasted no movement. In order for Xarden to have the same phenomenal reflexes, he would have had to open himself near fully to *mysteria,* yet this stranger had barely grasped it.

"Y'dax, you are tense. What ails your mind?"

Xarden knew he could not lie to Y'tal. "I was just thinking about how fearsome you will be on the battlefield when the next Great Servant comes. I was remembering your Trial of Body. Your strength still amazes me."

Y'tal's voice remained cold and high. "Y'dax, do you fear me?"

"Very much, Lord Y'tal," Xarden answered with honesty. His own voice wavered, sensing Y'tal staring at him through that massive hood of his. "I fear nothing more."

Y'tal turned away and gestured for Xarden to continue following him. "I feel that the others have begun losing that fear. They no longer believe I am as strong as I once was. Y'xon is terrified of me, and he is right in doing such. However, the twins, the rogue, and even Mali have faltered too often. They are thinking too independently, and it shall be their ruin if they continue on that path. When I join the battle, they shall remember who I am and learn their place once more."

"Shall the other Y'mordi, the real seventh, come before then?"

Y'tal shook his head. "No, I believe that they shall not be prepared to come into the battle until after I have reasserted my place. I do not fear for them, though. The seventh will be more than terrified of me. Of this, I am quite confident."

Xarden considered Y'tal's words for a moment as they turned a corner around the castle. The sky was black with clouds of Darkness, yet it felt so relaxing to Xarden. Having his heart's ties to the Darkness was responsible for that feeling of respite. "Y'tal, what about Mali? You said that he does not fear you, but he is more servile than even I. Do you doubt his loyalty?"

For a moment, Y'tal was silent. "He is loyal to the Darkness, but I do not think that he serves me fully. This past decade, he has acted more and more nervous around me, as if he *is* hiding some great secret. However, I feel that soon he, too, shall know his place."

"I see . . ." Xarden had not been paying too much attention to Mali, then, if what Y'tal said was true. "Have you heard any news about the possessor of the Emperor Regin?"

"No, Mali has reported to me, but he has not found out anything useful yet. The Emperor Regin shall make an attack against Apolis on the day of the disq tournament. Hopefully, by that time, Emperor Helius shall be dead on Earth. Arnim was able to communicate to me that the program Ragnarok initiated without problem, but she is still seeking the Emperor to ensure he is dead."

Xarden nodded. "So, for the most part, everything is going according to our plans."

"Yes," agreed Y'tal. Finally, they had stopped in front of a statue of the Dark Lord, Dagan. His colossal form towered over them, and its obsidian eyes stared down at them as if it commanded them even in his absence. "Y'dax, Xarden, the way of the Darkness has changed so much since his time, has it not?"

"I would agree. No longer is the Darkness at its previous level of power. Now, we hide in the shadows, preying upon the weak and sneaking around like rats. The Dark Lord would certainly say we have fallen. We shall rise again, Lord Y'tal. You do not have to worry about that."

Y'tal lowered his head. "Yes, we shall rise once more. The Hand of the Darkness is my guide, and it always brings us closer to redemption."

Xarden raised an eyebrow in confusion. "Pullatus," he started, reverting to Y'tal's more informal name, "What is on your mind? Something ails you."

"I couldn't care less what happens to Maksimilian or Valdridge or any of the others. I want to know where that stranger is—the one who attacked us ten years ago on Earth. I want to know who he was and how he became so strong."

Xarden took one step back in surprise. He had no idea that Y'tal was still obsessed with the events of that stormy night on Earth. The person had dressed in the same black robes that they all wore. He had protected the Guardians of Light and helped them escape to Gevás where that Golden Dragon had been able to find them with ease, despite Mali's devoted efforts to kill them. "Pullatus, there is nothing we can do about that guy. Nothing. All we can do is hope that we run into him again, and then you can have at him." However, Xarden sensed that his words did not truly help Y'tal. "Honestly, Lord Y'tal, it would not be wise to obsess over it. It can only bring you grief."

Y'tal replied, "Are you one to talk about obsession, Y'dax? Are you not obsessing over a past that is centuries old? At least with my obsession, something can be done about it."

Xarden had never heard Y'tal snap like that. He did not open his mouth in response. He knew better than to incite the head of the Y'mordi's rage. Together, the two stared up at the statue of their former king. Xarden wondered what had happened to the Dark Lord, Dagan, whenever he stared at the figure, but no answers revealed themselves.

Finally, Y'tal spoke. "Xarden, Gevás is still in the middle of a great shift. The Darkness shall rise soon. It shall rise with the coming of the next Great Servant, for we will all reveal ourselves then, and, when we do, the world shall fear us as they once did. Once we have the fourth Great Servant in our grasp, we will be much closer to the end of this struggle."

In Y'tal's words, Xarden sensed hidden knowledge. "What do you mean, Y'tal? Has the Hand of the Darkness spoken to you again?"

"Yes. With the coming of the fourth Great Servant shall come the others in rapid succession. We are nearing the final battle. We do not even have twenty more years before that happens. It is that close, Xarden. Can you not feel the pull of the Darkness as it prepares to unleash its full expanse across the Water Realm of Gevás?"

Xarden opened his heart to receive the pulses of the Darkness that filled the Dark Realm. He could certainly feel its anxiousness deep within the shadows' many folds and layers. "Yes, Y'tal. It is definitely there. The Darkness is eternal, and it is on the verge of breaking loose into the other Realms."

"You are wise, Xarden. I thank you for your advice today. You have helped clear many of my thoughts and have soothed my worries. Now, I implore you to return to your duty. Find the rogue, Maksimilian. If you can, take it upon yourself to look for clues as to the Emperor Regin's possessor as well. Forget this nonsense about learning who the other parts of your heart are. Such thoughts will do you no good as they will only distract you from your primary cause. Resist the urge to seek such knowledge. There are only three in the universe that know the truth: your original form, Master Valdridge, and myself. The only time that that number shall change is when one of the three dies. Now, you are dismissed, Xarden."

Xarden summoned a Gate and returned to the Water Realm to search for Maksimilian. He could not believe that Y'tal had admitted that he knew who the other parts of Xarden's heart were. Usually, Y'tal was silent about Xarden's past and did not reveal how much he knew, but now it was clear that the leader knew everything—possibly more than Valdridge. Had Y'tal talked to Xarden in his original form? Was there some connection between Xarden's past and Y'tal's? He did not know, but they were still things to think about. Now, more than ever, his curiosity was insatiable. He needed to know more, but how could he with Y'tal watching his every move like a sea serpent waiting for a dying animal to finally pass? It seemed as if he would have to lie low for a while until Y'tal's eye had passed on to another of the Y'mordi before he could act so freely again. Hopefully, he could do it before the next Great Servant appeared. When that happened, Y'tal was going to crack down on even the slightest of offenses. What Y'tal had given him today was only the greatest warning of what the future would hold for the Y'mordi.

"Y'tal, what are you hiding?" Though Xarden had been advising Y'tal for centuries, he still failed to understand the enigmatic leader of the Y'mordi, and he figured he probably never would. He raised his head to behold the Temple of the

Spirits. "Alright, I suppose I should begin searching for some clues. Here is as good a place to start as any. Maksimilian was certainly not in the Southern Continent. He might as well be here." And with that, he began his search, completely unaware of the fact that Y'tal was still watching him from the shadows of the Dark Realm through an orb in the throne room.

Mali stared out at the massive legions that marched before him. All of the Emperor Regin's armies had assembled, and Mali sensed the intense power that his sorcerers wielded. Mali knew he could defeat any one of the Emperor's soldiers, but, together, they would be quite the force. The Emperor Regin was much more powerful as well, now that his Darkness had been fully awakened. He had nearly doubled the strength of his military by creating several battalions of Shadows. Although many of the Emperor's soldiers were anxious around the Shadows, their faith in their Emperor was unwavering.

Mali could not believe that the Great Servant was going to launch such a dishonorable attack on Apolis. Whoever was possessing the Emperor was base and classless, and Mali did not approve in the slightest; even as one of the seven Lords of the Shadows, he knew and respected honor. As such, however, his duty was to aid the Emperor Regin and protect him if a battle ensued. More than anything, he had to be ready to take the Emperor Regin's blood if he was near death. The Y'mordi could not afford to lose him.

Mali sighed. He had spent so long sifting through the Emperor Regin's library, but he had found nothing on the legendary—if not mythical—Dusk Lyre. He had not encountered even a regular lyre mentioned in any of the books. A more intriguing task had been trying to understand the puppeteer's hold on the Emperor Regin. He wondered if any of the other Y'mordi had found any clues that might lead to the possessor's identity.

None of the Y'mordi had made communications with him since he had come to the Emperor Regin's side. It was not as though he had expected to hear from them, but he had hoped that Randir was having luck finding that woman. Randir really did need something more solid nowadays. For centuries, he had kept to himself and his memories—his memories of Ophelia.

"What are you doing on the balcony?"

Mali did not have to turn to know that the Emperor Regin was standing right behind him. "I was watching your terra, Lord Regin. With such a force, I cannot see Apolis surviving this attack. With your newfound Darkness, your plans will come to fruition."

"Yes, you are correct. The Emperor of Light will fall, and this world will fall prey to my power. No longer will the Light shine to illuminate the streets of the cities. This time, the anima will not go back into exile. This time, we shall annihilate them all. They should not even be on this planet."

More groups of soldiers marched in front of the fortress, humans mixed amongst the Shadows. It reminded Mali of the first Obsidian Wars when the Dark Lord, Dagan, used both humans and Shadows in his armies. The only differences were that the Dark Lord's armies had Demons, the Y'mordi, and about ten or eleven times the size of this army. Still, Mali was reminded of those epic wars.

The Emperor's words haunted Mali. While the Emperor Regin would naturally only hate the anima, the possessor clearly hated both anima and the Light, a curious combination for the person controlling an emperor. "Lord Regin, what is your ultimate goal?"

"My goal—is to conquer all worlds with my Darkness, using this body as my vessel."

Mali tried to act surprised, but the Emperor Regin shook his head. "I know that you know this is not the real me. I am not completely stupid, Lord of the Shadows. How long did you think you could fool me?"

"I was not—" Mali began but stopped when he sensed the Emperor Regin grasp at *mysteria*. Mali summoned a katana just in time to block a strong sphere of Darkness. "What are you doing?"

"I told you: I am going to conquer this world, and, in my new world, there will not be a place for someone like you. Quite frankly, you disgust me, and I could use your power."

In the high-ceilinged library of the castle, Mali leaped over the Emperor Regin's head to avoid another blast and summoned his second katana to block another flurry of dark spells when the Emperor Regin turned to face him. Although his blasts of Darkness were strong, they were slow enough for Mali to block them with ease. Mali took a few steps backward, giving himself more room in the large library. Though he wanted desperately to fight back, he knew he could not damage the Emperor Regin at all or else he would be quite clearly going against orders. He had to stay with him, but he also had to stay alive. "Lord Regin, what are you doing?" he implored. "Stop this nonsense!"

"Oh, but I am only getting started!" Then, the Emperor Regin cast a spell that Mali had not been expecting. A wave of Darkness emitted from the Emperor Regin's outstretched hand, knocking Mali to the wall and holding him there. As soon as Mali reached for *mysteria,* he found that he could not cast any spells. The Emperor Regin was preventing him from doing so.

"What? How did you—?"

"Really, all of those are quite trivial questions, Y'lam. A better question would be of what is going to happen to you next."

Before Mali could protest, the Emperor Regin rushed forward and pulled something from his robes, wrapping it around Mali's neck. It snapped shut with a metallic click, and Mali realized it was a golden collar.

"What is this?"

The Emperor Regin laughed. "That pretty collar is an artifact from the first Obsidian Wars—a treasure that Lord Ferro kept hidden in his treasury. Only I can remove it, and it binds you to me: when I most need strength, I will sap it from you." He chuckled again. "Really, you should be glad. You have been wanting to serve me better, and now you have your wish. Enjoy your new home, Y'lam, my little, little lamb."

With Mali's pained screams drowning out the Emperor's laughter, the Emperor Regin left the library and closed the door, leaving Mali in utter darkness. Probably as a test, Mali felt his strength being sucked out of his very soul, as if a sudden depression had overcome him, leaving him feeling exhausted and spent. It felt as if it were the opposite of an adrenaline rush.

Still pinned to the wall by the spell of Darkness, he sobbed. The collar felt like a burning ring of metal on his neck, and he was confident it had left a mark there on his flesh. "Randir, where are you when I need you?" he muttered. He felt the Emperor Regin suck more life out of him through the golden collar, and Mali begged for even the pleasure of passing out. However, the pain, like his screams, only increased in intensity.

13

Deceit and Truth

I T WOULD SEEM YE'RE correct, Miss Stehl," Mirah responded promptly. "Dey are attacking Apolis da day of da ternament. Dey won't hold anyt'ing back."

Tilgé agreed, "Yes, and the fact that they are using Shadows now only makes them even more intimidating. The Emperor Regin has truly fallen if he is resorting to serving the Darkness. Honestly, what could he be thinking?"

Stehl paced in their hotel room, considering the events of the day. They had certainly found no trace of the Enigma Brigade, but what the Emperor Regin was planning disturbed her. It was true that she had left both the Emperor Regin's and the Emperor of Light's armies, but she did not think that siding with the Darkness was the right path, no matter how much she despised anima. "How could he do this? He is becoming as bad as the Enigma Brigade."

Tilgé countered, "He is far worse than the Brigade now. At least the Enigma Brigade serves the Light. At this point, the Brigade would fight him in a heartbeat if they knew how dangerous he truly was. He is of the Darkness now."

"What he has done is wrong, Tilgé, but he is not yet a

murderer."

Much to the others' surprise, Mirah added, "'Yet' is an important word dere, Miss Stehl. If we don' do somethin', he *will* be a murd'rer."

"We?" Stehl asked, confused.

Tilgé grinned as Mirah continued, "Well, ye're agains' innocent people bein' killed, aren't ya? Den, we have to stop him before dis gets outta hand, don't we?"

Finally stopping her pacing, Stehl leaned against a wall. "It's not murder, though. It's war."

Tilgé added, "Isn't that what you said Maksimilian had said?"

Stehl could not remember telling Tilgé that, but it was true. Maksimilian had said that he had done everything for the purpose of better serving his Emperor. "What are you saying, Tilgé? Are you with Mirah in that we *should* do something about it?"

The silent grin on Tilgé's face was enough answer for her. She sighed in submission. "Well, what do you two lovely gentlemen have for an idea to get through the heavily guarded fortress?"

"Well," Tilgé began, putting his hand to stroke his chin, "I heard rumors earlier of a ghost in the castle. Apparently, people heard screams coming from one of the higher balconies."

"So? What does that have to do with us exactly?"

Tilgé rolled his eyes. "Everything! If someone was screaming up there, then that means that it could very well be a small prison or something. I am sure that the Emperor Regin will not be spending any time tonight in a room where he just had someone beaten or killed, you know?"

Stehl looked out her window to see one of the turrets of the castle. "I don't know, Tilgé. I feel like we are stepping into water too dark here."

Mirah added as he stood, "I'll stand by ya, Miss Stehl."

"As will I," Tilgé concluded. "With Brawn at your right and Brains—myself—on your left, no guard would have a chance to harm you."

This time, Stehl rolled her eyes. "Since when did you two decide to become such a close team?" She saw their smirks. "Fine, let's get out of here and see what we can do."

Grabbing their cloaks, they stepped out the door and headed through the hotel as quietly as they could. They passed no one as they exited the building, and once they were outside, they clung to the shadows, minimizing the chances of their being seen. They crept across several streets, and Stehl watched the turrets appear closer and closer.

Then, they heard the scream themselves. They were not high-pitched, but they were loud and long, echoing through the city. Stehl reacted immediately, running toward the direction of the sound and not caring if someone spotted her. She heard Mirah and Tilgé struggle to keep up with her, but the sound of their footsteps never faded.

Once they reached the castle, the screams stopped, giving way to a grave silence that made Stehl's heart beat only louder. "How are we going to get up there?" she muttered when she saw how high that particular balcony was.

"The old-fashioned way, of course," Tilgé said as if it were the only possible answer. "Come on, we have to take care of the guards if we want to get through the front door."

Stehl nodded and followed Tilgé and Mirah to the front of the fortress. Several guards walked across the upper balconies, and even more walked in the front courtyard guarding the door.

Mirah muttered, "Some o' dem are not armed. Dat means dey can prob'ly use *mysteria*."

"We don't need to fight them!" Stehl snapped as softly as she could. "We are wanting to sneak in here. That's why you guys thought of the balcony in the first place!"

"Well . . ." whispered Tilgé. "I might be able to get you up there with *mysteria*."

Both Mirah and Stehl looked at Tilgé with their mouths agape and eyes wide. Stehl hissed, "You can use *mysteria*, and you didn't tell us?"

Tilgé folded his arms. "Well, I don't like using it that much. I would much rather use a sword or a real weapon. *Mysteria* makes a cheat out of life. I just didn't see a need to tell you. It's not like I am that good at it, anyways."

Stehl shook her head. "Well, can you get us up to that balcony at least?"

"Should be able to." Reaching for *mysteria* for the first time in a while, Tilgé felt his stomach churn. He tested the water above them to see if there were any wards, and he was surprised to find none leading up to the balcony. "This seems fishy . . ." he muttered as he lifted the three of them with a Water spell, affecting the water pressure and the current to lift them higher and higher until they were at the level of the balcony. Steadily, each of them climbed onto it.

Tilgé looked back to see if the sorcerers in the courtyard had sensed his limited *mysteria*, but they seemed not to have noticed. Before the three entered the room, Stehl turned to Tilgé and grabbed the collar of his shirt, pulling him close so he could hear her whisper. "Don't ever keep a secret from me again," she said softly. Though the words seemed harsh, she was smiling playfully as she said them. Then, she turned back and followed Mirah into the room. The place was completely dark, as if not even the lights of the city below caught the shadows here.

"Hey Tilgé, could you get us some light?" she muttered. She knew she was going to enjoy making Tilgé use *mysteria* when she could.

He groaned and summoned a glowing ball of Light. Stehl raised her Sword as soon as she saw the black-robed man pressed against the wall, his hands held high against a wall by invisible forces. "What are you doing here, Lord of the Shadows? Are you responsible for these Shadows that have been put into the Emperor Regin's armies?"

The Lord of the Shadows raised his hooded head, and Stehl could see the river of tears that streamed from his sparkling golden eyes down his cheeks to land on a golden collar that tightened around his neck. "Help me . . ." he muttered.

Stehl did not hesitate in cutting through the invisible chains with Kohana's Fang. The Sword cut right through the spells, and the Lord of the Shadows fell to the metallic floor. Both she and Mirah bent down to help the man. "Hey, are ya alright?" Mirah asked.

The man's voice choked, and his arms went to his neck, pulling at the collar to no avail. "That fool . . . Only he can take this damned thing off me."

"Who did this to you?" Stehl asked.

It was then that the Lord of the Shadows fully realized that three humans had helped him. His eyes gazed deep into Stehl's, and he cleared his throat. Though his instincts commanded him to do so, he could not kill her. "Why would you help me? Can you not sense that I am a Servant of the Darkness?"

Stehl frowned. "Yes, I can tell you are one of the Lord of the Shadows. So what?"

"Why did you help me? If you knew I was suffering, you should have let me suffer." The Lord of the Shadows was still knelt on the floor, not yet confident in his ability to stand.

"I helped you *because* you were suffering. Did the Emperor Regin chain you like that?"

The Lord of the Shadows rubbed his wrists. The way he had been hanging had only increased his pain after being stuck there for hours. His arms ached from being stretched like that for so long. "Yes, he did. He decided he no longer truly needed me, except to drain power from me."

Suddenly, Stehl changed the subject. "You wouldn't— you wouldn't happen to know where Lord Ferro is, would you?"

His eyes widened, more in surprise than in confusion, and Stehl noticed that. "Lord Ferro? What do you mean by that? Lord Ferro has been dead for centuries—"

Stehl shook her head. "I know who he is, and I know that you know. Do you know where he is?"

Recognition dawned upon the Lord of the Shadows then. "Are you Stehl?"

This time, Stehl was taken aback. Tilgé and Mirah exchanged confused and nervous glances before looking back at the Lord of the Shadows and Stehl. "Yes, how did you know that?"

"My name is Mali, and I'm a good friend of Victor's." Mali wrapped a hand around his collar, trying to loosen it. "He's talked about you a lot. The last time I saw him, he went off looking for you."

For a moment, Stehl felt a fluttery feeling in her stomach, and then the sea of happiness became a flood of rage. "Well, what makes you think I would want a serpent-headed jerk to be looking for me? He's rude and snobby and rough and cruel. Besides, I have two perfectly good guys right here." She gestured to her two bodyguards and then realized that she had included Tilgé in the same category as Mirah. She immediately turned to look at Mirah, but he was just smiling, as if he did not mind that Stehl had introduced Tilgé in such a manner.

"Well, regardless," started Mali, rising, "I have not seen him for a few days. I am sure he is done searching the Southern Continent, but I cannot say more than that. I can only guess that he shall be at the disq tournament in a few days. He would have to think to check for you there." He almost keeled over, but leaned against the wall. Mirah and Stehl rose to help him, but he waved a hand dismissively. "I am not even going to ask how you got mixed up with the Y'mordi, but I suggest that you be careful. Not all of us are as friendly as

Randir and myself. I might have killed you myself, had you not mentioned Randir."

Tilgé snarled, "I'd like to have seen you try. What are you even doing here, snake?"

Mali's features hardened. "I was here serving the Emperor Regin, but I think that he has made it all too clear that my services are no longer needed. I recommend that none of you approach him now. He is becoming too strong." He raised a hand to summon a Gate but found the dark hold still on his heart. "Damn it!" he hissed.

"What is it?" Stehl asked.

"I can't even summon a Gate. The Emperor Regin barred my heart from casting any spells."

Stehl stood back as she said, "Alright, hold still. This shouldn't hurt . . . shouldn't, anyways." Before Mali had any time to protest, Stehl raised Kohana's Fang to point at Mali's heart. As she closed her eyes, the Sword glowed a silvery hue and shot a beam of its light at the Lord of the Shadows. The light filled the room, dissipating the shadows the Emperor Regin had placed in the room. When the light cleared, everyone noticed that Mali was smiling.

"It has been a long time since I have seen that Sword, Stehl. The last time I saw it, it was in the hands of the great Tatsu himself. Now, if only you had the Sword of Destiny, I could be rid of this collar as well. For now, thank you. I shall leave you."

"What was that all about?" Tilgé roared at her inside the hotel room. Mirah was in the shower, and the two of them were finally alone. "For how long have you been fraternizing with the Y'mordi? You never told me any of this."

"I don't fraternize with them! I hate them just as much as you do!"

"Clearly not!" He flung a chair to the ground. "You were getting all googly-eyed at the mention of that one Y'mordi's name, Reindeer, or whatever it was. Besides that, you just saved one of their lives, too. I had thought we were going into the castle to do some justice, not start serving the Darkness!"

"Do you honestly think that that is what I am doing? Serving the Darkness? Well, last time I checked, you helped! And you certainly didn't complain while we were there. So why didn't you say something if you felt so strongly about it?"

Tilgé's face stayed red, but he averted his gaze, not wanting to say what was on his mind.

"Go on—what was it, Tilgé?"

"I just went along with whatever you did, okay? I trusted you, and I thought you knew what you were doing. I thought that maybe I was seeing things the wrong way, that maybe you weren't in league with those monsters after all." He sat down on one of the still-standing chairs.

Stehl sat in the chair beside him. "Tilgé, I will say this for the fifth time, and the Great Spirit so help me, you had better listen: I am not in league with the Lords of the Shadows." She sighed. "I hate them . . . just as much as you, or Mirah, or anyone else in this world does, but they are not my primary enemy. I have a score to settle with the Enigma Brigade, and I am not going to truly be happy until I've killed every last one of the ones that took part in the massacre that day ten years ago."

Tilgé threw his hands up. "But you don't even know the people in the Enigma Brigade! I'm not even so sure that I would *let* you kill Bryco if we came across him. He saved my life, Stehl, and I can't let you just go around killing them without care. It's not like everyone in the Brigade did it because they enjoyed killing," although he made the mental note that he had enjoyed it when he had done it. "Most of them were probably just following orders. I mean, you saw Maksimilian yourself. Did he seem like the type of person you can really argue with? Especially if he is your Captain?

No matter what duty your heart preaches, in war, you always follow your commanding officer. Surely, that was something you were taught?"

Stehl's face was bright red. "Of course I was taught that! I was taught everything a soldier is supposed to know, and don't you for one second think that I was less of a soldier than anyone else! They admired me in this city."

Tilgé sneered. "And then there came the rumors of you and the Y'mordi."

Stehl aimed a punch at Tilgé's nosem but changed the direction the last second, hitting his shoulder hard.

Instead of yelping in pain or even fighting back, Tilgé rose, kicking his chair onto the floor, and walked to the door. He slammed it shut behind him, leaving an angry Stehl. Mirah came out of the shower with a towel around him. "Hey, what was all dat noise about? I heard da door slam."

"Nothing. I would rather not talk about it." She turned around and looked out the window, wondering if she would see Tilgé pass in front of her on the street.

"Y'know what ya need, Miss Stehl? A night on da town. It's been a while since you an' I had a real date. Let's go on one tonight. Whaddaya say?"

Stehl gave a faint laugh. "I really don't think I'm in the mood, my love."

"Oh, sure y'are." He took Stehl's hand into his, guiding her from the chair. "Jus' put on some real pretty clothes, an' I'll be back in a minute in me own spiffy clothes. Then, jus' you an' me, alright?"

She sighed with a smile. "Alright. I'll be ready."

When Mirah came into the room, she was wearing a green dress, something she had kept in her pack for a while but had never really worn. Mirah gave a wolf whistle as soon as he entered. He was dressed in his own red tunic and coat, an old look for the time, but one that made Stehl smile all the same.

Neither of them was used to seeing the other in such fine clothing. Stehl certainly found it better to dress as a man still, and Mirah still wore the navy garb occasionally. Usually, they each dressed as comfortably as they could, without sparing any time for beauty or handsomeness.

"Are ya ready, Miss Stehl?" Mirah asked as he offered his arm.

Her smile widened as she came closer to him. "I told you I would be." She wrapped her arm around his, and they exited the hotel, grinning. They walked down the street, arms linked. The fluorescent street lights made glowing pools across the sidewalk, but the two never stepped in those pools. Rather, they walked straight down the middle of the street, relishing each other's company in the dark of the night.

Mirah eyed several of the taverns they passed, but he did not so much as think of suggesting to go there with Stehl. He wanted this night to be as romantic as possible, and a bubbler was not on the menu. Finally, he saw the very place he had been seeking: a fine restaurant called Brillig's. It was more than a little expensive, but Mirah still had quite a bit of salt from his time in the navy.

"Ha, I didn't think you knew that Brillig's even existed," Stehl said.

"Yeah, I've only been 'ere once do'. I'm sure ye'll find it a treat."

Without responding, Stehl snuggled her head against Mirah's thick arm. She took a deep breath and realized he had put on his best cologne, giving him a nice warm smell of freshly fallen amber leaves from a maple tree after a crisp current billowed the branches. She hugged him more tightly and relaxed in his scent as they entered the restaurant. The place had a few people chatting amongst themselves, enjoying some expensive cariok, a drink far more upper-class than a bubbler.

Mirah gestured the number two to a waiter, and she

seated them at a comfortable bench with a golden-flame candle flickering between them. Though Stehl had been one to oppose the use of *mysteria,* seeing a fire colored differently from blue enchanted her—especially this one with its aureate hue.

"What can I get you all to drink? Could I bring you a bottle of the house cariok?" said the waitress.

"We will take a bottle of marygeiss actually."

Stehl put a hand to her mouth. "Mirah, you don't have to—"

However, he shook his head with a playful smile. "I know I don't, but dat doesn't mean I won't." He turned his head back to the waitress. "The marygeiss please."

"Yes, sir. Are there any appetizers I could bring you while you look over our menus?" As she said this, she handed each of them a rather complex yet ornate menu.

"No, ma'am, we will be fine. T'ank ya."

She bowed politely and headed to the cariok counter to get their marygeiss.

"So, Miss Stehl, how many times 'ave ya been here?" Mirah asked.

She shook her head. "In all my time at the Capital, I have never been here. I've heard a million times how it is the trendiest place around the Capital, but I have never eaten here. Many of the soldiers I worked with took their wives here to calm them down when they were in pissy moods. I can see why it would have made them feel better. This place is amazing!" Indeed, the place was beautiful. The golden lighting was dim, but the candles were bright. The tables were all well-polished, and a pleasant current swept through the restaurant, spreading the smell of pine and mint to create a truly calming atmosphere.

"Well, I am sure that ye're in fer a real treat. Dis is not an easy place to get into."

Realization dawned on Stehl. "Wait, you had tonight

planned? This place needs reservations?"

Mirah chuckled. "Yeah, I did, and I can tell ya, Miss Stehl, it was well worth it."

Despite herself, Stehl blushed.

Mirah smiled back at her. Tonight, he wanted to be as romantic as possible. He truly loved Stehl, and that love was all he wanted. He did not expect for her to show her love to him in the bed tonight, and he did not expect for her to discard their new companion Tilgé for him, either. He liked Tilgé and wanted him to stay with them. Mirah did not even care if Stehl loved Tilgé, as long as she loved Mirah, too. He wanted her love, and he wanted to keep loving her. He could not ask for more.

The waitress came back over and placed a glass in front of each of them, pouring the bubbling marygeiss into the glasses. "Have you guys decided what you would like to order?"

"Hardly," grumbled Mirah, confused as to how anyone could have decided what they wanted to order in such a short time. "Give us a few minutes, please."

The waitress bowed again before leaving them.

Stehl and Mirah unfolded their menus and looked through the lists of items, searching for something that would catch their eyes. "What do ya think, Miss Stehl?"

Stehl laughed before saying, "Mirah, if you call me that one more time, I will start calling you Mistah Mirah, and I know you won't like that."

"Alright . . . love." They shared a smile before returning their eyes to their menus.

"I think I might just get some skander. It's a Southern dish I learned to love back in Apolis." She took a sip of the marygeiss and almost melted from the sweet, intoxicating taste of the drink. "And this stuff is amazing, Mirah!"

"Yeah, it's pretty good stuff. I t'ink I will be getting da same. It's been a while since I had skander, too." He pressed the button on the wall with the black word "Waiter" printed across its plastic surface.

The waitress came up to them eagerly, "What can I get for you today?"

"Two of the parsnic skander dishes if ya please." Mirah's features softened as he reached his massive hand across the table to hold Stehl's hand. "I want everyt'ing to be perfect for ya."

Stehl placed her other hand on top of Mirah's. "It already is. It really is."

"What are we doing out here again?" Mirah asked.

"We are looking at the stars, love. Aren't they dazzling tonight?"

Mirah rolled over and wrapped one thick arm around Stehl's middle before looking her in the eyes and saying, "Yes, they most certainly are."

"Oh, stop it. You're not even looking at the stars." She pointed upward to reiterate her point, but Mirah was entranced just watching Stehl's eyes sparkle.

"Sure, I am, just not da ones in da sky."

This time, Stehl did not argue. She had only been stargazing once before, and that was with another man, but it still felt good to do it with Mirah now. "When you look at the stars, what do you see?"

Mirah turned a head to look at the sky again. "I see a bright future, one wit' ya, me, and maybe even Tilgé. All of us, happy as skander in a whir'poo'. What about ya? Whaddaya see?"

Her smile faded, and a meek sigh escaped her lips as she sat up. "I thought that I would know by now, but I really don't. I look up at the stars, and it feels like I'm still missing something, no matter how good my life is. I mean, I have you. I have Tilgé. I have the disq tournament to look forward to. So, why am I not happier, love?"

Mirah stuck a hand in his suit and said, "Dis may help,

Stehl." He pulled out a beautiful, red rose. Unlike the other three continents, the Eastern Continent had a custom of engagement, and that was the presenting of the rose. When a man gave a woman a rose, it was a clear sign of love and the willingness to give her the life of her dreams.

Stehl put a hand to her mouth in utter astonishment. "Mirah, you had this planned all along?"

Mirah rubbed the back of his head. "Maybe a bit . . ."

She could not contain herself and wrapped her arms around him in a tackling hug, tightening her grip as much as she could. "I love you, Mirah. I love you so much."

He hugged her back, but tried not to hurt her in doing so. "I love you too, beauty."

"Mirah, I don't know what I would do without you." She let him go and took the rose from his hand to smell it. Being crushed in his suit, it smelled more like Mirah than it did a flower, but she did not mind. She fell back down on the seaweed and looked up at the stars with a grin. Mirah lay down as well and sighed, content with the knowledge that Stehl loved him as much as he loved her.

Then, before he knew it, her hand reached over him to the ground to his left, and she pushed herself on top of him, though it felt more like she *slid* on top of him. "Stehl, what are ya—?" he began, but her finger went to his lips, cutting him off.

"Now, it's my turn to give you something," she whispered so quietly in his ear. As soon as her lips had come close to his ear, his hairs stood on end. He groaned as she placed her hands on him.

The morning sunlight was what woke her the next day. "Mirah? Mirah? We need to get up," she muttered, as she shook his hairy shoulder. That was when she realized that they were both lying there naked in the middle of the Capital's park. "Hey, get up! We need to get dressed before someone sees us!"

At those words, Mirah rose and began pulling his clothes on. Occasionally, Stehl would throw him a piece of clothing that was scattered in her own pile. They laughed as they rushed to hide their nudity.

Stehl started as they exited the park, "Alright, we need to get back to the hotel and talk to Tilgé." She was thinking of the fight they had last night. He had been pretty upset, though he had most certainly been the one in the wrong. He was not going to get an apology out of her, no matter what, but she still hoped he was not mad at her. "Come on, let's hurry up."

Mirah obliged, still holding her hand. "Stehl, why are ya in such a hurry?"

"Well . . . we had that pretty big fight last night. He was mad at me for knowing one of the Lords of the Shadows, and I told him that I was by no means in league with them or anything. He just didn't believe me . . ."

"I'm sure he's fine, Stehl."

As they walked, they passed several battalions of soldiers who were making their final preparations for the coming battle. Stehl stopped. "Mirah, the Emperor Regin is doing so many things wrong. We can't just let him do this to the people of Apolis, not without honor."

Mirah shook his head. "No, we can't."

As they approached the hotel, they noticed the front door was cracked open—an unusual occurrence, considering the strict personality of the innkeeper. Mirah pushed the door fully open, and the two of them beheld the massacre in front of them. Everyone who had been in the lobby was dead, their blood drenching the floor.

"Tilgé . . . where is he?" Stehl asked.

Ignoring the bodies, the two of them ran up the stairs to their room, the door to which was also open. Stehl pulled her Sword out of its sheath and pointed it at the red-haired man in the room. The man was holding Tilgé by the neck, and Tilgé struggled against his grip.

"Stehl..." he gasped.

Maksimilian turned his head to face Stehl and Mirah. He tossed Tilgé aside as if he weighed nothing, and Tilgé's his head slammed against the wall, leaving a gruesome blood stain there.

"Tilgé!" Stehl exclaimed, but she did not move. She kept the Sword pointed at Maksimilian.

"Girl," Maksimilian warned, "Tilgé is mine. I own his life, and I shall soon end it. You would be wise to forget about him now, lest you be killed as well."

Stehl's jaw clenched tighter than it had before, and she felt a well of rage surge within her. "You're him ... Maksimilian, the Captain of the Enigma Brigade, aren't you?"

Maksimilian's smiled faded. "How do you know my name, girl? Did Tilgé tell it to you?"

"Yeah, he told me alright, but I knew you well before that."

Mirah edged over to the desk, where he knew a gun was hidden.

"How would you know me, girl?" Maksimilian smiled again. "I have never seen you in my whole life, and I have been around for quite a while."

Stehl took a few steps closer to the murderer and said, "Oh, but don't you remember from ten years ago? I saw you at the Emperor Regin's fortress, when you massacred almost every person in there."

Maksimilian only said, "Could you be friends with Captain Terrell?"

It was Stehl's turn to smile. "Pretty close. I *am* Captain Terrell." She charged at Maksimilian.

With ease, Maksimilian raised a barrier of Light, but he was astonished when Stehl's blade went straight through the barrier, stabbing into his side. His eyes widened in pain, and he aimed a blast of Light at Stehl, knocking her backward and pushing the blade out of his flesh. His hand went to the wound, and his fingers turned red in the stream of his own blood. "How?" As he looked down, he noticed the Spirit Sword he carried was glowing. "A Spirit Sword . . . Is that . . . Kohana's Fang?" He could not believe it. He had sought that Sword for centuries without ever hearing a word about it. "How did you manage to find that blade, girl?"

Mirah pulled out the gun and fired a shot at Maksimilian quickly, but the former captain raised the massive Behemoth and blocked the bullets. He aimed a blast of Light at Mirah, knocking him against the wall beside Tilgé.

Stehl called, "Mirah!" She struggled to stand, but she managed to do so and held her Sword upright, ready to fight. "Maksimilian, you're not getting away this time. You've hurt me too much, and you certainly aren't going to get away with hurting my men."

"Your men?" Maksimilian scoffed. "I told you: Tilgé is mine. He belongs to *me*."

"Why? Just because you put a bounty on his head?"

Then, Maksimilian realized the truth. He turned to face the heavily breathing but awakening Tilgé. "Oh, you didn't tell her the truth, did you? You poor fool . . ." Maksimilian's grin seemed to split his face, and Tilgé felt the urge to spit at that wicked smile. However, the strength evaded him.

"Stehl . . ." Tilgé started, wanting to say it himself rather than Maksimilian relishing in saying it himself. "Maksimilian targeted me . . . because I was actually a member of the Enigma Brigade myself. I served him for years, and then he tried to have Bryco kill me. But, Stehl, I'm different now. Ever since then, I haven't wanted to kill. I'm tired of the fighting. I'm tired of all of it."

"Tilgé, shut up," Stehl said. "Right now, all I care about is you, Maksimilian. I am tired of you making others suffer." She charged again, but this time, Maksimilian was ready for her. He dodged the stab and grabbed Stehl's wrist, controlling her momentum so that the Sword fell out of her hand and into his, and she ran into the wall. Maksimilian turned with a sweeping stroke, planning to separate her head from her shoulders with her own Sword.

In a searing flash of pain, he screamed, and the Sword, along with his right hand, fell to the floor in a bloody spatter. Tilgé attempted another attack with his now blood-stained dagger, but Maksimilian dodged the attack and ran to the door. "It pains you to see others suffer, Captain Terrell? Well, how about I go and have some fun at the disq tournament? Then, we shall see who is the one in pain."

He left through a Gate.

Tilgé approached Stehl, struggling to keep his own balance. "Here," he said, offering her his only good hand. She turned to face him, but she did not grab it.

Staring up at him, her eyes a cold fire, she said, "You lied to me."

He withdrew his hand, curling his fingers. Though Stehl's glare tore at his heart, he steeled his own face, not revealing his own misery. "Very well then. I shall leave you, and I wish you luck."

As he reached the door, Stehl asked, "Where are you going?"

He did not turn around but said, "I am going to finish Maksimilian off. He is weak now, and I should have sought him out long ago. He's my problem, and I'm going to take care of it."

"How do you think you're going to stand against him with just one hand?"

Tilgé smiled. "Well, now, I'm not the only one with one hand. He and I . . . we're even now." He lowered his head. "I never realized how alike the two of us were. We both killed for pleasure, and we both claimed we acted in the name of the Light. I never knew how wrong we were until I was kicked out of the Brigade. And now—I have to set things right. I guess this is goodbye, Stehl."

Stehl lowered her own eyes and did not say anything.

"Now, listen 'ere, the pair of ya!" Mirah barked, struggling to sit up.

"Mirah!" Stehl exclaimed as she saw him try to stand. Tilgé turned to look, taking a step forward to help.

"I won't have none of it!" Mirah said. "Stehl, I know ya love Tilgé, so don' be actin' like ya could never speak to 'im again." Then, he turned his head to the former Brigadier. "And you, what makes ya think that we are goin' to let ya go off by yerself to fight Mister Big-Ugly-and-Redhead?"

Tilgé said, "Mirah . . . I lied to both of you. I couldn't expect either of you to forgive me for that."

Mirah shook his head. "No, Tilgé. You yerself said dat dat was da you from six years ago. Ye're different now, an' I'm sure even Mister Big-Ugly-and-Redhead could see dat. What ya did in da past was wrong, but ye've been doing everyt'ing to make up for it since den. Now, both of ya, pick yerselves up, and let's take care of dis Maks guy once an' for all."

Tilgé did not respond. He looked to Stehl for her response. She stood and sighed. "Mirah, can you give us a minute?" Her voice was stern, the tone that Mirah had learned all too well to be her do-not-argue voice. He nodded, and Stehl and Tilgé walked into the hallway, closing the door behind them.

"Tilgé, what Mirah said bears some merit, but you still lied to me. I trusted you, and you lied to me. I don't see how I can ever trust you again with that."

"I'm sorry, Stehl, I really am. It's just . . . I've wanted for the past six years to be free of the Brigade, but I have been constantly hounded by Maksimilian and my own memories. When I met you, I wanted to get to know you without you having to know that part of me—that part that I have been trying to get rid of for six years. I wanted a fresh start, I guess, but the past has a way of catching up to you."

Stehl stepped over to Tilgé and wrapped her arms around his middle. He smelled of sweat and fresh rain. "Tilgé, I love you."

His eyes widened. "You . . . do?"

She nodded against his chest. "I do. I love you the same way I love Mirah, and I know he is okay with that. Honestly, he's right: I couldn't bear to lose you. You're a reminder of my past, something that I cherish now, and I see a future with you, me, and Mirah, together."

Then, Tilgé hugged her back. "I'll stay with you, Stehl. I will if that's what you want. I would give anything to just be with you."

Stehl pulled back and said, "Well, for starters, we need to go after Maksimilian, or he will kill everyone at the disq tournament. We still have a couple of days, but it will take us a while to get there." She started to pull away, but Tilgé pulled her closer and pushed her head against his, his mouth wrapping around hers. When he kissed her, she felt as if fireworks were going off in all directions. When she kissed him, the former Brigadier realized he had never shared a kiss with a woman before, and he smiled as he kissed her. He wrapped his arms around her back, while she grabbed his biceps.

"Alright," he said with a warm smile as he let her go. "I think we can go now. We have the Captain of the Enigma Brigade to kill."

"Right. Let's finish this," she said, still dazed from the passion of his kiss.

14

Steps in the Darkness

RANDIR HAD SCOURED the city for a while, but once the Emperor Regin had his troops moving through the Capital in formation, he knew to hightail it out of there. Having given up on finding Stehl on the Eastern Continent, he tried the Western. He certainly did not think the Stehl he knew would be in the West, one of the anima-infested continents, but he also could not find her in the Capital: wherever she was where he had not expected her to be, and that alone was reason enough to examine the other large cities of Gevás, including the filthy continents of the North and West.

He approached the legendary Pyramid, the largest city in the Western Continent, and marveled at its alien construction. The whole city was hidden inside a gigantic pyramid, larger than a skyscraper ten times over, and, inside, the inner walls held screens that changed the lighting of the city from day to night and even altered the heat. It was a complex system that Randir had never fully understood.

As he approached, he opened his heart to *mysteria* and masked his presence in the warm scent of Darkness, evading any sensors the defense system of the Pyramid might be using. He was going to play it safe this time, or at least safer than he had in Apolis. It was not that he was worried he would run into a Guardian or anything. Rather, the people here were more prone to have a rebellion in the middle of the day if something ran amok.

The Western Continent in general had always perplexed him. It was a mixture of humans, anima, griffins, and even a few dragons. Somehow, the humans had lived with the filthy non-humans and had little trouble with them. Randir simply could not understand it. He had always considered the Western people so primitive in their ways of thought—a reason that was strong enough to convince him to rarely travel to the West. It was a symbol of the foreign and unnatural union of two cultures, a symbol he could not readily ignore. Yet, if Stehl was here, it would be worth the search.

He saw people traveling through the city gates, tall, black oak doors that appeared in the middle of each side of the Pyramid's base. He approached the passing lines, some entering the city and some exiting. He needed to get into the city without being caught, and that meant not running into anything. If that happened, one of the guards would surely cast an anti-*mysteria* spell, a trick that was becoming more and more popular in Gevás, Randir had noticed. However, he realized he needed to use *mysteria* to get in here. The traffic in and out of the Pyramid was ridiculously bustling, and it would take a miracle to get him in there.

Then, a simple thought came to him. With his Dark spell keeping him invisible, he stepped through the line to stay on the guard's side of the line going into the city. Stepping closer to the guard, he summoned his hammer. He looped it around the guard's foot and pulled, tripping him to the ground. With a leap against the wall, he sailed over the guard's head and was on the other side.

"What was that?" the guard roared in confusion.

"Hurry up and check my ticket. I don't have all day," a

rude aristocrat asked the guard as he stumbled to find the right words.

However, Randir was already inside the Pyramid. Though the sky outside the Pyramid had been gray and stormy, the weather there was bright and sunny, almost as warm as the Eastern Continent was in the middle of the summer. People walked through the streets like a colony of ants, everyone fully aware of where they were headed and oblivious to the thousands of lives that surrounded them. The daily processes here were devoid of thought. It reminded him of back home in the Capital. In the daytime, that city was once as bustling as this one, but, with the war going on, he did not think that such times of jubilation and business were at hand. After entering a side alley, he released his spell of Darkness and reentered the busy street, blending into the crowd perfectly despite his black robe. He allowed the water to rise in heat around him, knowing that no one would really notice, not in a capital like this one. How in the world was he going to find Stehl in this crowd? He had to make some kind of sign, but doing that would require throwing all secrecy away.

What could I do to catch her attention here? he pondered in frustration. His eyes drifted up to the warm sunny sky, the artificial atmosphere, and an idea came to him. *What if I mess with the stars? I wonder if she would see them . . .* He could not mess with the technology: he was not that savvy with technology-based *mysteria,* but he could certainly make balls of flame that blazed in the sky, making her name. First, though, he would have to wait until nightfall.

He trudged through the town, wondering what could keep him occupied until night came. As he walked, he passed taverns, theaters, and merchants' kiosks. Randir found the day life of cities to be dull: he preferred the night life, when the real fun began. That was when people performed their festivities of dark and light, and they brought out their wild, unbridled passions. In the daytime, the only thing on people's minds was to get to work as soon as possible or to find a place to eat for a quick lunch. He considered turning into a Red Dragon just to cause chaos in this bustling city, but he thought better of it. His ability to shift was premeditated by his being a Prophet of Fire. However, he was not the only one of the Y'mordi who could change form at will. They were not anima, at least not *true* anima. Randir had seen Xarden once turn into a sea serpent, but that was a transformation that occurred through *mysteria*. Ixion had fittingly turned into a rat on multiple occasions. However, Randir had suspicions that Ixion could very well be an anima after all. But, Randir's own ability to shift was not *caused* by his being a Prophet; it seemed to coincide. The form of the Red Dragon was his true form. He had been born neither on Earth nor Gevás. He was from Menx, a world of supreme technology and a mystical power known as nesis, which granted a certain control over things that *mysteria* simply could not handle.

While caught in his thoughts of the past and his home-world, he sensed something. It was a presence of Darkness, a person marked by the Shadows. "There is a Servant of the Darkness, even here?" he muttered. Randir followed his heart, allowing it to steer him in the direction of the Servant. Finally, he came upon a kiosk where a large man in bright clothes was selling disq merchandise in preparation for the coming tournament. Randir waited in the short line until he was at the front.

"What can I get for you, kind sir? Have you already bought your tickets for the tournament? They are on sale to-day!" The man's jovial expression was clearly a mask for his darker nature, Randir knew.

"What? Is there no discount for a fellow Servant?" Randir said, trying to reveal to the man that he was one of the Y'mordi without saying such out loud.

The man raised an eyebrow in mild surprise. "A fel-low Servant, huh? That's a pretty curious thing to be saying around these parts, stranger. What can I do for you?"

"Well, for starters, do you have somewhere private we can talk? Somewhere a little *darker?*"

The man's hesitation subsided. "Sure, man. Right this way." He set out a sign that said he was out to lunch and activated a security barrier around his kiosk to prevent any thievery. He gestured for Randir to follow him into the nearby inn. The building itself looked pretty dingy in quality, but it was clean. Randir opened his heart to sense what was going on in the hotel. He could feel a couple sleeping nearby, a woman lying to the innkeeper, and a few old men concentrating on a board game in the main lobby.

"It's just up one floor," the man said, "so, we'll take the stairs." As they walked into the stairwell, he asked, "So, what part of the world are you from, fellow Servant?"

"The Palace of Shadows. I am one of the Y'mordi."

"One of the Y'mordi, huh?" said the man with a smile. "It's not often I get a visit by one of you guys."

"Whom else have you met?" Randir asked.

"Oh, it was—um—well, his name sounded like 'platypus,' but I know that wasn't it."

Randir stopped as the man opened the door to his floor. "Pullatus came to talk to you?" Though Y'tal was the leader's name amongst the Y'mordi, to those not in the loop, he was Pullatus.

They walked into the dimly lit hallway. "Yeah, he was a little short and had a high voice, but he knew how to inspire some fear, that's for sure. I didn't much care for him, but I guess I don't have much choice, being a Servant and all. I am here to serve the Darkness, and as such, I did what he asked, and you can be sure to tell him I did."

Randir shook his head, perplexed. "What did Pullatus tell you to do?"

"Oh, he didn't tell you? You must not be too high up the ladder then, huh?" The question made Randir's blood boil, but he did not say anything. "He asked me to sell disq tournament merchandise rigged with explosives. At noon of the first day of the tournament, the whole arena is set to explode. Pullatus has a whole network of tampered merchandise across Gevás."

Randir could not believe what he was hearing. The first thing that came to mind was of what could happen to Stehl if she went to the tournament. "How could he do this without telling us?"

"Oh, he didn't tell any of you about it?" the man asked, opening the door to his room. Randir noticed the man's nervousness. He was sweating, though his face did not betray any such hesitation. "Well, he did it alright. So, here's my place. It's not much, but I guess it's my home for the week."

Randir looked around. The room looked like it had to be one of the finer ones in the hotel. It was well-kept, and a tall window was over the bed, allowing warm, artificial sunlight to pour into the room. However, his mind was more on Stehl's potential fate, assuming she went to the tournament. He realized there was a good chance she would not be there, and he hoped that that was the case, even if it meant more time he could search for her. At least, she would still be alive. "What is your name, Servant?"

The man sat on the bed, though it appeared to be more of a hop, Randir noticed. "I am Yarng. So, what can I do for you, Y'mordi?"

"Well, I suppose for starters, you can tell me more about what Pullatus has planned for this tournament plan. He has not informed any of the rest of us, and I demand to know what's going on."

Yarng shook his head. "No can do, General. As strange as it sounds, I think I fear him more than I fear you, and if he doesn't want you to know about it, then I am not going to get myself killed for it."

Randir summoned his hammer and swung it, shattering

Yarng's knee and filling the water with a resounding crack, accompanied by Yarng's screams as he collapsed. "Now, Yarng, there is a considerable difference between Pullatus's and my interrogating styles. He has a way of threatening and making you believe he will do it." He stepped closer to Yarng. "I don't even give you the blessing of a threat. I will take out your other leg if you don't start talking, Servant. Now, do you think you have some information?"

Yarng whimpered, holding his deformed leg in his shaking hands. "I—I—I don't know all the details, but—but Pullatus said he wanted as many Servants as possible to—to—to sell disq merchandise that was rigged with explosives. It's set to blow on noon of the first day of the tournament." Randir raised his bloody hammer again. "Don't hurt me! Don't—don't!"

"Oh, shut up! You already said all that. What else did he tell you?"

"He—he—he said he was using it for a trap, a trap for a guy that messed with him years ago. I don't think he told me anything else."

Randir lowered his hammer: He could sense the Servant was telling the truth. "I have got to stop him. He cannot just kill off all those people, especially if Stehl is in there. I don't care how mad he is about that guy that messed with him back on Earth all that time ago. His plan ends here."

He summoned a fireball in his black gloved hand, and Yarng stuttered, "What—what are you doing?"

Randir aimed his hand at the man and unleashed a stream of Fire, incinerating the man instantly and lighting the room on fire as well. Ignoring the dying screams, Randir exited the room and the hotel, sensing the whole place going up in red flames, clear signs that the arson was committed by a mage. Still, he could not use a Gate to get away: ever since the Third Obsidian War, all the major cities had created new Gate defenses, and in this city, it was impossible to even summon a Gate. However, he did not feel more vulnerable, only annoyed.

The people outside ran in fear of the spreading Fire, screaming and trampling others in their terror. None of them noticed Randir exit the hotel, but the sound of sirens blared through the water, warning of the approaching law enforcers

He reached the kiosk that Yarng had been using and examined the security barrier with his heart, seeking a weakness. By the looks of the device, it would be hard to crack it through the slow and analytical way as Xarden or Arnim would probably handle it. He created a barrier inside Yarng's, protecting the goods he wanted to examine before trying to destroy the barrier. Summoning as much *mysteria* as he could muster for one spell, he released a blast of Fire in the form of Lava.

At first, the barrier held under the powerful spell, but then it shattered from the pressure and power of Randir's *mysteria*. He grabbed one of the pieces of merchandise Yarng had been selling. They were rigged with explosives alright— Y'tal's spells of Darkness that would likely cause a spell of such dark force that the whole stadium would be utterly destroyed, along with everyone in it. Of course, one small trinket such as the one he held did not have that power, but with the quantity that Y'tal was probably dealing with, that place would be a crater.

The sirens were getting much closer now. They would be at the hotel in seconds.

Randir looked around, seeking an escape route. He needed to get out of here as quickly and quietly as possible.

"Victor, over here!"

Randir turned to see Mali standing in an alleyway, gesturing for Randir to come closer. Randir ran to his friend and felt the other Y'mordi alter his appearance with a Light spell, and he now looked like any other random citizen of the Pyramid—not that there was a unique look to a person in the Pyramid. However, in his black robes, he did appear ominous. "Hector, what in the name of the Dark Lord are you doing here? You're supposed to be watching the Emperor Regin!" His voice was not angry, and his tone certainly did not reflect it. Rather, he smiled at seeing his close friend.

Mali exchanged a smile of his own. "Let's get going. I can keep us hidden for a while." As he said this, he allowed a Light spell to keep both of them invisible to others. "So, what brought you here to the Pyramid? Have you found out anything about that Stehl girl yet?"

Randir shook his head in sadness. "No, I have not, and it would seem as if Y'tal has a dastardly plan. I figured that Stehl would be the kind of person to go to the disq tournament soon, and so, I had planned on searching everywhere else until that time, but I just found out from a Servant that Y'tal has rigged the whole arena to explode at noon at the start of the tournament. If Stehl *does* go there, she will die."

In response, Mali's eyes widened. It was then that Randir noticed the golden collar around Mali's neck. Mali started, "Why would Y'tal do this?"

Still staring at Mali's collar, Randir replied, "He wants to catch the guy who messed with him on Earth ten years ago. I think he's going a little too far, though. I don't know where Stehl is either . . ."

"That, I can sort of help you with." His smile faded as he realized what he had done. "Well, actually . . ."

"What? What is it?"

"Well, I kind of ran into her at the Emperor Regin's fortress."

Randir grabbed Mali's shoulders. "She's at the Capital?" His face lit up. "That's amazing! Why didn't you say so sooner?"

Mali brushed Randir's arms off. "Because I told her you would be looking for her at the disq tournament. I came looking for you to tell you that she would be there. Y'tal was the one who told me where you were. I am to tell you that you have been slacking on your duties and are to get back on the proper track immediately."

"What about you?" Randir asked, slightly offended. "Haven't you left your post?"

Looking down, Mali responded, "Well, I kind of had to leave the post. It got to the point where I could no longer handle the Emperor Regin."

"And what's with your new necklace?" Randir's tone was becoming angrier with every passing second. "Did Y'tal give you that as a prize for being his little dog?"

Mali lifted his head to look straight at Randir, and his eyes watered. "No, Victor, he did not. The damned Emperor Regin stabbed me in the back once I activated the Darkness in his heart, and he trapped this damned thing around my neck. Y'tal couldn't even remove it, so now I *am* stuck being a dog for a while. It's bonded me to the Emperor somehow. Even in death, it came right back."

Randir met Mali's gaze. "In death? Do you mean . . . that Y'tal . . . ?"

"Yeah, Victor, he killed me to see if it came back—as if I had no problem with experiencing any pain. The collar came right back, and I think the only way to get it off might be to use the Sword of Destiny, but it's not like the Emperor of Light will hand that over if I ask politely or anything, so why don't you just back off! And, you can very well take care of yourself now that I've got you out of your own mess and told you where your bride-to-be is." Mali stormed off down the alley, fists clenched.

"Hector, wait!" Randir called, but Mali was already gone. He wanted to chase after his friend, but he had other problems to worry about right now, namely Y'tal's plan for destruction at the disq tournament. He followed Mali's *mysteria* scent to find the best way into the main area of the city without being seen. Then, he went his own way to get out of the city. He needed to get to the Northern Continent and find a way to either disarm all of those bombs or stop Stehl from going into that arena, and neither of those were particularly easy things to do.

He turned back to where the alley was as he ran. "Hector, I'm sorry, but I have got to go and find her. When I get back, we can get that stupid collar off and worry about Y'tal. I'm sorry . . ." He turned back toward the exit and ran in that direction.

Mali stood there, hidden by his own illusions, and listened to every word that Randir said before he ran off toward the exit. His eyes were still tear-rimmed, but he did not cry. He did not know whether to be furious, disappointed, or even content with Randir's actions. Sure, Mali felt betrayed since he had helped Randir so much, but Randir was following his heart. Knowing that he would be giving up his friend and his place with the Y'mordi, Randir was going to find Stehl. She had looked pretty enough for Randir's tastes, and she very well might have a matching personality, what little Mali had seen of it.

"Victor . . . you take care of Stehl, and I will try talking to Y'tal. Good luck," he muttered as Randir faded around the corner.

15

Into the Volcano

DRAGE OPENED THE DOOR to the room to find that Feranx was already getting dressed. *"Drage, I had begun to wonder if you had left me,"* the green screen said. Drage could not help but notice that Feranx had had to delete a piece at the front of the screen before sending Drage the screen: he had probably started typing "your Majesty" at the front of that message; Drage smiled. The griffin was learning.

"No, I did not. However, the Ring felt that we needed a full night's rest before we tackled the problem of the next computer. How do you feel?" He admitted to himself, however, that it did not matter if Feranx was feeling well or not: they had to leave soon.

"I feel well. Thank you. I apologize for sleeping so late."

Drage shook his head. "No need to apologize. We needed the rest. Well, let's head out. We need to take care of this computer problem."

"I make, you break, my break, your ache."

"What's that supposed to mean?" Drage asked. He had never heard such a phrase before.

Feranx laughed silently and replied, *"It is the motto of*

the tech guild in Apolis. It's meant to represent our relationship with customers. Of course, we never share it with the customers, but it's sort of our inside joke. We make the stuff people want, but then they break it. People can be so ungrateful. And when we ask for a break or even just a day off, we only get more complaining. Society needs people like us, not only to make their latest gadgets, but also to fix them. We make a living by making other people's livings easier. It's not exactly the ideal life, but living in the big city makes the pay almost worth it."

"*Almost* worth it?"

Feranx lowered his beak nervously, realizing he was talking to the Emperor of Light, and it was ungrateful to speak of bad working conditions to his own generous employer. "*Well . . . perhaps I am just being a little harsh.*"

Drage shook his head. "Nonsense. Speak what is on your mind, but just walk with me as you do. We *do* need to get ready to go against the next module."

"*Alright . . . well, all of us in the guild live in the city now, but even with the demand of our tech knowledge, we barely make enough to support our own families in Apolis. The cost of living is off the charts in Apolis as the highest cost of living in Gevás, and our salary isn't that great.*" Though it was hard to hear a tone in Feranx's typed words, Drage could see the griffin's nervousness in his face. The griffin's ears were lowered, and his head was half-bowed in submission.

Drage laughed, trying to diffuse Feranx's worry. "Hey, it's fine. If I cannot listen to the people I govern and hear their problems, I am not doing a very good job as leader and representative of them, now am I?"

Feranx's ears perked up, and he smiled. "*No, you would not be.*"

They descended the stairs as Drage continued, "The days of my father and his predecessors are over, Feranx. The exile they all allowed to exist is gone, and I shall not have the non-humans of my people live in fear." Drage caught one of the griffin's eyebrows raise at the phrase "my people." "Yes, even the non-humans are my people. I never created a distinction between the two in my mind. I have an anima in my Enigma Brigade, along with a woman, for the first time. There is not a non-human in my Council, but I happen to be really good friends with one—my sister-in-law, actually."

"*Your sister-in-law is a non-human? How?*" Feranx ventured.

Again, Drage could not help but laugh. "Well, my brother happened to fall in love with a horse anima from the Northern Continent. You've probably heard of her. Her name is Lilian."

Feranx stopped walking and typed rapidly with a look of urgency on his face. "*Your sister-in-law is Lilian? She is still called a hero in the Northern Continent! Everyone just said she married a human. She married your brother?*"

"Yep, she most certainly did. They have two kids now, although one of them is actually adopted. The adopted one is a squirrel anima, and their other kid is very much a human, a quiet little boy named William." Thinking about Matthew's kids made Drage think about his own: Apollo, Ace, and Alison. Right now, he even missed seeing the miscreant Ace. "My point is that I am trying everything I can to get rid of the barriers that my family caused. I do not want for there to be any grudges between humans and non-humans. I think it will take a few years, but I definitely think it can happen."

Feranx smiled. "*Drage, I am glad that you are the Emperor of Light. Many of my people had been skeptical about you before you took the Throne, but you have shaped up to be a splendid leader, and I am sure that, if your ancestors realized how much you are doing to unify my world and yours, they would be proud of you.*" He placed a claw on Drage's shoulder before they exited the hotel and walked onto the beach. The whole Ring of Elders was there waiting on them.

Drage started, "Alright, we need to head back to the

destroyed module and use it to get to the next one. We won't know if this next one is Cronus 624 or another strong one. Regardless of which it is, we will need to destroy it." Then, he immediately corrected himself. "Well, do not destroy it, but disable it. Once it is disabled, Feranx and I can get it to take us to Cronus 624 if this one is not it."

Elizabeth added, "And, remember what you were taught! Do not stay still for one second. Always be in motion and focus more on defense than offense. I have no intention of losing a single one of you today."

The Elders all bowed to her in understanding, and they summoned their staves, their annoyingly uncomfortable mounts that flew them back toward the disabled computer. Feranx summoned a green screen on which Drage could ride, and they shot off into the clear, blue sky.

The wind blasted against Drage's face, and he realized then how much he had missed feeling that pleasant breeze on his skin. He had spent way too much time in the water the past few years. At first, he held onto the edge of the soaring screen, his body pressed flat against the digital surface. Then, he tried raising his body. He was able to get his rear into the air, but he knew that if he let go of the edge of the screen, he would fall off.

Feranx noticed his struggles and opened his beak in a silent laugh. He pressed a few buttons on his digital keyboard, and the screen morphed to trap Drage's feet, holding him to the green surface. Drage laughed in amazement at Feranx's abilities. Steadily, he let go of the edge of the screen, one hand at a time. He found he could stand fully, even with the wind pressing against his body at full force. Spreading his arms wide, he embraced the wind and roared triumphantly into the sky.

Cameron spoke to Helen as the two rode their staves side by side. "For the Emperor of Light, he sure seems like he's letting loose . . ." Cameron could remember when he had first met the Emperor of Light. He had only been the heir to the throne at that time.

Helen rolled her eyes, kind of glad she was seeing her brother again. The last time she had seen him had been to see his wedding five years ago. "Yeah, he's always been like that. I guess the fresh air is good for him. He's probably had it pretty rough these past few years."

"It sounds like a rough life . . . being the Emperor of Light. He seemed crazy when I first met him. I can't imagine what the responsibility has done to him."

"Well, it certainly couldn't be easy, Cam." Though it often irritated him, Cameron allowed his girlfriend to use whatever name she wished. "Still, he's got it pretty good over there too . . . He has a wife he's been in love with since high school. He has three kids. He owns a humongous palace, and he has a Sword that can cut through anything. He has it made for the most part, I guess."

Cameron smiled. "Yeah, I guess he does. The griffin is pretty interesting, though. I don't think I've ever seen one, not even when I was in Gevás. I guess that was because the exile was still in effect, though."

Helen put a hand on Cameron's. "Drage was always a dreamer. I guess it's only fitting he lives in a dream world."

"But it's not a dream, Helen. It's very much real. And if Cronus 624 does any more damage, there will be more living humans on Gevás than here on Earth."

Helen's expression became dark. "We have to take out that stupid computer, or it could wipe this world out."

Cameron countered, "No, we have to disable it."

Suddenly, Helen glared at her brother as she muttered, "Assuming Mister Big-Shot knows what he's doing . . ."

"Do you doubt him, Helen?" called her mother as she flew down to their level. "Do you think he is wrong?"

Under the pressure of her mother's powerful gaze, Helen turned her head. "Yeah, I do think he's wrong, but I will follow him anyways. He's my brother, and I trust him." She had always trusted her brother, even when she had messed around with him and teased him as kids. Even though she remained the eldest, she had a lot less to worry about than Drage did, and he was probably the more mature of the two now. Helen was willing to admit this possibility, albeit with a little jealousy. "I trust him," she repeated.

Elizabeth nodded, appearing content with the response. "And you, Cameron? Do you still hold the word of the Emperor of Light to be true?"

"Yes, master, I do." Even though six years had passed, Helen and Cameron remained to be Elizabeth's ever eager apprentices. Cameron constantly found new things to learn about *mysteria,* and he was always appreciative of Elizabeth when she taught him a new spell of *mysteria.* While Helen focused more on battle magic, he preferred to learn more constructive spells.

"Good. We are approaching the computer module. Be prepared to use all that I have taught you. If this is the 624 model, then we are in for quite a challenge." Then, Elizabeth flew over to Drage and Feranx. "Drage, we are nearing the computer. Are you and the griffin ready?"

Drage nodded and yelled, "Yeah, Feranx will open a Gate large enough for all of us once we are close enough to it for him to siphon its energy and data."

Feranx typed, *"I can see the computer, Drage!"*

In response, Drage leaned forward on the screen, propelling himself forward just a little faster, bringing him to the front of the group. The massive computer came closer and closer to them as they soared through the afternoon sky. The Ring came to a gradual stop, and Feranx hooked his own system up to the disabled computer. He enlarged one screen so that everyone could read it: *"Gate activation in 3 . . ."*

Drage muttered with a smile, "He has to be dramatic with everything."

The countdown continued, and Feranx activated the Gate to the next Cronus model. The Ring, Drage, and Feranx flew into the massive Gate that hovered above them.

Instantly, they found themselves flying in blistering heat, a stark contrast to the pleasant breeze they had been feeling only moments before. Fires blazed around them, and a sea of lava spread beneath them. Ahead, a massive computer stood on a ledge shooting fireballs toward them. Drage realized they were in the middle of a volcano.

The Elders concentrated all their efforts on dispelling the fireballs that raged around them, and that task alone took up their concentration. Drage dodged a few fiery spheres himself and yelled to Feranx, pointing. "Get a screen in there! The quicker we disable this thing, the better!"

The griffin nodded and sent a screen in that direction. Controlling the screen, he made it weave between the spells, but the Cronus model targeted it and shot it down before it could get even close to its body. He sent Drage a message, *"Some more cover would be great!"*

"I'm on it!" Drage called back. Then, he said to the Elders, "Hey, if you see Feranx send a screen toward Cronus, try deflecting the computer's attacks. We need that screen to capture data from the computer. We can't do anything until Feranx can do that without his screens dissolving every three seconds!"

Elizabeth nodded. "Alright, Elders, you heard him: protect the griffin's screens!"

The Ring changed formation. The front Elders cast wards around the moving screen, dissipating each of the computer's fireballs, while the middle ones protected the group from the sides and allowed an opening for Feranx's screens to pass through. The Elders at the rear circled around the griffin, protecting him in case a stray fireball came their way while Feranx was still maneuvering a screen. Drage fell into formation at the front and used his Sword to slice through several fireballs. They circled around the computer, not daring to get too close. It was hard enough blocking its attacks from this far away where they could see the blasts coming.

Feranx released another screen through the opening the Ring of Elders had made for him. Again, once it got close to Cronus, the computer destroyed the screen. *"Drage,"* he messaged, *"this isn't working. Think of something else."*

He wanted to yell to Feranx that he was working on it, but he knew the griffin would not be able to hear him. Instead, he called to his mother, "Hey, are you sure there isn't something we can do to stun the machine without damaging it?"

Elizabeth called back, ducking to avoid a fireball, "Drage, if we can't disable it, we need to destroy it! We can't hold it off forever!"

Drage looked around desperately, trying to figure out what other options they had. "Um . . . Hey, how strong of an Ice spell can we get going?"

"As strong as you need it. Why?"

"If we create a strong enough spell, we should be able to chill the air so that any fireballs it shoots at us will disappear before it even gets near us!"

Elizabeth immediately began barking off orders. "Middle ranks, prepare heat barriers around everyone. It's about to get really cold. Front ranks, keep those shielding spells going, and rear ranks, as much Ice *mysteria* as you can muster! Now!"

The front Elders magnified the size of their barriers, trying to protect everyone just by themselves now. Drage flinched as an Elder near him burst into flames by a stray fireball. He felt warmer before he felt colder. The heat barriers surrounded each of the Elders, along with Drage and Feranx, as the other mages prepared their spells of Ice. Once they were sure that everyone was protected by an aura of suitable heat, the Ice spell filled the air, and just as Drage had predicted, each of Cronus's fireballs turned to mere wisps instantly. The sudden change in temperature made Drage along with many of the Elders to shiver for a moment.

"Feranx, try a screen!"

Complying, Feranx summoned another of his green screens and sent it whizzing toward the computer. Mere yards from the machine, Cronus destroyed it with a bolt of Lightning.

"Damn it . . ." Drage muttered in frustration.

This time, Helen was the one to complain. "Drage, we have to destroy it now. Your ideas are up."

"Keep the Ice spell going!" he roared as he leaned forward, causing himself to speed toward the Cronus model. Drage raised the Sword of Destiny and held it in front of him, trying to protect as much skin as possible. He whispered into the blade, "Oh, Great Spirit, if you can hear me, protect me."

Bolts of Lightning shot toward him, and he moved his blade fluidly, blocking each strike. His reflexes were all instinct, and he hoped the piece of the Great Spirit that resided in the blade aided him as he came closer and closer to the machine. The closer he came, the harder it was to deflect the attacks. He heard his mother and sister call his name far behind him, but he did not think about them. He had to focus on staying alive and getting as close to this computer as he could.

The force of those Lightning spells was powerful, and the constant beating against Drage was really wearing him down. He watched as his blade began to glow. At first, he thought his Sword had been charged with electricity, but then he realized that the Spirit was responding to his requests. It was starting to move of its own accord. He released his grip on the Sword, and it floated around him, deflecting each spell. Drage smiled as he circled the base of the computer repeatedly. Then, Feranx's words appeared on the screen on which he stood. *"Alright, Drage, I got it. Hold on just one second there."*

However, Drage did not have to really do anything. The Sword glowed blue as it danced around him, blocking every attack the computer attempted. Then, much to Drage's own surprise, the Sword of Destiny struck the computer, and the bolts of Lightning ceased. The Sword fell back into his hands, and the Ring flew closer to Drage and the computer.

Feranx typed, *"Drage, what happened? I only got a part of the code. Why did you attack it?"*

Drage shook his head. "I didn't."

"And how did you get your Sword to protect you like that? You weren't using *mysteria,"* Helen commented.

"I didn't do it," Drage repeated in exasperation. "This is a Spirit Sword, possessed by a piece of the Great Spirit. Sometimes, it comes to me and aids me. I got close to the computer to allow Feranx to crack the code through the screen I was using, and the Spirit Sword protected me itself. I did nothing."

"So," began Feranx, *"the Sword attacked the computer?"*

While many of the Elders looked skeptical, Drage could tell that Feranx was ready to believe anything he said. "Yeah, it did." Feranx nodded, and Drage realized that he was as confused as the griffin was. Why would the Sword attack the computer if it knew that Drage was trying not to damage it?

"Well," Feranx said, *"I can still try to figure out the rest here. I did get quite a bit of code, but it will take me a while to decode, at least a few hours."* His feathery ears were flattened in slight shame at his own inadequacy.

Drage noticed his ashamed tone and consoled, "Hey, it's fine. We can wait a while if we have to. You just start cracking the code."

The griffin nodded in response as they flew out of the volcano. Now that they were high in the air, Drage could see they had been on a volcanic island. There was a fairly large city on the island, but from here, it looked quite idle. Ocean went in every direction as far as the eye could see, but the sight was hardly beautiful to Drage. He had seen plenty of water in his lifetime.

"We're lucky that Drage thought of that when he did, Helen," Cameron tried again, using the voice of reason that she clearly did not want to hear.

"Yeah, well, we lost one of us today because of his stupid idea."

"It's hardly stupid if it would have saved that Elder's life if he had only thought of it sooner. His idea was a good one, and we all should have thought of it sooner." In actuality, Cameron was upset about the lateness and sloppiness of Drage's plan, but Helen was steamed, and he did not like it when she was this mad. "Hey, it will all be fine. Once Feranx has that code fixed up, we will know if we got rid of the right one and where the next one is if it's not. We are just one step closer to restoring this world." He grabbed her hand and held it between his own.

She relaxed. "I know . . . It's just . . . I think he could have done a better job."

"Hey, you said it yourself: he has not had it all that easy. He had to become an Emperor before he was done with college. That's a lot of responsibility. I think we can cut him a little slack. Besides, think how many people he will have saved once this world is restored."

Elizabeth walked over to the two of them. "What are my two apprentices chatting about now?"

"Nothing . . ." Helen grumbled. "How close are they to completing the code?"

"Well, Drage said it will still be a while. He said he feels pretty bad about it, even if he did not have that much control over it. And Feranx is feeling even worse since it is taking him so long to work on the code." Elizabeth looked back to where Feranx and Drage were talking. Even though her son was back on Earth, he still seemed so distant. She was not sure if it was because of the technological apocalypse that the Y'mordi had created or if it was something wrong with her son.

Cameron ventured, "And what have you decided about the restoration after Cronus 624 is taken care of?"

"Well, Drage is of the impression that his brother Matthew has enough skill in Time spells to undo what was done here to a certain point. However, even Drage is a little skeptical. It is our greatest hope for the moment."

Helen snapped, "So what makes Drage our fearless leader now? Isn't that your job?"

Elizabeth's face flushed. "Yes, it is my job, and you had better remember it, apprentice." Helen cringed at being called apprentice immediately. "He is an Emperor in his world, and he has come to help us with our problem. He has knowledge of the makings of our enemy, the computer's masters, the Lords of the Shadows, and he has a Spirit Sword, an item that has not been seen on Earth for centuries. If you want to tell him to leave, be my guest, but do not be mad at me if he chooses to respect his duty more than a mage's apprentice and refuses."

Without another word, Elizabeth stormed off. She was getting too old to have to deal with her kids fighting. Though she spent so much of her time with her daughter, she had always held Drage to be the star child. After all, he had grown up to be a fine man with a loving wife and three amazing children of his own. He definitely had a steady job as the Emperor of Light, and he held the responsibility well. He was an expert swordsman, and he had inherited her skills in *mysteria*. He was charming, dutiful, generous, and mindful of the difference between right and wrong. In essence, he was everything that she had hoped he would become.

Helen, on the other hand, was still in the dating process,

and had a quaint little house in Maine with Cameron. Though Elizabeth had protested, the two had been living together even before they had started dating. Sure, Helen had a job. She worked as a veterinarian, and Elizabeth did like that Helen helped out all the little animals. There was always plenty of disease in the animal kingdom, and Helen's cause was certainly noble. Still, she was not an esteemed doctor, a well-off lawyer, or even an emperor as Drage was. Helen merely worked with animals.

Of course, Elizabeth was proud of her daughter. She was glad to have Helen for an apprentice, and Helen learned quickly enough, though her passion and craving for more advanced spells became annoying.

Sighing, she approached Drage and Feranx. They were each sitting on chairs that an Elder had constructed for them out of Earth. Feranx was typing away on his green light keyboard, while Drage examined the screen in front of them and would occasionally nod at some message that Feranx had sent him. Elizabeth found herself wondering how the griffin was mute. Was it a birth defect? Childhood trauma? A psychological condition?

Drage turned to face her, and he smiled. His face still had that boyish grin to it, but he had grown some facial hair: a goatee, some fuzz on his cheeks, and a full moustache. "No, it's not done yet, Mom. It will still be a while." His voice had changed a few half tones deeper too, displaying his maturity, but she still could not quite see him as a man yet. She smiled back at him when she remembered he was in his late twenties.

"Alright, well just let me know the second the code is finished."

The griffin lowered his ears and typed something to Drage, but she could not see it. Still, Drage responded, "Hey, it's fine. Just keep working on it. Take your time."

Elizabeth almost flushed at how lax Drage was being about it. "We don't have time to spare, you know."

Drage glared at his mother and stood from his seat, gesturing for her to follow him away from Feranx and the computer. "Hey, leave him alone. He's doing all he can. It's my fault he didn't get the full code, but he's blaming himself for it."

"Drage, we really don't have time here. Every second, more people could be dying from this computer's crazy rampages. We really don't have any time to just waste."

"No, but you also don't have room to negotiate. He is going as fast as he can, and the slightest error can make him have to start over. He already feels nervous, so he definitely needs to take his time, and I am not going to rush him especially with all the hard work he has been doing. You don't see me bossing around your Elders, so don't tell my mechanic what to do." His voice was stern and commanding, but far from rough. Still, Elizabeth was taken aback by the tone. It had been the same voice that John had used all those years ago when he had wanted her to do something.

"You really have grown up," she said. "You're just like your father."

However, these were words that Drage had not wanted to hear. "No, I am nothing like him. He was cruel and abused the people of his world just for his own comfort. He held his own pride over justice, and that was his downfall, too. I am nothing like him," he repeated.

"Your father was not a bad man, Drage. He did many great things, whether you choose to realize it or not." She shook her head, wanting to change the subject already. "Anyway, how are Aria and the kids doing?"

Drage appreciated the change of subject and sighed. "Aria is doing well. She usually has her hands full with the kids, but she stays happy. Apollo has sadly taken a liking to expensive food, and Ace is a real handful."

"And what about Alison?"

Drage smiled. "You should see the way she smiles. You

really should, Mom." He looked out at the clear ocean around them. "I never saw myself being this much of a fatherly figure, you know. I mean, sure, I thought I would have kids someday. Who doesn't? But it was just an idea, not something . . . real, I guess."

Elizabeth laughed at his explanation. "Well, you are *really* a father now—of three kids, no less. Just be sure to raise them as well as I raised you."

However, at these words, Drage grimaced. He had every intention of raising his kids a little differently. When he had been growing up, he had been without a fatherly influence. His father had been in Gevás his whole life. Also, his mother had not been strict enough on following the right path. As he had experienced growing up, his heart had fallen easily to the Darkness, and he did not want the same to happen to his own children. He wanted to raise them fully in the Light. He had been raised right in several regards, and for that, he was grateful to his mother, but she was not perfect. "Oh, I know," he lied.

A green screen filled his vision, catching him off guard. *"Hey Drage, the code wasn't as bad as I thought! I finished it!"*

Drage ran over. "Feranx, what is it? What have you found out?"

Feranx was typing away frantically trying to get as much information across as quickly as possible. *"The one we destroyed was not Cronus 624 but Cronus 623, the second strongest of the models. However, just by disabling the two that we did, we have slowed the rate of Ragnarok exponentially! Once we take out 624, the program will be terminated."*

"This guy should be easy. I mean, how hard can it be? All we need is for your screen to get near it for a few seconds, and problem solved."

Feranx rubbed the underside of his beak in slight disbelief. *"I don't know, Drage . . . The one we just went against was pretty strong. We are not going against an offshoot this time.*

This will be the real thing, your program intertwined with the most powerful of Darkness. The last thing you want to do is underestimate it."

In understanding, Drage nodded. "Alright, fair enough. Can you use it to create a Gate to 624?"

Feranx nodded. *"Shouldn't be a problem."*

Elizabeth begged for information, "Drage, what is it? What is he saying?"

"It doesn't matter," said a voice behind them, one that only Drage had heard before. "None of you are going to get close to Cronus 624."

All three of them turned to face the newcomer, a stranger in a brown robe. Drage smirked. "I wondered when you would show yourself, Y'mordi scum."

16
Spade, the Mysterious Stranger

"D ID WE CHANGE ERAS again?" Aria asked, trying to understand the *mysteria* that Matthew had used.

"Yes," he responded. "We are in the era in which the Seeker of Paradise lived, 600 years before our time. Somewhere here, he is seeking Paradise, I guess. The question is how to find him."

Lilian asked, "Well, you said you found a book on him, did you not, Aria?"

"Yes . . ."

"Maybe we could find the author of that book more easily than finding the Seeker." Lilian smiled as she offered this simple tip. The mystery surrounding Ace was not as fierce and compelling to her as it was to Drage, Matthew, and Aria, but she was interested nonetheless.

Aria shook her head. "I don't remember who wrote it. I should have thought to remember it." Her eyes lowered. "How are we going to find him?"

"Perhaps," began Matthew, "we could do something to let him find us. Whatever we do though, it has to be relatively subtle. We do not want the attention of the Y'mordi.

What could we do that Ace would pick up, but the Y'mordi wouldn't?"

"What about a Time spell?" Lilian offered.

"A Time spell? Oh yeah, my dad said that Ace could use Time more effectively than any of the Keepers could. Perhaps if I could just create a surge through this era, Ace would feel it and come to the source." He had told Aria and Lilian about seeing his father again and about his true genetic background. He wanted to tell Drage. Somehow, telling his brother things finalized the status in his mind. It was not that he needed his brother's approval, but it still comforted him to know that there were no secrets between them.

He let his heart feel for the stream of Time, and its compelling aura lured him to sink into its depths. He resisted the powerful urge and just touched the surface of that stream. He had never created a surge in the stream, but he figured that this would be the only way to do so. At first, a trickle of his *mysteria* entered the stream, making it glow in his heart. Then, it increased in brightness as he strengthened the amount he put into the stream. In a quick burst, he released *mysteria,* and the stream of Time vibrated with his energy in waves. If Ace was truly in this era and was as adept at Time as his father had led him to believe, then Ace would have sensed Matthew's presence by now.

"Alright, if he doesn't think it's a trap, he will be here soon." They were still inside one of the meeting rooms in the Palace of Light. If Ace did arrive, Aria realized they would need to relocate in case someone did walk into the room. There was no point creating unnecessary complications. However, they were all nervous now. Aria and Matthew had waited so many years to know who this mysterious stranger was, and now they might finally learn the answers.

"Matthew, Aria, Lilian—what are the three of you doing here?" They turned in surprise to see a man in a black robe with a hood pulled over his face standing in front of a Darkness-based Gate that had appeared in the room. He continued, not moving, "You are supposed to be in your own time. This is against the laws of Time, Matthew. You should know that."

However, Matthew knew he was not breaking a single one of them. "Are you Ace Helius?"

The man was silent. Aria said, "Hey, people are coming down here. I can sense people coming from a few rooms away. Do we want to continue this chat elsewhere?"

Matthew did not. He froze time outside of the room. "Care to answer me?" he demanded.

"Yes, I am Ace Helius." Everyone stood stark still, the three Guardians of Light taking in Ace the Seeker of Paradise and Aria's son. "This is not your time, so why are you here?"

Aria put a hand to her mouth. "You're . . . my son, after all?"

Ace snarled, and Matthew felt a dark gaze through that hood piercing his heart. "Matthew, you might know the laws of Time, but how well does she?"

Matthew replied in a flat tone, "What makes the Prince of Light hide in the shadows like this? What has made you snap so at your mother and your uncle?" Then, Matthew felt a surge in the Time stream himself, and Aria and Lilian were frozen solid in the spell. He clenched his teeth. "You stopped time for them, too? What was the need for that?"

"What was the need for bringing them along if you knew that they could not be responsible with the powers that Time grants? However, I suppose you can ask what you need of me. You are one of the Keepers, after all, are you not?"

Matthew grimaced. "You know very well that I am."

Ace gestured to the seats in the council meeting room. "Shall we have a seat? I am anxious to hear what knowledge you seek from me."

Complying, Matthew sat in the chair opposite and began, "What is Paradise, and why do you seek it?"

Ace crossed his black-sleeved arms across his chest. "Huh, I told you about that when you first came to Gevás, and you kept that little bit with you for a while." When he noticed Matthew's blank expression, he decided to answer the question. "Though all five of the worlds were born into this universe with hearts connected, they will not always be so. Each world experiences a Climax, a point of no return where a master conflict can decide the fate of the world for the rest of its existence. When all of the worlds have passed their Climaxes, a sixth world, Paradise, will appear only to a select few. Each world has some legend regarding what is on Paradise. Many say that it is your dreams made reality. Others say that Paradise is an eternal garden, a place of new beginnings and everlasting hope."

"Why do you seek it, Ace?"

"I have my reasons, and none of them are ones I am willing to discuss with you. I am assuming you have more questions, though?"

"Yeah, how did you find us on Earth? How did you know we were going to be attacked by the Shadows?"

Standing, Ace approached the large windows in the back of the room. "Well, I had not intended to help you. In actuality, I had been in that era, tracking down a werewolf. As I did, I found the Y'mordi. It was a little hard for me to get through Elizabeth's barrier since it protected the community from those with tremendous Darkness in their hearts. Nevertheless, I made it through the barrier in time to get Aria out of there, but by the time I arrived at your house, the Shadows had already surrounded the place. I'm sure you remember that it took me little effort to take them out, but I can tell you that Pullatus, or Y'tal as he is known to the Y'mordi, was far from happy about my little visit. As it turns out, I am one of the loopholes in the stream of Time. The Keepers clearly were not too happy about that either, as you can imagine."

Matthew nodded in understanding. "Yeah, I will bet

they were not happy about that at all. So," began Matthew, rising to join Ace by the window, "do you serve the Darkness, or the Light?" He felt it was one of the more important questions now. Though Ace had clearly helped them on numerous occasions, he had always worn the black robe of the Y'mordi and used spells of Darkness. Even his Gate had been constructed from the shadows.

At first, Ace was silent. After a few seconds of that silence, he sighed and responded, "I belong to neither. I neither walk the road of the saint nor the road of the assassin. I am a rogue, and what's more important, I am an illusion."

Matthew shook his head. "You said that last time, too. I thought you had meant it was because you were treading through a different era. Is that not the case?"

"No, it is not. I am less real than you could probably fathom. In all honesty, that is a mystery that Aria could solve more easily than you could, but I am not going to give her the opportunity. Once I unfreeze the flow of Time, I am leaving this era, myself. I sought the werewolf here as well, but he was just not here, either. I have one more era I need to visit, and then I am returning to my own time."

"When is that?"

Ace smiled beneath his hood. "You know better than to ask that question, Matthew."

"You do not call me uncle, and you do not call Aria your mother. Did you leave your family as well? Have you separated all connections with them?"

Then, Ace's tone grew more solemn. "No, I could not do that." He turned to face Aria. "I miss her. I wish I could go back to when I was just a boy and run into her arms, fade into her embrace, and lose all worry. I wish it were that easy." He sighed. "But, she is not my mother. Because of our differences in era, the Aria I see now is nothing but a memory."

Matthew stepped closer to Ace and hesitated. He ignored his nervousness and put his hand on Ace's shoulder.

"Are you alone?"

Ace turned his head so that Matthew could see a bright smile on his face, but none of the features above that. "And that is the right question, Matthew. Sadly, I don't have a good answer. On this world, I will always be alone, for evermore. Four more worlds of loneliness, and I should be in Paradise."

They both sensed a presence moving toward them despite the solidity of time. The doors opened, and another figure in black stood there. The figure spoke quickly and in a gruff voice, "Hey, I've been looking for you! We need to get out of here. Wulfgar *was* here, and he has moved on to— Who is this?"

Ace lowered his head. "As if you don't already know . . ."

Matthew raised his raven-engraved staff and ventured, "Excuse me, but who are you?"

Just as quickly as Matthew had brought out his own weapon, the newcomer held out his hand, and a silver katana appeared in it. It glowed with a magnificent blue light, and Matthew immediately recognized it to be the Sword of Destiny. Though its form had changed, its hilt and glow were definitely the same. "How is that—possible?" Matthew asked in disbelief.

The mysterious stranger explained, "It is possible solely because I will it to be so, Master Helius. The Sword of Destiny has not chosen me to be its greatest wielder, but it has taken a liking to me nonetheless, and I am obliged to wield it. Spade, we need to get out of here, now!"

Matthew raised an eyebrow, looking to the man he thought was Ace. "Spade?"

The man he thought to be Ace sighed. "Yeah, I lied. I am not Ace. He's Ace. My name is Spade Helius. I told you: I am an illusion, and I am not meant to exist."

The real Ace added, "And don't you forget it. Come on. We need to go."

"Wait!" Matthew implored. "Who are you?"

Without even summoning a Gate, the two were gone. Matthew could not sense their hearts anywhere, so it was not that they had become invisible. They were just gone, completely vanished. "What just . . . ?"

"Matthew, where did he go?" Aria asked behind him.

He turned to see that time had unfrozen for everyone. Lilian asked, "He froze time, did he not? For us?"

"Yes, he did, and I feel more confused if anything."

"Matthew, so who is this Spade character, and who was the other guy?"

"I told you: I don't know. Why would he lie like that? It makes me wonder how credible all the other stuff he said was. Could Spade just be a nickname, perhaps? No, I cannot believe that the way he talked about you was not a yearning for a past relationship. I do not know. It is so confusing."

Lilian came over to him and held his hands in hers. "Matthew, do not worry about it so much. You learned at least some things. You now know what Paradise is and how it can be found. You know that these people are not enemies, and you know that this stranger can wield the Sword of Destiny. Those are pretty powerful facts."

Aria rolled her eyes in her own frustration. "Yes, but those facts left pretty powerful questions, too. How are we going to find him now?"

Matthew shook his head. "I do not think we will. I think that was the last time we will see that guy, Ace or Spade, in a different era from our own. We will just have to see if Ace grows up to be this mysterious character or not." When he noticed Aria bite her lip and look downward, he asked, "What's wrong? You look like something else is on your mind."

"Yeah . . . kind of . . . It's just that I recognized something else about Ace—I mean Spade."

"What is it?"

"Well, I think he is part of another mystery actually. He

revealed something without meaning to."

"Oh?" Matthew asked.

"I will explain later. For now, we have other things to worry about: namely, what we are going to do with Valdridge once we get back to our time." She trailed off, her eyes lowering. "I sure hope Drage is doing okay . . ."

While Lilian and Aria discussed the problem of Master Valdridge, Matthew sat on the roof of the castle alone. His thoughts were going in a million directions, and none of them concerned the politics of the Emperor's Council. Since speaking to the Keepers, he had felt the itch to transform into a raven again and just fly off into the sea—a foolish venture. He was more than satisfied with his life, so why did he want wings so badly?

He wrapped his arms around his legs and rested his chin on his knees. He was certainly content with the way things were, but having the pressures of an Emperor of Light were really just too much. He now had more information on the Seeker of Paradise, but he did not know what to do with it. With so much new responsibility, he felt helpless to the powers that surrounded him. Relaxing his feelings, he felt for *mysteria* and created a current with a Wind spell, making the sea revolve around him. Even such simple tricks as these were comforting to him. He found his inner peace here in the middle of the waves, and inner peace was necessary for effective thinking. He considered Master Valdridge. What Darkness had enveloped his heart? What mysteries enshrouded his past? He could not begin to guess.

"Hey, what are you doing up here?" Lilian asked, using a Gate to appear by his side. She sat down beside him and held his rough hand in her soft, pale hands.

Matthew sighed. "Just thinking, I suppose."

"About what? What is on your mind?" She wrapped an arm around his neck and leaned her own head against his shoulder. "Tell me."

"There are so many mysteries now. There could be a traitor in the midst of the Emperor's Council, and we might be expecting an impending attack on the city during the disq tournament. Plus, now we are worrying about the mystery of Ace and Spade, the Seekers of Paradise. What connection does Spade have to Ace? I do not know what to do with all of this. I think I should try to find Drage on Earth."

Lilian ruffled Matthew's hair with a stray hand and muttered in his ear, "Why do you not use your abilities? You could talk to Lord Helius instantly. Just change time to a little while before he left and talk to him about what you should do. Then, erase his memory of the moment. Could that work?"

Matthew's eyes widened at the brilliant solution. "Lilian, that is a great idea!" He grabbed her head in his hands and brought his lips to hers, kissing the outline of her mouth tenderly before standing. "I will be right back, okay?" he said, preparing to travel the stream of Time once again.

Lilian stood up as well and said, "Alright, but when you get back, I want to ride with you. We have all the time in the world, and I want to have a moment with you before we get back to our time fully."

"Ride with you?"

She smiled in the way that only a true love could smile. "You cannot expect me to believe that now that you have flown once, you do not seek to try it again? You fly, and I run. Do you not want to experience the great open sea with me?"

Matthew gave her a tight hug. "You know I do. I will be right back."

"Drage, is that you?"

His brother jumped. "Hey, Matt, what are you doing here? You are not even supposed to be here until tomorrow morning!" They were in the computer room, where DATA resided. "How did you even know about this place?"

"Drage, listen to me. I am coming from a few days from now. I learned how to travel through Time, and something terrible happened once you left for Earth."

"Left for Earth? I—?" When Drage realized how serious Matthew's face was, he stopped. "What is it, Matt?"

"Do not ask any really pressing questions. I will try to explain the situation as best as I can, and then I need your advice. Then, I am wiping your memory of this whole conversation, okay?"

Drage swallowed. He did not feel particularly keen about having his memory altered. "Sure."

Matthew took a deep breath before beginning. "Alright, so here's what happens. When you leave, you make me take over the responsibilities of being Emperor of Light for just a few days, but things go awry. For starters, Aria believes that there is a Darkness that is messing with Master Valdridge. We are trying to figure out a way to solidify the Council's voting him out of the group."

Drage muttered under his breath, "That traitorous snake . . . I knew he was up to something." He considered what Matthew was saying for a moment and wanted to ask a hundred questions, but he remembered Matthew's words and said, "Fine, have my signature." He found a scrap metallic sheet nearby and inscribed some words on it, giving Matthew his vote to remove Valdridge. Then, he placed an Imperial Seal on it, making his word solid and final. "That's one problem down, right?"

With a nod, Matthew smiled. "Yes, it most certainly is. The next problem is of the Emperor Regin. He accepts the truce for the disq tournament, and then he plans an attack on Apolis. What should I do about that?"

Again, Drage gritted his teeth, not believing he was hearing this. "I do not want you to attack him, at least not in a typical warlike fashion. If he comes demanding a real battle, bash his brains out. See if I care, but we shall play the defense. He has never been so aggressive as what you are saying. Something must have changed indeed." He walked over to DATA and caressed its metallic walls. "Matt, I want you to use DATA. I'm sure I have shown her to you already, but I want you to use her defense system to protect Apolis. She can do it . . . I'm sure of it."

Matthew grimaced at the idea of Drage's incomplete computer being the savior of Apolis, but he merely responded, "How do I use it?"

"Just say, 'Activate Genesis.' I want to show my people that I can protect them even while I am away, and DATA can do that much, I am confident. Still, do not hesitate to engage Regin directly if you have to. I want as little bloodshed in my kingdom as possible."

"Alright, sounds fair to me." Matthew ran a hand through his hair as he sighed.

"Is there anything else?"

He considered telling Drage about the mystery of Ace and Spade, but he decided it would be a waste of breath. "No, I will see you later." Using a flash of Time, he wiped Drage's memory of the past few minutes and transported himself back to 600 years prior when Lilian awaited him on the top of the Palace of Light.

"How was it?" she asked with a smile.

The current he had created seconds earlier in this time still moved around him, fading, and he laughed. He did not realize how effective and useful the powers of Time could really be. "It went amazingly. Drage gave me the power to shut down any complaints in the Council, first off. That is one problem solved. Also, he told me he wants me to use DATA to protect the city."

"Against the Emperor Regin? I suppose if he truly did build a master computer, it could be powerful enough to defend Apolis on its own. However, I will not lie. I am slightly

skeptical—only slightly, but that is still something. Do you
have faith in his plan?" Her silver eyes bore deep into Matthew's own eyes, and he felt himself question what Drage
could be thinking.

"Yes, I think that he knows what he is doing. I trust him.
The computer will work." Matthew said this last sentence
with confidence, his voice loud and strong.

Lilian nodded, satisfied with his words. "Alright, and
now we ride. Shall you freeze time for Aria so that we are not
really leaving her?"

Matthew nodded. His wife was such a thoughtful woman, and he loved her for that. "Let's go." He froze time for
Aria, who was still down in the Palace of Light, probably for-
mulating some plan or another. Now, the only things that
could move in this great big world were Lilian and him. Of
course, he allowed the water to move as well. Otherwise, it
would have been just a wall to them.

They both leaped off the top of the building, Matthew
turning into a raven and Lilian reverting to a horse. Lilian
used her own *mysteria* to manipulate the water around her,
allowing her to run across steps of Ice on her way to the gorgeous fields that sprouted white flowers outside of Apolis.
Her white mane flipped left and right across her neck, and
those white, silken strands flailed in the current when she
tossed her head to whinny at the blue sky above them.

Matthew flew only feet above her and to her left. His
wings were black as night, but the sun shimmered off them,
giving a leathery appearance to his now-small body. He
closed his beady eyes and let out a sound of his own, a cry of
joy. His talons opened and closed, embracing the feel of the
sea in his grasp.

The world soared past them: trees, flowers, animals frozen in Matthew's spell, mountains, and the occasional house.
Matthew had never felt so free. He glanced down at his lover,
his wife, his Lilian, and he smiled—as much as a bird could

smile. She looked up at him as well and communicated, "I love you, Matthew. I really do."

He clicked his tongue in pleasure and replied mentally, "And I love you. I wish this moment could never end."

Together, they rode the current, and, in that moment, they were one. He was the night, and she was his bright and shining moon.

"He seriously thinks that it can protect the city?" Aria asked. "I don't see how that will happen. He gives his skill with technology way too much credit."

Lilian said, "Do you have an idea, Lady Aria?"

"No, Lilian, I don't." She sighed. "We shall go along with Drage's plan for now, but hopefully, this is all just a silly rumor, and the Emperor Regin is not really going to attack us." She knew it was wishful thinking, but she did not see a reason to give up hope yet. If DATA failed, without the armies prepared, it would be up to the Guardians to fight off the armies of the Eastern Continent. Hopefully, Drage would be back before that attack happened.

Matthew said, "That settles it. It is time to go back to the present." Then, he noticed Aria's fists clench. "Hey, is something wrong?"

Aria shook her head. Something had clicked in her mind. She at least knew what Paradise was now, but she was not sure what that meant to her, either. Now, the thing that most concerned her about the Ace and Spade mystery was that they both had a piece of the same heart.

17

Lady Chiara

THEY WERE BACK IN their own time, back at the meeting of the Emperor's Council. Aria stormed into the room waving Drage's sealed sheet of metal. "Master Valdridge, I challenge your position in the Council. I demand your removal." All eyes shot toward her.

Valdridge roared, his face flustering, "What is this nonsense?"

Matthew nodded in agreement with Aria. "We, along with the Emperor of Light, feel it is in the best interests of the Kingdom of Helio for you to be removed from the Emperor's Council. You have acted against the good of the Council and the Emperor himself." His face stayed stern and steady.

Mistress Leona approached them and examined the sheet. She raised it up for the others to see. Once she grasped *mysteria,* it reacted with the sheet, making the Imperial Seal visible, rich with Drage's identity.

Ocrum protested, "Why are we doing this now? We have a battle soon, and we cannot be fighting on the inside like this!"

"Regardless of any protests," Mistress Leona began, a slight sly smile on her face, "the Emperor of Light has decreed it so. Valdridge, you are no longer welcome here."

Valdridge's face turned crimson, and his fists clenched. He had not expected something like this to happen all of a sudden. He wanted to unleash a barrage of *mysteria* on everyone in the room, but he knew he could not do that. Still, he could not just do nothing either. He was well aware of what the Y'mordi would do to him if he came back to them stripped of his title. "You all cannot be serious," he pleaded. "I have done nothing wrong."

Mistress Leona summoned a Gate through which Valdridge could leave the Palace and enter the city.

Shaking his head, Valdridge summoned his own *mysteria,* not able to take it any longer, and he let a bolt of Lightning fly toward Mistress Leona. The Prophet blocked the spell with a simple barrier and prepared her own counterattack, tossing the table at Valdridge by making powerful vines push the table from underneath.

Valdridge leaped over the table, showering golden arrows of pure Light down on Mistress Leona. Aria dispelled the arrows with a quick flick of her wand and then shot a fireball at him. However, it was Master Ocrum who blocked the fiery attack with a sword. It was seven against two. Though Valdridge and Ocrum threw spells as quickly as they could, the others of the Council had them bound in invisible chains of *mysteria* in seconds.

"Let me go!" Valdridge roared. As if his words had willed it, the chains dissipated into Darkness, and he threw a blast of blistering Light at Aria. She had not seen it coming with Valdridge being chained, and the blast hit her arm. She screamed in intense pain. Before anyone could attack Valdridge, he placed a hand on his chest and fired a bolt of Lightning through it, and his eyes went cold. His body fell onto the cold floor, a black mark staining the wall behind him where the Lightning had shot through his body.

The Prophets Master Marqest, Mistress Quella, and Mistress Leona ran to the collapsed Aria and beheld her blackened arm. Leona and Marqest exchanged worried looks before moving the moaning Empress.

Matthew followed them, "Hey, is she going to be alright?" He could not believe what had just happened. In one second, Valdridge had badly injured Aria and killed himself. However, he knew that the suicide meant nothing if Valdridge had really been controlled. If that was the case, then Valdridge was just a body for the possessor to use, and that person was still out there somewhere.

Marqest ignored Matthew's question and spoke with Mistress Leona. "Can you heal it at all? You are the Prophet of Nature. If anyone can, it is you, Mistress Leona."

She shook her head. "The spell went right through to the bone. All the flesh is dead, cancerous. If we let it fester, it could kill her. You know what we have to do, Master Marqest."

The older man nodded grimly. "I will do it, then. I am good with such things." Without saying another word, he prepared his concentration for the spell he was about to perform. Mistress Leona felt for *mysteria* and focused on keeping Aria's mind away from pain, removing all sense of feeling from her body. She knew that this was going to hurt. Then, Marqest grasped quite a bit of *mysteria* and felt his form shift to Water, preparing a deadly sharp current—sharp enough to cut through flesh and bone. He let the Water spell blast right through the top of Aria's arm, severing it from her shoulder.

Despite Mistress Leona's attempts to make Aria feel less pain, Aria still cringed. The spell had worked well for Aria, but she would feel more pain as the day went on. Mistress Leona could not hold that spell forever. Marqest cauterized the wound with a rapid Fire spell, and Aria clenched her teeth in pain again. Still, she did not say anything. Every piece of her wanted to protest Mistress Leona and Marqest doing anything else to her, but she knew that anything they did would be for her own good.

Marqest muttered to Mistress Leona and Matthew. "She should be fine . . . minus the arm, of course." He stood and faced the other members of the Emperor's Council. They stared at Marqest sadly and then looked to the trapped Ocrum. He still struggled in his enchanted chains, desperate to escape, but he was trapped well.

"What a waste . . ." Mistress Leona said, breaking the silence. "We could have found out what Darkness was possessing him."

Gradually, Aria's eyes lowered as Mistress Leona cast a spell to put her to sleep. Matthew said, "Drage has a plan for protecting the city. He does not want to make a direct attack on the Emperor Regin, but rather wants to use a secret weapon of his." He knew that the Council did not know about DATA, but now he would have to tell them regardless of what secrecy Drage wanted.

Mistress Leona and Master Marqest gave him a look that demanded him to continue.

"Drage has created a master computer called DATA, and it has the ability to defend this city by itself."

Marqest raised an eyebrow. "That is quite the claim. How have you communicated with his Majesty?"

Matthew responded, "I traveled through time to right before he left and talked to him about what would happen. He does not know about it now because I wiped his memory afterward. Still, his orders remain the same, and we are to follow them immediately."

"It actually does not sound like a half bad idea," Marqest said, stroking his silvery beard. "If we can show Regin what this computer can do for defense, he would be terrified to see what it could do for offense, and he should retreat immediately—a battle won without force. His Majesty is quite clever. Of course, this is all assuming that the computer *does* work as well as he hopes. We do not know what types of forces Regin will be bringing into this battle."

A knock rang through the room, and all heads turned to the humongous double doors of the throne room. Matthew walked over to it, being the one who was supposed to be in charge. Once he opened the doors, a white-robed servant entered the room. His back was bent low, and his face was twisted into a silent fright. "Master Matthew, an anima named Nilram is here to see his Majesty. He says it is an important affair of the Enigma Brigade."

Matthew nodded. "Send him in."

A massive, golden-furred lion leaped into the room over the servant's head. "Where is his Majesty?" he roared.

Matthew communicated without words, "He is not here. He has asked me to take his place. What is the problem?"

The lion anima looked taken aback by the mental response. While for everyone else in the room, the two just stared at each other, they spoke to each other clearly. "The Captain of the Enigma Brigade has been captured by King Lomeo. The people there are plotting against his Majesty and might start a rebellion soon."

Matthew's eyes widened. "Where are the other Brigadiers now?"

"They are waiting outside, my Lord. You have got to do something!"

"This could not have happened at a worse time . . ." Matthew communicated these words, but he said them rhetorically. "What is your name, anima?"

The lion sat back on his haunches and bowed deeply before Matthew. "I am Nilram."

"Alright, Nilram, if we are going to save the Captain, we must be quick. The Emperor Regin shall attack us soon. How many are waiting outside?"

He started walking with Nilram to the exit and sent a

thought to Lilian, "Hey, you can come, too. We have to go west a bit. King Lomeo has imprisoned the Captain of the Enigma Brigade." Lilian responded by reverting into her horse form and trotting beside Matthew. He turned to the Council and said aloud, "Hey, take care of Aria. I should be back before dark. Master Marqest, can you handle standard defense preparations while I am gone?" The old man gave a nod to Matthew.

Exiting the palace with a lion to one side and a horse to his other, he approached the three humans who were waiting outside. "Are you three other members of the Brigade?" he asked.

Then, he recognized Gaspard. The swordsman smiled and said, "Master Matthew, it would be a pleasure to see you again if only it were in better circumstances." The two had chatted only briefly in the past with Drage, and Matthew had forgiven him for his fighting the laws of Apolis. Gaspard had not been a truly evil person, only misguided.

"I agree. Now, we must hurry to Lomeo's keep." He drew his staff and tapped it against the ground, summoning a Gate of Wind, the air bubbling through the water from the Gate. "I have been given orders by the Emperor of Light himself to take his place in his temporary absence, and you are to take orders from me as you would from him."

"Yes, sir!" the Brigade chanted in unison. Matthew was far from the commanding type. He had had professional training at the Capital years ago, and he had led many fierce battles over the years. However, he simply did not have the authority that Drage wielded.

He charged into the Gate with Lilian and the Enigma Brigade close behind him. As they moved, he sensed Lilian create brown robes around all of them, giving them disguises in Terin.

The main street of the capital of Varyx was bustling. People crowded the street from left to right and as far as the eye could see in either direction. They chattered, and Matthew could hear occasional words such as "rebellion," "war," "scumbag anima," "foolish Emperor," and even "kill him." Up ahead, he could barely make out a wooden scaffold, a platform on which a handful of people stood. It seemed to be the real center of attention here.

He pushed his way forward through the crowd, saying "Excuse me!" when he could and just pushing others when he could not. He needed to see what was going on, especially if such black words were hot on the tongues of the civilians.

Once they were within sight of the scaffold, Gaspard put a hand on Matthew's shoulder. "Look, there's the Captain." He pointed at a man in a white uniform of sorts. It held a red phoenix on its front, the same emblem as the Phoenix Regiment that Aria commanded. He was kneeled on the wooden planks, and his face was grim with resolution. Clearly, his hands had been tied behind his back, but he had an air of dignity about him.

Behind him stood the fearsome executioner, a tall and muscular man. He was shrouded in black, and his muscles bulged against the cloth. His face was dark, with a few scars lacing his skin in numerous places. Neither his build nor his scars were what intimidated Matthew, though. It was the axe he held in his hands that sent shivers up Matthew's spine.

Another person stood on the podium, King Lomeo. He was dressed in fine, golden robes and wore a great crown on his head, but Matthew saw through the disguise. Gaspard muttered, "That is not King Lomeo. That is one of the Y'mordi."

"Yes, I know. It is Ixion, and he's come back to mess things up again."

It had been so long since Matthew had seen the wicked Y'mordi known as Ixion, and, apparently, Ixion had been preparing for this moment for a long time. Then, Matthew realized how rigged all of this truly was. The Y'mordi set up a trap on Earth for Drage, and while he was gone, they prepared a rebellion in Varyx. "I wonder if they have something to do with the Emperor Regin's breaking of the truce . . ." he muttered. "Valdridge . . ." That had to be the answer to all of this chaos. That snake had probably been working for the Y'mordi, giving them information and telling them all of Drage's plans and actions. This war was between the Y'mordi and Drage, not the East and the South.

"We have come to the end of an era!" Ixion roared to the crowd. Matthew begged for the crowd to boo him off the scaffold, but they cheered, deluded by his poisonous persuasions. "And with the death of this era, we begin anew. The time of the Emperor of Light has ended, and we shall bring to power the rule of humans once more. Nonhumans shall quake before us, as they did when Apolis was pure and Lord Mentiris ruled." Again, the crowds cheered as if Ixion's words were their salvation from an eternal darkness.

Gaspard pleaded, "What's the plan, Master Matthew?"

Matthew noticed how quickly Gaspard reached for the sword at his hip. It looked to be a long katana. He eyed it with familiarity. "Is that not the blade of Maksimilian, the former captain of the Brigade?"

"It was, Master Matthew," Gaspard said with pride. "He stole my Sword, and I simply returned the favor."

Matthew shook his head, displeased. Still, governing the Brigade's manners was Drage's job and not his. "The plan is for us to hurt as few people as possible. We need to expose Ixion for the traitor he is. If we just kill him, the people will still hate us. It is crucial to get them back on our side by humiliating Ixion."

"What is the plan?" Lilian repeated, meaning that the plan was not concrete enough to actually act upon.

"We have to make Ixion reveal his true form. I cannot challenge him to a duel because he does not have pride. I cannot negotiate with him. He is foolish."

"Is he a gambler?"

Matthew looked Lilian in the eyes. "He is. We could definitely use that." He turned back to Ixion. A game was going to be how he defeated Ixion, and Time was going to be how he won that game. Still, the question was of which game he should choose. It did not help that Matthew was not much of a gambler himself. Drage had went to some of the gamerooms of Apolis a few times, but Matthew had not particularly enjoyed himself. Gambling seemed vile no matter which world it was. He shook his head. Whatever game they played would have to have Ixion's approval, anyways.

With a sigh, he froze all time except for Lilian, Ixion, and himself. Lilian and Matthew stepped forward and climbed onto the scaffold. Ixion was dumbfounded. "Ixion," Matthew began, "I want to challenge you to a game. You have terrorized this city long enough, but I will not kill you if you are up to my challenge."

Ixion was taken aback at first, but then he relaxed. "A game, huh? What do I get if I win?"

Matthew had known this was going to come up. "You get a Spirit Sword: the Steel of Life."

At this offer, Ixion's eyes lit up. "Okay, what do you get if you win?"

"I get to fight you." Ixion's smile faded. "Right here on this scaffold with everyone watching. You can shift to your true form. I would hate for anyone to think you were foolish by staying in all that kingly finery."

"Fine with me. What is the game?"

Matthew shrugged. "Your call. This is your city after all."

"That's right!" Ixion laughed. "It is my city. So, I shall hide a blue rose in the city, somewhere in the city. Hold on one second." The Y'mordi summoned a Gate and disappeared somewhere in the city, but Matthew could not sense where he had reappeared. He heavily considered unfreezing time and escaping with the Captain of the Enigma Brigade, but he knew he needed to defeat Ixion at his wicked game. Finally, Ixion came back through his Gate. "Now, you will have an hour to find the flower—starting now!" Ixion summoned an hourglass and set it down on the scaffold.

Matthew ran away from him, dodging the solid people and grasping *mysteria* fully. How was he going to find such a flower using his Time spells?

An idea came to him as he ran. He could keep a general awareness of Time to see where Ixion had been in the last few minutes. Such a search would warn him if he stopped by the place where Ixion had put the blue rose. Still, he could not make such an awareness so large that it covered the whole city. He would have to come across that area by chance, meaning he needed to run as fast as he could and cover as much ground as possible.

Equipping a Time spell to speed himself, he raced through the city, using an aura of awareness that extended about twenty yards around him in all directions, an invisible orb of sensitivity that should alert him to Ixion's last Gate. This city was too large to cover in an hour, though. He was relying mostly on luck. It was also hard because the people were all frozen solid, so it was as if he were maneuvering through a dense thicket. It was not merely running he was having to worry about. He also had to dodge and weave through the people. The workout brought him to exhaustion after ten minutes, and he still had no sign of the blue rose.

Already, his breath was becoming ragged, no longer relaxed and slow, but choppy and short. Each step warranted an exhale, and then an obvious idea came to him. He stopped in his tracks and froze time for both Ixion and his hourglass. That would give him an infinite amount of time, though he only really needed enough time for him to find the blue rose.

He sighed in relief. Now, he could find the flower without worrying about a time limit. He was starting to love being a Keeper of Time. It had more benefits than he had imagined. Shifting into a raven, he soared through the water, maintaining his orb of awareness.

The water chilled his feather-covered flesh, and each sweeping current brought him close to shivers. Still, he focused his full energy on enlarging his orb and locating the Gate that Ixion had used to hide the flower. As Matthew soared higher, he was amazed at the massive forests that surrounded the city. Those had certainly not been there the last time he had come to Terin. Some vestiges of the forest extended themselves through the boundaries of the city, allowing vines and bushes to add a wild side to the outermost buildings. He curved his body in the direction of the closest edge of the city. Perhaps if he circled the edge of the city, he would find the trace of the Gate and the flower in the undergrowth. Ixion had said it would be *in* the city, so it could not possibly be in the outer forests. That did not stop him from hiding it in the inner forest.

As his black body sped toward the walls of the city, he let out a long breath. Flying was so much easier than running, and it was faster as well. Within seconds, he was at the walls, yet his orb showed him no sign of a Gate having been there moments before.

Seeing the world through this Time spell was strange. In his heart, he could feel the remnants of people all around him: he was sensing what had happened in these places for the past few hours. Though he was limiting his senses to the past few minutes when Ixion would have used the Gate, he could still catch the slightest traces of what had occurred in these places before that. He continued to fly around the city, skimming the outer limits. Still, he found no trace of a Gate, and there was certainly no blue rose.

While he flew, he thought about his father and his newly discovered heritage. He was part-anima and part-human, and his son probably was, too. It was clear to him now that his son was more anima than human. Still, what animal would William be? A raven? There were good chances of it if William was indeed to be the last Keeper of Time. Another question was if Ace was really Drage and Aria's son. If Ace was, then would he learn the ways of Time through William? There were so many possibilities there, and Matthew could not fathom which one would actually occur. He sighed again as he completed his circuit of the city. The flower was certainly not on the edges of the city. He would have to look deeper into the streets and alleys.

His head turned to the massive castle that served as the centerpoint of the capital of Varyx. Having another clear goal in mind, he flew toward it, flapping his wings a little harder to push himself higher into the sea. His orb became less confusing, the higher he went. The transports of the past tapped his senses lightly, but it was overall clearer.

He could see the whole city from there. It was not as if he could make his orb cover the entire area from there, but at least it gave him a vantage point from which he could see his next destination. Then, he felt it. On the very top of the castle, a Gate made its way into his senses: it was where Ixion had placed the blue rose, lying on a high windowpane. Matthew clicked his tongue against his beak in joy as the small blue petals came into view. Snapping the flower into his beak, he flew back toward Ixion, Lilian, the Enigma Brigade, and the rebellious citizens of Terin.

As he landed, he shifted back into his human form, the flower falling into his open hand. With his other hand, he clicked his staff against the ground, and time resumed itself for Ixion and Lilian again. "Alright, Ixion, here is your blue rose."

"You . . . you cheated!" Ixion stammered, but Matthew was not going to hear any complaints. Immediately, the Keeper unfroze time, and everyone gasped as Matthew raised his raven-engraved staff against Ixion, their king Lomeo.

However, Ixion was not going to let himself fall so easily.

Shifting into his black robes, he summoned his two long daggers and blocked the staff strike. As Matthew twisted the staff around to strike Ixion with the other end, Ixion jumped over the twirling wood. While Matthew's attacks were flowing and rapid, Ixion's counterstrikes were choppy and loose, without focus. Each maneuver was a struggle for Ixion, though he had already successfully defeated both Mali and Randir not too many days ago.

The crowd was at a loss as to for whom they should cheer. Though they had wanted their king to win, seeing him in the garb of one of the Y'mordi, they were more willing to accept the stranger as the good guy, there.

Matthew aimed another strike at Ixion's head, and to fend it off, Ixion manipulated the wood scaffold on which they stood: a plank came to life and grew a branch that moved upward, halting Matthew's attack mid-swing. This parry gave Ixion the time to make an attack of his own. Before the battle had even started, Matthew had planned on not using *mysteria* to aid him unless Ixion did the same. By reanimating that part of the scaffold, Ixion had broken that implied truce. Matthew froze the dagger in time and struck Ixion's chest roughly with his staff, knocking him to the edge of the scaffold.

"You would kill these people's king?" Ixion snarled, hoping to manipulate his audience.

Matthew shook his head. "That will not work, Ixion." He turned to face the crowd. "People of Terin, I hate to inform you that your so-called king is none other than one of the legendary Lords of the Shadows. He has been fooling you from the start, and he is probably responsible for your past king's death. Do you stand by him while he cowers so? Or do you stand by the Light that your kingdom has preached and followed for centuries, as brothers to the nation of Helio?" He had never been a real speaker. Still, he was not in the mood to let Ixion win this battle by manipulating the people of Varyx.

Ixion noticed the people's expressions become thoughtful, considering his betrayal, and he leaped at Matthew. He just had not expected for Matthew to freeze him in place and then swing his staff directly into his face with full power.

The force of the strike rang through Matthew's arm as Ixion was thrown backward along with a spray of blood from his nose. A few brave people in the crowd cheered, and the Enigma Brigade and Lilian came to stand on the scaffold. Gaspard went to free his captain, and Lilian tapped her husband's shoulder, "Matt, what are we going to do with him? Take him back to Apolis and put him in the Labyrinth?"

Before Matthew could answer, Ixion crawled onto his knees, blood still trickling from his broken nose and mouth. "You fool . . . you would cross one of the Y'mordi as if it were child's play? You truly have a death wish, then." He placed a hand on the scaffold, opening a Gate in the wood itself, and he fell into it. It closed behind him before Matthew or the others could do anything about it. He was gone.

Matthew turned to face the crowd. All eyes were planted on him, imploring him to tell them what to do next. Even Lilian and the Brigade were looking to him for guidance. He felt a lump rise in his throat. He was just not leader material, and now he had the politics of a whole kingdom in front of him. His first instinct was to tell the people to continue about their normal lives until later, when Drage could sort this mess out, but he could not just let a whole people live without law. "Did the old king have any descendants?" he asked the crowd with anxiety. Everyone turned to look around, chatting with their neighbors, but that chattering hit Matthew like a roar.

Finally, one voice called out above the swelling noise, "Here's his niece!" It was a young man who had called out to Matthew. The man was probably five or six years younger than Matthew himself and wore simple workman's clothes: a white shirt that clung to his skin, showing his scrawny frame, tight black pants, and durable but filthy black shoes. He held the arm of a girl who looked about Matthew's age, but could have been a little older. "This is his niece!"

Matthew addressed the woman herself, "Excuse me, my lady, could you please come up to the scaffold please?" He tried to imply that he did not want the man to accompany her, and his stupid grin faded from his face as he realized the implication.

The woman herself was dressed finely. In a white dress, she made her way through the murmuring crowd. Her expression was blank and maybe slightly fearful. Matthew offered her his hand as she came to the scaffold, and he helped her onto it. "Alright, so are you indeed the former king's niece, my lady?" he asked gently.

She nodded with nervousness. "I am, but—I do not know how to lead a whole country! I was never taught: the king's son was the heir, but Lomeo—the Lord of the Shadows—took over, and during his rule, that son died. I may be the king's niece, and I did live in the castle as well, but I was not taught everything about ruling. Forgive me . . ."

Matthew clasped her hand in assurance. "My lady, do not worry about it. If it would please you, I shall summon one of the members of his Majesty's Council, and that member shall assist you until his Majesty himself can handle the situation. Would that be alright with you? If you do not think you are fit for even that role, then that is perfectly understandable."

The lady looked out upon the crowd before muttering, "Someone has to step up, yes?"

Matthew swept a hand through his hair. "I think so."

"If it is indeed for only a couple of days, and I would be with a member of his Majesty's Council, I think that would be fine . . ."

"Gaspard," Matthew said, summoning the Brigadier. "Return to the Palace and inform the Council that I need one of them to come and assist Lady . . . ?" He turned to the lady, imploring her to give him her name.

"I am called Chiara, my Lord." She said the last part hesitantly. It was then that Matthew realized he had not yet told any of these people who he was, though it was quite clear he was in league with the Emperor of Light.

He turned back to Gaspard. "Yes, inform them that Lady Chiara needs immediate assistance. I shall stay here and await your return. Go," he implored. Instantly, Gaspard summoned a Gate and disappeared into Helio. Matthew looked around and beheld the anxious crowd. "Um . . . Lady Chiara, do you think you could . . . ?"

She blushed at the suggestion. "Of course, my lord." Facing the crowd, she said, "If I may have your attention please, I shall be taking temporary leadership over the kingdom until a more suitable ruler may take the throne. For now, you may return to your normal activities. Thank you!" With that, the crowd dispersed, but the murmuring became a booming chaos of chattering. Chiara turned to Matthew, "How was that?"

Offering an unsure smile, he said, "It seemed fine to me. Now, if you will excuse me, Lady Chiara, I must speak with the Captain." He mustered a polite bow before turning and approaching Captain Bryco. "Are you well, Captain?"

The other Brigadiers moved into formation after having chatted very briefly with their leader. "Yes, Lord Helius. I cannot express my gratitude to you enough. You saved both my life and this kingdom from utter ruin. I apologize for having failed his Majesty."

Matthew shook his head. "Nonsense, Captain. This kingdom is now successfully under control, and, although quite indirectly, you were the moving force behind this transition. I believe his Majesty will be quite pleased with your overall work, Captain."

"Thank you, Lord Helius," replied Bryco, making a deep

bow to Matthew. Matthew squirmed. He was not used to being treated so formally. He had still not become accustomed to people calling him a Lord yet, much less the Enigma Brigade bowing to him.

A Gate appeared, and both Gaspard and Mistress Leona walked onto the scaffold. "Mistress Leona," began Matthew, "this is Lady Chiara, the niece of the late king. I trust that you can aid her in managing this kingdom's affairs until his Majesty can assess the situation?"

Mistress Leona pursed her lips, but she nodded. They were in dangerous times, and Matthew knew she would be sorely needed at the Palace. Right now, however, Varyx had to be handled properly, or else the kingdom might be led astray as it had under Ixion's influence.

Not wasting any more time, Matthew opened a Gate, and he, Lilian, and the Brigade stepped through it to come to the gates of Apolis. Soon, the Emperor Regin would attack the city, and DATA would need to be prepared to defend Apolis.

18

Emperor in the Shadows

STORM CLOUDS TWISTED in the sky above his city. The current howled between each building and each alleyway, animating the debris and trash of millions of people. Despite the shadow the cloudy layer set on the city, the sun's beams shone through and lit up the occasional metallic skyscraper on one side. The current pushed its way through those technological behemoths and wormed its way to the castle—to his castle.

The balcony on which he stood was metal itself, though it reflected no light. It was a small extension to the castle, allowing only a few feet of space to walk with a silvery rail that guarded that whole space. The Emperor Regin's gloved hand tightened on the rail. Then, it relaxed. His body was old and weak, an ancient artifact of some primitive age enchanted by the Darkness. Yet, there was nothing primitive about the Darkness itself. It was something that Mali had failed to understand, and it was something that evaded Xarden's knowledge as well.

Still, with the Emperor Regin's full dark capabilities now in hand, the possessor found it much easier to control the body and cast aside the voice of the body's former owner. It was a terrible body, a worthless husk. All the same, even while the body was cheap and frail, the heart held such power in it, a power that even the possessor envied. It was the Darkness that came with being one of the Great Servants of the Darkness, one of the seven chosen by the Hand of the Shadows, and that meant a very close connection to the Great Lord Dagan.

The possessor could feel that power build in the Emperor Regin's soul, the power to hate, to fear, to burn, to kill. The power to unleash havoc on a billion worlds seemed to fill that heart, and the possessor intended on using every last ounce of that power. Gevás would be his. With this power, the Light would fall.

He reached his sense out to touch Mali again and snarled when he could not feel his presence. Somehow, the Y'mordi had escaped the bond the collar had on him. He probed at his spell harder. In the darkness of his heart, he could see the golden glimmer of that collar. Mali had not been able to remove it entirely, though many enchantments had been removed. With a grin, the Emperor Regin relaxed even more. While he certainly had no control over the Y'mordi now, he could still locate that particular one whenever he so chose. He was one of the first kings to actually have such power over the Y'mordi.

At the mere will of his heart, three Shadows appeared behind him and knelt. "How goes the preparation of the armies?"

The one on the right spoke in the cold, raspy voice that was characteristic of Shadows, "It goes well. The humans and Shadows have been intermingled flawlessly, and your force is now so tied to the Darkness that no army, man or Shadow, could stand against it."

The Emperor Regin sneered at that last comment. Shadows were quite heavily tied to the Darkness, being embodiments of that force itself. Therefore, it stood to reason that they would try to manipulate and use him as much as the Darkness itself would. Whether he willed it or not, the Darkness still saw him as but a tool now, nothing more than a weapon to use against the Light. He would have to show the world that he was here to stay, and he would fall no easy prey to the Darkness. "Are my people content with the shift in power?"

"No, my Lord," spoke the middle Shadow. "There is quite a lot of unrest amongst your people, and rumors fill the street. Still, they serve you."

Sneering again, the Emperor Regin waved a hand. As the Shadows faded back into Darkness, he clenched the railing again. They were all fools: the Shadows, the Y'mordi, the Guardians of Light . . . Every last one of them expected him to fail, to not be able to defeat Apolis alone. What they failed to understand was the vast amount of power he now held. Not even the Y'mordi dared come near him again.

As he looked down upon his city, he saw one battalion marching through the streets. It was composed of both his armored soldiers and the Shadows. Seeing the two groups intermingled in this way was chilling. Human and Shadow were never supposed to fight together. The Dark Lord, Dagan, had either possessed his humans when he mixed their forces with Shadows, or kept them entirely separate. However, there, in the Capital, the two were fighting alongside one another. It was scary, even for the Emperor Regin and his cold possessor.

"Hmph, these are my people, but they're just that: they're just people." Yet, even as he said it, he felt a pang of sorrow, not regret. Shadows dampened one's spirits simply by being near. His people were suffering, and he was allowing it. "They're just people," he repeated. Turning away from the scene, he re-entered his chamber.

Standing there in the shadows of his room was a short

man in a black robe. "Who are you?" the Emperor Regin demanded in a growl as he rose a hand to prepare a Dark blast.

The dark figure took a step closer with arms folded, hood well covering his face. "Hm . . . interesting . . . I never would have thought it was you possessing the Emperor Regin."

The Emperor Regin froze in his tracks. He had been discovered after all.

The figure continued, "That was quite a nasty thing you did to Mali, you know."

"Lord Y'tal," the Emperor Regin acknowledged. "He had it coming. He was becoming annoying and disobedient."

Y'tal laughed at the Emperor's words. "I see. You have certainly caused a lot of trouble, though. You have become an annoyance yourself." The current pushed into the room, swaying both the Emperor's and Y'tal's robes. The Y'mordi stepped forward to walk onto the balcony. "Still, you have this whole kingdom to yourself. You are using your treachery and your lies to destroy those Guardians of Light."

The Emperor Regin snarled, "No, I am doing this to destroy the kingdom of Helio altogether. This is not about the Guardians at all. This is about putting those anima back in their place, along with putting the Darkness back at its rightful throne." He followed Y'tal back onto the balcony. "However, if some Guardians get killed along the way, I will certainly not complain."

He raised his hands and held up seven fingers. "Draconis has returned to Sharl Drake." One finger went down. "Marqest is being watched by that Servant we have in the Emperor's Council, Valdridge, and Lilian, the filthy horse anima, is sleeping with the human Matthew." He lowered three more fingers. "Empress Helius is going to try to lead Helio alongside Matthew, and the Emperor of Light is still trapped on Earth—if he's not dead already." He lowered two more fingers such that he was only holding his pointer up now. "And last but not least is that snake, Randir." As the hand turned into a fist, he growled, "I certainly wouldn't mind if a lot of them were killed, but that is not my goal here. I will bring down Helio one way or another."

"Hm, a real politician, I see. Yet you care naught for your people?"

The Emperor Regin wanted to snap back, but his words caught in his throat. Turning away from the Y'mordi, he stepped into the room as if to ignore the dark man. "I am becoming attached to them, it seems, these people. While I was in this for power alone at first, some part of me wants to protect them, and I realize that I am not doing that now."

"Does your Darkness falter?"

Turning, he said, "What?"

"I said, 'Does your Darkness falter?' It would seem that in your becoming strong, you have also become weak and have forgotten the amount of work it took for you to become strong. Your goal is destruction. Your goal is death. Your goal is Darkness. Yet, you cower now and care for the wellbeing of your people."

The Emperor Regin sat down in his massive chair and sneered, "I fear you, Y'tal. I fear you more than you could ever realize." These words seemed to relax the Y'mordi. "But, I have found the strength of former days, and I shall use it to serve the Darkness, even if that is not serving you. The Darkness fills me. It wants to use me and twist me, as much as you want to use and twist me. You do not realize how strong a hold I have over the Emperor Regin's body. With a mere whim, I can move all the blood in his body to where I really am. True, you could stop me. But maybe not. It's a risk, Pullatus. Is it one you are willing to take?"

Quicker than the blink of an eye, Y'tal threw a shard of Darkness at the Emperor Regin that shot straight through his lower leg, the shard solidifying into the wall behind him. The Emperor Regin howled with pain as he clutched the leg and fell back against the wall.

Y'tal summoned the shard back and absorbed it fully. "Now, I have your blood, Great Servant of the Darkness. You have nothing to use against me."

The Emperor Regin glared up at the Y'mordi from his weak position on the floor, his leg still bleeding. "Heh...heh heh...that's what you think. At least I know who it was that kicked your ass back on Earth all those years ago. And that's information you will never drag out of me."

Now, Y'tal was silent and still. The current slowed to a stop. The slightest twinge of fear stabbed at the Emperor Regin's possessed heart, but he waited.

"Do you challenge me, your Majesty?"

The Emperor Regin struggled to stand with pained gasps. "No, of course not, Pullatus. However, what you need to be asking in reality is what the hell are you doing." Instead of stopping his tongue as his thoughts warned, he pushed forward. "You preach to all not to step too far into the Darkness, and you have gone even too far for yourself. You no longer seek to raise the Darkness to its potential. You seek to raise yourself, and this stranger who kicked you in the balls is your number one target. It is the only thing you see sometimes, and it brings out the flaw in you. If you obsess too much, then you will have fallen prey to the Darkness, and that stranger would have beaten you even after that fight."

He awaited his limbs to be stricken from his body or his eyes to be burned out of their sockets, but Y'tal remained still. He said not a word. He made not a movement. The current made not a movement, and the light seemed to dim outside, leaving the two of them further enshrouded in darkness. Finally, after what seemed like hours, Y'tal turned around. "Your Majesty, continue your work here. The battle begins in two days. It seems that Apolis will be expecting your attack. Valdridge is dead. I am not quite sure of how much the Council knows, but this will not be the ambush you were expecting." He threw a tremendous sword that appeared from nowhere to the Emperor Regin, who caught it in surprise and barely managed to stand upon catching it.

"What is—?"

"It is a replica of the Behemoth. It is not a perfect replica but powerful nonetheless. As long as you do not bring it across the path of the other Spirit Swords, you should be invincible with it."

"It is . . . possessed by the Darkness," the Emperor Regin managed.

"As you yourself are. As the seven Y'mordi are. We all shall find eternal freedom in the embrace of the Darkness." He summoned a Gate without the slightest movement and stepped into it, vanishing into shadows.

The Emperor Regin heaved out a massive sigh. He had just lectured the head of the Y'mordi and had only suffered an injured leg. He had been sure he was going to die. His eyes glanced down at the massive buster sword in his hands. It glowed with a faint purple light. It was certainly imbued with the powers of the Darkness, but no piece of the Great Spirit resided in this blade. If anything, the very idea of it would intimidate most he encountered.

He swung the blade forward in experimentation, and a sharp disc of Darkness shot forward, slicing the rail in two easily. He grinned to himself and stepped forward onto the balcony again. The war was almost over, but it was certainly about to go out with a bang.

Arnim lowered her hood to reveal her flowing blonde hair. "I will not let any of you get to Cronus 624, so prepare to die." She raised her two pistols and placed her arms into a position one would hold when wielding a bow. Her face was cold and held no emotion.

She watched the others tense and draw their pitiful weapons. Immediately, she could pick out the Ring of Elders as the mages who were riding their staffs. With a quick sense of the strength of them, she felt instant surprise: these mages were stronger than the average sorcerer back on Gevás. She shifted her focus to the other two individuals of interest: the Emperor of Light and his griffin mechanic. While the griffin was flying with his wings, the Emperor was riding on a screen of green light.

Her own muscles tensed as she considered her strategy. Clearly, they were already on the defensive, and she liked that. Still, it made her uneasy. Even with the advantage of being able to use *mysteria,* she wondered how much these people had learned. It certainly had to take some strength to fight the Cronus models and even fly as they were. How had they gotten this far?

To ensure that the model was destroyed and could no longer be used, she shot a bullet at the machine and changed its properties as it flew, converting it into some unknown metal that could pierce through the machine's metallic hide and ruin its insides. The sound of the gun set everyone off, and spells were instantly flying toward her. With quick Earth spells, she created platforms of Dirt in the air and leaped from one to the other, dodging the flurry of fireballs and Lightning bolts. Even in midair, she aimed her pistols in their direction and fired away at them. Her bullets were fast and deadly with accuracy, yet the Ring had everyone well-protected with invisible barriers.

Suddenly, the barrage stopped, and the Emperor of Light flew toward her on his green screen. He jumped off it to land on one of her Earth islands that was adjacent to her. None of the Ring shot a spell toward them. Arnim watched him assume the Way of the Dragon, and she resumed her stance as well.

"Why are you fighting us, Y'mordi? Why are you after Earth in the first place?" The Emperor's voice had certainly become deeper and more commanding since she had last seen him.

She grunted as she lowered her pistols. "I am fighting you to kill you. You are in the way of this planet being utterly destroyed. Stand down so that I can make this easier on you. Death comes to us all. Why make it overly painful?"

The Emperor of Light tensed. His knees bent, and his teeth clenched. "You're not going to kill any of us, filth. We're going to save this world, and you will be the only one here to die unless you move out of *our* way!" Without any further warning, he charged the Y'mordi, his Sword flashing.

With another grunt, she raised her pistols and leaped backward to dodge the Sword. She sidestepped before aiming a quick volley of shots at the Emperor, who blocked each attack without any clear effort. She snarled as her body twisted in the air. How were his reflexes so fast without the full capabilities of *mysteria* at his disposal? None of the Ring shot any spells toward her, though even their abilities were a mystery to her. Cronus 624 was supposed to have shut off all connections to *mysteria,* yet everyone here could wield *mysteria* with as much ease as if the barrier was not there at all.

She cast a rapid spell of Sand in an attempt to blind the Emperor, but he dodged the cloud. In retaliation, he swung his Sword, and a disc of blue light shot toward her. It took her little effort to create an immediate barrier of steel to block the attack.

"Dammit . . ." she muttered under her breath. "I can't even touch him. I'm just not strong enough . . ." She looked to the side and saw the Ring of Elders and the griffin watching. While she could sense the Emperor preparing an attack to destroy her barrier, she aimed one pistol in the direction of the griffin and fired a shot. The Emperor of Light was entirely oblivious to the bullet that moved in the direction of his mechanic. The Ring saw it move but had been commanded to hold and therefore did not have their typical reflexes at the ready, and they had not expected such an attack.

The griffin saw the pistol pointed at his beak. He saw the

bullet leave its barrel. To his fortune, he had already been extremely tense and ready to defend himself. As soon as he saw the pistol move in his direction, his claw moved, and a green screen moved at a speed faster than any bullet to push him upward out of the way of the shot. While Arnim focused again on Drage, Feranx soared and flipped in the air without the use of the screen, and, as he fell downward toward Arnim, he summoned a screen that converted into a long, thin bar of light in his claws. Arnim sensed his descent too late and turned to face her new opponent. The spear-shaped screen forced itself downward with the griffin attached, making him slam the spear down through her chest.

Arnim gasped as she felt the rod impale her body. She could feel Darkness seep out of her back along with several streams of blood. Her body dissipated into her shadows, and black was the only color to fill her vision.

"There is nothing here," she muttered in frustration. It felt like the hundredth time she had searched through the Academy's records, but she could find nothing on the Demons. "Where are those monsters . . ." She had been searching every record she thought would be tied to the Demons, but every result seemed to bring her further away from her ultimate goal.

"Ms. Cabot, what a surprise."

Sarn wheeled around to see the Grand Master Dean standing in the center of the room. "Oh, Grand Master Dean, forgive me," she managed with a deep yet quick bow.

The man walked forward in his gold and red robe. "You are certainly adamant about finding these Demons, are you not, Ms. Cabot?"

"Y-yes, sir. Ever since I heard that Lord of the Shadows talk about them, I've been intrigued." What was the Grand Master Dean doing here? What was going to happen? She prepared to grasp *mysteria* at a moment's notice. She was not sure she could defeat the man, but she might have to try.

"Have you ever heard the story of Pleityr and Meridan?"

Sarn froze.

"At the time of the First Obsidian War, this Academy was founded. There were two particularly gifted students here at that time. They were twins, Pleityr and Meridan, both beautiful, both incredibly intelligent. Their parents had dropped them off at the Academy when they were just children, yet the Grand Master Dean at the time helped them rise up in this new world. They became adept mages through their training here."

Sarn grasped *mysteria,* but the Grand Master Dean showed no reaction to it.

"They were excellent students, easily the best in the whole Academy. That is why it came as a surprise to the Academy when they joined Dagan and became Lords of the Shadows. Meridan became Y'nir the Guardian, and Pleityr became Y'nas the Messenger. Together, the two burned down the Academy, killing almost everyone in it. It was Dagan's ultimate test for them, and they passed. In a way, they gained a discipline in the Darkness. They learned to betray and hate."

"Why are you telling me this?" Sarn growled.

"Because someone needs to remind you of the past, Y'nas. You cannot keep going forward like this, destroying all around you as you destroyed this place once. You had a home at one time, Y'nas. We would give it to both of you again if you were willing. The Academy's doors are always open—"

"Shut up!" Sarn summoned a blast of Force to attack the Grand Master Dean, but the spell dissipated before it reached him. She threw another one and another, barraging him with as much Force as she could conjure. Each attempt turned to nothingness against him, though. Finally, she stopped, clenching her teeth and exhaling heavily.

"Y'nas, what made you do it? Was the lure of power really so compelling?"

Sarn said nothing, but lowered her eyes.

"Was it worth it?"

This time, Sarn's eyes snapped up to meet his, and her eyes were rimmed red with tears. "No, it wasn't worth it!" she snapped. "I hated doing that to this place. It was my home. It was *our* home. Then, we saw it burned to the ground. No matter what, I will never be able to forget the sound of those flames and the sounds of people dying. But . . . we didn't have a choice. If we didn't do it, we would have been killed—discarded like old tools. And we had to join them because . . ." She trailed off there, too embarrassed to speak any further.

"Because of what?"

She clenched her teeth as she said, "Because we knew and saw that Darkness was the greatest Element there was. And I . . . more than anything, I wanted to help the Academy. As the War grew more intense, I wanted to do something to help. The Academy had done so much for me, and I had done *nothing* for it. I thought that by becoming an Y'mordi, I could have the strength to protect it from falling. Meridan tried to stop me, but when I became insistent, she decided to help me and become an Y'mordi too."

"You never sought to betray the Academy then," the Grand Master Dean said. She could not tell if he was surprised or just repeating what she was saying.

"No, I would never have wanted that! I didn't want that . . . And, when the Academy rose again . . . I didn't know what to feel. I'm still not sure how I feel about it. It's the same place, but it came about without us this time. It's not the same. We felt like we were part of the Academy when it first was constructed. We didn't think . . . that it could just blossom again without us in the picture, as selfish as that may sound."

"Pleityr," the Grand Master Dean started, and Sarn's face softened at being called her true name. "If there was a way to sever your ties to the Darkness, would you do it?"

"I would in a heartbeat. Arnim would too."

"Arnim?"

"Oh, sorry, Meridan. I forget that we had our own names, back then."

The Grand Master Dean turned his back to Sarn and called out to the input module. "Computer, search records for the Dusk Lyre."

"Alright, Y'lam, you said that you wished to speak to me about some matter?" Y'tal spoke softly as he sat in his massive chair in the Palace of Shadows.

"Yes, Lord Y'tal," replied Mali with a quick bow. "I have learned that you intend to cause a massive explosion at the disq tournament. Is this correct?"

At first, Y'tal was quiet. Finally, he responded, "It is correct. Do you contest this plan of action?"

Mali winced. He could already tell that Y'tal was on edge and ready to do something nasty. "I—yes, Lord Y'tal. When both the Emperor Regin and the Emperor of Light deny that it was them, there shall be extreme unrest, and people will realize that it was we who did it."

"Will that truly matter if the Emperor Regin succeeds, though? If he destroys Apolis and crushes the Light, will it matter to people if we are real or not?"

Mali opened his mouth to speak but realized the truth of Y'tal's words. "My Lord, I mean no disrespect, but I truly doubt that the Emperor Regin can defeat Apolis."

"Oh? Why is this? He was certainly able to best you."

Again, Mali winced, but he explained, "Lord Y'tal, he might have bested me through deception and trickery, but he is no general. I have seen the way he speaks to his armies. He does not have the full support of his people. If the people do not know what they are truly fighting for, they are not united. If they are not united, they cannot possibly defeat the armies of Emperor Helius."

A Gate appeared beside Mali, and Xarden came out of it, immediately kneeling. The Gate closed behind him. "You called, my Lord?"

"Yes, Y'dax. Y'lam here believes it unwise for me to obliterate the disq tournament."

Xarden lifted his head. "Oh?"

Y'tal gestured toward Mali. "Repeat what you said to me."

What was going on? Why did Y'tal summon Xarden? Mali forced, "I think that it would bring us out to the open and to the public unnecessarily."

"It won't matter, assuming the Emperor Regin wins," Xarden said.

Mali shook his head. "I really don't think he will, though. In order to lead effectively, you have to have the support of your people, and his people are only becoming more suspicious. His armies are not united. And, if he does not have unity, then he cannot defeat the armies of the Light."

"What do you think, Y'dax?" Y'tal asked.

Xarden lowered his eyes. "Even the Great Lord Dagan had political prowess. People begged to join his armies. The one who controls the Emperor Regin does not have that power. His might is great, but not so his political influence. He knows that. That is why he is rushing this attack. He knows he is losing his support."

"You make it seem as if he were desperate," Mali countered. "Everything I've seen of the man belies anything but desperation at this point."

Y'tal ignored Mali. "What would you suggest, Y'dax?"

"So far, the Emperor poses us little threat. Even if he does fail, he provides chaos to the world. The less order there is, the easier it will be to topple Apolis."

"Allow me to frame it a different way," Y'tal continued. "Do you think the Emperor Regin is acting in the best interests of the Darkness?"

The air was still around the three for a few seconds. Both Xarden and Mali noticed the cold, calculating tone of Y'tal's voice. Without a sound, Y'tal stood, and the other two stepped backward, fright overwhelming them as he raised a gloved hand. The Darkness in their hearts stirred, and pain filled their bodies as Y'tal manipulated that Darkness to force them to the floor in a bowing position. Shaking, both of the Y'mordi managed an inaudible apology.

"Know this." Y'tal stepped forward, passing the two of them to approach the front door of the throne room. "The Darkness is rising again, but so is the Light. If you falter, if you err one single time and put your own motivations above those of the Darkness, the shadows will drag you under. *I* will drag you into the pits of Hell itself. I tire of these games." The doors to the main hallway flung open without him touching them. "Mali, you are to return to the Emperor Regin. He misses his little pet." Mali's eyes opened wide, but his mouth stayed clamped shut. "Xarden, I have learned of the identity of the possessor for the Emperor Regin." Y'tal released his hold on the two. Mali summoned a Gate and vanished without another word.

Xarden rose carefully and waited for Y'tal to continue.

"Come on out, *possessor.*"

A side door opened, and Xarden's mouth opened wide as he recognized the possessor. "You . . . you did this?"

Ixion grinned widely as he brought a blue rose to his nose and inhaled its soft aroma.

19

A Rose for Stehl

STEHL AWOKE WHEN SHE realized they had stopped. Stretching, she turned to see Tilgé exiting the transport to fill up the tank. Mirah, as expected, was passed out in the back seat, his snore filling the vehicle. She yawned and opened the side door to get up and stretch. As Tilgé paid the station attendant to fill up the transport, she stared at him, thinking. This thin, aggressive man had been an enigma to her: despite spending years tracking down members of the malicious Enigma Brigade, she was now traveling with one. She cared for him, and she sensed his affections as well. He was the Brigade, and, despite her bitterness at being lied to, she felt no animosity toward him. In his position, she would have done the same. For the Emperor's sake, she had lied to the Emperor Regin about her own sex and had posed as a male soldier for ages. She realized she was not much different from Tilgé. However, admitting that did not make her feel much better.

Tilgé came back toward the transport. His eyes met Stehl's for a moment, and then he looked down, his face florid. Without a word, he sat down in the driver's seat, closed the door, and gripped the steering wheel while the attendant injected gas into the rear of the transport. After stretching one more time, Stehl returned to the passenger's seat and closed her door, too. She did not hide her gaze as he had. She watched him fidget with the grooves in the steering wheel, his nail tracing up and down it. He gave her a sideward glance, and then looked sharply back at the wheel. "Why do you keep looking at me like that?" he muttered. "Do you hate me?"

A bump on the rear of the transport alerted them that the attendant was finished, and Tilgé started the vehicle, making it float in the water and propel itself forward. Stehl looked out at the murky water before them. "Where are we?"

Tilgé smirked. "Yeah, you crashed pretty hard last night." He looked down at the clock embedded in the steering wheel. "It's about noon now. We are just about to leave the Eastern Continent. That was our last stop for a while. I wanted to make sure we had a full tank before sailing intercontinentally."

Nodding, Stehl replied, "Sure, makes sense."

Tilgé flexed his fingers around the steering wheel. "What are you thinking? I have to know."

"I think," she started, "I'm still processing it."

Tilgé nodded.

Minutes passed. Tilgé's eyes seemed centered on one spot in the distance, and Stehl looked everywhere except at him. Once, she even glanced back at Mirah and was surprised when he opened one eye and mouthed, "Go on" before closing the eye and resuming snoring. Stopping herself from smiling, she faced forward again.

After taking a deep breath, she started, "Okay, let me just talk through it with you . . . but no interrupting, alright?"

Tilgé was silent.

"Alright." She turned her body more to face Tilgé, but she looked mostly at her hands, talking as much to herself as she was to him. "Back when I was a soldier for the Emperor Regin, I had only one concern: to serve and protect. I wanted to be a hero. When I walked in on you g—the Brigade attacking the Emperor's staff, I saw it as a means of some variety, a chance for me, personally, to be a hero. I wouldn't rest until I saw all of the Brigade dead."

She gestured to the back seat. "When I ran into Mirah, he loved me despite my obsession, but he also showed me what else there was to life besides fame and glory. I've been happy traveling with him. He's a gentleman, and he makes me feel special. I love him for that.

"When I met you, I felt special again. But, it was in a different way." She saw his fingers grip the steering wheel a little more tightly. "You re-awakened my sense of adventure, my sense of purpose. Half the time, you're as crazy, rude, and demanding as I am. And I love that about you. The Light knows I. . . . I love you, too.

"Then, I found out you were one of *them,* a Brigadier. Don't get me wrong: I was pissed at you. But . . . it was mostly because you had lied to me. I know *why* you did it. I know you *had* to do it. But, I still didn't like being lied to, y'know?"

Tilgé opened his mouth but then closed it sharply. "And," she continued, "it felt like I didn't really know you. Like it had all been a lie, a farce." She reached over and grabbed his arm. "But, I really don't think that's the case. Even after everything the other day, you are still here. You've been nothing but apologetic. I believe you. After meeting Maksimilian, I can see how he'd be a person tough to argue with. And after we stop him at the tournament, I think we will finally be done with this chapter. I will be content with that."

Tilgé blurted, "And us?"

Stehl released his arm and hesitated. "Tilgé, when you were in the Brigade . . . how many innocent people did you murder?"

The man in the driver's seat was silent, and his jaw

clenched.

Stehl felt her face flush. "I will forgive you on one condition. You have to promise me that you will not kill another soul as long as you live."

He turned and looked at her in full. "What?"

"You heard me." She touched the hilt of her sword, which was between her legs under the seat. "You and I both want to leave our pasts behind us. No more war after this. No more fighting. We could live out our whole lives without ever having to kill again. Besides that, you and I have killed enough outside of the law that, if we were found out, we could both be put to death. Even in self-defense, we have not the right to raise a weapon. If we fall, we fall."

"What about Maksimilian?"

"He can be the one exception for both of us. But after that, no more killing. That's it."

Tilgé hesitated himself before repeating, "And, you will forgive me if I promise this to you?"

"Yes."

Sighing, he responded, "Alright." He nodded. "I promise it. Aside from Maksimilian, my hand will not be the cause of any more deaths. If it means more time with you and being in your good graces again, it is more than worth it."

Stehl's mouth fell open. "Tilgé . . ."

"I mean it. I still . . ."

When he paused, Stehl pressed, "What is it?"

"Nothing, damn it!" Tilgé roared. His face flushed, and he squeezed the wheel tightly. "I made your promise. Now let me think for a while. Is that too much to ask?"

Stehl was torn between arguing for the sake of arguing and crossing her arms in anger, but she decided to just let it go. She had a guess of what he had wanted to say, but she did not want to even acknowledge it. She looked out the window and peered through the opaque water to search for stray fish.

Tilgé watched her out of the corner of his eye. His fingers

flicked across the steering wheel as he sped up the transport. He loved her. He knew that she loved Mirah, and that Mirah loved her. Yet, Tilgé loved her all the same. Despite being the thing she had hunted for much of her life, she did not hate him. Glancing in the mirror at the snoring Mirah, he considered it might be a good idea to talk to him about all of this. Closing his eyes, he muttered under his breath, *"Eldra,"* and felt the shimmer of a Light barrier separate he and Mirah from Stehl. He tested it. "Stehl?" She did not turn to face him, only stared out her window. "Stehl?" Still nothing. He shook his head. *Mysteria* made little to no sense to him. He knew light was physical. It affected matter much like water did: it was invisible, yet moved everything around it. Somehow, a barrier of Light could, if strong enough, be a barrier of sound, stopping sound waves in their tracks as easily as bending reflected light. "Mirah," he called. "Hey, Mirah, wake up."

The corpulent man spread out across the back seat snored one final time before opening his eyes and sitting up. "Oh, hey, Tilgé, everyt'in' alrigh'? Are we dere yet?"

Tilgé shook his head. "No, Mirah." He flicked his head toward Stehl. "She can't hear a word we say right now . . . I wanted to talk to you privately."

Mirah stretched, his bulky arms pressing against the cushioned backs of the seats. "Alrigh', what ya wanna talk about?"

"I saw you got Stehl a rose."

"Yeah, I did. What of it?"

Tilgé swallowed. "I . . . I want to give her one, too."

Mirah laughed and clapped a hand on Tilgé's shoulder, making him jump in his seat. "Well, what's stoppin' ya?"

Tilgé clenched his jaw before muttering, "I don't know, Mirah. Three-way partnerships happen here, sure, but they're not common. And they're only *really* okay in the West. What will people think about it? Darkness, I don't even know if you are fully okay with it. Stehl might not even accept it. That's a lot to ask someone, especially someone from the East."

"She loves ya." Mirah paused to let that sink in. "She really does, Tilgé. Ya know ya have my blessin'. I t'ink it's good for her. She needs both of us, an' I jus' want her to be happy. Regardin' what everyone else t'inks, forget about them." Tilgé looked up in the mirror to watch Mirah's face, much more serious than usual. "As far as I'm concerned, we need each other. Who cares what the rest o' da world say?"

Tilgé smirked. "Stehl is stronger than that, Mirah. You're right: she wouldn't care what anyone else says. But her strength means she might not need me as much you claim. She doesn't need any man."

"Perhaps," Mirah said, "but she is strong enough to decide who she loves, too. If she wants ya, ya might as well offer da rose. No point in pissin' her off by waitin' for her to offer it to you."

Nodding, Tilgé remained silent. After a minute, he said simply, "Alright. Thanks, Mirah. I will think about this. I just do not want her to reject me, I guess."

"She may, but don't let that stop ya from tryin' again in da future, yeah?"

Tilgé froze. He did not want to think about rejection as an actual possibility. He had been hoping that Mirah would dispel all of his worries. "Yeah," he replied with a bitter taste in his mouth. *"Eldra."* The barrier collapsed.

"Alright, we're here," Tilgé said, waking Stehl from her sleep again.

Her eyes opened, and she marveled at the sight of hundreds of transports parked around them. "We're here already?" She opened her door and stood. "What time is it?" She looked to the sky and saw the sun was already setting.

Mirah followed her out and replied gruffly, "A little affer six, dear."

She smiled and looked to Tilgé. "Excellent. We can start

searching for Maksimilian before the tournament starts tomorrow."

Tilgé locked the transport as he got out. "Gonna be harder than even I thought, though." He looked around. "The place is packed already. It took about an hour just to find a spot to park, and we're about twenty minutes walking distance from the actual stadium."

"That's fine," she countered. "I don't mind walking after being stuck in a transport all day."

Mirah stretched before saying, "Well, I'm gonna find us a hotel. I could use some more sleep m'self. I'll let you two go searchin' yourselves. I'll shoot ya both a message wit' da address."

Stehl nodded. "Sounds good." Opening the trunk, she pulled out her rifle and hid it under her robe. "You ready, Tilgé?"

He came around and grabbed his own sword from the trunk, making sure Stehl did not see the rose hidden under his own coat. "Yep. Ready as I'll ever be." While Mirah went toward the ramshackle inns of the Northern Continent, Stehl and Tilgé headed toward the stadium and larger city in the distance. "Well, Stehl, have you ever been to Ruvion before?"

She shook her head. "No, I've never even been to the Northern Continent before."

"Really?" He was genuinely surprised. "I have been here too many times to count."

"On missions?"

Tilgé was silent at first and lowered his head. "Yeah . . ."

"So, tell me more about what kinds of missions the Brigade went on."

He looked sharply at her. "Are you sure?" After she nodded, he started, walking close beside her. "Well, for the most part, the Emperor of Light left us alone. Sometimes, Maks would talk with him, but usually he decided what Helio needed. These missions were typically espionage or assassination missions. We'd often go after terrorists or traitors. Mostly, the bloody work the Emperor wouldn't want on his hands directly. That's what we did."

"Sounds rough," Stehl said tersely.

Tilgé looked at her pleadingly. "Well, it was rough at first, but . . . after a while, you became used to it. I guess that's what makes it scary. You became accustomed to the violence of it all. It was just part of the job, y'know? I'm not going to say it was the *same* as war, but . . . it was *similar.* You become desensitized to it."

She nodded again. "I suppose it does make sense."

He floundered, "Stehl, it was . . . bizarre . . . surreal. Maks always validated our actions. We *knew* it was the will of the Light. We never doubted it for a second. We saw ourselves as the Light's dark angels. When your commander tells you that what you are doing is right, you just don't doubt that, y'know?"

"It's kind of like what I was doing."

Tilgé's head turned sharply toward her again. "What?"

"It is." She lowered her head to the cobblestone streets beneath them. "I have followed others just as blindly for most of my life. Between serving the Emperor Regin and even Lord Helius, I have never questioned those above me. These past ten years, I have never had a doubt in my mind that I could be wrong in hunting the Enigma Brigade. I saw them as just heartless monsters who were determined to kill and murder indiscriminately. Yet, I wasn't really much better the whole time. I murdered five of them, each in cold blood."

Tilgé went through the list of names in his own head: Fend, Warbrix, Seryl, Viso, and Grenn. She truly had killed all of them. Still, he was hesitant to lump her in with the rest of the Brigade. "Stehl, you are not like them." He grabbed her hand, and she looked at him with cold eyes. In that moment, he wondered if maybe she was exactly like them. "You are good and kind. Everything you did, even if it was out of revenge, was to set things right. You are *nothing* like Maks."

They walked down the street in silence. Tilgé's heart thumped in his chest as he looked at all the quaint cottages they passed. Ruvion was the capital of the kingdom known as Hurale. It saw the disq tournament two or three times a century, and it was always the height of commerce for the place. Tilgé knew little about the mountainous kingdom, except for the fact that it had sided with Maris at the start of the Third Obsidian War. Now, most of the people here were probably seeing the kingdom for their first time—Stehl included.

"Once we stop him, I *will* be nothing like him," she said. "I will be alive, and he won't."

"Well," Tilgé said with a sigh, "we have to find him first. Before he starts killing people."

"We won't let him."

Tilgé did not protest. He knew there was a good chance that Maksimilian had already started, but he did not speak this thought aloud. In fact, he wanted to simply change the topic. "Stehl, do you want to know how I got involved in the Brigade?"

She looked at him. "Sure."

"I was raised in the West in Arvon. It's mostly humans in that kingdom, but it's not that different from Ruvion with the tournament around. Well, fewer people, but the same ratio of humans to nonhumans right now. Somehow, we all got along. Maks met me on one of his missions. They were looking for some Servant of the Darkness, and the guy happened to work at my shop—I was a shopkeeper back then—and they asked me for his whereabouts. Well, when I found out the guy was actually a Servant of the Darkness, I flipped out. We all saw him walking through the front door, and I even saw Maks grab the hilt of his sword then. But I was quicker. I pulled a rifle out from under the counter, slung it downward softly so it rested on Maks's shoulder, and fired two shots into the guy's chest. I wasn't going to have that scum working in my shop."

He tightened his grip on Stehl's hand. "I was quicker to kill than Maks was, and he was super impressed. He offered me a job on the spot. But," he paused, "it wasn't the killing that I loved. It was being able to fight for what I believed in." He thought back to living in the West. "Back then, things made sense. I knew what I was doing. I had morals, and I stood up for them. I stood up for my country but not my leader."

Stehl raised an eyebrow. "What are you getting at, Tilgé?"

Tilgé did not slow down. "Stehl, Arvon was so different from the South. Back there, it was okay for nonhumans and humans to talk to each other. Killing wasn't punishable if it was defensible. There weren't laws that mistreated women. I won't say it was perfect, but it was just better. Better than how the East and the South act half the time." He saw the way Stehl's mouth opened in protest and intercepted her, "No, I am not speaking ill of either. It's just that I lived in a place that just didn't care. They looked out for everyone. Wasn't a great place for business or even a strong military. Yet, it was good for people. We were taught about loyalty and trust and honor and love." Tilgé pulled Stehl away from the main road and into a side alley.

"Hey, what are you doing?"

He stopped and turned her to face him. "Look, I know you are strong. You are independent, and you are easily the fiercest woman I have ever met. I know we have only known each other for about a week. I know you are promised to Mi-rah. But . . . the way I was raised . . . if you love someone, if you truly, *truly* love someone, you let them know. And, I want you to know it." He took a step back and fell to both knees before her. "You make me feel awake for the first time in years. I enjoy your company and your companionship, but

I want more than that. I may be a one-handed sadist, but . . . I love you, Stehl." After reaching into his coat, he pulled out a tall rose and presented it to her. "Please, will you give me the honor of being your beloved?"

She put a hand to her mouth, and her eyes widened. "But . . . is Mirah . . . ?"

He nodded. "I have his blessing here. He's okay with this being a multimony . . . if you are."

Maksimilian walked into the hotel and let his black robe swirl around him in the current that drafted in from outside. He had every intention of waiting until tomorrow before he began his massacre. His anger was riled. He had let his Steel of Life go to the Brigadier Gaspard, and he had lost a hand to that foolish Tilgé with his unlikely accomplice, Captain Terrell. Things could not have gone less smoothly for him. He wanted revenge on all of them. Considering the disq tournament tomorrow, he was not surprised to see there was a line to the innkeeper's desk. "Oh, come on, Behemoth," he muttered. "Grant me some luck here."

Still, the line did not move any faster. "Damn this waiting." He tried to count the heads before him to pass the time as well as to measure it. "One, two, three, four, five, six—" Then, he stopped. Backtracking in number, he realized he recognized one of the people in line. It was the large fool who had helped Tilgé and Captain Terrell, the one he had knocked out with little effort, the one in love with Terrell. With his remaining hand, Maksimilian brushed the hilt of the Behemoth. "Heh, I guess you're luckier than I thought."

Sliding it out of its sheath, he watched as its golden light illuminated the entrance of the inn. The people between him and his target turned to face Maksimilian, and they stepped back when they realized a sword had been raised in such a place of comfort. Slowly, the target must have sensed the strange glow filling the room, and he turned.

Maksimilian raised his sword as he stared, grinning, into Mirah's eyes.

Stehl grabbed the rose from Tilgé's hands, bent down to hold his face in her hands, and said, "Yes," before pressing her lips to his.

20

Final Preparations

YEARS AGO, CAMERON had stood against two Lords of the Shadows: Randir and Mali. Even at the mystical Stonehenge, he had exhibited great prowess with *mysteria*. When dueling Randir, he had been disarmed, and he had relied on wandless spells to stand against the Prophet of Fire. Now, he stood proudly amongst the Ring of Elders. He was still an apprentice, but he trained under the head of the Ring, Elizabeth. And, he was dating her daughter. He had never felt so close to greatness before. Yet, witnessing the synchrony between Lord Helius and his mechanic, the griffin, he was in humble and envious awe.

"I just can't believe this, Helen."

She looked over at him. The two stood on the white beach, facing the turbulent ocean. "What?"

"How is he so strong? He's almost my age; he's had little to no training; and he doesn't even use a wand. I just don't get it."

Helen shook her head but held his hand. "I don't either. Maybe it's just genetic."

He glanced sharply at her. "You can't be serious. I'm

not even sure that Elizabeth is that strong. His level of instinct and sensing . . . it's incredible. How do I get to be that powerful?"

"Well, that's why we are training, Cam."

Shaking his head, he said, "No, I've barely gotten any stronger in five years. She doesn't even let me try working without my wand yet. She knows I can do it, but she doesn't push me." Together, they looked out to the makeshift tent meant to protect the leading Elders and Lord Helius from the wind. "I want what he has."

Helen gripped his hand tightly. "No, you don't. He is in the middle of a war in his world, and he's struggled with worse things than a couple of Lords of the Shadows. He may be my little brother, but he's gone through more than I had imagined when we were younger. It had to be rough."

"Fuck this," Cameron said and turned away from her.

"What?" she called back in disbelief.

Turning back, he said, "I am not going to sit around and constantly be the apprentice. I've got to do something."

Smirking, Helen said, "And what are you going to do? We need to wait here until we have further orders."

He shook his head. "I want to help. I don't want to sit back and just be a witness to everything that's going on. We're not Elders, but we are part of the Ring. It's time we actually act on that."

"How do you propose we do that?" Helen caught up with him, but she did not move to hold his hand. Her face held a smile of excitement. Although she was quick to defend her brother, she more than agreed with Cameron about their own roles in this struggle.

As they walked farther away from the others, he started waving his hands as he talked. "*Mysteria,* it's different here on Earth. In Gevás, wandless spells are just easier. Emotion just matters more there. Here . . . here it is all about form."

"What are you getting at?"

Cameron stopped walking, and his leather jacket moved in the breeze. "I . . . I think you and I can lift the barrier on *mysteria*."

Helen's eyes widened. "What? How?"

"The fact that we can still use *mysteria* as long as we are using strong aids shows that it's not about being cut off from it. It's that the emotional aspects of *mysteria* are just blocked here. It's all about form."

"If that were true, then how can Drage still use *mysteria?*"

Cameron paused to consider. "It's that Sword of his. It just doesn't follow the same rules somehow. It makes form automatic."

"So . . . how do we get rid of the barrier?"

"Simple," he said, pulling out his cell phone. "I took a photo of one of Elizabeth's spells. It's a barrier-removing one."

Helen raised an eyebrow as she looked at the spell. It was a basic incantation from what she saw. "Um . . . are you sure this is going to work? It looks pretty standard to me."

"You remember what Elizabeth taught us? Even the simplest spells can have the greatest effect, given the proper aids."

"Well, what aids do we have?"

"We each have wands. We will be using the incantation. And, we will be doing it together."

She read over the incantation again. "I don't know, Cam. When you try to make spells that large, bad things can happen."

"It removes barriers, Helen. The worst that can happen is failure."

She nodded. "Alright, fine. We will do it, but I think we should make it the full ritual."

Cameron rolled his eyes. "Must we?"

"Every little bit helps," she said as she summoned her wand. "*Eldra.*" A light left her wand and began etching a glowing design into the sand, encircling them both and forming star-like symbols in the circle. "You have to help me finish this if you want our powers to be bound correctly."

"Fine." He took out his wand as well and repeated, *"El-dra."* His light joined hers, tracing over the circle and the stars. "Now what?"

"Blood is power, Cam."

He rolled his eyes. "Alright." He flicked his wand over his opposite arm and said, *"Lune."* A slice of Force slashed his arm, and a rivulet of blood trickled down his arm into the sand. By the time he looked up, Helen had done the same.

"Now, can you remember the *full* incantation?"

"No, I just looked at it, damn it!"

Helen smiled. "Then, repeat after me—and quit being such a baby. This was your idea." As if the glowing ritual marks around them had summoned it, a storm erupted above them, showering them with freezing rain and beating them with howling wind. Helen began waving her wand in a precise pattern, as if she were conducting the world around her in a tempestuous orchestra of wind and rain. *"Barrier."* The marks lit up in flames even as Cameron repeated the word. *"Este. Hindrun. Rhwystr. Obex."* She had paused after each word to let Cameron pronounce each one in turn. The wind was now trying to force them from the circle, resisting against the two mages' compulsion. "Alright, halfway there." Cameron nodded before she continued, *"Thyej. Shatter. Frantumare. Kowasu. Breek."* The rain drenched them, turning the sand into muck. With a final flourish of their wands upward, they yelled in unison, *"Séala!"*

A red sphere of energy exploded outward from the center of the circle, throwing them both yards away from it. But the storm had stopped.

Helen lifted her head. "Did it work?"

Before Cameron could raise his hand to try a spell, Elizabeth was upon them. "What the hell did you two do?" Her face was livid, and her hair flowed behind her in the now mild wind. Her eyes were wide, and her face almost snarling.

"I..." Cameron started.

"We," Helen interrupted, "were trying to destroy the barrier, the one between us and *mysteria*."

"How did you...?"

"We used one of the spells from your spellbook."

Fire seemed to leap from Elizabeth's eyes. "You didn't..."

Cameron showed her the phone, bracing himself for her to use a lightning bolt to disintegrate him on the spot. She took the phone and examined it. "This is just a basic barrier-breaking spell. Did you honestly think this would work? You felt the chances were so great, that you felt alright performing a whole ritual right here to let the Cronus thing know our exact location?"

Helen winced. "We didn't . . . we just weren't thinking about . . ."

"No, perhaps you weren't thinking." Elizabeth's voice was cold and harsh.

Just as she started to turn, Cameron said, "Hey."

When she turned back, she was dumbfounded: Cameron held a flame in his hand. He had used *mysteria* without an aid.

"Did you...?"

Helen stood up and cheered, "It worked!"

Elizabeth could not believe it. "How is that even possible? There's no way you two could have completely removed the barrier that easily. That barrier was supposed to cover the entire world. There's just no way."

Then, a Gate appeared, and Drage walked through it to stand beside them. "Elizabeth, the barrier's gone. What happened?"

Helen and Cameron were under the tent with just Drage, Feranx, and Elizabeth interrogating them.

"So," Elizabeth said, "you just used a ritual, and it overrode the barrier completely?"

"Yeah," Helen confirmed. "We had each other and our wands. We used the full magic circle, and we used the fifth level incantation."

Cameron added, "I think it has to do with form. I think form is more important here than in Gevás. Like, something as well-executed as our ritual always trumps something just done with emotion."

"Like my programming," Drage said. "My computer's programming taps into the powers of the heart, never the mind. When this is all over, I would like to learn more about this ritual process. I have never heard of it being so strong back in Gevás."

Elizabeth said, "I have heard of many strong rituals performed here, but never to this extent. Granted, I have never heard of a barrier like Cronus 624's either. It makes me wonder if the barrier was just weak."

"Perhaps it was," Drage agreed, "but you have to admit, it took these two to actually dispel it. They deserve commendation."

Helen, though silent, could not believe her brother was judging her, defending her to her mother. It was like he was not aware they were even siblings.

"Perhaps," Elizabeth said between pursed lips.

"For now though," Drage said, "Feranx and I are rested from the battle against the Y'mordi and insist we move on. Now that the barrier has been lifted, Cronus 624 will not stand a chance against us all. This should change our strategy considerably. We can now more effectively take advantage of distraction techniques."

"We've been through this already, Drage." She slammed her knuckles down onto the magically constructed table. "We are not using the Ring as bait for you. This is their fight as much as it is yours, and we cannot put all our chances on one person. That is not how we are going to do things."

"Hey," Drage said, gesturing toward Feranx. "It's not just

one person. He's with me, too."

"Can I—" Helen started.

"No," Elizabeth interrupted. "You may not. You are both dismissed. We have heard what we needed. You are to report to the rest of the Ring and await further orders. You are to go nowhere else. And you are not to cast any spells until instructed. Do I make myself clear?"

"Yes, master," they said in unison before leaving the tent.

"Now, you, Drage," Elizabeth started.

Drage raised a hand to silence her. "No, Elizabeth." She noticed him referring to her as if she were not his mother. Stunned by his forcefulness, she closed her mouth. "I may not be as gifted or knowledgeable about *mysteria* as any of the Ring. I concede this willingly. However, Feranx and I are the only ones who know its potential and its battle strategies. We are also the only ones who know how to disarm it. This machine was made to be impervious to most attacks, especially spells. With the barrier gone, the Y'mordi could pour into this world and decimate your Ring. If you will not take my leadership, then the Ring will fall. Do not risk their lives over foolish pride."

She folded her arms. "You sound just like your father."

Those words hit him like a hammer, but he did not protest it. "Feranx and I will outline Cronus 624's potential attacks, and I want the Ring to have ritual circles prepared. The power that Cameron and Helen exhibited when they destroyed the barrier . . . I want that power quadrupled in defense of Feranx and I. I want to be able to stand before the module with no fear and no danger. Do I make myself clear?"

"Yes," Elizabeth said, "your Majesty."

His jaw clenched, but he turned around and headed out of the tent. Summoning his Sword, he charged it with energy and released a lightning bolt of blue into the heavens, causing the members of the Ring outside to jump in shock. "Your head has instructions for you," Drage bellowed. "We fight in an hour."

As Helen passed Drage, she could sense his heart, and the furious Light that raged in it scared her. She had never sensed a heart so drenched in power. He seemed like a god: glowing with divinity and burning with wrath. She swallowed. Drage was a completely different person. For the first time, she feared someone even more than her mother. Entering the tent, she saw her mother had her fists clenched as well, but the anger coming from her was nothing compared to that of Drage.

21

Empire of the Blue Rose

XARDEN APPEARED IN the island south of Varyx and was met with a rush of freezing water. Even in this cold, his skin adapted. "You wanted to see me, Y'tal?"

The shorter Y'mordi stood at the edge of the island, looking out into the murky abyss. "Yes, Xarden. The time has come. Tomorrow, the Emperor Regin will fall, and we need to be prepared for the next Great Servant."

Xarden pulled back his hood, and his face was contorted into surprise. "What? You *know* Regin will die tomorrow? How?"

"The Darkness has told me this. Come, let us walk." Y'tal gestured with a gloved hand toward the water in front of him, and Xarden stepped forward. Xarden focused on the orb in his robe and created a bridge of ice that extended into the water as they walked. "I do not know that the Emperor Regin will die, but that he will fail. Even with Ixion's controlling, his power will be insufficient to stop what the Guardians are planning."

"And…" said Xarden," what *are* the Guardians planning?"

"They still have significant strength with their master

computer, and it would seem that Matthew has gained much power since we last encountered him. He will lead Helio to salvation despite our attempts."

"So, what are we to do?"

"I plan on at least evening the odds. Perhaps we can take down some of Helio's defenses all the same."

"How do you plan to—"

"Xarden," Y'tal said under his breath, silencing Xarden even with the whisper. "I need your strength ahead, but now I also need your ear." They continued to walk into the darkness on the magically constructed ice path.

"Yes, my lord."

Y'tal did not address Xaren directly. "It would seem that the Darkness is becoming wilder, more uncontrollable. The remaining Great Servants are all coming close to power. If the Y'mordi follow the instinct that Ixion had, then we shall rise to our former glory as well. We are entering a new age, an age of Darkness." Xarden lowered his head in thought but did not continue. "I know you may have doubts, Y'dax, especially since the Light has been winning these past few skirmishes." He sensed Xarden look at him sharply at the word "skirmishes." "Yes, that is all they have been. These petty wars do not concern us. They have been minor seeds of chaos. When we garner the blood of the Great Servants, the power of the Darkness will be unstoppable. Let the Guardians think that they have figured us out. Their proud ignorance will be their undoing."

Up ahead, the darkness increased as if they were walking into a cloud of black smoke, yet there were no cloudy tendrils around the edges. The darkness was merely there, a sphere that lacked light. "Nevertheless, the point remains that you all have failed me." Xarden winced. "Only Ixion has shown strength these past few weeks. Everyone has grown to be far too independent, yourself included." Lowering his head further, Xarden feared what was coming. "Do not fret, Y'dax.

Now is not the time for retribution. As I said, I called you for your aid."

The darkness now loomed over them, a mighty shadow that could have swallowed the Palace of Light. Xarden ventured as they stopped, "What is this? It does not feel like *mysteria*."

"This, Y'dax," Y'tal said, "is a barrier constructed by the Great Lord Dagan himself."

Xarden's eyes widened. "What? How could this be?"

Y'tal raised his hands to the heavens. "This is the home of the Demon Epofis."

The ice cracked under them as Xarden lost his concentration momentarily. "You brought me here to—"

"Yes," replied Y'tal. "I brought you here to help me awaken it. It is high time for the world to know we exist. It is time for them to remember what fear is."

Xarden considered the darkness before them. "Y'tal . . . forgive me, my lord. But, once we do this, we cannot go back. The Demons bring Shadows in their wake. The world will know the legends are true. You said it yourself: we are still weak. The Continents could combine their forces against us, and I do not think we could stand against them, even with the power of the remaining four Demons."

"You are only partially right." He turned his hooded face toward Xarden. "When Ixion realized he was tired of being treated like scum among us seven, he broke through a form of barrier. He found his old power instantly, as if it had been waiting there for years, and indeed, it had. It was not training that brought him back to power; it was will."

Xarden raised an eyebrow. "What kind of barrier do you mean, Y'tal?"

"The Dark Ways . . . They were what fostered our power. When the Dark Lord fell, a kind of cloud fell over our hearts, not constructed by Darkness, but just that sheer power."

"Kind of like the barrier that keeps the Demons at rest."

Y'tal nodded. "Yes. However, the barriers are fading. The Darkness is rising. The Great Servants are appearing, and the Demons are breaking free, too."

"And," Xarden said, "the barriers on our own hearts are weakening."

"Yes, but we still have to break out of them ourselves."

"How long did it take you, Y'tal?"

"Ten years."

Xarden did not respond at first. He processed that. This barrier had to have been at its strongest back then. For Y'tal to be able to break through it was an impressive feat. Xarden highlighted his mental note not to get on Y'tal's bad side. "And you and Ixion are the only ones, right?"

Y'tal nodded again. "Yes, though the false Y'mordi will not have such an awakening."

Xarden knew he would get nowhere pressing that point. "Well, how do we break through *this* barrier?" he said, gesturing toward the dark cloud in front of them.

"Easy. We just have to awaken the Demon. He can break through the barrier on his own once awake."

"So, we just need to get its veins flowing, huh?" Xarden clicked his staff against the ice beneath their feet. The orb at the tip of the scepter glowed purple, and a purple cloud surrounded the orb.

Y'tal smirked. "Exactly." The smaller Y'mordi raised his hands to the cloud, and Xarden sensed the thin stream of *mysteria* connecting Y'tal to the cloud. As usual, Xarden noticed that Y'tal was hiding his full capacity. He was certain that even this thin stream of energy was stronger than Xarden's own best. Xarden focused his energy outward, and a purple beam shot into the dark cloud. The light disappeared within its depths, and Xarden could not tell if his energy was even reaching through the void. Concentrating harder, he let the powers that connected him to the Darkness seep into his spell. His will ran into something solid in the dark.

"Is that?" he asked.

"Yes," Y'tal said, his tone impassive. "That is the Demon."

Xarden was amazed at the surge of energy he felt in that obstruction. Gradually, he pushed his *mysteria* against it, willing it to awaken.

Two diamonds of red light appeared in the cloud. The horizontal diamonds were as large as either of the Lords of the Shadows, and it took Xarden a few seconds to realize those diamonds were the beast's eyes. Epofis, the Dread Serpent, had awakened.

In a deafening explosion, the cloud of darkness burst outward, sending black currents across the two figures. Xarden quailed as he beheld the massive serpent, coiled and writhing. Its scales were like glistening pearls, and its eyes were blood-crimson. Coiled, it was two-thirds the size of the Palace of Shadows.

With its head reared back, it shrieked, piercing the water with its wrathful cry. Xarden forced his hands against his ears, trying to mute the deafening tone. The Darkness in his heart throbbed at the sheer force of the Demon's presence.

"Silence," Y'tal said.

Suddenly, the beast snapped its jaws shut and pointed its angular nose down toward the two. Its ruby eyes fixated on Y'tal, and its tail flicked as if in irritation. Opening its jaws to reveal rows of needle-like fangs, Epofis hissed, "Y'taaaal, what has happened here?"

Y'tal's voice never rose in tone or volume. "It has been almost a thousand years since the Second Obsidian War, Epofis. Although the world has changed, we find ourselves returning to where we were back then: the Darkness is on the rise. We need your aid."

The serpent seemed to consider, growling under its breath. Then, its eyes widened. "Waaaait. What has happened to Naeth?"

Y'tal shook his head. "Naeth is no more. He is the only

one of your kind to fall. A young anima trapped him in his cave and destroyed him with *mysteria*. This same anima now stands at the head of your enemy's forces. You may consider this vengeance, or you may consider it showing that you are better than Naeth. I do not care what your motivation is, as long as you get the job done."

Epofis's eyes thinned into slits, leering at Y'tal. "Have the great Y'mordi truly fallen so low? You cannot handle some individuals?"

Xarden took a step back, fearful of both Y'tal and Epofis now.

Y'tal replied, "Do I need to remind your kind of the power I wield?"

Epofis slunk back even as it hissed. "Noooo, Y'tal. I merely question those who follow you blindly. Even Y'dax cowers in fear of me now. If you want blood on this day, I shall paint the world's aquasphere a thousand shades of crimson and maroon. I am Dread, Y'tal, and the world shall know me again."

Smiling beneath his hood, Y'tal said, "Good. I need you to fight alongside the Emperor of the Eastern Continent, a man named Regin. He is under the possession of Y'xon."

The serpent hissed, "That sssssnake?"

"Yes. Like you, our powers have been slumbering. So far, only Y'xon and I have broken our own barriers."

Epofis angled his head toward Xarden. "Shall I lift this one's barrier, Y'taaaal?"

"No," Y'tal said. "His heart is still Divided, and he will need to have his heart restored before that is even an option for him."

Xarden's jaw dropped. "Not an option . . . ?"

"I ssssee . . ." Epofis said. "You must guiiide me to Y'xon, Y'tal. This new world will only confuuuuse me."

Y'tal turned to Xarden. "Do you think you can handle guiding him?"

"I . . . yes, my lord." Xarden bowed before his master.

"Then," hissed the serpent, "hop on." It lowered its humongous head, and Xarden leaped from his ice platform onto the Demon's neck. He swallowed nervously once before the Dread Serpent took off into the night, the dawn trailing in its wake.

Y'tal muttered as the two sped into the dark, "You will know the truth soon, Y'dax. That you will."

Mali screamed in a high pitch as the Emperor Regin stood before him, sapping every ounce of strength from Mali's body. "Good boy . . ." the Emperor chuckled. Releasing the draining force, Mali collapsed onto the ground, his fingers scraping the floor in agony.

"I'm . . . I'm not your dog."

The Emperor Regin kicked Mali in the side, rolling him onto his back. "You might as well be."

"Why are you doing this?" Mali put one hand around the golden collar that strangled his neck, trying to pry it open desperately.

"Even though using this vessel gives me greater access to the Darkness than I can alone, I cannot control it as easily as he can." Mali felt the collar tighten around his neck. "But, by stealing your strength, it is as if I am the Emperor Regin entirely. The layers of separation between he and I vanish through your strength. I feel invincible."

Although Mali could feel the confidence brimming in that shadowed heart, the Emperor Regin did not look strong. His face was gaunt with dark patches across it. His skin clung to his bones, and his voice seemed to become raspier each time he spoke. Mali begged, "Please, just release me. I will do anything."

The Emperor Regin began to walk away as he spoke, "Drivel. There are many you serve, Y'lam, but you would not serve me willingly. I assure you of that."

"Please, just set me free," Mali repeated.

The Emperor Regin gave Mali a sidelong glance. "Anything, you say?"

Mali felt the pressure on his collar slacken. He hesitated. "What is it you would request, Lord Regin?"

"You and I are two old souls, Y'lam. I could not ask you to bind yourself eternally to my service. Even I know you would not go as far as that. I want you to bind yourself to three of my wishes, as long as they are within your power and do not directly violate your responsibilities with Y'tal."

"And . . ." Mali said, "you will let me go? You will remove the collar if I bind myself to this agreement?"

The Emperor Regin turned to face Mali fully. He held out his hand, and a black and purple smoke wound around it. "With the Dark Lord, Dagan, as my eternal witness. After I remove your collar, you will fulfill three demands of my choosing, as long as they are within your power and do not directly go against your laws as an Y'mordi."

Mali raised his own hand to meet the Emperor Regin's, and the dark wisps swarmed around their handshake, and they each felt the Darkness surge within their hearts, reminding them of their promise.

Struggling to stand, Mali said, "Alright, now get this thing off of me."

The Emperor Regin smiled and shook his head.

Mali's jaw dropped. "What?"

"The binding merely was that *when* I remove the collar, you will have to do my bidding. I am not quite ready to do that just yet."

"You . . . you cheater," Mali hissed. "How long do you intend to keep me like this?"

The Emperor Regin walked over to the balcony, coughing and holding a fist to his mouth. "Damn body . . . Mali, I will not keep you like this forever, but for a while yet. It seems that adding your strength to the Darkness the Emperor is already wielding is only furthering the destruction of his body."

"The destruction . . . ?" Mali started to follow the Emperor Regin toward the balcony, though he felt the farthest thing from concern.

"The Great Servants of the Darkness . . ." he managed between coughs, "they are able to wield a larger amount of Darkness than most people. However, they are still very much *human*. They are not like the Y'mordi, bound to the Darkness. When a Great Servant comes into power, they are suddenly faced with an impending death. I'm channeling too much Darkness too quickly. But, it is too late. The dawn comes, and with it, the end."

Mali frowned. "I know you, do I not?"

The Emperor Regin straightened his back and looked into Mali's golden eyes. With a smirk, he replied, "Yes, you do, Mali." His voice was double, a much higher voice accompanying the Emperor's bass.

Mali's jaw dropped again as he stepped back. "Is that . . . I-Ixion?"

Chuckling in that doubled voice, the Emperor said, "Yes, Mali. Stunned a bit?"

"Yes, why would you . . . why are you . . ."

"I have been sick and tired of the submission. I am done with playing the lowest of the Y'mordi. It would seem that, besides Lord Y'tal, I am the first to break through the barrier placed on our hearts by the Darkness."

"What barrier?"

The Emperor Regin summoned a ball of dark energy in his hand, letting it hover a few inches from his palm. "After the Final Battle, the Darkness receded. It was not just us who went into hiding. The Demons were hidden, and our own connection to most of the Dark Ways vanished. Our powers were stinted. However, now the Darkness is on the rise again, for the first time in almost a thousand years. I have broken through the barrier over my own heart, and now I am one of the strongest Y'mordi there is. I incited a rebellion in Varyx. I have led the Eastern Continent to war against Lord Helius. Yet, I fear that now, at the pinnacle of my triumph, this body is too spent."

Mali grasped the collar around his neck. "Why the collar, though? Why are you doing this to me? You had your vengeance on me a while ago. You *killed* me, for Darkness' sake."

The Emperor Regin flashed Mali a cold look. "You act as if knowing my identity makes it okay for you to be informal with me." He fired the dark sphere at Mali, and Mali's clothes dissipated into wisps. Mali fell to his knees, naked save for the thick golden collar. "I shall rise in the ranks, Mali. You are below me. You shall be my dog until I have my first wish for you. Only then, as per our binding, will the collar fall from your neck. Until that time, you *belong* to me. Of course, I cannot force you to do anything, really. The collar serves as an energy conduit between us. I can sense where you are at any time and take your strength whenever I need it. I can bring you low through fear of pain, if nothing else. But, you still have your free will. However," the Emperor Regin said as he loomed over the naked, bruised, and shivering Mali, "if you are a good dog, I will not drain you for the rest of the day."

"Alright," Mali whispered.

The Emperor Regin sent a jolt of pain through the collar, and Mali's back arched as he writhed on the stone floor. "Alright, what?" the Emperor Regin chided.

"Yes, master!"

"Good dog." The Emperor Regin released his hold. "You may learn yet."

Coughing, he looked back out the balcony. He squinted at a shape he saw in the distance. "Damn that fool, Y'tal." Mali was unconscious on the floor and could not hear the

Emperor's words. "He has awakened one of the Demons." The white serpent glided with the sun toward the Emperor Regin's castle.

"Sarn, what have you been doing? You were supposed to still be at the Academy," Arnim said.

Sarn could not contain her excitement, however, and grabbed her sister by the shoulders in her chamber in the Palace of Shadows. "Arnim, you will never believe what has happened."

"Try me."

From her robes, Sarn pulled out a small instrument, an amber harp with golden strings. The instrument was shaped like a U and easily fit onto Sarn's forearm. "Do you have any idea what this is?"

Arnim shook her head.

"This is the *Dusk Lyre!*"

Arnim raised an eyebrow, unimpressed. "What is the Dusk Lyre?"

Sarn waved her hands dramatically as she talked, "This is the best thing ever! It will give us the power to cut off our ties to the Darkness! We can be human again!"

Arnim stood and grabbed Sarn's arms, shaking her in the process. "Are you crazy? It's not safe to talk about that stuff here."

With a smirk, Sarn brushed off her sister's grasp. "Oh, stop it, Arn. I used a simple ward outside. Even with Pullatus's super senses, they will be confounded here. It seems that he is distrusting of all of us, anyway. He won't have a clue as to what you and I are planning. He has bigger things to worry about."

Testing the ward cautiously, Arnim felt outward with her heart. Satisfied, she placed a hand on the lyre, marveling at its workmanship. "This . . . it's an artifact from the Obsidian Wars . . . How did you find this?"

"The Grand Master Dean gave it to me!"

Arnim's eyes widened. "What? Why?"

Sarn's face turned more serious, then. "He knew who I was. I don't know how, but he did." Arnim did not interrupt here, although Sarn paused. "I . . . he called me by my old name. He called me 'Pleityr.' He knew yours, too. He reminded me of what we used to be back when the Academy first opened. And he . . . he told me there was a way out of our situation if we wanted it. He told me about how the Lord Lux had created the Dusk Lyre to force the Y'mordi to return to their old selves, but, after the Lyre was finished, it turns out that the Y'mordi had to willingly use it themselves for it to work."

"He knew us," Arnim repeated.

Sarn nodded. "Yeah, he told the story of Pleityr and Meridan like it was out of a children's book."

"Or like it was part of the Academy's history . . ." Arnim added. She traced a finger across the lyre. "Having a normal life again. Are you ready for that, Sarn?"

"Yeah," she said. "I am."

"What will we do?"

"Does it matter?" Sarn shrugged. "We could fight Y'tal. We would join the war. We could go be hermits somewhere, for all I care."

"We could return to the Academy."

At this suggestion, Sarn's eyes twinkled. "Yeah."

"Well, how do we make this thing work, then?"

Crossing her arms, Sarn replied, "Well, that's the catch. There's a certain Song we have to play on it. Not even the Grand Master Dean knew what it was or even where to start looking."

"A Song . . . Do you think the Grand Master Dean giving it to us could be a trap?"

Sarn shrugged again. "It very well could be just a means of getting rid of some Y'mordi. But even so, it would help us, too."

Arnim nodded. "Well, I guess now we just have to look for this Song. And we have no leads whatsoever?"

"All he said was that the Dusk Lyre had been created by combining powers of Light and Darkness together."

"That doesn't help much." Arnim stood and went to her small book collection. "I have never heard of any Song having Elemental power itself. I would think the Song itself would have to have Elemental powers of Light and Darkness, too, but I can't imagine a song that has that kind of power."

"We will find it, though, right, Arn?" Sarn pleaded hopefully.

Arnim put a hand on one of her books. "Absolutely. Anything for you, sister."

22
Program Genesis

MARQEST BEGAN THE meeting, "So, is Drage's program ready to go?"

Matthew nodded. "Yes. I spoke with the computer, and everything is in order to defend the city. If this computer is as powerful as your COM was smart, then Apolis should be well-fortified by the computer alone." Matthew was in awe at how the Council room had shrunk since Drage was last here. While it had been eight then, now it was only four: Master Jallun, Mistress Quella, Master Marqest, and himself. Aria was still recovering from the loss of her arm, and Mistress Leona was aiding the new Lady Chiara in Varyx. Ocrum was being imprisoned in the Labyrinth beneath the Palace. "The question now is of how we want to approach Regin's forces and how we want to approach this matter publicly."

Mistress Quella said, "Well, what do we know about the forces that are coming to attack us here?"

Matthew pressed a few buttons on his side of the table, and three holographic pictures appeared over the table for all to see. "These are some of the images provided by our scouts." Each one of the images showed several of Regin's armored troops standing beside equally armored Shadows. "His armies have begun to include Shadows."

"He's been messing with the Darkness," Marqest muttered.

Nodding, Matthew continued, "This is relatively new development, though. At least, this is the first our scouts have seen of it, and, furthermore, people seem to just now be gossiping about this. There seems to be some civil unrest about this at the Capital."

Mistress Quella said, "And heavy artillery?"

"If the Emperor Regin has any," Marqest said, "he would not be making that information public. He's working in Darkness now, and his movement will likewise be concealed. Correct, Lord Matthew?"

Matthew nodded. "These are the only detailed photos our scouts were able to take."

Marqest said, "So, you are right. The only questions are what to do and what the public should hear."

Mistress Quella started, "That should be obvious. We should focus on defense. We should keep our troops here, outside the gates."

Matthew heard Master Jallun speak for the first time in three weeks, "We need to make this come off as if it is not an anticipated battle, but just a standard defense."

"Why is that?" Matthew asked.

Marqest offered, "Simple. It shows Regin to be the liar and traitor he is. It will unite the people in hatred of him; paint us as innocent even to his followers; and it will show that we are as true to our word as we claim."

"How do we set up a standard defense that can fight Regin without it being clear that we were anticipating an attack?" Matthew said.

Mistress Quella pressed a few buttons on the table to show a map of the city. "Look. The Emperor Regin is just going for a standard ambush, right? He will try to rush the main gates. He's not going to go for over-the-wall tactics for this. So, just casually make sure the guard is focused on the front."

Marqest interrupted, "Are we not trusting that Lord Helius's computer can take care of this?"

"It depends," Matthew responded. "Are we trying to win this fight, or merely neutralize it? Drage seemed pretty confident that Regin's troops would not be able to get past DATA's defenses, but he didn't say whether the computer could completely defeat them, either."

"Well," Marqest said, "if we are to trust his Majesty, then we have to assume that only a basic force is needed to supplement DATA's potential."

Matthew stood, looking down at the holographic map. "I will be helping at the first sign of Regin's forces."

Mistress Quella raised a hand to stop him. "Absolutely not. We are already absent one ruler. If you fell in the battle, who would lead us?"

"I will not fall." Matthew stared intently at Mistress Quella, waiting for her to challenge him, but she did not. "If I did, you would do what you do: lead in place of the Emperor. But, I will not fall."

"So," Marqest said, "this will be you and a few troops fighting the whole of Regin's armies?"

Matthew paused before replying, "No, I shall rally the Phoenix Regiment and the Enigma Brigade to help."

Master Jallun raised a brow. "How do you hope to manage both of these? Lady Helius is incapacitated, and Lord Helius is away. Both of the forces' leaders are out of commission."

"Which," Matthew said, "is why they will follow me. To protect their absent leaders."

Marqest nodded. "Then, it is settled."

A banging sound erupted against the door. The Council leaped to their feet, and they heard a shrill voice from behind the door, "Master Helius! Master Helius!"

Matthew ran to the door and flung it open. Standing there was Captain Zel, a leader of some of Apolis's scouts. "What is the matter, captain?"

The man was clearly out of breath as he saluted before sputtering, "Sir, Master Helius, one of our scouts just reported in with an image for you, sir."

"Show me," Matthew demanded, gesturing toward the table.

Captain Zel bowed quickly and stepped over to the table, connecting his personal device, which was attached to his arm, to the table's port. Suddenly, a massive image hovered over the table. It showed a tremendous white serpent floating above a battalion of Shadows.

"What in Lux's name is that?" Matthew said in disbelief.

Marqest's tone was grim. "I recall that beast from the Obsidian Wars. That is one of the Demons of legend, the Dread Serpent. The Lords of the Shadows must be working in conjunction with the Emperor Regin."

"One of the . . . Demons?" Matthew repeated.

Master Jallun started, "That cannot be, Marqest. We do not even have proof that the Lords of the Shadows exist, much less that the Demons have returned. This is some cheap trick Regin is employing."

Marqest said simply, "If you are wrong, are you willing to offer your life for putting the people of Helio to death for your words?"

Master Jallun shut his mouth.

Matthew said, "Wait, Lilian destroyed one of the Demons a while ago. A Spider. She made it seem like it was super easy, though."

Marqest shook his head. "The Spinner of Lies was the first of Dagan's creations. By far, it was the worst and weakest. The Dread Serpent was the middle child of the Demons."

Matthew turned to Captain Zel. "Thank you for bringing this to my attention. Anything further to report?"

Captain Zel nodded. "Only this, sir. Our scout could not get a picture of it, but he said he saw the Emperor Regin riding atop the serpent with a naked man at his side. The man had a golden collar around his neck and blonde hair."

"Thank you. You are dismissed."

The captain saluted again and exited the room, shutting the door behind him.

Matthew turned back to the Council. "This changes nothing about our plans as far as I am concerned. Marqest, try to dig up any info you can on the Dread Serpent in battle, and bring that to me within the hour. Mistress Quella, go and see Lady Helius. Tell her to summon the Regiment for me. Master Jallun, do the same for the Enigma Brigade. Bryco is the captain, and he has temporary quarters here, in the guest wing. This meeting is over."

As they stood, Marqest asked, "And you, Master Helius?"

"It's time to see what this computer can do."

Matthew stood before the massive computer, its black screen wide in front of him. "DATA, awaken."

The main screen lit up with a blue aura, and smaller screens brightened similarly. On each of the screens, a blue feminine face appeared, with blue gridlines behind her. "Hello, Matthew. How may I assist you? Is it time to enact Program Genesis?"

Matthew was taken aback. "How did—how did you know I was going to ask you that?"

"Simple," the face said with a creepy and sly wink. "You told Master Dragenopn before he left."

"But you . . ." Matthew started. "I didn't wipe your memory."

"Correct."

"And you didn't tell him?"

"No, why would I have told him?" was DATA's quizzical reply.

Matthew shook his head. "Never mind. Um, can you tell me a little more about Program Genesis? Drage didn't tell me too much about it, except that it would help."

All of the smaller screens shifted to show various weapons, from elaborate guns to mechanical swords. "Of course, Matthew. Program Genesis was Master Dragenopn's plan to create a new era for Helio—an era that involved genuine protection of the people and brought Apolis's defense system to rival that of its defenses in the Second Obsidian War."

"But back then, Lord Lux was able to afford wards around the whole city. There hasn't been power as impenetrable as his in centuries."

"Until me," DATA interrupted with that wicked smile. "Right now, Genesis cannot reach its full potential. I am still incomplete. However, I have enough of the code to be able to be a hindrance to the Emperor Regin's forces."

"What does that hindrance entail specifically?"

"Three phases. The first phase is Defense. This allows me to place an entirely invincible barrier around the whole city of Apolis. Neither *mysteria* nor missile can breach its power. However, we could fire from within."

"Ok," Matthew said, nodding. "What is the second phase?"

"Counterstrike. There is an electric framework mere feet beneath the ground all around the city. I can transform that framework into a living minefield. With my other components, I would be able to use whatever Element I desired, but presently I can at least cause some explosions from it."

"And the third phase?" Matthew was genuinely impressed with Drage's handiwork, now more than ever. If DATA spoke truly, then the Emperor Regin's forces truly would be stopped at the door.

"My third phase is Destroy. I simply cannot enact this phase, though. I would have to have the missing information. It would allow me to take a more versatile form and actually enter the arena of combat as a nearly invincible warrior."

Matthew cursed himself for not considering the potential limitations of the program because of its missing components. "Well, it still sounds like Program Genesis can help us out plenty. You need to activate it now. The Emperor Regin is on his way with one of the Demons, a snake."

DATA responded calmly, "Do not worry. I cannot defeat Regin or the Demon, but they cannot get past my defenses, either. Rest easy in your decision to keep the guard at the usual level."

"Huh?" Matthew regarded the computer with suspicion. "How did you know about *that?*"

"Master Dragenopn gave me ears throughout the Palace. I hear everything . . . well, except what goes on in the bedrooms."

Matthew's face flushed. "I . . . just do it. Activate Program Genesis."

Suddenly, Lilian's voice rang in his mind. "They are here."

Matthew summoned a Gate as DATA said, "Program Genesis activated." Matthew now stood on the front walls of Apolis, and he looked out at a massive portal in the distance, from which legions of Shadows and men stormed. Above them all was a white serpent that wound its way through the water toward them. He noticed that Lilian, Marqest, Bryco, and a Regiment officer were there.

Immediately, he spoke to the two officers. "Captain Bryco, officer of the Phoenix Regiment, if ever your groups needed to stand, it would be now. We—"

Bryco interrupted. "Just tell us where we are needed, sir."

The Regiment officer joined his side, "Yeah, just tell me what you need the Regiment to do."

"You both . . . you're willing to take orders from me?"

Bryco started, "Well, we kind of owe you after helping with Lomeo."

"And," the Regiment officer continued, "Lady Helius is

injured now. We have to protect her."

Nodding, Matthew said, "Alright. The city is protected. We just have to push Regin, the Demon, and their armies into a retreat. I have some troops who will vanguard the front of a barrier we've created."

"Wait," the Regiment officer said, "you're not calling the terra or navy?"

"No." Matthew looked at her with wild and passionate eyes. "We will do this alone. I need the Regiment to be a two-part force: defend all of us with barriers, and cast light missiles all through the enemy."

The officer created a Gate. "Yes, sir." She was gone, leaving Bryco to receive orders.

"Alright, now, Bryco. I need the Brigade to engage the army in combat. Do everything you can to decimate these forces."

Bryco's eyes widened, and he crossed his arms. "I mean you no disrespect, sir, but we are a unit trained in one-on-one combat. We are not exactly equipped to be a formidable force in grand-scale battle."

Matthew stepped forward and placed a hand on Bryco's shoulder. "And you don't have to be. We only have to create a retreat. If you can create a visible frontline, then that will force Regin and his damned snake to engage in combat with me. Alone."

Lilian spoke behind them on the wall. "No, Matthew. You can't do this alone."

Marqest added, "She is right. Matthew, you are needed here. You should not even be out there fighting." He tapped his scepter against the battlements. "Matthew, this is reckless." When Matthew lowered his gaze, Marqest pressed. "What is this really about? Why the insistence all of a sudden? You are supposed to be the level-headed one between you and Lord Helius."

"That's just it, though." Matthew faced Marqest. "If I am

taking his place, I need to do what he would do. I am thinking of what he would say. He would not let anyone fight for him. If he learned that the Y'mordi were behind the Emperor Regin's poisoning, he would fight them directly. This is no longer a war about race. This is about good and evil, right and wrong."

Marqest turned to look at Lilian. "Make sure the alarm is sounding, Lilian. Then, see to it that the Brigade and Regiment are ready." Lilian summoned a Gate and fled, her white hair streaming behind her. "Now, Matthew, I do not care what your brother would do. You are not him. You are the son of Master Derek Janus. Do not let his legacy die in vain."

Matthew's jaw clenched. "No. Do not try to make this personal, Marqest. This is about all of Apolis, all of Helio. We do not have the manpower to fight back against Regin."

Marqest laughed. "And you think you have the power to stand against the force of the Y'mordi alone? And against a Demon at that?"

"It's not about power." Matthew summoned his own raven-imbued staff. "It's all about time." Placing a foot against the low wall, he vaulted himself up and over the battlements, saying, "I'll be back when the Emperor is defeated." Marqest gave him a wide-eyed look that only softened when he saw Matthew transform into a raven in flight.

Marqest stood there and watched the black bird soar toward the approaching army. With a hand stroking his beard thoughtfully, he murmured, "Matthew may be right. All of this. It is not about power, for the Light or the Dark. It's about time. The Darkness is rising, back to what they were a thousand years ago. This world is beginning to reach a point of no return." He heard a groan behind him, and he turned to see Aria standing there. With a quick bow of his head, he said, "Lady Helius, what are you doing out of your room now? You should be resting."

She shook her head with a grimace. Standing there in a

white robe with one sleeve completely slack, she appeared frail, not her usual formidable self. "I am fine, Marqest. What has happened?"

Marqest spoke softly, "The Emperor Regin has ambushed us. He rides on a Demon, the Dread Serpent, to meet us."

"What defenses have we?"

"Master Helius has utilized Lord Helius's computer DATA to construct a barrier around Apolis. He also has a small battalion of guards, the Enigma Brigade, and the Phoenix Regiment to defend him. The Council and I tried to convince him not to enact this crazed plan, but he insists on it."

Aria nodded but did not respond.

Marqest noted that the concern on her face had dissipated. "Are you not worried for his safety?"

With an eyebrow raised, she responded, "Why would I be? This is Matthew we are talking about."

Marqest gripped his staff tightly with one hand and gestured to the approaching battle in the distance. "Do you not see what is in store for him? The strongest army in the East, now fused with Darkness, is headed by a Dark-ridden Emperor astride a serpent as large as the Palace of Light. You are not worried? You are as mad as he is!"

"No," Aria replied, looking out at the Demon as it approached. "I will be helping him."

Marqest's face went livid. "Light knows I will let you do no such thing. I will knock you unconscious myself before I—"

His mouth stopped moving when he saw Aria's sharp glare. "Master Marqest, back down." Marqest held his staff with both hands, as if unsure whether he would actually strike the Empress of Light. "You may be more knowledgeable with *mysteria* than I, but can your passion meet mine right now?"

Marqest lowered his eyes, "No, my Lady."

Aria turned back to the field of impending battle, and,

as she did so, she sensed Marqest move his scepter to strike: she anticipated it with a wall of flames, pushing Marqest back and almost off the wall instantly. Rolling her eyes, she summoned a Gate and went toward the front of the barrier where Matthew, the Brigade, the Regiment, and some guards awaited.

Matthew stood at the head of the group and did not look back when she arrived. He merely looked straight ahead, anticipating the Dark forces that approached. Aria frowned. Together, they had stood against the evil horse anima Maris, the power-crazed Gaspard, and years of war in this watery world. Yet, now, before the Demon and the Emperor Regin, Matthew seemed more afraid than he ever had.

As she walked toward Matthew, the Dread Serpent reached them. Its white body coiled in the water above them, and its ruby eyes glared down at them, fury burning in those ageless gems. Even she stopped when it opened its fanged mouth and spoke, "How daaaare you stand in my way, huuuumans?"

Matthew replied, his voice sonorous enough to even shake Aria's concern. "Your threats do not concern us, Demon. Only the rider on your head has that power!"

The Serpent's eyes thinned into diagonal slits, and its head reared back as if to strike. But a third voice roared above them, "Stop, Demon! Let me down to speak with these humans."

Hissing in frustration, the Demon lowered its head, and a silver-armored figure leaped from its crown onto the ground in front of Matthew and his comrades. The Emperor Regin, despite his refined armor, looked frailer and weaker than ever. "Where is Lord Helius? Is he too much a coward to face me?"

Matthew gripped his staff, his fingers pressing hard into the wood of its length. "We would not waste our lord's strength on a wasted toad like you, Regin. What are you even

doing here? Go back home, where it is safe and warm." Aria
marveled at Matthew. She had never seen him attempt such
wit and outward strength. "Or better yet, go and visit the
disq tournament in the north. Or, have you forgotten about
that?"

The Emperor Regin's face contorted into a snarl. "Foolish boy, have you no respect for your elders?" He smirked.
"How do you even expect to stand against me all by yourselves? It looks like there might be thirty of you, thirty-five
at best. Epofis has killed more than that in one strike, and I
have been known to be close to that number myself. If you
are the only defense Apolis has to offer, the city deserved to
fall in the first place."

Aria spoke up then, causing Matthew to whirl back and
regard her with wide eyes, "Lord Regin, this city is well fortified with the technology the Y'mordi sought to steal from
us. The city needs no men to protect it. We are here to drive
you back."

Regin's growl was familiar to both Aria and Matthew.
"You will all die here, and all your city's hopes with you."
Holding out a hand, he summoned his replica of the Behe-
moth. "The legacy of the Guardians of Light ends here."

Members of the Enigma Brigade widened their eyes at
the sight of the weapon, but no one said anything about it,
not even Matthew and Aria who were, at this point, used
to combatting it. Aria smirked, "Are we supposed to be impressed with your toy? We've beat baddies who knew how
to wield that thing much better than you." Indeed, it seemed
that the Emperor Regin had trouble keeping the sword upright, its tip only inches from the frozen soil.

Glaring, he looked up at the snake. "Mali, get down
here."

As Matthew looked to the top of the serpent, he watched
as a pale figure dove down to the ground, and the body crumpled upon hitting the dirt. A golden collar encircled the

man's neck, and his blonde hair nearly matched it in color. Matthew recognized the blonde Y'mordi, and sympathy touched his heart, yet he did not move.

The Emperor Regin barked, "Mali, use what energy I have left you and kill these foul-mouthed bastards."

Silence reigned for a moment. Mali did not move at first, and no one said or did anything in anticipation. Even the Dread Serpent was anxious to move. The dawn's light began to pour over them, and the current swept by them as if they were mere stones in the landscape.

The naked figure stood to his feet but did not raise his head. As he summoned two katanas, though, the Regiment began casting spells. In response, the Shadow-fused army of the Eastern Continent charged, and the battle for Apolis began, on the same soil where Maris' blood had been spilt ten years earlier.

23

The Crystal Trident

TILGÉ AND STEHL HAD been searching the nearby hotels for hours, with the sun already almost at its peak. It was almost time for the disq tournament to start, and they had not seen or heard from Mirah since the previous night. They had rested for a couple of hours in the transport throughout the night. Despite their frequent calls, however, they had heard nothing.

Tilgé exited one inn with his head lowered. "Nothing," he said grimly.

Stehl turned away, face livid, and searched the dwindling crowd, her eyes daring in twenty directions. "Damn it. Where could he be?"

"Stehl . . ." Tilgé started softly.

"What?" she replied, turning toward him sharply, her tone full of frustration.

"I think we may have to consider what may have happened . . ."

Stehl clenched her jaw. "Do you really think . . . ?"

"Yeah . . . Maksimilian must have got him."

Tightening her fists, Stehl hissed, "If that red-haired

freak hurt him in any way, I'll chop off his other hand and shove it down his throat this time."

Tilgé nodded and ran a hand through his hair. "This is bad, Stehl. We have no idea where he is."

Stehl grabbed him by the handless arm and pulled him in the direction of the stadium and the crowd. "We know where he is going to be, though."

"What? The tournament?"

She did not turn back. "Yeah. The bastard said he would start killing people there. It's time we find him before he finds others to hurt. Maybe if we find him, we will find Mirah, too."

Tilgé pulled back and stopped. "Stehl, stop for a damn second and look me in the eyes."

Whirling on the spot, she demanded, "What is it? We can't just stand here and wait for him to start killing people."

"Shut up!" At this point, a few passers-by gave them looks of concern, but no one stopped or said anything. "Listen to me for just a minute, okay?" Stehl crossed her arms and set her jaw, but did not say anything. "Alright, so have you ever encountered a shark before?" She shook her head. "Well, this is how they act: They sense their prey. They start to circle the area. They size up their prey and the area around. They come in and do a test bite. If they like what they taste, they come back for more. Bite by bite."

Stehl shivered despite herself. "So?"

"Maksimilian is like a shark. Despite his red hair and his personality, he is a cold and calculating killer. If he indeed has Mirah, he hasn't killed him yet. He will use Mirah as bait. He has sized us up, and now he's coming back for more."

"Bite by bite," Stehl repeated, looking back toward the stadium.

"Exactly. He won't start anything until he's confident that we are watching. He's not committing himself to a massacre for his sake. He wants us to feel like any innocent deaths are our fault."

Stehl turned back to Tilgé, her face set with a calmer determination. "Alright, so what do you suggest we do?"

Tilgé pointed out toward the massive stadium. "We go to the stadium. Have a seat. Then, we wait. Maksimilian will not start unless he is sure we are probably there. It's probably about eleven o'clock, now. Nothing will happen until the tournament start. So, we just need to wait until he makes the first move."

Stehl gestured with a hand for Tilgé to follow her as she started to walk toward the stadium, following the crowd. Once he caught up, she asked, "What about if he is on the opposite end of the stadium killing people? Won't security just be the first to show up?"

"No," Tilgé said with confidence. "He will do it near us. I guarantee you he will see us before we see him."

Nodding, Stehl continued to push forward with Tilgé at her side. Among the crowd of anima, griffins, and humans, they looked perfectly normal. They each had hidden weapons, and they were both itching to fight. This seemed like the end, the final battle against Maksimilian. Stehl realized she now had two lovers to protect, and Tilgé, for the first time ever, realized he had someone to protect. Walking through the crowd of people into the tremendous silver gates of the disq stadium, they were two of the only people not excited to witness the outcome of today's game. They merely hoped that minimal blood would be spilled.

Various flags adorned the path to the stadium, their colors a stark contrast to the dull murk that filled the Northern waters. Stehl went through the colors and emblems in her head: Helio, Immyx, Hurale. Many of the flags she did not recognize, yet she tried to guess based on the various animal emblems. When her eyes scanned a flag with a shark as its emblem, she swallowed, thinking about what Tilgé had said about Maksimilian being like a shark. It was hard to process all of this.

After years of trying to decimate the Enigma Brigade, her search had boiled down to killing one ringleader, Maksimilian. Now, she was even engaged to a former Brigadier. As they paid for their tickets, Tilgé handing money off to the vendor, Stehl marveled at her one-handed partner. Tilgé was strong and masculine; a gentleman, yet an ass. He challenged her in ways that Mirah never could. She thought guiltily about how she and Tilgé had slept together in the back of the transport a few hours last night. It seemed wrong, now that it appeared that Mirah was in the malicious hands of Maksimilian.

Blushing, as she stepped into the bustling stadium, she looked up and marveled at the intricate silverworking of the architecture. As people pushed past her and Tilgé, she said in awe, "I never knew the North was capable of structures like this. Did the East fund this?"

Tilgé laughed. "No, star." Stehl blushed deeper at the pet name but did not respond. "The North has griffins, some of the best architects in Gevás. Did you know that the Palace of Light was built by griffins back around the First Obsidian War?"

"No, I thought griffins were all just thieves and rapists."

Tilgé gave her a hard look. "You can't be serious."

She returned the look. "I am! In the Capital, that's all I ever heard about them."

Shaking his head, Tilgé smiled. "Well, hopefully, exploring the world with Mirah and I will change that mindset a bit."

"Exploring the world?"

Now, it was Tilgé's turn to blush, and he rubbed the back of his head. "Well, Mirah and I talked about it . . . settling down sounds nice and all. But, maybe it would be nice to just travel and see the world a bit."

She nodded, and, as she opened her mouth to respond, a booming voice resonated through the stadium. "Ladies and gentlemen, anima and humans, and everyone else out there, welcome to the 2016 Crystal Trident Tournament!"

Stehl looked out to behold the packed stadium go wild with applause. It was her first time truly taking in the stadium. It was a bowl-shaped stadium, with a large glass diamond in the center. The diamond rotated slowly in place, a sparkling blue water filling its interior. A ring of athletes stood around the pinpoint base of the diamond, wearing slick pants that showed off their musculature. Most of them were shirtless, but they each had a colored collar that matched the color of their pants, revealing their represented kingdom.

Tilgé started to pull Stehl by her arm. "C'mon. We need to get seated. We're in others' way."

She looked back and saw the impatient frowns of the people behind her who were waiting to find a good seat. "Oh, sorry," she said, half to Tilgé and half to the angered spectators. As she followed Tilgé through the rows of seats, higher into the stadium, she kept looking over her shoulder at the diamond. In the stadium near the Capital, the playing field was a sphere.

Tilgé said, "Alright, let's sit down here." As they seated, Stehl broke her gaze from the disq playing field and perused the stadium, hoping to catch a flash of red amongst the crowd. However, her search was fruitless.

The announcer began, "Hailing from the forests near the Pyramid, welcome Kelton Efrain!"

The crowd cheered again as a lean, dark-skinned man with a green collar used a Gate to enter the center of the diamond. With his appearance, a green pyramid appeared around him, the main symbol of Arvon. As he swam downward to one of the bottom panels of the glass, he laid back against it and waited for the next athlete.

"Hailing from the icy plains of Helio, welcome Jiron Mackey, the star player of the Southern League!"

Stehl turned to Tilgé after the crowd finished cheering.

"So," she started, holding his hand, "how exactly does disq work?"

He raised an eyebrow at her and tightened his hand around hers. "You've never seen it before?"

She shook her head and looked back at the diamond. "I mean, I've seen kids playing it in the street. I see them throwing around a disk of *mysteria,* and they always try tossing it to each other while going around or through obstacles. That's all I really know, though."

Tilgé let go of her hand and pointed out toward the athletes. "Well, you know that each athlete represents a kingdom. There should be fifteen in total . . . but I only see fourteen. One might have been sick or injured."

Stehl nodded and pointed to the diamond. "Yeah, and they are all setting themselves up on the walls of the arena."

"Yeah, that's what's called the disqspace. An enchanted glass contains it, so that it can't be broken, at least not from the inside. Each kingdom has their own unique disqspace, from pyramids—"

"Let me guess, Arvon?"

With a laugh, Tilgé nodded and continued, "Yes, all the way to an hourglass shape or a spiral. It creates unique variance with each disqspace."

"Alright, so, do the obstacles vary with each area, too?"

Tilgé shrugged. "Sometimes. But sometimes, they stick with standards, too. Clouds in the water that slow you down . . . Gates that transport you to other parts of the disqspace . . . walls that you can crash into . . . currents that speed you up."

"Swimmers!" called the voice that filled the stadium. "Take your positions!" After having swum around the disqspace to rouse glee from their fans, the athletes assumed ready positions against the walls of the space.

"So," Stehl continued, "what's the goal?"

Tilgé stared intently at the diamond, as oblivious to the

events happening around them as Stehl was. "You have to get as many points as you can. You get points by disspelling an enemy's disq or by tapping white orbs. You lose points by being hit with a disq."

"And whoever has the most points wins?"

Tilgé winced. "Not quite."

"On the count of three! One!"

Tilgé finished his thought. "For this tournament, there are ten rounds."

"Two!"

"Each round kicks out the weakest player after a time limit."

"*Three!*"

The athletes were off, and the water in the diamond began swirling instantly, even as the diamond rotated faster.

"Wow," Stehl muttered. "They have to basically race to find those orbs against those kinds of currents?"

Tilgé nodded again and laughed. "Yup. At the same time, they can create Elemental disqs to try to hurt their opponents. Only thing is, though, that those disqs bounce off the walls. They can even hurt the original caster."

This time, Stehl winced. "Spirits of Light . . . that sounds harder than I imagined it would be. I'll stick to sharpshooting, thanks."

Tilgé smiled at first and then snapped to reality. "Speaking of sharpshooting . . . where is our red-headed demon? It should be about noon now."

The two looked around, particularly behind them, scanning the faces around the stadium for Maksimilian's trademarked red hair. The only red they saw was in some of the occasional griffins in the crowd, however. As they searched, the crowd cheered and booed as various athletes gained and lost points. Stehl sent a cursory glance at the diamond and was amazed at the now four colored disqs that bounced among the walls of the disqspace. She shook her head, impressed, before returning to her search. "Where is that damned man?"

Then, she felt the card in her pocket buzz. Mirah was calling them.

She rushed to pull the card from her pants, and, when she did, a white image of the caller appeared above it. Standing there on the flat of the card was Maksimilian.

Stehl fought her instinct to crush the card in her palm. Over the crowd, she managed to speak to the figure. "Where did you put my fiancé, you bastard?"

Even before he spoke, Stehl saw the seats behind Maksimilian. He was here somewhere. She stood and started moving even as he spoke, Tilgé close behind her. "Oh, he's around. I thought I would let you know before I started killing people. I wanted to make sure you arrived in one piece." The smug grin on the man's face sent blood rushing to Stehl's face.

"Where are you? I can't kill a snake if he doesn't come out of his cowardly hole." Though this was said low, Maksimilian heard it, and his grin vanished.

"By the end of this tournament, there will be so much blood on your hands, Captain Terrell. I hope you are prepared for that."

Tilgé grabbed her by the shoulder and pointed in the distance. They saw him, standing at the top of a section of seats, he seemed to loom over the seated spectators before him, a serpent waiting to strike.

Stehl pocketed the card, not caring what else Maksimilian had to say. Even from this distance, she could see him reach under his cloak, as if to grab his Sword. With a snarl of her own, she reached under her own cloak and grabbed her gun. Tilgé moved to grab her and stop her, but love held him back. As she whipped the gun out in front of the crowd, many people gasped in surprise, and a few shrieked in fright. The sound was lost in the general sounds of the crowd. Maksimilian raised his Sword, and Stehl aimed her gun with lightning speed and fired, the one sound that resounded even over the din of the crowd.

The bullet went right over Maksimilian's shoulder, and he fell back in surprise, turning toward the pair in shocked anger. At this point, the whole crowd was searching for the source of the gunshot. Those around Stehl and Tilgé began to scatter in a panic.

Stehl could not fathom how her bullet had missed his head. Her skill should have been good enough; how had he been so lucky?

With a grimace, Maksimilian raised his Sword and swung in a wide arc, sending blood-spurting bodies into the fleeing mass. The screams intensified as people began to realize that danger was stemming from two different points.

"Damn it!" Stehl yelled as she reloaded her rifle to fire again. Tilgé ran forward to engage Maksimilian, still quite a distance away. Even as security officers ran to disarm Maksimilian, he sent an arc of golden energy through them, felling them among the rows of seats. The red-haired man saw Stehl raise her rifle, and he held his Sword in front of him. As Stehl fired, Maksimilian expressed little surprise that the bullet collided with the edge of the blade, splitting it so that both halves of the bullet shot in either direction of his face, neither touching him. Although Stehl was dumbfounded, Maksimilian was learning when to rely on his blessed luck.

Then, Tilgé was upon him. The two single-handed former Brigadiers locked blades instantly, but Tilgé was now the faster of the two. Maksimilian, even with his Light-enhanced speed, could not match Tilgé's speed with the bulky Behemoth. Tilgé grazed a shoulder with his sword, and then the back of Maksimilian's leg. Maksimilian struggled to keep the Behemoth between them, and he growled as he dodged the attacks, only able to make one attack for every three or four of Tilgé's. Tilgé ducked under each of Maksimilian's horizontal slashes and leaped to the side when Maksimilian made downward strikes.

Stehl jogged over to them while they fought, leaping over bodies and seats as she made her way. She knew she could not shoot while Tilgé was engaged, but she could at least get closer and see if an opening would reveal itself. Heart thumping in her chest, she ignored the bodies and blood that murked the water, and she focused solely on Maksimilian and Tilgé, willing her lover not to be hacked to pieces by the claymore-wielding maniac.

Right as she was close enough to be comfortable to fire again, Maksimilian landed a kick on Tilgé's chest, sending him falling backward onto a metallic row, his back landing hard on an edge before he sprawled face down two rows further down. Stehl ran forward, not knowing what she could do. As she ran, she saw Maksimilian raise his Sword, a golden glow emanating from its length. She stood between Maksimilian and Tilgé. She raised her rifle and aimed it at Maksimilian, knowing that it would do her no good.

She fired.

"Stehl!"

Her heart leaped for a split second as she recognized the masculine voice, and then her eyes closed, expecting the arc of the Behemoth's energy to split her in two.

A clanging sound resonated through the water.

She opened her eyes and saw that her Sword had left its sheath, floating in front of her. Its silver glow stunned everyone around. Reaching out to grab it, she saw that Maksimilian was fleeing the stadium at a run. Tilgé was in hot pursuit. Trying to get over her own bewilderment, she stepped to follow, but a hand stayed her where she was. Before even turning, she realized that she had recognized the voice behind her.

"Randir." She turned and stared into his blazing eyes.

Although he was in his black robes, his hood was pulled back so she could see the scars on his face and the smile on his lips. "Stehl . . . I've . . ." He shook his head. "Look, Y'tal has a bomb system set up under the stadium. It's going to blow this whole place up. You've got to get out of here!"

"What?" she asked in disbelief. Looking around, she saw that there were still people fleeing the stadium. "There's still people here, Randir. We've got to disarm that bomb."

Randir shook his head again. "No, there's no time. It's going to go off in about five minutes. And that's just a rough guess."

He raised a hand to summon a Gate, but Stehl pulled his arm back down. "No." Her eyes bore into his. "We need to save these people."

Seeing there was no arguing with her, Randir growled, "Alright, fine! Start helping people evacuate. I'll see what I can do with the bomb. But, hurry!" Without another word, he created a Gate and went to the underworkings of the stadium. Stehl ran to the entrance, helping some of the older people get out in a timely manner. As she did so, she realized her heart was beating for a number of reasons. Where was Tilgé? Where was Mirah? Where was Maksimilian? How had Randir found her all of a sudden? Could she get these people out in time? She could not think to answer the questions, so she focused on guiding people to the exit.

"Randir, you'd better hurry up . . ."

Her mind filled with an image of his face. The thought made her angry . . . happy . . . relieved . . . all of these at once.

With each passing minute, the remainder of the fans left the stadium, such that only Stehl stood in the massive aperture to the stadium. "C'mon, Randir. Where are you?"

A tremendous light filled her vision, and next came the deafening roar.

Seconds passed.

As the light faded, heat enveloped her, and she saw that a silver aura surrounded her and, beyond that, a cloud of smoke and fire. The bomb had gone off. She looked down at her Sword and realized the glowing blade had once again protected her. "How is this possible?" She looked toward the center of the stadium. "Randir, please come out." She stood there in the doorway, unsure of what to do, unsure of what she *could* do.

Finally, she decided to move. Walking forward into the smoke and flames, the silver aura protected her from the worst of the heat and from the black smoke. Metal debris covered the ground, and she had to climb to move past the entrance hallway of the stadium. Each step forced her to watch for broken glass and sharp edges of the metal. To make matters worse, the smoke hindered her vision such she could only see within the three feet in front of her provided by the silver aura. She marveled at the power of Kohana's Fang. She had witnessed it protect her from the effects of *mysteria* and indeed stop another from using it against her, but now it seemed to be actively protecting her, as if it were alive.

"Randir!" she called hopefully, realizing that, as colossal as the stadium was, there was little chance that wherever Randir was enabled him to hear her now. More under her breath, she said, "Dammit, Randir. Where are you?"

As if in response, Kohana's Fang glowed even brighter in her hilt. Stehl widened her eyes as she drew the blade. "What is it? Can you help me find him?" She lowered her eyes. "I know you don't owe me anything. You saved my life twice in the past half-hour. But if you could help me find Randir, it would mean more than you know."

She felt the Sword pull from her hands, and she let it go, amazed as it floated slowly through the rubble. Silently, she kept up with the magical blade, staying within its silver aura of protection. Remembering the layout of the stadium before it was destroyed, she realized she was now where one of the managing offices was. As soon as the Sword stopped moving, she saw the gloved hand beneath the rubble. "Randir!"

Crouching on her knees, she began digging through the

debris, pushing back wall panels and the charred remnants of computers that had been in the room. Although many of the edges sliced into her hands and arms, she only increased her fervor, her heart pounding as she lifted piece after piece. She could see his whole arm now.

His hand flexed then. "Randir? Can you hear me?"

Muffled beneath the debris, he managed, "Stehl, get back."

At first, she was confused. Then, she saw a red light appear in the palm of his hand. Falling backward, she started to crawl through the debris, trying to evade the spell Randir was about to cast. Once she thought she was a safe distance, she called out, "Do it!"

A red and fiery blast shot upward through the metal, and debris came flying toward her. Out of reflex, she held up her arm to deflect the objects, but the barrier held firm. Each piece of metal bounced off the silver shield. Lowering her arm, she saw that Randir was crouched on top of the debris, his black robe charred in multiple places, revealing his heavily muscled body. As she moved to help him, she saw there was another person with him, someone crouched beside him.

"Mirah?" she whispered as she increased her pace.

Practically falling on top of them, she grabbed Mirah's shoulder to set him upright. He almost fell back, but Randir caught him. The red-haired man shook his head. "He's out. Still alive, just unconscious."

Stehl sat back, relieved. "What happened?"

Randir wiped dirt off his face with a bare hand and replied, "I started working on the bomb, and then I sensed this guy in the room above. It was last minute, though. So, I just got up here and created a barrier around us. I hope no one got killed by the bomb, did they?"

She shook her head. "No. We got them all out."

"Good." Randir's stare was vacant, looking out into the rubble of the stadium. Turning his head back to her, he leaned forward and put a hand on her arm. "Hey, are you alright?"

At first, she smiled, and then she frowned. "Randir, how did you know there was going to be a bomb under the stadium?"

A snarl appeared on his face. "That damned Pullatus. He's the leader of the Y'mordi, and he's getting reckless. I found out from Mali back in the Western Continent."

"What were you doing there?"

Randir saw the cold look on her face. He wondered if she was asking if he had been doing anything dastardly. He shook his head and gave her a look of genuine worry. "I was looking for you."

Now, her eyes went wide. "For me?"

"Yes, I . . ." He stopped, shook his head again, and started laughing. "It's crazy. It's been years since I've seen you, Stehl. And I never stopped thinking about you."

A pained look spread across Stehl's face, and she started to reach a hand out to him. "Randir, I . . . I haven't stopped thinking about you either. And . . . I hate you for that . . . but I love you for it, too. But, Randir, now I'm . . ."

"Stop," Randir said, squeezing her arm. "I don't want to know. I just . . . I had to see you again."

Now, it was Stehl's turn to shake her head. "You didn't come here just to see me . . . or to stop the bomb."

Lowering his eyes, Randir said, "You're right." He stood amid the debris and put a hand into the folds of his robe. "I realize it is stupid now. I know that. But, I still wanted to give you this." He pulled out a rose, the third one Stehl had seen the past two weeks. Her mouth gaped at the sight.

"I . . ." she started.

"No, Stehl. I don't want you to say a word. I couldn't truly ask you to accept, but I can't bear the idea of rejection, either. So, just have a rose. Let a flower be a flower." He tossed it to her, and it landed at her bent knees.

As Randir turned as if to leave, Stehl struggled to stand and said, "No, wait."

Once she had risen to her feet, five Gates appeared around them, and Shadows poured onto the ruins of the stadium. Amid them stood a robed stranger. "Randir, I do not like that you have interfered with my plans."

Randir did not turn but muttered, "Lord Y'tal."

24
Falsehood

Y'TAL RAISED HIS HANDS toward Randir. "You call me your Lord, yet you find every way you can to disobey me. Do you not comprehend the chains that constrict you? Do you not understand the contract you signed in your blood?"

Randir turned to face Y'tal, and a massive hammer appeared in his hand. "You keep bitching about that like I actually care. I signed that damn thing a thousand years ago. I had been promised the world, and all I got was a shitty bedroom in a dark castle for a thousand years. Was it the reward you had hoped for, yourself, Y'tal?"

Stehl's head turned back and forth to regard both of the figures in astonishment. The hooded Y'mordi was much shorter than Randir and spoke in a high, childlike voice. She could not fathom why Randir was so intimidated by the stranger. She glanced once at Mirah to make sure he was alright, still breathing, and then she walked over to Randir's side, brandishing Kohana's Fang, its glow piercing in the murk of the water.

"Hmph," Y'tal smirked. "Will seeing this girl die for you be the reward you seek, Y'ran? Will her blood be the price of your obedience?"

Just as Randir prepared a fireball, Stehl swung with her Sword, and a ray of silver energy shot toward Y'tal. He sidestepped out of the beam's path the last second. Stehl roared, "If you plan to kill me, you're going to have to quit talking and start fighting, you coward!"

Randir growled lowly, "Stehl. Get out of here. Now."

Her head did not turn to address him. Y'tal spoke almost in a whisper, "Girl, do you understand that the man at your side is one of the legendary Lords of the Shadows? Does that not fill you with fear?"

"Stehl, go!" Randir repeated, tempted to grab her and throw her through a Gate.

"No!" Stehl cried, turning back to Randir, addressing him with fiery eyes. She whipped her head back toward Y'tal. "And you. For someone so small and young, you sure do act pretty high and mighty. I don't care what Randir is. I've known he's a Lord of the Shadows for years, and I've still loved him. There are lots of things I fear, but neither of you are among them. The past few years, I've fought the Enigma Brigade, Maksimilian, Shadows, griffins, and a fair number of sea serpents along the way. How in Darkness do you think you threaten or intimidate me?"

Y'tal smiled beneath his hood. "Girl, I hold the key to your lover's heart. I can crush him without lifting a finger, and I could subdue you with equal ease. I was the Dark Lord's closest confidante, and I am the Prophet of Shadows in this world. All Darkness succumbs to me. I have controlled both Maris and the Emperor Regin." Suddenly, the current swept past him, pressing against Randir and Stehl violently. "In this world, I . . . am . . . *Death!*"

With lightning speed, he flew with the current toward Stehl. Randir leaped between them and blocked Y'tal's charge with his hammer, the younger Y'mordi's grappling with the handle of the hammer and finally tossing both the hammer and Randir over his head, as if Randir were weightless. Stehl raised her own Sword and swung downward over Y'tal's head. Y'tal kicked to the side, his foot connecting with Stehl's stomach and sending her flying backward.

A gruff voice called out, "Stehl!" as she crashed into the pile of debris. Randir looked up to see that Mirah was getting to his feet, holding a small handgun out against Y'tal.

"Don't do it, you fool," Randir muttered.

As Mirah aimed the gun at Y'tal, Randir watched Y'tal prepare to destroy Mirah in one blow, but Randir shot a fireball toward the black-robed figure. Y'tal was forced to put some distance between all of them to dodge both projectiles. Stehl rose, blood trailing across her arms, and charged at Y'tal with her glowing blade. Y'tal sent an orb of black Darkness toward Stehl, but it dissipated against the blade, and the Y'mordi growled in frustration, leaping several yards in the water to avoid Stehl. "Why must you all resist?"

The Shadows that Y'tal had summoned upon arriving, which had stayed in their places watching their masked leader stoically, suddenly advanced upon the three, silver swords flashing through the clouded water. Stehl struggled to combat the rushing Shadows while keeping an eye out for Y'tal. Randir flew into the water, searching for Y'tal amid the murk, knowing not to engage the inconsequential Shadows on the ground. Mirah, on the other hand, was firing bullets at anything that came close to him. The water, though dark, was full of the clashes of swords and the blasts of Mirah's gun. But, Randir focused on finding Y'tal and stopping him from killing his beloved. His heart could not sense the dark presence in the vicinity. Yet, he knew that Y'tal had not left: he had only masked his heart from being traced or sensed. With a snarl, Randir summoned the fiery energy in his heart and transformed. His robes burned away, and his golden, glowing body elongated into a serpentine form, his arms and legs becoming bulkier while draconian wings formed upon his

back. The Red Dragon's crimson eyes scanned the murk with
new insight, and he spotted the Y'mordi leader instantly.
The Dragon's tortuous body sped through the water, its maw
opening to consume Y'tal in one swoop, but Y'tal vanished
into smoke before the Dragon reached him.

Snarling, Randir doubled back, searching again for Y'tal.
Then, he sensed Y'tal down with Mirah and Stehl. In frantic
fear, he shot downward, hoping to intercept whatever attack
Y'tal was planning. However, a sudden light appeared, small
at first, but increasing as the Red Dragon neared the ground.
The light grew to fill his vision, awakening his dark instinct
to flee back into the shadows.

Randir landed on the ground once the light had dissipated, and he was in human form, again robed. The murk
had cleared along with the Shadows, and a new figure stood
between Stehl and Y'tal—a one-handed man wearing tight,
silver garments. In his one hand, he held a simple sword.

Y'tal said, "Another male come to protect this girl?" He
smirked. "Y'ran, you would love a woman who already has
two lovers bound to her?"

Stehl interrupted, not allowing Randir to answer, "You
keep talking like that, kid. I can have as many lovers as I'd
like, and then some. They are my protectors, and they are my
lovers. For all your talk, do you think you can stop all four of
us? Between Tilgé's Light, Mirah's military experience, my
Kohana's Fang, and Randir's Fire, you are powerless here."

Tilgé called emphatically, "You heard her, Y'mordi."

Mirah nodded and added, "Return to da shadows."

Randir stood beside the others and, smiling, said, "War is
upon us in the South, Lord Y'tal. Focus your energies there.
You have no business here."

Y'tal spoke with a level voice, "What makes you think,
Y'ran, that you have authority to discuss what my business
is?"

Randir gripped his hammer tightly. "Your second-in-command. Your General of the Shadows. And, as such, I can advise you that dealing with random humans in the North does not advance your military situation between Lord Helius and the East."

The water seemed to get darker around them. "Y'ran . . ." Y'tal started. "You are a presumptuous fool. You have not the power you claim to wield." He held out a hand, palm directed at Randir. "Return what was lent to you. The time has come for another to rise out of the ashes of your pyre."

Screaming, Randir fell to his knees, clasping his heart.

"Randir!" Stehl yelled as she ran to his side. In an instant, a black sphere shot from Randir's chest into Y'tal's hand, washing the shorter man in a white glow.

"He . . . he . . ." Randir gasped as he crouched on all fours.

Y'tal turned away from the four lovers. "I would say I am sorry, but I am sure you will be delighted to hear that you were never meant to be one of us, not truly."

"What?" Randir breathed.

"Your soul . . . it was solely to act as a repository for the Dark Lord's power until the true seventh Y'mordi awakened. Now, I believe the time has come. Your connection to the Darkness is gone, as is your immortality and your name."

All were silent as Randir processed what Y'tal was saying. "I'm . . . free?"

Y'tal was silent at first and then looked over his shoulder at Randir. "Yes, you are. However, I shall give you and your lover one final gift." He extended an arm in Randir's direction and released a blue ball of energy. The action was too quick for anyone to stop it. Collapsed on the debris, Randir was frozen in Stasis.

"Randir?" Stehl cried as she felt Randir for signs that he was still alive. When she turned to look back at Y'tal, he was gone. Mirah and Tilgé came to her side to help her carry Randir back to the village.

25

Rent in the Space
Between Realms

AUGMENTED WITH THE gift of Time, everything slowed before Matthew. He watched the Dread Serpent rear its head back, ready to strike, and he saw Mali charge with a katana in each hand, by far the faster attack, as Mali was moving with the speed of Light. However, time held even Light in its sway, and Matthew was the last surviving Keeper of Time. The forces behind him were moving toward the massive armies behind Regin and the Demon, almost frozen in their momentum.

His eyes stared intently into Mali's. He remembered Mali most vividly from meeting him on the Varyx island ten years ago. Back then, the man had worn a white robe and seemed to be as powerful as any of the other Y'mordi. Now, Mali was markedly different. His whole body was covered in cuts and scratches. His skin clung to his ribs, and the emaciated man had a golden collar tight around his neck. Had the Emperor Regin made one of the Y'mordi a *slave?* He touched on the collar with *mysteria* and felt its power. Yes, whatever Regin had done, it was now trapping Mali under his spell. The flaming look in Mali's eyes was one of despair and fear. Despite himself, Matthew felt sympathy for the creature.

Lifting his staff, he aimed a strike a Mali's chest and unfroze time mid-swing.

As the sound of gunshots and flying spells rang through the water, Matthew's staff went between Mali's blades and rammed into the Y'mordi's sternum, creating a loud thud as the Y'mordi crumpled to the ground in pain.

Although surprised at Mali's instant defeat, Matthew leaped backward, narrowly dodging the Dread Serpent's lunge downward at him, which barely missed both Matthew and Mali. Matthew retreated toward Lilian and Marqest, growling, "Regin has Mali under some kind of spell."

A powerful beam of blue light shot through the water, coming from Apolis. The beam destroyed tens of Shadows at once. Marqest smirked. "Looks like Lord Helius was right. His computer has a pretty reliable defense system."

Aria ignored the remark and added, "If Regin has an Y'mordi under control, then he has fallen into Darkness as much as Maris had."

Matthew shook his head as he stared up at the Emperor atop his roaring Dread Serpent. "No, he's stronger in the Darkness, but he's ten times as weak, physically."

Aria regarded Matthew carefully. "What is the plan?"

"I need you three to handle the Demon. I can take care of Regin."

Lilian nodded and responded for all three of them. "We will do it. Go."

Matthew needed little encouraging and froze time long enough for him to morph into a raven, flying upward over the Serpent's head and landing on its back in his human form again, facing the Emperor Regin. Once time unfroze, Matthew started, "Well, Regin, I see you have been dabbling in the Darkness."

Even as the Serpent moved to attack the three mages on the ground, the two kept their balance. The Emperor

Regin laughed deeply, and it was now that Matthew realized the Emperor spoke with a doubled voice, a much higher voice speaking simultaneously with Regin's bass. "Foolish Matthew, you have inherited your brother's stupidity and arrogance."

Matthew swung his staff into a defensive position, gradually realizing his opponent was more dangerous than he had initially realized. "What do you know of me, Regin?"

The water darkened around the Emperor Regin, and Matthew could feel that dark power intensifying around them. "I know that you are a Keeper of Time—the last one, to my knowledge. And, I know how to counteract your spells."

The man rushed up the Serpent's back, his Behemoth raised over his head to strike at Matthew. As Matthew slowed down time to dodge the attack, he saw that Regin did not slow. He felt the blade sink into his shoulder, but he managed to release an explosion of Wind to knock Regin back before the sword could sink any further into him. The spell separated Regin from his sword, and Matthew turned with a pained grimace to see the blade three inches into his shoulder, hanging there. After placing his staff in his other hand, he used his now-free staff hand to wrench the Behemoth free. He tossed it out into the sea, and Regin gasped, "No!"

Matthew, blood pouring from his shoulder down his side, replied, "What will you do now without your weapon? I thought you guys could just summon it back, anyway?"

Regin just stood there and growled. Raising a hand, he created a silver sword from *mysteria* and rushed at Matthew again. This time, Matthew knew his Time spells would not work and blocked the attack with his staff, letting the bottom end of his staff twist its way into Regin's stomach, leaving the old man breathless. Regin fell to his knees on the Demon's scaly hide.

"I . . . I can't . . ." the man gasped.

It was then that Matthew truly realized how frail the

elderly man was. "Regin?"

The doubled voice smirked loudly, "Damn this body. I knew it would not last, yet it decided to wait until this battle to give in entirely? Oh, well." The old man keeled over, falling off the side of the Serpent and toward the ground.

"No!" Matthew called, leaping after him. His staff's orb glew with a blue light, and he shot it down toward Regin to slow the old man's fall. Right as the spell caught up with Regin, the old man cast a spell himself, and Matthew could sense it was a Gate. However, the two spells collided.

An explosion of purple light filled everyone's vision, and the wave of force sent everyone flying backward.

Matthew struggled to rise when he heard screams.

The Shadows had all dissipated, but the Emperor Regin's army, the Phoenix Regiment, and the Enigma Brigade had ceased fire. Before them was a massive purple and black sphere. It was almost as large as the Dread Serpent that hovered over it, and the sphere seemed to pull everyone toward it, the current flowing into it as dark energy poured out of it.

Marqest called out over the din of the sucking sounds of the sphere, "Master Helius! The Emperor Regin went in there!"

Nodding with grim determination, Matthew responded, "You all take care of the Demon. I'll be back!"

Grabbing his raven-etched staff, he ran toward the sphere, dodging a strike of the Dread Serpent on his way. As he approached the sphere, he felt it pull him harder with each step. Once he ran into it, it reappeared several feet behind him, and the world had changed.

The world around him was no longer water. Shadows pervaded every inch of the air, and he began choking on the black wisps in the air, his lungs crying for water. Collapsing onto the ashen ground, his eyes rolled until they spotted a prone body beside his own, that of the Emperor Regin, his face frozen in a perpetual scream.

"Emperor . . . Regin?" Matthew gasped, his hands grasping his throat.

"He's dead," said a high voice farther into the darkness. "You are a fool for following me here, Matthew."

Matthew closed his eyes and concentrated on clearing out his thoughts. He summoned Wind and forced water to pour through the Gate toward his face, giving him water to breathe again. Taking a deep breath of the cool liquid, he stood on the obsidian earth. "Who are you? Where are we?"

A familiar face stepped forward in the darkness. "Do you not remember me?"

Matthew's eyes widened as he recognized Ixion. "You."

Ixion was not wearing his traditional dark robes but a regal emerald suit of armor, his wiry hair billowing in the hazy wind. "Yes, Matthew. Your troubles started with me a decade ago, and they will end with me now, here in the Realm of Darkness." The green knight of shadows drew two long daggers and smiled at Matthew.

"The . . . Realm of Darkness?" The title made sense to Matthew. The air itself was fused with Darkness, and all of Matthew's senses felt weaker there.

Ixion did not respond but charged toward Matthew, daggers poised to kill.

Matthew transformed into a raven and dodged the dual swipe, reverting back into a human once he was behind Ixion. Keeping his flying momentum going, he swung his staff at Ixion's back, but the staff bounced off Ixion's impenetrable armor harmlessly. Ixion whirled back around, daggers flashing as he spun.

Matthew struggled to block each of the deadly slashes, twisting his weapon every way possible to block the dual weapons. He could tell that Ixion's movements were much more taxing than his own. At this rate, Ixion would be too exhausted to fight within minutes. Ixion must have sensed this, for he changed tactics. Jumping back, Ixion summoned a vine from the ground to wrap around Matthew's foot, trapping him in place. Becoming aware of the trick instantly, with each subsequent vine Ixion created, Matthew slowed time and batted away each vine. Before un-slowing time, he tapped the vine at his foot once with his orb, aging it to rot instantly.

No sooner had he stopped, Ixion was upon him again with his daggers in a fury. As the glistening blades only met the enchanted wood of Matthew's staff, Matthew recalled Drage discussing his own encounter with Ixion. Drage had said that Ixion's daggers were always tipped with sleeping poisons. That knowledge was a grim reminder that Matthew needed to not let Ixion even nick his body—ven that could prove deadly in this battle. Still, at the rate Ixion was going, Matthew knew it would be much less energy-consuming to play defense. A Wind spell would disarm Ixion instantly, but it would be easier to combat Ixion martially first to exhaust him. Matthew barely held onto *mysteria*, allowing Time to barely increase the speed of his reflexes, just enough to block Ixion's attacks with ease.

Then, Matthew sensed Ixion open himself more to *mysteria,* and the energy he felt terrified him. Ixion waved a hand, and a field of vines appeared behind him, each snaking their way toward Matthew. Gritting his teeth, Matthew realized his basic time-slowing spell would not be sufficient to stop all of these. Holding his staff centered with his body, he tapped the staff on the ashy ground and sent a wall-shaped blast of Force from the orb embedded in the staff, and the wave disintegrated the vines a couple of feet from Matthew's body.

As Ixion prepared another spell, Matthew tapped his staff again, freezing Ixion in time. Knowing that Ixion had some way to counteract the Time spell, Matthew shot a spear of Force at Ixion, and, even as the Time spell dissipated, the spear tore a hole through Ixion, and Ixion, with eyes wide, collapsed, transforming into wisps of smoke, leaving only the emerald armor on the ground.

Matthew exhaled deeply and breathed in again from the stream of water that connected him to the massive sphere. His eyes scanned the ground for the Emperor Regin, but the corpse was nowhere to be seen. He looked back to the sphere. If it was a Gate, why had it not disappeared once Ixion had been killed?

With nervous fear in his heart, he stepped back toward the sphere. As water enveloped him, he entered to see the Dread Serpent fleeing the battle, its winding body vanishing against the horizon.

Aria and Lilian ran over to Matthew, Aria calling with concern, "Matthew, are you alright?" Lilian expressed the same concern with her eyes, staring at Matthew's shoulder wound.

Matthew nodded. "Regin is dead."

Regin's troops heard this and started talking amongst themselves, though Matthew could not hear their words.

Lilian replied, "That is a sad truth. What about this Gate? Why does it remain now?"

Marqest joined their ranks. "This is no ordinary Gate."

All three of them turned toward Marqest. Matthew asked what they were all thinking, "What do you mean?"

Marqest looked up at the massive sphere. "Gates are simply connections between hearts, not just connections between worlds. Gates can also move between the seven realms of each world."

Matthew shook his head. "That doesn't make sense."

Aria explained, "Sure, it does. Each world has seven . . . phases, you can think. There is only one phase that people actually populate because the world only gives us the power to survive in one: the world's heart's true Element."

"So, just now, I really was in the Realm of Darkness."

Marqest gave Matthew a cold stare. "If that is truly where that Gate leads, it is a true danger."

Lilian said, "How do we get rid of it then?"

"Gates to realms are no different from Gates to worlds. I can sense the power of this one to see it is a realm Gate. But this is a Gate created from both Time and Space."

Matthew frowned at first. Then, his face softened. "I understand."

Aria looked to him. "What do you mean? I'm not sure I fully do yet."

"When Regin . . . no . . . when Ixion created the Gate, I used a Time spell." He noticed how everyone raised their eyes about Ixion, but no one interrupted. "The two spells must have collided. What does this mean, Marqest? Is this Gate just stuck here, or will a basic Time spell fix it?"

Marqest shook his head gravely. "This is what is called a Rent. In Dagan's old castles, there used to be Rents that connected this realm to the Realm of Darkness, making it easier for Shadows to seep into this realm. The only thing is that they only dissipated with Dagan's destruction. Rents are destroyed when the creator dies."

"But, I killed Ixion," Matthew countered.

"No, Ixion cannot truly die." At Marqest's words, all looked at Matthew with wide-eyed looks on their faces.

Matthew sighed. "Damn it."

In the council room, the Emperor's Council decided what actions would need to be taken.

Leona having returned from helping Lady Chiara, said, "The soldiers of the East have returned to their continent, and Immyx is placing the next-in-line on the throne. While they are grieving, we need to return his Majesty to our throne."

Aria nodded. "I, too, am worried about my husband."

Matthew said, "I will go to Earth and find him."

"No!" Marqest snapped with finality. "For once, you will do as you are told. You will stay here."

Matthew stood and barked at the elder man. "No,

yourself. I am tired of these games. I am done with this role as Emperor of Light. I renounce the Crown for the moment. The Council can handle the affairs of Helio for a few hours while I grab Drage. Last time you let me lead, I caused a Rent right outside Apolis. I killed the Emperor Regin. And, the Dread Serpent escaped, too."

Leona said softly, "Matthew, go to your brother. We will take care of things here."

Marqest turned and glared at her, but he did not argue. With Valdridge's death, Leona was the head of the Council, and Marqest knew his place. He nodded to Matthew, showing obeisance.

Matthew turned and fled from the room, despair burning his soul. He was a failure.

26

At the End of the World

LORD DRAGENOPN HELIUS, Feranx the Royal Mechanic, and the Ring of Elders flew through the Gate, one by one, to enter the final sanctuary for Cronus 624.

Cold blasted them instantly. All around them were ice-and-snow-capped glacial mountains. The sky was gray with clouds, and their breath froze in the air. This place was perpetual winter, and it bit at the humans with savage rapacity, unfeeling, uncaring, and mercilessly. In unison, the Elders cast multiple Heat spells to keep the party warm. They would need to feel their fingers if they were to cast the proper spells they would need ahead.

Drage and Feranx headed the group, with Drage standing on a green screen and Feranx flying with his wings. The two held grim but determined expressions, their eyes piercing the cold with warm vigilance. They flew over peaks and slopes, valleys and crevices, all treacherous landscapes that promised various threats and dangers.

After minutes of traversing the ice, they saw a central valley with a lone metallic spire at its core. Drage muttered its name to himself, "Cronus 624." He signaled with a hand for the group to land well in advance of the monster, the monster he himself had caused to be borne. "Elders, get in position. Keep a safe distance: we do not yet know its range of attack."

Now taking his word as command, all the Elders except Elizabeth scattered. Elizabeth approached her son cautiously. "Are you certain about this, Lord Helius?"

Drage was silent in response, and Feranx lowered his eyes, feeling awkward at the interaction. Drage's eyes following the flying dots in the horizon, bidding them to hurry to their places so they could begin the defensive rituals. Once he was sure they were in their places, Drage nodded, and the screen rose again with Feranx alone in tow, heading toward the final module.

What had seemed from afar to be a solid tower now was much more complex. The computer was made of two solid columns, the top one hovering three yards above the lower. The whole structure was the height of a ten-story skyscraper, yet it was much thinner and cylindrical. Metallic panels orbited the two halves, and Drage wondered if these were as versatile as Feranx's digital screens. Red lights adorned the whole structure, and, at points, wires poked from the base of the thing, connecting it to some unseen power source buried beneath the ice.

Then, the ground below shook, and Drage held out an arm, halting both himself and Feranx. The shaking stopped immediately. A deep voice boomed across the valley. "Dragenopn Helius, you are here to arrest the execution of Program: Ragnarok, are you not?"

Drage called back, well aware that the computer would be able to hear him even if it were a whisper from this distance. "Yes, Cronus, I am. Your programming has been corrupted."

"Forgive me," the computer replied, "for my programming anticipated that this would be one of your rhetorical ploys. I am disinclined to believe you."

Feranx marveled at the computer's intelligence. He sent a green screen of text toward Drage. *"Drage, are you sure you're sure about this? There's a good chance we could all die."*

Drage responded without facing the griffin. "That is a risk I am willing to take." He addressed the computer, "Cronus 624, if your programming deems it so, then you are right to distrust me, but still hear my pleas. When you examine your code, do you not see that contradictions abound? Your code has been corrupted. I created the base set, and my enemy stole you away and inserted code to make you more aggressive and deadly. Let me restore you to your full glory!"

"No," the computer said, its voice almost shaking the ice itself. "The ice of this wasteland will be your tomb. If you believe yourself to be my master, then come and test your creation!"

Drage muttered under his breath, "Gladly." He looked sideways at his mechanic. "Feranx, report."

A green screen flew in front of Drage's face. *"Sir, the computer has a barrier all around the area. None of the Ring's spells will be able to penetrate it. It seems that the barrier controls all use of* mysteria *inside it . . ."*

"Communicate this to the Ring, then. They will need to destroy the barrier before they can start defending us." The ground began shaking once again, and the panels that were once hovering around the module started spinning toward Drage and Feranx. "They are going to need to hurry, though. Cronus will not wait for them."

Summoning the Sword of Destiny, Drage flew forward. The rapidly approaching tiles spun dangerously toward Drage. With Sword flowing through the Way of the Dragon, Drage split each panel into pieces. The debris fell lifeless to the ice below, melting straight through the glaciers. Eight panels later, Drage realized Cronus was done with those. Now, as he looked at the machine, he saw it was changed. Three cylindrical protrusions extended from the top half of

the module toward Drage. "What are . . . ?" Once he saw a
red light, he instinctively raised his Sword. A beam of glaring
red light shot toward him, pressing hard against the Sword
with incredible force. When the beam stopped, Drage saw
that his sleeves had been burned off, and his hair was singed.
Still, he was unharmed.

Feranx flew to Drage's side. *"Sir, with a cannon that
strong, we can't approach until the Ring is able to destroy the
barrier!"*

"Watch me!" Drage roared back in anger. He pointed his
Sword at the module, and the blade glowed with an intense
blue aura. Releasing the energy with a growl, Drage shot his
own beam of energy toward Cronus, still a little over a mile
away. He watched it pierce the barrier, but the energy dissipated well before it could reach Cronus. "Damn it!"

The computer roared back, "An excellent attempt, Lord
Helius. It is my turn again." Again, Drage saw the flash of
a red light, and he held his Sword up to block the attack.
This time, he focused some energy through the Sword, and
the barrier it created dissipated the beam without burning
Drage.

"I have to get closer," Drage said, urging his screen to fly
forward. As soon as it reached the barrier, it shattered, and he
fell fifteen feet down into the snow.

Feranx rushed forward, descending as he did, and landed
on the ground beside Drage. His eyes were wide with fear for
his leader. As he grabbed Drage's shoulder to check on him,
Drage pushed the hand away.

"Drage," Feranx typed. *"We are not as powerful here.
You're going to get us killed!"*

Drage stood, ignoring the snow that clung to his skin
and clothes. He was vaguely aware that, being through the
barrier, the Elders' Heat charm was removed. "No, my Sword
will be able to reach him, here."

Cronus 624's voice resounded. "Lord Helius, your

mechanic has a point. You are inside my barrier, and you are powerless here. Do you have any last words before you are roasted where you stand?"

With a smile, Drage said, "I didn't realize that about you, Cronus."

"What?" the computer replied.

"When I programmed you, I put quite a bit of myself in you, so I guess it is just as easily a fault of mine."

"Of what do you speak?" Cronus repeated, his tone revealing his impatience.

"A love for the dramatic. I will have to fix that later."

"You fool!" the module said angrily.

"No, you are the fool. I didn't need you to be weakened. Just for you to keep talking to buy some time." Even as he finished the sentence, blue light flickered above them as the barrier dissipated from the Elders' ritual.

"No!" Cronus 624 roared.

Drage and Feranx took back to flight, and Drage swung his Sword, its energy renewed. Each swing sent a blue arc of force toward Cronus 624, and the computer sent a few more metallic panels toward Drage to fend off each deadly arc. Drage called to Feranx, "Tell the Elders to prepare the next ritual!" Out of the corner of his eye, he saw Feranx typing a few commands that went to screens that were in front of each of the Elders, a simple but direct means of communicating. "What is your next trick, Cronus?" he said as he began to close the distance between him and the computer.

As if responding to Drage's words, the tower transformed. The bottom column pulled upward, and the wires stretched and snapped like roots of a falling tree. The column above moved sideways and hovered beside the other one. The two columns began rotating around one another and moved away from Drage and Feranx. "Trick, you say?" the computer repeated. "I shall disturb your circle! Your Ring of Elders will fall to me."

Gritting his teeth, Drage willed his screen to accelerate to pursue the moving computer. More cannons appeared from the rear of the cylinders, and spheres of red energy blasted toward Drage.

With his Sword free to use its full energy, he was able to block the smaller blasts with ease, but the force of them slowed his speed, setting him further back. "Stay away from them!" Drage roared as he fired a beam from his Sword toward the computer. The two cylinders stopped where they were and divided, creating a space large enough for the beam to pass through and hit a glacier harmlessly. Suddenly, the cylinders shot toward Drage. Not expecting the attack, he began firing erratic blasts of power toward them, hoping at least one shot would connect.

The two barrels fell onto their sides, and the wires that stuck out from the bottom of one connected to the top of the other, creating a huge, mechanical set of nunchucks. At the center point between the two cylinders, a sphere of Lightning appeared and fired toward Drage. Right as it was about to electrocute Drage, Feranx swooped in and grabbed Drage by the shoulders, lifting him over the attack. The griffin threw Drage so that he landed on the backs of one of the cylinders. Immediately, he stabbed his blade down into the core of one of the cylinders, knowing it to be the one that did not contain the hard drive for the module.

The other cylinder, the one with wires attached to its base, aimed a cannon at Drage, and he leaped from the cylinder's side, barely dodging the laser. He felt the heat on his back and rolled through the snow as he heard the other cylinder explode behind him.

Upon stopping, he stood and turned, prepared to parry another blast from the computer. However, it was rooting itself into the ice again, and, to his amazement, a red ring of symbols appeared on the ice around it. "What is it . . . ?" he started. Then, a column of fire appeared around the module.

To Drage's terror, the column began moving in his direction. Running in the opposite direction, he called, "Feranx! Could really use that screen right about now!"

The heat increased behind him, and the red light washed over him. He sweated even as he felt the cold seep through his shoes to his feet. At lightning speed, a green screen collided with him, carrying him out of the path of the fiery tornado the computer had summoned. Grunting, Drage climbed on top of the screen. "Could have been a little more gentle," he muttered, though he knew the griffin could not hear him wherever he was. Drage looked out into the distance and saw a few pinpoints that were undoubtedly Elders completing the next ritual. "They had better hurry up." He looked down for the computer and saw it was preparing a tornado made from Wind this time. Rolling his eyes, he willed the screen to descend toward the computer, more prepared to fight it this time.

Even as he sped, though, a shimmer of Light spread around him, and he realized the second ritual had worked. The Elders had erected a barrier around him. Now, as long as the Elders could hold that spell, the computer could not attack him with any spells. Cameron and Helen were right: ritual magic was stronger than *mysteria* in this world.

However, as he flew to the computer's level, he saw that Cronus had stopped constructing a tornado and was instead transforming again. The panels that made up its exterior began shifting. Drage stopped, uncertain of what was happening. Feranx flew beside him and typed a message, *"Drage, what is it doing?"*

Drage's eyes widened as he realized the computer's final stage. "It is becoming anthropomorphic." The panels and wires connected in such a way that the computer now took the form of a man on the ice, with an electric rod in the grip of one robotic hand. It turned what would have been its head toward Drage and Feranx, and the two beheld the large red light become the thing's eye. Its voice still roared at them with the same intensity, "You cannot halt the force of Ragnarok! This world is mine to destroy."

It flew toward them with surprising agility, and Drage ran forward to meet it.

Feranx, too, constructed green bars from his screens, but he did not see a way to engage the computer as Drage was. The two became a mesh of swordplay: Drage striking fluidly at the enemy computer, and Cronus rotating and twisting to defend its mechanical limbs and to electrocute Drage in the process. Drage's reflexes were perfect, each strike a natural movement as if the Sword were just an extension of his own body. The computer, though less graceful, anticipated each move with perfect precision. Never before had Feranx seen such an intense battle between man and machine.

He began typing on his keyboard. In order to stop this without destroying the program entirely, Feranx would have to accurately construct the code that would halt the Cronus entirely. After watching it fight and defend itself, Feranx had a much better idea for how the code would have to be structured. It relied on a series of pseudo-intelligent parameters and aggressive functions. It could definitely be done, but, as Feranx had complained frequently of late, it would take more time than he liked.

In Drage's mind, the battle was much slower than it appeared. Each strike was intentional, a specific response to his combatant's move. He had faith in Feranx's abilities. All he had to do was hold out until then. Not even the Elders could help at this point, and he knew that.

Drage noticed suddenly that the mechanical warrior was increasing its speed, even pushing Drage to his limits. He gritted his teeth as he had to focus more, his reflexes gradually becoming slower than his ability to sense the next move. Trying to create some distance between him and his opponent, he manipulated Light to give him speed, but Cronus matched it. The computer was learning. Drage realized that his computer program was adaptive: based on Drage's moves, it would learn how to better defeat him, like a fatal game of chess. Cronus 624's single red eye bored deep into Drage's eyes, and he cringed under the crimson glow. "Damn it," he muttered. He called to Feranx impatiently, "Would you hurry it up?"

With his concentration interrupted, Drage felt his Sword fly out of his hands, and Cronus whirled his electric staff to stab Drage in the chest, but the rod transformed into a vine of flowers. The vine fell apart once it touched Drage, and he staggered backward in surprise. Cronus looked down at his hands, as if in disbelief. *The Elders . . .* Drage thought with a smile. Summoning his Sword, he severed one of the computer's arms and pushed it back.

"Get back, Drage!" he saw on a screen that appeared in front of him. Taking heed immediately, Drage fell back into the snow as a green screen shot through where he had just been standing. It wrapped around Cronus 624's body.

The computer roared through the valley, "No! Get this off of me!" But the screen was already affecting the computer's programming, halting it where it stood. As it froze, the red light on it blinked three times, and then completely deactivated.

With a sigh of both exhaustion and relief, Drage stood, walked over to the darkened computer, and reached under its metal panels to touch its core. He knew the button to locate. Within seconds, he had removed the disk that contained the computer's base program. Cronus 624 had been shut down. "We did it," Drage muttered. He turned and saw that Feranx was beaming, his beak curved into a smile.

27

The Keeper of Time

ELIZABETH SPOKE LOUDLY for all to hear, "Master Helius, we implore you to do your best."

Matthew clenched his fists, "I appreciate your faith in me, but I am still very new to this. You are asking me to correct a major event in Earth's time, hence affecting an entire world. I have neither the power nor the moral authority to do so."

Drage mused on the absurdity of this situation. Both he and Matthew were Elizabeth's sons, yet they all were in authority roles that necessitated the need for such formality. Elizabeth had thankfully learned that these matters were not resolved by playing "the mother card." Still, Drage hoped that Matthew would be able to do *something* to fix all of this. A lot of Earthans had died the past few days. If Matthew could not fix this, he did not think it could be fixed.

Another Elder said, "You are the only Keeper of Time, are you not?"

Matthew nodded. "Yes, Elder. That is correct."

The Elder continued, "Then, you alone have the power to do this."

Matthew lowered his head, staring at the white tile floor of the Council's meeting room. "I fear it is not that simple, Elder."

"Explain this to us, then," the Elder said, leaning back in his chair and folding his arms on top of the long desk the Elders now shared.

"The past is immutable, Elders. I can affect things in the future, but the past can't change. Not really. Usually, I would go back in time to *learn* something, not to change things. In achieving the reset you seek, Cronus would back in power, and, even if we stopped Cronus earlier, then the events in my own world would be changed, too, for Lord Helius would have returned sooner."

"So, you just plan to leave Earth in its state of chaos and destruction?" Elizabeth asked through a clenched jaw.

Matthew turned to look at Drage who leaned against a wall behind him. Realizing Drage was not going to help him here, he turned back to the Elders. "No, Elders . . . but it is still not in my power to change. Lord Helius has explained to me that you have been increasingly learning of the power of ritual magic. Is this correct?" The Elders nodded but said nothing. "What I suggest is that you find a way to fabricate memory. I can use my powers to restore the physicality of this world: the buildings, the technology, the landmarks. But, you all will need to create new memories for the people. How many have actually died from the Ragnarok program?"

Helen spoke up for the first time, "A few million."

The number hit Matthew hard. He swallowed before continuing, "It is not in my power to bring them back . . ."

Helen finished his sentence, "But, our memory ritual would be able to create logical explanations for the deaths for their families and friends."

Elizabeth stood and pressed her knuckles against the table. "You mean to tell me that Gevás sent a terrorist program into Earth, that it killed *millions* of us, and the most you are offering is damn building renovations?"

Finally, Drage stepped forward. "You know quite well that the Y'mordi are not exactly the chief representatives of Gevás. If what Matthew says is true, then that is indeed the best that Helio can offer Earth. We are truly sorry for your loss, but we cannot do more than this."

Elizabeth sat back down, lips pursed. "We will speak with you both again in an hour."

The two bowed before the Ring of Elders and walked out the door of the conference room.

"How are you holding up?" Drage asked.

Matthew nodded, staring out at ruined Boston. "I'm alright, but I'm shaken. Things fell apart in Gevás, but things don't seem to have went much better here, either."

Drage crossed his arms. "No. The Y'mordi were ahead of us this time. Not even I expected things to be this bad here, even anticipating their trap." Matthew was silent. "So, Regin was being controlled by Ixion, huh? That little rat was basically controlling the entire war."

"What are you going to do?" Matthew asked, still not looking at Drage.

"The Y'mordi have made themselves public. Now, the world will be at war against the Darkness. I anticipate that the Demons will start awakening more fully now, and the Shadows will more easily seep into this world through that Rent of yours."

Matthew winced at Drage's final words. "I'm ... I'm sorry, Drage. I lost control of the situation. I tried ... to be like you, and I could not have failed more."

Drage stepped forward and put a hand on Matthew's shoulder. "No, Matthew. You did more than I ever expected of you. Had you not been there, the situation could have gone a lot worse. You kept the Council in check. You kept the Darkness at bay. You ended the war with the East. You did more this past week than I have done since I've been crowned."

Turning to look at Drage with tear-rimmed eyes, Matthew said, "I just don't see it that way. The Darkness is coming into power. I may have ended a battle, but the war is only beginning."

With no response this time, Drage lowered his hand. "Earth will be fine. Its birth rate is skyrocketing. It will be back on its feet in no time. You and I need to concentrate on Gevás. We have to figure out what the Y'mordi are planning and stop them ahead of time, for once. We must have faith in the Light." Drage gave Matthew a worried glance. "Will you be alright?"

"Have faith in the Light . . ." Matthew repeated. "Yeah, I'll be fine. Just give me some time."

Drage nodded and headed back into the Council room, sensing they were ready. Matthew did not follow.

"Master Helius," Elizabeth began, "you start preparing your spell. We will create a ritual to enhance the spell's effects and range so that it restores all the physical damage created by Cronus. Our ritual should also affect the memories of the people of the world as well."

Matthew nodded in the center of the rune-drawn circle. Lowering his head, he tapped his staff into the white circle on which he stood, and the whole ring lit up with green flames. He focused on the process of rejuvenation, reversing objects through time to their state a couple of weeks ago. As he focused this energy without releasing it, he heard the Elders chanting around him.

"*Auka. Millorar. Verbessern. Forbedre. Styrke. Enhance. Aumentar. Itejbu.*"

He felt his power start to increase, welling over his usual maximum, and his senses began failing him, only aware of the power he grasped.

"Laienema. Espandere. Ehangu. Hirogeru. Leathnú. Ut-vide. Razširiti. Expand."

The power was still there, but he felt it extend past the circle, past the roof of the building, even past Boston. Tears started streaming down his face. He felt as if he were grasping the whole world at once, and it tore at his heart. "Please . . ." he muttered, begging for the ritual to end, to end this overwhelming feeling.

"Muisti. Memoria. Cuimhne. Jì yì. Geheugen. Nco. Iranti. Memory."

Matthew fell to his knees, his head now pounding. He started to scream.

"Construct. Kreye. Lumikha. Kujenga. Oluşturmak. Yaratish. Kurti. Krijoj."

The green fire whirled around them, wrapping around each of the Elders and Matthew, burning them but leaving no mark.

"Séala!"

The green flames shot outward and dissipated. Matthew collapsed on the roof, immediately unconscious.

When Matthew came to, he saw that Drage was standing over him. They were still on the roof of the skyscraper. "What . . . what happened?"

Drage looked down at Matthew and crouched before him. "Hey, how are you doing? You passed out once the ritual was over."

"The ritual . . ." Matthew put a hand to his head and felt the memories wash over him. "Oh, yeah . . . Did it work?"

Drage gestured with his head toward the edge of the roof. "See for yourself. Do you need a hand?"

Matthew nodded, and Drage lifted an arm and helped Matthew stand so they could walk to the edge. What Matthew saw amazed him. The skyscrapers were all back to normal. Traffic flowed in the streets below as if nothing had happened. A plane flew overhead, and the sky was clear and bright. "Everything . . . it *did* work."

Smiling, Drage nodded. "Thanks to you, the Elders were able to restore this world. Sure, some lives were lost, but I'm starting to learn that's just the price of war."

Matthew looked down at the city. "I don't like this . . . it feels wrong."

Drage raised an eyebrow. "What do you mean? We saved this world."

Shaking his head, Matthew said, "No, we helped to destroy it. Whole lives were just written off. Their spirits will never be at rest. The Council will be dealing with those angry spirits for years to come."

"Then, that's their problem." Drage was already looking back out at the city.

Matthew stared hard at Drage. "When did you become so cold?"

Drage did not turn to face Matthew again. "Being an Emperor means you do not have certain luxuries. It is my place to choose which lives matter more than others. I have to sacrifice some to save more. Those choices . . . they harden you . . . so you can make the same choices again later."

Matthew was dumbfounded.

Drage turned and walked away, saying, "Get some rest before we return to Gevás."

28

The Phoenix and the Lion

THE ENIGMA BRIGADE stood before Drage in the Throne Room of the Palace of Light. All five of the members were kneeled with heads bowed. All feared to look up at the Golden King.

The deep voice of the Emperor boomed over them. "Captain Bryco, much has been amiss during the time of my absence. What have you to say for yourself?"

Bryco did not raise his head and spoke simply. "I apologize profusely, your Highness. We failed against the Y'mordi in Varyx, and we were saved only by the traitor Maksimilian, whose Sword Brigadier Gaspard was able to acquire. Even against the Dread Serpent, we failed you, your Highness."

Even without looking up, Gaspard felt the Emperor's gaze fall upon him.

"Gaspard, show me the Sword."

Gaspard kept his eyes lowered but drew the Steel of Life for the Emperor to see. Gaspard's mouth opened wide as the blade's green glow reflected on the tile floor. It had not held such a light for him yet. Although he was in awe at the brilliance, he smiled inwardly at the knowledge that he was in the possession of one of the legendary blades again.

The Emperor noted that his own Sword glowed a shimmering blue in response to the presence of the sister weapon. The Brigade heard the Emperor rise. "I shall be confiscating this Sword from you, Gaspard."

Gaspard's eyes widened, and he clenched his jaw, stopping himself from crying out in protest. He merely lowered his head further.

The Emperor stretched out a hand, summoning the blade with only his heart. To Gaspard's stunned disappointment, the Steel vanished from his hands in sparks of green light. They heard the pop of the Sword reappearing in the Emperor's hand. As Gaspard lowered his hands to the floor shakily, he heard the Emperor speak again, "Thank you, Enigma Brigade. I confiscate this blade for multiple reasons. With it in your possession, Maksimilian will always seek you out. He may seek you out anyway, but it will be your life he seeks, Gaspard. However, you are all aware of the risks you take by being in the Emperor's service." They heard him turn back to his throne. "You will be rewarded for your dealing with Varyx and restoring it to glory. As far as I am concerned, your attacks were a success."

"Sir—" Gaspard choked.

The Emperor snapped, "Brigadier, shall I remind you of your place?"

Gaspard was silent, though he felt his face turn livid.

"Brigadier Gaspard, stand." Gaspard stood, keeping his head lowered so as to not look directly at the fearsome Emperor. "Hold out your hand and call to the blade. If your heart can wrench the Steel of Life from my grasp, I will allow you to keep it." In a sharper voice, he said, "Call to it."

Gaspard could not help but look up at this challenge. And he was scared. Still, he stretched out an arm and closed his eyes. He searched with his heart, calling to the blade as he had called to the Great Spirit years ago in the Temple of the

Spirits. "Please," he muttered under his breath. However, the blade did not move from the Emperor's grip.

"You may kneel again, Brigadier," the Emperor demanded. Once Gaspard was on his knees again, his face drained of its color, the Emperor continued, "Captain Bryco, see to it that Gaspard is punished for his impertinence. We have more pressing matters at hand than a single weapon."

"Yes, your Majesty," Bryco responded simply.

"Now, I want the Brigade to handle a new mission until we have decided where things stand with the impending Darkness. I am tired of this nuisance Maksimilian appearing everywhere. Apparently, he was responsible for the massacre in the Northern stadium, and possibly the explosion, though our intel is gradually suggesting the two occurrences may not have been connected at all. I want the Brigade to hunt this man down and bring him to me alive. I have a cell waiting for him in the Labyrinth, and I would so hate for him to be without a home. I will secure you whatever footage you need from the security cameras that were at the stadium. I want wanted posters for his arrest around. I want him as soon as possible. Do I make myself perfectly clear?"

"Yes, your Majesty!" the Brigade cried in unison.

"Good, you are dismissed. Captain, I would like a word, however."

The Brigadiers summoned golden Gates and vanished, leaving only Bryco kneeled before the Emperor. "You may stand, Bryco."

Bryco stood and relaxed visibly. "Yes, your Majesty."

The Emperor stood and waved the Steel of Life experimentally. "You are aware that the Brigade will become public knowledge now, correct?"

Bryco swallowed. "Yes, your Majesty."

"Bryco, I have no problem making this knowledge public, but you need to work harder on keeping our operations covert. The more rumors go around of the Brigade's location, the more your enemies will be able to locate you and anticipate your actions. Right now, both that damned Maksimilian and the Y'mordi will be searching for you. Especially since Maksimilian believes you are in possession of the Steel of Life. From what I gather, this blade grants its wielder immortality . . . so long as he does not kill with it. Maksimilian has likely been around for hundreds of years, not exactly an Ancient, but still not trustworthy."

Bryco nodded in agreement.

"One more thing. My wife has brought to my attention that the Regiment and the Brigade are fighting over symbols. I would like to propose a new mascot for the Brigade."

"Yes, your Majesty?"

"The lion."

Bryco smiled, thinking of Nilram.

"In honor of our first anima Brigadier," the Emperor said with a smile.

"I very much appreciate and applaud your creativity, your Majesty."

"Good. I shall see to it that one of our mages stops by your headquarters to enchant your garb with the new design. I have instructed her to also work on creating more versatile garb for Nilram, anyway, for his changes."

"Very good, your Majesty."

The Emperor nodded. "Yes. Well, send in the Regiment on your way out."

Bryco bowed and headed toward the front doors.

Aria led the Phoenix Regiment into the Throne Room, and her heart thudded against her chest as she beheld her husband. The light-hearted boy she had fallen in love with on the beach years and years ago was dead. Before her sat a powerful ruler, hardened by war and death. Still, her confidence never wavered. Although she stood, the Regiment behind her kneeled before the Emperor. "Dragenopn," she said, using the Emperor's full first name, showing her affection without reducing him to a nickname, "you summoned us." This was not a question, but an acknowledgement.

"As requested, my Lady, the Phoenix symbol has been restored to you."

Aria beamed. "Thank you. What will be the symbol of the Brigade, now?"

"A lion," the Emperor said with a smile. It honors the anima in our forces, as well as serves as a subtle call to the griffin who served me on Earth, Feranx."

"Very good," she responded. She waited before adding, "Surely, you did not summon the entire Brigade just to inform us of the mascot shift?"

"No indeed," Drage said, standing, "I wanted to enlist the Regiment in a special mission, but I did not want this to be just an appeal to its leader."

Aria nodded cautiously for him to proceed.

"I am fully aware that the Regiment is your personal military force of sorcerers, and I applaud you all tremendously for your work against the Emperor Regin and the Dread Serpent. However, as the Darkness continues to rise, both of them will be the least of our worries. The East is allying once more, though with us as an ally again. Now, the Darkness is our prime enemy."

"Yes," Aria agreed.

"And at its head are the elusive Y'mordi, the seven Lords of the Shadows. If possible, I would implore the Phoenix Regiment to seek out and hunt them."

"Forgive me, Dragenopn, but why us and not your Brigade?"

The Emperor gave her a cold look. "Because, my Queen, the Brigade is specialized in physical combat. Death would only return the Y'mordi to the Realm of Darkness. In order to stop them completely, they must be placed in Stasis. Then, we could start to collect the bastards in the Labyrinth. I think only one of the Brigadiers might be able to place people under Stasis, while I bet most of your Regiment can handle the task easily."

"Yes," Aria agreed. "We will add this to our priorities, Dragenopn."

"Thank you," the Emperor said with a sigh.

"Regiment," Aria said.

The Phoenix Regiment stood promptly and bowed. "Thank you, your Majesty!" they cried in unison. Aria walked through the line, and in double-file they followed her out the doors.

Staring hard at their backs, the Emperor shook his head. "I would hate to be the Y'mordi right now."

Content with how the meeting with her husband had gone, Aria walked toward the nursery, smiling at their squeals of delight. The door was already open, and she stood there, leaning against the doorframe. Her own children were playing with Matthew and Lilian's. Apollo, Ace, and Alison were all running around, chasing each other, while Senagul was playing a video game, occasionally looking over at William looking at a book, not understanding what he was seeing. Aria shook her head. Even with the chaos Gevás had experienced the past couple of weeks, her children were still as innocent and heavenly as ever.

With her smile still on her face, Aria walked away from the room and moved down the hall. For the moment, she wanted to bask in this feeling of success. Drage was home again. The war was over. Her children were safe. With a sudden grimace, she looked at where her arm used to be, but shook her head. "At least it wasn't my wand arm," she muttered softly.

She pressed her fingers against the ivory walls as she walked, deep in thought. She felt pride at their success. She felt pride for her children. Yet, she knew that things were far from over. She was no closer to knowing who had Gifted her. She was no closer to understanding the mystery of Ace.

Her musing brought her through several hallways, upstairs and downstairs, until she found herself at the mystical door to Drage's master computer, DATA. Turning around once to see if anyone had followed her, she eased through the door and stared at the blue-screened behemoth.

"Empress Aria. How are you today?"

Aria beamed up at the computer. "I'm doing well, DATA. Yourself?"

The screens transformed to create a warm but very human cerulean face. "Doing splendidly. Is there any way at all that I can assist you today?"

"I'm not sure. I'm not really sure what I came down here for."

"When Drage finishes my programming, I would be able to sense what you needed. Alas, I cannot yet."

Aria nodded. "Of course." She paused awkwardly. "You did an excellent job defending the city, DATA. We could not have done it without you."

"Perhaps not," the computer said matter-of-factly. "But the same goes for you."

Aria repeated DATA's words. "Perhaps not." She turned as if to leave and then stopped herself. "Actually," she started, turning back, "how complete are your records at this point?"

"How do you mean?"

"I mean, compared to Master Marqest's old database COM or the Academy's Archives?"

The digital face smiled. "I have copies of COM's system, and I have access to most of the Archives. Plus, Drage set me up with personal intel-retrieval programs so that I can monitor certain points on Gevás at all times, adding to my own database."

Aria brightened. "Is there a way that I could make use of your data from time to time? Especially for the Phoenix

Regiment?"

DATA's feminine lips pursed. "Technically, it is up to Drage. But, it is also not in my programming to deny service to anyone. So, I could help as long as he does not tell me otherwise."

"Good. I may need your help answering a couple of personal questions, or at least find starting points for where to look."

"Certainly," the computer responded.

29

Fade to Black

FINALLY ALONE, THE Emperor of Light sighed. He had seen the Enigma Brigade, the Phoenix Regiment, and his Council, all of which had severe issues with authority. He considered the Council's proceedings after he slumped back against his Throne. Mistress Leona would be the new head of the Council in wake of Valdridge's death. Ocrum was being held in the Labyrinth and would undergo interrogation soon. The Emperor could not believe that two Servants of the Darkness had been working so closely under his nose. He found himself wondering how long the Y'mordi had held direct access to information from the Palace of Light.

Stroking his forehead, he sighed again. "The war with the Darkness is beginning." He held out both of his hands and summoned his two Spirit Swords. With these in his grasp, fighting the Y'mordi would be much easier. In one hand, he held life, and, in the other, strength. These would be tools for his victory now.

He winced as he thought about the devastation he had left behind on Earth. He almost regretted having gone there at all. Despite his foreknowledge, he had walked right into the Y'mordi's trap, and it had almost cost him both Earth and Gevás. As he made the Swords vanish, he realized he needed to quit trying to play the hero and stay the leader. Gevás did not need a wild-eyed, passionate rescer; it needed someone to guide it.

As he thought these things, his eyes started to droop, and, within minutes, he was snoring on the golden throne.

Matthew sat down amongst the children and laughed as they all ran around him, all except Senagul, who was still playing some game, and William. "Uncle Matt, Uncle Matt!" Apollo cried, running toward him with a picture in hand. "Look what I drew!"

Matthew frowned at the picture. "What is it, Apollo?"

"It's a picture of Aunt Lilian!"

Indeed, Matthew could barely make out the figure of a horse, and he smiled. "Well, why does she have a horn?"

"Well, she's so pretty, I thought she must be a unicorn."

Alison fell against her sister and cheered, "Unicorn!"

Matthew picked up the youngest girl and set her on his lap. "Aunt Lilian is certainly not a unicorn. Imagine saying 'hello' to her if she were a unicorn. She'd practically stab you with a horn."

"Oh," Apollo said, putting a thumb in her mouth, deep in thought.

The Khaosdog said across the room, "Apollo has been getting better at her drawing, though."

Matthew smiled back at the woman. "I can see that. Have you been giving her lessons?"

She nodded and went back to reading to William.

Matthew turned to look for the last child, Ace. He found the boy sitting in a corner, playing with toy transports. Although the boy was not looking up, Matthew could sense something strange in the boy. He did not want to admit it, but it felt like Darkness. His inner raven's eye stared at the boy and made a mental note to keep his eye on the mysterious Ace. Times were changing.

"So, what are we going to do?" Tilgé asked, arms folded as he leaned against the wall anxiously.

Stehl shook her head, staring forlornly at the frozen body on the bed.

Mirah added, "It shouldn't be 'ard for a mage to fix 'im."

"I know that," Stehl said, "but any mage could sense what he is. We'd all be locked up in the Emperor's Labyrinth as soon as we're discovered. We can't take him to a mage."

Tilgé rolled his eyes. "We're going to have to take him to a mage. Otherwise, he will stay frozen in Stasis forever."

Stehl glared at him. After a few moments, her glare softened. "I know . . . it will just have to be more of a black market mage."

"I thought da guy said dat he had turned Randy normal again?"

"We can't be sure. Can we?" She intended that last question for Tilgé.

He shrugged. "I can still sense Darkness on him, but the Y'mordi are good at hiding that anyways, if they have a mind to." Tilgé regarded the man on the bed with concern, but there was not rage or disdain on Tilgé's face. In some ways, he envied the man's physique. Stehl had changed his clothes from the black robes to simple gray sleepwear. Tilgé could see the swells and curves of Randir's musculature through the thin clothing. At this point, Tilgé could not pass judgment on the man. He, too, had committed crimes.

Stehl responded, "Fine. We will just have to find one of those black market mages. Do either of you know any?" When both of them shook their heads, she said with determination in her voice, "Then, let's start looking."

"Mali," the high voice whispered.

"What is it, Ixion?"

The naked Mali sat beside Ixion's chair, the golden collar still tight around his neck. Ixion smiled down at him. "We need a new strategy to take another kingdom."

"Another?"

Nodding, Ixion urged with glee, "Yes, I took Immyx and Varyx with ease. I wonder which kingdom I should start with next. This time, I'll even have my own personal servant."

Mali grumbled, "I wish you would just make a damn wish already."

Ixion chuckled. "Not until I have to. Don't fear. It will happen soon."

Mali stared off into the distance, looking out through the bars of the cage beside Ixion's seat, and dreamed of the freedom to live and the freedom to have his revenge.

Poised in a high motel near the ruins of a disq stadium, Maksimilian watched mages work to restore the stadium to its former glory. He gritted his teeth anxiously. His plans had gone terribly wrong. Not only had he failed to kill Stehl, Tilgé, or Mirah, but he had also failed to live up to his promise for a massacre. With the bomb that destroyed the stadium, his short-lived massacre was overwhelmed in the media. Of course, Lord Helius knew about it, and there was now a warrant for his arrest. However, he knew he could avoid getting caught. He placed a hand on the hilt of the Behemoth and grimaced. The damned blade was too cumbersome for him to wield in a one-on-one battle. It gave him the luck to dodge Stehl's bullets, but when it came to actually fighting, the heavy Sword was just too much.

So far, he knew that Stehl had one of the Spirit Swords, Kohana's Fang. He also knew that the fool, Gaspard, had his Steel of Life. Lord Helius still had the Sword of Destiny. Having the Behemoth himself, Maksimilian knew where four of the five Spirit Swords were. He smiled to himself. Now, he just had to find the final Sword and take back the others.

But first, he needed help. He needed to regain some of his old power. In order to do that, though, he needed to speak to the one Emperor of Light who had valued his talents, Seth Mentiris. And, Maksimilian happened to know the one man who knew what dwelled beyond the grave. As Maksimilian packed his belongings, he envisioned the name of the mysterious Prophet he would seek: Lot Manes.

Y'tal's black robe flowed silently behind him, long and draping. Its end glided across the tiled floor of the Palace of Light. This place was nauseating to him: the gold, the white, and the damned light. Each step brought him closer and closer to his goal. Now, in the middle of the night, the castle slept, and the Prophet of Darkness walked among them, not bothering to raise his guard or sneak through the castle floors. He was confident.

His smile faded. Well, the whole castle was not asleep; the one he sought was quite awake. He proceeded through the halls, anxious to reach his destination, the mythical place where the Emperor of Light kept his glorified computer program. Even with Valdridge discovered, Y'tal still had his spies, and poor Ocrum was not one of them. He just happened to have sided with the one man on the Emperor's Council who was a Servant of the Darkness. Y'tal sneered. He was confident that Ocrum's torture would have been pleasant to watch.

As Y'tal walked, he felt the energy seeping through the final floor, the layer of the computer DATA. He paused, staring at the tremendous mirror at the end of the wall. "Not very subtle, are we?" he muttered as he pressed forward. Holding a hand out to the mirror, he released only the slightest stream of *mysteria,* cloaking him entirely from sight, hearing, smell, and even *mysteria.* He entered the colossal computer room and marveled at the blue-screened wonder.

However, his interests were not on DATA. After all, a computer could not be destined to be the next Y'mordi. Instead, he looked at the young woman speaking to the computer.

List of Characters

Ace: A mysterious stranger who, on multiple occasions, saved Drage, Matthew, and Aria when they first came to Gevás. Aria has spent much of her life trying to decipher who he is, and Y'tal wants him alive.

Ace Helius: The son of Drage and Aria.

Aksel: A mountain climber on Earth.

Alcar: The Dean of *Mysteria* at the Academy.

Alison Helius: A daughter of Drage and Aria.

Apollo Helius: A daughter of Drage and Aria.

Aria Helius: The Empress of Helio and one of the seven Guardians of Light. Although she was born and raised on Earth, someone anonymous Gifted her a strong finesse with *mysteria,* and she was able to tap into her latent powers when she traveled with Drage and Matthew to Gevás. Now that she is an Empress, a member of the Emperor's Council, and the leader of the Phoenix Regiment, she is determined to solve the mysteries of Ace and the person who Gifted her.

Arnim (Y'mir / Meridan): One of the twin Y'mordi. Always following her sister Sarn into danger, she joined the Y'mordi out of the desire to protect Sarn, and, blessed with Darkness, she now wields two guns and the Earth Element to decimate her foes.

Barrius: Manager of the Twenty and Silas Inn.

Bastion: Marqest's brother, who is said to have split his heart in two. Fought in the Second Obsidian War.

Black Joker, see *Loki.*

Bral Helius: Former Emperor of Light. He was the first of the Helius line to rule, and he is renowned for saving Draconis with the Dragon's Clause.

Bryco: The captain of the Enigma Brigade. He was born in the Capital, but now lives lavishly in Apolis.

Buay: Ixion's original master. However, once Ixion learned all there was to know about thieving, he killed Master Buay in his sleep.

Cameron Kane: A youth on Earth who once idolized Drage. He is now an apprentice to the head of the Ring of Elders, Elizabeth.

Chiara: A lady in Varyx.

Compendium of Myriads (COM): A master-intelligence computer that belonged to Marqest on Heaven's Isle.

Cronus 624: A master-intelligence computer that mixes Marqest's programming for COM, Drage's programming for DATA, and the power of Darkness. The Y'mordi send this weapon to Earth in an attempt to destroy the world.

Dagan: The Shadow King and former Prophet of Darkness. After coming to Gevás with his brother Lux, he sought the power to rule the world himself. As he stepped deeper into Darkness, he started a series of wars against his brother and divided the world politically. In the Final Battle, both Dagan and Lux vanished without a trace.

Digital and Arboreal Total Archive (DATA): A master-intelligence computer designed by Drage to be central intelligence unit in Helio as well as a large-scale weapon and defense program. Still incomplete.

Derek Janus: Former Prophet of Wind and Council member. His wife, Elizabeth, took their children away when she started seeing Lord John Helius, and he grew insane as one of the Keepers of Time. However, upon meeting his son again, his mental state began to recover, and he once again engaged in the affairs of the world. In protecting both Matthew and Drage, he was killed in battle with the Y'mordi Xarden.

Divine Dragon of the Heavens: The mythical Dragon that ended an ancient war on Sharl Drake by giving a crown of power to one race and condemning others. The myths are still in question.

Dragenopn Helius: The Emperor of Light and one of the seven Guardians of Light. Having lived most of his life on Earth, he has only recently moved permanently to Gevás to accept his place as Emperor of Light and start a family. Now his sole purpose is to rid the world of the Darkness the Y'mordi have been releasing upon it. He wields the legendary Sword of Destiny.

Elani: Queen of Sharl Drake. She is the one who started the rebellion that led to Cairon's overthrow.

Elizabeth Helius: Head of the Ring of Elders. She is the mother of Drage, Matthew, and Helen, and she has been married to both Derek Janus and John Helius. Now, she leads the Ring of Elders in protecting Earth from abuse of magic and *mysteria*.

Epofis: One of the five Demons. Also known as the Dread Serpent.

Fend: A former Enigma Brigadier. Shot and killed by Stehl.

Feranx: A mute griffin who serves as Drage's personal mechanic. He communicates through a personalized computer.

Gaspard: One of the Enigma Brigade. He formerly was a worshipper of the Great Spirit, but after manipulation by Y'tal that led him to challenge Drage, he was hired to protect Drage instead and wielded the legendary Behemoth in battle.

Grand Master Dean: The head of the Academy.

Great Spirit: Supposedly, the original life form found on Gevás. Once acted as a deity over the world until Dagan divided the Spirit into five pieces, each of which later possessing a sword.

Grenn: A former Enigma Brigadier. Shot and killed by one of Stehl's men.

Hector, see *Mali.*

Helen Helius: Elizabeth's apprentice and daughter. She is just now in her twenties, discovering the powers of *mysteria* she has inherited from her mother, and she is training alongside Cameron.

Ixion Medora (Y'xon): The lowest of the Y'mordi. Acting frequently as the spy and assassin, Ixion uses daggers and poison spells to quickly kill his enemies. In the past, he has been trod upon by the other Y'mordi, but after years of re-training, he is hoping to become feared once again.

Jallun: One of the members of the Emperor's Council.

Jiron Mackey: The disq star of the Southern League.

John Helius: A former Emperor of Light. His son is Drage, and he once wielded the Sword of Destiny. He was eventually killed by Maris after bringing the Guardians of Light to Gevás.

Kelton Efrain: Star disq player of the Pyramid.

Khaosdog: Owner of Khaosdog's Wonder Works.

Kibou Gerlach: A wolf anima known as the Werewolf who once terrorized the Northern Continent as he hunted creatures of Darkness.

Kusvor Cairon: A Black Dragon tyrant who assassinated the previous king Vran and flipped the racial discrimination in the world. Having turned out to be one of the Great Servants of Darkness, the Y'mordi awakened dark powers within him, only to have Draconis defeat him in battle anyway. Not content with his defeat, the Y'mordi killed him and dragged him into the Realm of Darkness.

Lara: A squirrel anima who gave birth to Senagul. Died of natural causes.

Leif: A professor who was attacked by an Y'mordi at the Academy near the end of the Third Obsidian War.

Leona: The Prophet of Nature and a member of the Emperor's Council. She has been the most consistent mentor for Aria. She is married to Master Valdridge.

Lilian: One of the seven Guardians of Light. She is a white horse anima who married Matthew and had a child named William with him. They also adopted the squirrel anima Senagul after his mother died.

Linda Daghda: The former Prophet of Earth. After awakening Aria's powers with *mysteria,* she was killed by Ixion in an act of vengeance.

Lly: A Blue Dragon who held Draconis's heart before she was killed by the Y'mordi Sarn.

Loki: The mythical Black Joker who is said to be sealed somewhere on Earth.

Lomeo: The new and enigmatic king of Varyx.

Lux: The first Emperor of Light. Upon discovering Gevás with his brother Dagan, he sought to establish a royalty-based empire connected to worship of the Light. When his brother contested and sought his own power, Lux made war against the Dark forces that spread through Gevás. In the Final Battle, Lux vanished along with his brother.

Maksimilian: Former Captain of the Enigma Brigade. After disagreeing with Drage's humanitarian approach to the specialized force, Maksimilian left in search of the five Spirit Swords, proudly wielding his own Steel of Life that has kept him alive since the first Obsidian Wars.

Mali (Y'lam / Hector): One of the Y'mordi. Originally a servant under Lord Lux, he defected to the Darkness when he did not receive recognition for his servitude. Now wielding Light as a weapon with two katanas in his hands, he fights for the Darkness. However, his bond with Randir has led him to question his service, and he now conspires with Randir to break their bonds.

Maris: One of the Great Servants of the Darkness. He was once an esteemed mage and horse anima known as the Black Hope. However, when Y'tal awoke the Darkness that was his birthright, he went insane with power and started the Third Obsidian War to destroy the exile against non-humans. After losing a battle against Drage, the Y'mordi killed him and dragged him into the Realm of Darkness.

Marqest: Formerly a Guardian of the Emperor of Light and now one of the Guardians of Light and a Loyal Servant. He serves on the Emperor's Council now as the Prophet of Water. As an Ancient, he frequently acts as a neutral party and offers assistance with his master-intelligence computer COM.

Matthew Helius: One of the Guardians of Light and a member of the Emperor's Council. Now married to Lilian and with two kids, Senagul and William, he struggles to balance family life with offering advice and assistance to Drage.

Meridan, see _Arnim._

Mirah Silverpike: A former naval general and shipyard owner. After meeting Stehl, he abandoned the military life to join her assassination mission.

Morgana La Faye: A former Prophet of Water who once made the Prophecy of the Guardians. Now, she is imprisoned in Stonehenge on Earth.

Neith: One of the five Demons, a spider that was sealed in a Northern cave. Was slain by Lilian.

Nilram: A lion anima who is one of the Enigma Brigade.

Ocrum: One of the Emperor's Council. Serves frequently as Drage's military strategist.

Ophelia Ferro: Randir's deceased wife. She was the Queen of the Eastern Continent. One of Randir's Trials required him to kill her.

Paldas: One of Lux's generals.

Pleityr, see *Sarn*.

Pullatus, see *Y'tal*.

Quella: Prophet of Earth and a member of the Emperor's Council.

Randir (Y'ran / Victor Ferro): A Guardian of Light, the second-in-command of the Y'mordi, a General of the Shadows, and formerly the King of the Eastern Continent. After the Guardians of Light surfaced, he questioned the leadership of Y'tal and became a rogue who has tried to assassinate the Great Servants of Darkness by himself. In the process, however, he has revived his bond with Mali and found a new bond in Stehl. He seeks to break his connections to the Darkness without Y'tal noticing.

Regin: The Emperor of Immyx. After Maksimilian killed most of his staff years ago, he has become more reclusive and has let his kingdom fall into turmoil, with many wondering what has happened to him.

Rexam Draconis: A Guardian of Light and the King of Sharl Drake. Formerly, he was a Guardian to the Emperor of Light, but at the urging of several Dragons on Gevás, he returned home to help in the civil war and bring peace to the world of Dragons. He is married to Elani.

Sarn (Y'nas / Pleityr): One of the twin Y'mordi. Impetuous and feisty, she often drags her sister into danger. She wields a long, metallic chain and harnesses the power of Wind.

Scyllma: A Dean who teaches the Elements.

Senagul (Sena): A squirrel anima who was adopted by Matthew and Lilian after his mother died.

Seryl: An Enigma Brigadier shot to death by Stehl.

Seth Mentiris: A former Emperor of Light who exiled all non-humans, turned the Enigma Brigade into an assassination squad, and banished Marqest.

Stehl (Terrell): A former captain and general who once used a potion to pose as a man. After witnessing a mass murder by the Enigma Brigade, she spends her life hunting the Brigadiers down in revenge. Wielding Kohana's Fang, she rides with Mirah in her search.

Sume: A member of the Enigma Brigade.

Thera: A member of the Enigma Brigade.

Tilgé: A former member of the Enigma Brigade. After Maksimilian ordered his death, Tilgé had to fake his murder by cutting off one of his hands as evidence that he died. He now seeks meaning outside of the Enigma Brigade.

Ulrill: A Silver Dragon who was a spy for Elani.

Urin: Aria's Second in the Phoenix Regiment.

Valdridge: The Prophet of Light and head of the Emperor's Council.

Victor Ferro, see *Randir.*

Viso Tharlam: A member of the Enigma Brigade as well as the Emperor's Council.

Volwyth: A Red Dragon who serves as Draconis's Advisor.

Vran: Former king of the world of Dragons.

Warbrix: Former member of the Enigma Brigade. Gunned down by Stehl.

William Helius: The son of Matthew and Lilian.

Xarden (Y'dax): Advisor of the Y'mordi. He wields an iron scepter with Water and Ice spells as he tries to figure out his past and where the other pieces of his heart reside.

Y'dax, see *Xarden.*

Y'lam, see *Mali.*

Y'mir, see *Arnim.*

Y'nas, see *Sarn.*

Y'ran, see *Randir.*

Y'tal (Pullatus): The leader of the Y'mordi. Childlike in appearance, no one has ever seen his face, but many are aware of his brutal cruelty. He hunts for the blood of the Great Servants of Darkness while also seeking the mysterious stranger who attacked him on Earth when he tried to kill the Guardians of Light.

Yarng: A Servant of the Darkness who sells disq merchandise.

Zel: A captain of Apolis scouts.

About the Author

JONATHAN W. THURSTON has thus far published three books in his Spirit Sword Saga, and his experimental noir horror novella, *The Devil Has a Black Dog,* was published by Red Ferret Press in 2018. Currently, he runs the publishing house Thurston Howl Publications, the Furry Book Review program, and is an editor for Weasel Press. He also is a graduate student and teacher of English at Michigan State University, while reporting for the Michigan LGBT paper, *Between the Lines.* In his spare time, he reads, drinks coffee, plays with his dog—who thinks she is a cat—and studies the historical significance of equestrianism and beekeeping.

www.ingramcontent.com/pod-product-compliance
Lightning Source LLC
Chambersburg PA
CBHW072105250626
47159CB00007B/2310